Kristian Moen is Lecturer in Screen Studies in the Department of Drama: Theatre, Film, Television at the University of Bristol. He has published and presented on topics including nineteenth-century visual culture, cinema and modernity, and the relationship between cinema and fantasy.

FILM AND FAIRY TALES

THE BIRTH OF MODERN FANTASY

KRISTIAN MOEN

I.B. TAURIS

LONDON · NEW YORK

Published in 2013 by I.B.Tauris & Co Ltd
6 Salem Road, London W2 4BU
175 Fifth Avenue, New York NY 10010
www.ibtauris.com

Distributed in the United States and Canada
Exclusively by Palgrave Macmillan
175 Fifth Avenue, New York NY 10010

Versions of some chapters were published previously. Portions of
Chapters 1 and 2 originally appeared in a somewhat different form as
"'Never Has One Seen Reality Enveloped in Such a Phantasmagoria':
Watching Spectacular Transformations, 1860–1889", *Comparative
Critical Studies* 6, no. 3 (2009): 361–72. Chapter 5 is a substantial revi-
sion of an article that was published as "'The Well-Organized Splendor
of a Growing Culture': Sites of Fantasy and *The Thief of Bagdad*", *Early
Popular Visual Culture* 8, no. 1 (2010): 63–73.

International Library of the Moving Image: 8

ISBN: 978 1 78076 251 7

A full CIP record for this book is available from the British Library
A full CIP record is available from the Library of Congress

Library of Congress Catalog Card Number: available

Printed and bound by CPI Group (UK) Ltd, Croydon, CR0 4YY
Text designed and typeset by Tetragon, London

MIX
Paper from
responsible sources
FSC® C013604
www.fsc.org

For my mom

Contents

List of Illustrations ix

Acknowledgements xi

Introduction xiii

Chapter 1 · "A Dream We Make Wide Awake": 1
The Nineteenth-Century Féerie

Chapter 2 · A Cinema of Transformations: 39
The Film Féerie and Georges Méliès

Chapter 3 · Fairy-Tale Aesthetics: 75
Early Film Theory and *The Blue Bird* (1918)

Chapter 4 · Mary Pickford and the Fantasies of Stardom 113

Chapter 5 · Sites of Enchantment and 141
The Thief of Bagdad (1924)

Chapter 6 · Delimiting Fairy Tales: 175
Snow White and the Seven Dwarfs (1937)

Afterword · Mutability Lessons 211

Notes 229
Bibliography 255
Index 269

List of Illustrations

1   *Cendrillon ou La pantoufle merveilleuse: grande féerie en*   p. 3
5 actes et 30 tableaux, 1879. Bibliothèque nationale de
France.

2   G. Webb and Co., Poster advertising *Ye Belle Alliance* at   p. 14
Covent Garden Theatre, 1855. © Victoria and Albert
Museum, London.

3   Joseph Nash, "The Indian Court", 1854. © Victoria and   p. 24
Albert Museum, London.

4   Odilon Redon (1840–1916), *Le Soleil noir* (*The Black*   p. 55
Sun), c. 1900. New York, Museum of Modern Art
(MoMA). Oil with incising on board, 12 3/4 x 9 3/8'
(32.4 x 23.8 cm). Gift of The Ian Woodner Family
Collection. Digital image © 2012, The Museum of
Modern Art/Scala, Florence.

5   *A Trip to the Moon* (Méliès, 1902).   p. 56

6   *Cinderella* (Méliès, 1899)   p. 60

7   *Bluebeard* (Méliès, 1901)   p. 61

8–11   *The Kingdom of the Fairies* (Méliès, 1903)   p. 70

12   Pierre Puvis de Chavannes (1824–98), *Winter*, 1896.   p. 99
Oil on canvas, 93.3 x 146.5 cm. © National Gallery of
Victoria, Melbourne, Australia / Felton Bequest / The
Bridgeman Art Library.

13   *The Blue Bird* (Tourneur, 1918)   p. 100

14   *The Blue Bird* (Tourneur, 1918)   p. 104

15   Jules Chéret (1836–1932), *Folies-Bergère. Loïe Fuller*, 1897. Colour lithograph, 120 x 80 cm. Bibliothèque nationale de France.   p. 105

16   *Cinderella* (Kirkwood, 1914)   p. 120

17   *The Golden Chance* (DeMille, 1915)   p. 120

18   *Cinderella* (Kirkwood, 1914)   p. 121

19   *The Golden Chance* (DeMille, 1915)   p. 121

20   *The Thief of Bagdad* (Walsh, 1924)   p. 152

21   *Seventh Heaven* (Borzage, 1928)   p. 170

22   *Snow White and the Seven Dwarfs* (Hand, 1937)   p. 184

23   *Snow White and the Seven Dwarfs* (Hand, 1937)   p. 185

24   *The Scarlet Empress* (von Sternberg, 1934)   p. 201

25   *Snow White and the Seven Dwarfs* (Hand, 1937)   p. 208

26   *Ball of Fire* (Hawks, 1941)   p. 209

27   *Sleepy Hollow* (Burton, 1999)   p. 219

28   *Harry Potter and the Deathly Hallows Part 1* (Yates, 2010)   p. 224

29   *The Adventures of Prince Achmed* (Reiniger, 1926)   p. 225

Acknowledgements

THIS PROJECT HAS GONE THROUGH MANY METAMORPHOSES since the idea of fairy tales in film first began to fascinate me, and I would like to thank and acknowledge those who have helped and supported me as the book came into being. Thank you to those at the University of East Anglia who helped me so much during this book's first incarnation as a PhD thesis: my astute supervisors, Justine Ashby and Yvonne Tasker, Peter Krämer whose intellectual generosity never failed to surprise me, and Jonathan Tooke, Charles Barr and Andrew Higson, who provided much valued encouragement. In countless discussions, Corin Depper always offered critical acuity and a delight in ideas for which I am deeply thankful. Staff at the Archives Municipales de Toulon, the Bibliothèque nationale de France, the British Film Institute, and the Library of Congress were tremendously helpful, and I thank them. I also acknowledge the support of the Canadian Social Sciences and Humanities Research Council for their funding during my PhD study. At the University of Bristol, as the book took shape, Alex Clayton and Sarah Street were instrumental in helping me out and keeping me on track, and I thank them along with my colleagues Catherine Hindson, Simon Jones, Katja Krebs, Jacqueline Maingard, Richard Misek, Angela Piccini and Martin White. Thanks also go to Liza Thompson at I.B.Tauris for her patience and guidance. Finally, I am deeply grateful to Carole Zucker and Mario Falsetto for their inspirational teaching and generosity, Sherry Kelly for her perceptive insights, and my family and my wife Eventhia for their fantastic support.

Introduction

While the spread of urban-industrial technology, the large-scale disembedding of social (and gender) relations, and the shift to mass consumption entailed processes of real destruction and loss, there also emerged new modes of organizing vision and sensory perception, a new relationship with "things", different forms of mimetic experience and expression, of affectivity, temporality, and reflexivity, a changing fabric of everyday life, sociability, and leisure.

– Miriam Hansen (2000)[1]

The cinema screen is the modern miracle placed within everyone's means. This luminous picture window opened in the wall is the will-o'-the-wisp, the clearing in which fairies dance. It is the place of dreams in a prosaic existence; it is a refreshment of the eyes after the fatigue of withering labour.

– Émile Vuillermoz (1919)[2]

IN THIS BOOK, I EXAMINE HOW CINEMA MADE FAIRY TALES modern. I look at a range of fairy tales, but perhaps not in the ways we have grown accustomed to think of them. Rather than approaching fairy tales as "the purest and simplest expression of collective unconscious psychic processes",[3] "a love-gift to a child",[4] a premodern idyll, a retreat into childhood simplicity, a site of escape or an opportunity for moralism – though addressing these implications – I trace how film fairy tales negotiated the modern world. To be more specific, I focus on how fairy tales in film and film culture, during the first decades of the twentieth century, emphasized spectacle and mutability in ways that resonated with modernism and an experience of modernity. Cinema's fairy tales elaborated on this through their narratives, their uses of film aesthetics, their visions of transformation and their associations with stars and cinemagoing, both exploiting and naturalizing new artistic and cultural forms, and new contexts of social and individual identity. Marshall Berman characterizes modernity as, partly, "an environment that promises us adventure, power, joy, growth, transformation of ourselves and the world…"[5] Film fairy tales showed this, often spectacularly, by highlighting the marvels of technology, the enchantments of consumer culture, the transformative potentials of social mobility and other apparently wondrous facets of modern life. As Berman continues, he adds that this experience of modernity can take on a darker hue, "at the same time, threaten[ing] to destroy everything we have, everything we know, everything we are." If this is a tension at the heart of a modern experience, it is also found in cinema's fairy tales, which sometimes dissolve identities, forms and meanings in a filmic vision of instability and spectacular wonder.

Cinema did not entirely reinvent the form of fairy tales, but rather extended their long-standing associations with transformation and metamorphosis. Marina Warner writes, "More so than the presence of fairies, the moral function, the imagined antiquity and oral anonymity of the ultimate source, and the happy ending (though all these factors help towards a definition of the genre), metamorphosis defines the fairy tale."[6] Similarly, Jack Zipes writes that "if there is one 'constant' in the structure and theme of the wonder tale that was also passed on to the literary fairy tale, it is *transformation* – to be sure, miraculous transformation. Everybody and everything can be transformed in a wonder tale."[7] Such transformations could take many forms, such as the changes of a protagonist through their quest or a journey, the coming to life of inanimate objects, the event of a magical metamorphosis or the realization of fantasy through a "faith in the transforming power of the imagination".[8] Cinema's fairy tales fastened upon such transformations, drawing out their visual appeal, aesthetic forms, narrative potentials and experiential qualities.

In what is usually regarded as the earliest book of English-language film theory, *The Art of the Moving Picture*, Vachel Lindsay describes fairy-tale transformations as "fundamental in the destinies" of cinema. He writes that film fairy tales should make use of cinema's capacity to "transfigure": "Substitution is not the fairy-story. It is transformation, transfiguration, that is the fairy-story, be it a divine or a diabolical change."[9] The qualities that Lindsay singles out from fairy tales – including animate objects, mutable places and transformations – were central to his understanding of how cinema might offer a ground for envisioning a new social sphere built upon a changing basis of vision and experience. This was not an isolated view. Fairy tales were sometimes seen as central to cinema as a medium, providing a model for understanding the imaginative and artistic potentials of this modern form of art, entertainment and technology. While diverse in their implications and formulations, filmmakers who wrote about cinema such as Georges Méliès, film theorists such as Hugo Münsterberg and Émile Vuillermoz, stars such as Mary Pickford and Clara Bow, and films such as *The Blue Bird* (Tourneur, 1918) and *The Thief of Bagdad* (Walsh, 1924) all engaged with the potentials of cinema to show fairy tales and transformation in ways that resonated with a changing social and cultural sphere.

Cinema absorbed fairy tales not just from traditions of oral tales and print culture, but also from other contemporaneous forms and media. Fairy tales, particularly from the nineteenth century onwards, were not just stories, but also theatrical spectacles, books, illustrations, facets of advertising and a host of other cultural and artistic manifestations. An exploration of how cinema drew upon this assemblage allows us to see better the scope of modern fantasy. It also allows us to see better cinema's own intermediality, particularly during a period of rapid change in its first decades. Film fairy tales vividly illustrate a dynamic process of media and institutional formation, as cinema's uses of the visual, narrative and formal material of fairy tales well into the 1930s often made overt use of media hybridity and intermedial borrowings. At the same time, though, fairy tales were also associated with cinema's own distinct identity; the marvellous experience of filmgoing, the onscreen and offscreen transformations of film stars, and the seemingly magical potentials of film aesthetics all contributed to ideas of cinema as a medium with its own specific manifestations of fantasy.

Cinema's uses of fantasy and fairy tales resonated with modernism as well as modernity. While films and writers on cinema would sometimes draw upon specific ideas and trends in modernism that used fantasy, such as Symbolist theatre and painting, a wider conception of modernism was crucial to film fairy tales. Miriam Hansen writes of how modernism can be seen to "encompass a whole range of cultural and artistic practices that register, respond to, and reflect upon processes of modernization and the experience of modernity."[10] Through its "vernacular modernism", Hansen explains, cinema was "the single most inclusive cultural horizon in which the traumatic effects of modernity were reflected, rejected or disavowed, transmuted and negotiated."[11] Some of the most prominent examples of film fairy tales during the period this book focuses on negotiated modern life through fantasy. Attuned to a world of instability and transformation, cinema's fairy tales were especially conducive to contending with the effects of modernity; while often set in far-off realms of fantasy, they nevertheless helped articulate the ways in which we might see, understand and feel the effects of a changing modern world.

Stephen Watts's analysis of Walt Disney's films in the 1930s offers an excellent example of how fantasy and fairy-tale films navigated modernism and modernity. Writing of how a "sentimental modernism" came to inform Disney's enormously influential and popular films, Watts describes their "overarching framework in which visual verisimilitude and a free-flowing modernist sensibility supported each other with a kind of tensile strength."[12] Negotiating tensions between traditional and modern aesthetic forms, Watts outlines five features of "sentimental modernism":

> First, it blended the real and the unreal, naturalism and fantasy, and manipulated each in an attempt to

illuminate the other. Second, it secured nonlinear, irrational, quasi-abstract modernist explorations comfortably on the cultural map by utilizing certain tropes from the Victorian past – an exaggerated sentimentality, clearly defined moralism, disarming cuteness – as familiar artistic signposts. Third, it willingly dug down through layers of consciousness to engage the fluidity of experience and action, but always returned to embrace rationality. Fourth, it animated the world – literally – by ascribing intention, consciousness, and emotion to living and inanimate objects alike, but did so in such a way as to downplay the presence of evil and tragedy. Fifth and finally, it good-naturedly satirized the pretensions of high culture and sought to invigorate it with the vitality of popular culture.[13]

I return to discuss this in a later chapter, but for now what I want to emphasize is that rather than being unique to Disney's films, this conception of sentimental modernism offers a valuable insight into fairy-tale films from the first decades of cinema. A range of films, as well as features of film culture, exploited and contained the possibilities of fantasy in the depiction of a dynamic, changing and unstable world.

Of course, no totalizing viewpoint can take into account all the uses and implications of cinema's fairy tales. My focus on their relationship to modernism, modernity and transformation should not be taken to deny the importance of other elements, but rather to shift our attention to the pivotal, and often neglected, role that fairy tales had in elaborating a modern form of cinematic fantasy. Rather than emphasizing issues of narrative or adaptation – which are treated extensively in Jack Zipes's study of fairy-tale films, *The Enchanted Screen* – I focus on the interrelation between film, film culture and fairy tales in the development of cinema as a site of spectacular fantasy that responded to a context of modernity.[14]

In order to follow the different paths of cinema's modern fairy tales, this book crosses national boundaries and historical periods.

It begins with two chapters focusing on the emergence of fairy tales as spectacular entertainment in France, in nineteenth-century theatre and in film around the turn of the twentieth century, and then shifts to American cinema from the 1910s up to the early 1940s. *Film and Fairy Tales* changes location in order to account for the most prominent and influential examples of fairy tales in cinema during this period. Moving from the mid-nineteenth century to the mid-twentieth century, it examines the place of fairy tales in cinema during an historical juncture in which modernity and consumer culture changed the social fabric of America and Europe. During this period, after its beginnings in the 1890s, cinema underwent a series of major changes including a shift towards feature-length narrative films, the rise of the star system, the establishment of movie theatres and the introduction of new technologies of sound and colour. Part of my aim in focusing on this period is to suggest the breadth of fairy tales in cinema despite shifting aesthetic and institutional forms. Moreover, this period is bookmarked by two of the most prominent examples of fairy-tale films: Méliès's marvellous fantasies at the turn of the century and the first feature-length Disney animation, *Snow White and the Seven Dwarfs* (Hand, 1937).

Examining cinema's fairy tales over the course of these decades becomes an opportunity to show both the durability of fairy tales in cinema and their shifting contours. I trace how film fairy tales took on different forms, attributes and implications in different periods of cinema history. As such, I approach film fairy tales more as a mode of cinema than a genre; Christine Gledhill describes a mode as

> adaptable across a range of genres, across decades, and across national cultures. It provides the genre system with a mechanism of "double articulation", capable of generating specific and distinctively different generic formulae in particular historical conjunctures, while also providing a medium of interchange and overlap between genres.[15]

Cinema certainly did not draw upon fairy tales in exactly the same ways throughout its first decades, and part of my aim is to show how, at different moments in the history of cinema, different uses of fairy tales emerged. Throughout the work, this is explored not only through the analysis of films and a wider field of culture, but also through the discourse circulating around cinema. Whether examining the popular press and fan magazines or the writings of filmmakers and theorists, I remain attentive to how the relationship between fairy tales and film was commented upon, analysed and celebrated. A diverse range of commentators and artists demonstrated an ongoing fascination with fairy tales and their cinematic potentials.

I begin with a chapter that examines how fairy tales were presented as popular spectacles on the French stage in the féerie, or fairy play. By the middle of the nineteenth century, this genre was a rival to melodrama and vaudeville in its public appeal, with its prominence lasting until around the turn of the century. Although localized around French – and particularly Parisian – theatre, the féerie's influence extended internationally, perhaps most markedly in English pantomime. The form of the féerie shifted over the course of the decade, incorporating new technologies of spectacle and becoming increasingly dependent on extraordinary expenditure. What remained consistent, however, was that the féerie departed from the narrative basis of fairy tales by emphasizing stage effects, spectacular imagery, marvellous tricks and transformative worlds. For example, the employment of new technologies of lighting and stage machinery in a play such as *Aladin* (*Aladdin*) in 1863 displaced an emphasis on narrative with an onstage aquarium, sudden marvellous changes of scenery, and a dreamlike conclusion of shifting lights and forms.[16] The genre's impact extended beyond the confines of the stage, with the tropes of fairy tales, the discourse of fairylands and the term féerique used to characterize other visual spectacles of modernity that emphasized transformation and opulence, such as the international displays and illuminations at world's fairs. Drawing out these various manifestations of spectacular fantasy, I explore how féeries and related forms were discussed, understood and characterized in the popular press at the time, as well as in the writing of prominent authors such as Charles Baudelaire and Émile Zola. In particular, the influential writings of Théophile Gautier on this genre offered an account of how the transformations of spectacular fairy tales could become connected to a conception of artistic modernism and modernity as interrelated sites of destabilizing, oneiric and phantasmagorical change.

With the emergence of cinema in the 1890s, the féerie was absorbed into a new medium of visual wonder, becoming one of the most popular of early cinema's genres. Offering extended versions of so-called "transformation views", film féeries presented fairy tales and other fantastic subjects to an international audience. Rather than simply inhabiting the framework of their theatrical or narrative predecessors, however, film féeries projected a novel use of their forms and attractions, most markedly in the films directed by Georges Méliès. For example, films such as *Cinderella* (1899) and *The Merry Frolics of Satan* (1906) showed the sudden transformations through film editing of domestic spaces and everyday objects, such as a dining room or a clock, into images of technological threat and dreamlike anxiety. Moreover, the féerie formally and discursively emphasized an understanding of cinema based upon transformation. Extending influential analyses of early cinema in works by Tom Gunning, André Gaudreault and others, this chapter approaches the féerie as offering neither the temporal continuity of narrative nor the discontinuity of spectacle, but rather a kind of cinema based on depicting an onscreen world as a state of change. I explore the forms and implications of such transformations, as well as the ways in which they were linked to fairy tales, cinema, modernity and modernism. This is examined through the analysis of a range of materials, including contemporaneous film catalogues and advertisements, case studies of major féeries such as *Cinderella* and *The Kingdom of the Fairies* (Méliès, 1903), Georges Méliès's own writing on the genre in "Cinematographic Views" (1907), and a contemporaneous context of Symbolist art and writing.

Despite enormous changes in cinema over the next few decades, the visual tropes and imaginative resources of the féerie would continue to shape film fairy tales. As befits their subject matter, cinema's fairy tales were mutable: mediated by changes in cinema as an institution, drawn into new contexts of visual culture, interrelated with other approaches to fantasy, and used to negotiate and imagine different facets of modern life. Chapter 3 examines how film aesthetics, film theory and the discourse circulating around cinema during the 1910s drew upon fairy tales. During a period of institutional consolidation and a turn to feature-length narrative, fairy tales continued to resonate with prominent accounts and manifestations of cinema's aesthetic and social potential. These facets helped situate cinema itself as a site of enchantment, a place of marvellous potential within the everyday, and a new form of public art. I focus particularly on two manifestations of this. First, through an analysis of the early writings of film theorists including Vachel Lindsay, Émile Vuillermoz and Hugo Münsterberg, I argue that fairy tales helped inform and shape an emergent conversation around cinema's potential as a modern medium for expressing fantasy, transformation and enchantment. Second, through a case study of *The Blue Bird* (Tourneur, 1918), a film based on Maurice Maeterlinck's féerie, I trace how a prominent example of cinema's fairy tales drew upon modernist theatre and visual culture in order to envisage cinema as a site of fantasy.

While the scope of *The Blue Bird*'s integration of fairy-tale tropes with cinema was unmatched in the decade, its aesthetic approach and its vision of cinematic potential were by no means unique. Fairy tales were not simply present in individual films, but were also figured through an emergent star system. Chapter 4 examines three interrelated questions. How did the star system draw upon fairy tales in the 1910s? How did stars contribute to the popular imagination and reflexive display of cinema's fantastic qualities? How were offscreen star personas presented in terms of fairy tales and fantasy? In order to draw out the importance of fairy tales to the star system, I focus on perhaps the most popular star of the 1910s: Mary Pickford. Examining Pickford's starring roles in fantasy films, while also elaborating on a wider context of fairy-tale stars, this chapter explores how a vernacular of fairy tales, and fantasy more broadly, helped shape stardom and the institution of cinema.

Chapter 5 examines how fairy-tale films participated in new contexts of fantasy in consumer culture and modern life. Consumer culture, in particular, became an increasingly dominant context in which fairy tales were situated. This chapter takes *The Thief of Bagdad* (Walsh, 1924) as its main case study, examining how it was shaped by an intermedial milieu of spectacular fantasy. Exhibited with Orientalist trappings designed by the theatre impresario Morris Gest, using fairy-tale tropes to accentuate the visual allure and transformative potential of places and objects, *The Thief of Bagdad* was characterized as a new kind of film in the popular press, trade journals, theoretical writing on film and its own publicity. The film's fantasies were closely related to the inscription of spectacular fantasy in two sites outside of cinema: department stores and illustrated fairy-tale books. The film's evocation of these sites was not simply intertextual borrowing; through its formal tropes, its reception and its publicity, the experience of viewing the film was linked to the experience of immersing oneself within a fantasy world. Drawing on the work of T. J. Jackson Lears and William Leach, this chapter examines the way in which this use of spectacular fantasy situated the film fairy tale within trends in consumer culture and the new commercial aesthetic. In doing so, the film celebrated a modern world of wonders where fantasizing and desiring were worthy goals in themselves, part of "productive consumerism", part of what it might mean to be a modern citizen.

While films like *The Wizard of Oz* (Fleming, 1939) can be seen as a continuation of earlier traditions of the féerie and the consumerist fairy tale, the final chapter examines films in the 1930s and early 1940s that substantially reworked and renegotiated the promises of transformation and fantasy found in fairy tales. *Snow White and the Seven Dwarfs* (Hand, 1937) aestheticized itself in terms of a beautiful object and a quality book, drawing on trends in publishing and in children's literature. Other films also envisioned a more self-contained and limited scope of fantasy in modernity, including Claudette Colbert's sardonic star turns in *Bluebeard's Eighth Wife* (Lubitsch, 1938) and *Midnight* (Leisen, 1939), and the ironic allusions to fairy tales in *The Scarlet Empress* (von Sternberg, 1934), *The Good Fairy* (Wyler, 1935), *Rebecca* (Hitchcock, 1940) and *Ball of Fire* (Hawks, 1941). These films can be seen as part of a trend in which the association of fairy tales and modernity becomes gradually muted or sharply satirized. Particularly in the 1930s and 1940s, but also evident in the previous decades, some of the most prominent fairy-tale films began to question the value of fantasy. Whether contained in a book, shown to be artificial or seen as deceitful, fairy-tale transformations began to be shown less in terms of cinema's potentials to negotiate modernity and more as charming or illusory distractions from the conditions of modern life.

An afterword, in which I discuss contemporary film fantasy, brings the book full circle. Here, I look at how cinema has continued to draw upon fairy tales in terms of transformation and spectacle. Focusing on the reflexive exploration of cinema's relation to fantasy in *Sleepy Hollow* (Burton, 1999) and *Harry Potter and the Prisoner of Azkaban* (Cuarón, 2004), I explore how the figuration of mutability is central to an understanding of their visions of fairy tales and fantasy. This resonates with a wider context of technological and cultural change, extending the long-standing and fundamental relationship between transformation, cinema and fairy tales into a contemporary frame.

1

"A DREAM WE MAKE WIDE AWAKE"
The Nineteenth-Century Féerie

IN 1841, THE AUTHOR AND CRITIC THÉOPHILE GAUTIER wrote that "the time for purely optical spectacles has arrived."[1] The theatrical genre of the féerie – or "fairy play" – fit this category neatly. In a review of the féerie *La chatte blanche* (*The White Cat*) in 1869, Gautier summarized the form: "What a charming summer spectacle is a féerie! That which doesn't demand any attention and unravels without logic, like a dream that we make wide awake…"[2] For Gautier, the play's story, which was loosely based upon Catherine d'Aulnoy's fairy tale, is eclipsed by spectacle. Rather than a staging of a traditional fairy tale, the play is a "symphony of forms, of colours and of lights" in which "the characters, brilliantly clothed, wander through a perpetually changing series of tableaux, panic-stricken, stunned, running after each other, searching to reclaim the action which goes who knows where; but what does it matter! The dazzling of the eyes is enough to make for an agreeable evening…"

Gautier's valorization of the play's visual spectacle over its story was not simply due to an esoteric or poetic conception of the féerie. Other reviews in the mainstream Parisian press, to stay briefly with the example of *La chatte blanche*, offered a similar account of the play. Émile Abraham in *Le Petit Journal* asked rhetorically, "You don't really care about the play, do you?"[3] Instead, he suggested, a reader is simply waiting to hear about the new entertainments and spectacles; he obliges, satisfying their curiosity through a discussion of the ballets, the music, the marvellous sets, the costumes and the dazzling onstage transformations. In *Le Temps*, Francisque Sarcey described the play's emphasis on spectacular events and the general lack of coherence, noting that "one can put the beginning at the end, and vice versa. The pieces never hold together."[4] With such plays, he suggests that the role of the authors should be seen as significantly less important than those who design the decor and stagecraft. The theatre director and critic for *Le Constitutionnel*, Nestor Roqueplan, drew attention to a significant effect of the play's fragmentary and spectacular qualities, writing of how its "twenty six tableaux have passed in front of the public's eyes like the facets of a prism, like the chimeras of a dream."[5] Elaborating on a tradition, partly drawn from Romanticism, that linked fairy tales with childhood wonder, Roqueplan goes on to describe how such plays could satisfy basic yearnings, creating an experience akin to infancy "where there is for us neither time, nor space, nor beginning, nor end, where we are still so near to the hand of the creator and so far from the disillusioning contact of things, which seem to us to have little of the divine assurance." A dazzling vision, an incoherent collection of brilliant spectacles, a product of industry and technology, a marvellous dream, a return to childhood wonder: rather than only specific responses to *La chatte blanche*, these various accounts highlight different ways in which the spectacular fantasies of the féerie were described and understood.

As the word "féerie" indicates – "*fée*" can be translated as "fairy" and "*féer*" as "to enchant" – this theatrical genre was based upon fairy tales and other fantastic subjects.[6] The féerie was among the most significant forms that fairy tales took in nineteenth-century popular culture.[7] Often lasting for several hours, féeries provided a multifaceted entertainment of dance, comedy and action while exploiting new technologies and extravagant stagecraft. These plays staged and restaged material drawn from sources such as the late-seventeenth-century French fairy tales written by Charles Perrault (such as "Cinderella" [Figure 1] and "Donkeyskin") and Catherine d'Aulnoy (such as "The Deer in the Woods" and "The White Cat"); the genre also used source material outside of the French fairy-tale tradition, including *The Thousand and One Nights*, the novels of Jules Verne and new fantasy plays. While the centrality of fairy tales to

Figure 1. *Cendrillon ou La pantoufle merveilleuse: grande féerie en 5 actes et 30 tableaux*, 1879.

the féerie might suggest a specific appeal to children, such plays addressed a wide audience. They were particularly significant in Paris during a period in which theatre was playing an expanding role as popular entertainment for a mass audience.[8] The genre of the féerie found enormous success with *Le pied de mouton* (*The Sheep's Foot*) in 1806, and its place on the Parisian stage – as well as its form and spectacular appeal – was further consolidated during the 1830s and 1840s with plays such as *Les pilules du diable* (*The Devil's Pills*). While the genre's popularity would wax and wane for the rest of the century, it continued to be a major attraction, presenting an ever-increasing spectacular scope and incorporating contemporary technologies and subjects. Although the féerie had faded as a central form of commercial theatre by the early twentieth century, it had continued to be among the most lucrative genres – as well as among the most expensive to stage – until the end of the nineteenth century.[9]

Some viewers were simply baffled by the extraordinary spectacles of fantasy that were presented in féeries. For example, noting that he had neglected to mention many of the dazzling scenes and marvellous transformations in the féerie *Rothomago* in 1862, the reviewer for *La Presse* asks, "But how can one analyse a kaleidoscope in movement?"[10] This chapter does just that, analysing the kaleidoscopic spectacles of the féerie. I trace how their entwinement of fantasy, spectacle, popular entertainment and technology partly redefined the framework in which fairy tales were seen and understood. I focus particularly on the ways in which féeries emphasized the spectacle of visual transformation, embellishing their fantastic and fairy-tale source material with stunning images of characters, objects and onstage worlds in a state of metamorphosis. In nineteenth-century visual culture, féeries were not unique in their depictions of transformation as a visual appeal; for example, Charles Rearick writes of the late-nineteenth-century luminous fountains at the Château d'Eau, illuminated boats on the Seine and spotlights on Loïe Fuller's swirling costume at the Folies-Bergère, noting how "féerique was the way French observers described such sights – dreamlike, fairyland brilliant, like an enchanting world of 'The One Thousand and One Nights'."[11] In "The Birth of Film Out of the Spirit of Modernity", Tom Gunning describes how one example of these féerique spectacles, Fuller's extraordinary performance of movement and luminosity, could be

seen to embody a contemporary form: "Like the modern experience of shock that violently disarranged concepts of solidity and
objectivity and conveyed the seeming insubstantiality of modern
experience, Fuller's dance displayed motion as a matrix from which
form was born, a possibility of continuous transformation."[12]
The féerie anticipated and, in some respects, moulded such vivid
depictions of visual metamorphosis. In doing so, the féerie also
partly recast fairy tales as a form of spectacular transformation.

The implications, uses and potentials of transformation and
fantasy in visual culture are, of course, diverse.[13] Focusing on
the relation of the féerie to transformation, I aim to ground this
discussion in a specific manifestation that played a central role in
changing contexts of art, fantasy, technology and popular entertainment in the nineteenth century. This was to have a significant
impact on important facets of modernism and modernity, where
the marvels of the féerie were interrelated with new approaches
to art and culture. In order to examine these issues, I focus on
how féeries were described in the influential writing of Gautier,
whose observations on the féerie's relationship to fantasy and
transformation would prove to be crucial to later discussions of
the genre. I then turn to examine how the féerie and its spectacular transformations were situated within a wider intermedial
context of spectacular fantasy, especially towards the end of the
nineteenth century, in the mass press at the time. Exploring the
form and impact of the féerie in configurations of fantasy, this
chapter elaborates on how the genre's dazzling visions of transformation, enchantment, technology and spectacle fashioned a
modern form of fantasy.

Spectacular Transformations

Early féeries, around the turn of the nineteenth century, offered
narrative simplicity with a sometimes moralistic intent. While
this partly stemmed from their relation to a fairy-tale tradition,

it also drew upon the theatrical context in which the féerie became established. Following the French Revolution, as Paul Ginisty notes, féeries emerged alongside the important genre of melodrama; they were often staged at the same theatres and were written by the same authors who, Ginisty suggests, "after having made their contemporaries tremble, wanted to make them laugh."[14] Despite the apparent differences between the fantasies and marvels of féeries and the depictions of social conflict and morality in melodrama, the two genres did share several important characteristics. Like melodrama, the féerie staged an innocent character's journey through a forbidding landscape, building its narrative around the protagonist's struggle to find their place in society.[15] While melodrama showed Manichean oppositions of innocence and villainy, féeries showed the conflict of love and tyranny, figuratively elevated through good and bad fairies. Premiering in 1806, *Le pied de mouton* helped establish the typical narrative structure of the genre: a character, opposed by a figure with supernatural powers, journeys through extraordinary lands on a quest with the help of a good fairy and a magical talisman (in this case, an enchanted lamb's foot). Usually, this quest would involve a romantic pursuit that defies social restrictions, and all would end happily. While often embellished with manifold complications, humorous interludes, numerous secondary characters and ongoing episodic interruptions, this simple structure provided the basis for the féerie narrative.

But the stories of féeries were often subsumed by their onstage wonders. Roxane Martin describes how, in the first decades of the nineteenth century, the moralistic narratives of féeries were largely displaced by an emphasis on spectacle. The féerie, Martin explains, would situate individual stage settings, typically described as "*tableaux*", as discrete sites of spectacle.[16] While melodrama might employ the tableau to depict different stages of a character's life, the féerie would emphasize it as a sight of spectacle and stage transformation.[17] Instead of complementing a narrative progression, the tableau became a semi-autonomous site for the display of marvellous images and effects. This shifted the féerie towards an episodic structure, diminishing the importance not only of the narrative but also of a traditional didactic structure built around oppositions between good and evil.

The féerie's emphasis on spectacle and individual tableaux in place of morality and narrative coherence became particularly pronounced during the period of the July Monarchy, in the 1830s and early 1840s, and would remain a central feature of the genre for the rest of the century. During this period, Gautier wrote his first reviews of féeries, elaborating on their characteristic fantasies and spectacles. From the mid-1830s to the early 1850s, Gautier was a regular contributor of short articles (*feuilletons*) for the major newspaper *La Presse*, quickly establishing himself as one of the most influential and well-known commentators on French theatre in an emergent mass press. His féerie reviews would prove to be particularly important for understandings of the genre; for example, the definitions of the term "féerie" in prominent reference works used quotes from Gautier, and major reviewers later in the century, such as Auguste Vitu at *Le Figaro* and Francisque Sarcey at *Le Temps*, would allude to and discuss his writings on the genre.[18]

In terms of narrative, Gautier sometimes characterized féeries as simply indescribable: "It is impossible to make a report, scene by scene, of such nonsense"; "You can pretty much guess that the summary has nothing to do with what goes on"; "We won't try to make a summary of the play".[19] Describing another féerie, he wrote, "We don't follow the authors in this maze of tricks, of *changements à vue*, of transformations, through the detonations of the puns… that escape the possibilities of analysis; it's the carnival of human reason."[20] Through such comments, Gautier pointed to a minor role for the narrative, emphasizing episodes of spectacle instead. Moreover, while sometimes pointing to an underlying structure that depicts a timeless struggle between good and evil in the féerie, Gautier would often mock their rudimentary morality. His review of *Le sylphe d'or* (1839) notes the division between good and evil, but implies that such a Manicheanism is simply an excuse for different spectacles: "It's always the same thing: a bad genie who has at their disposal firecrackers, ethyl alcohol and traps; a well-meaning fairy who has the right to the cardboard clouds, the tinplate suns, the garlands of paper flowers and the Bengal fires of the apotheosis."[21] The good and bad fairies are reduced to irritations for Gautier as he goes on to recount a scene where the famous Harlequin, Jean-Gaspard Deburau, is struggling with the moral dilemma of whether or not he should steal a pâté. Suddenly, a little devil appears in a "whirlwind" from a stage trapdoor and announces, "I am your evil genie." Deburau calmly takes an axe, rolls up his sleeves, spits in his hands and slices the genie in half. Then his good fairy, dressed in a dazzling sequin dress, emerges from a cloud to announce, "I am your good genie." Deburau takes his axe, spits in his hands and cuts the fairy in three. And the play goes on as if these interruptions had never happened. Gautier concludes his account of dispensing with these figures of good and evil approvingly: "This scene should really be placed at the beginning of all the spectacular plays." For Gautier, the féerie offered – and should offer – spectacular fantasy rather than moral lessons.

Gautier drew particular interest from the rapid transformations that would effect a stage of instability, and that were a major spectacular feature of féeries. Such transformations took different forms: *changements à vue*, "the rapid replacement of one decor by another before the spectator's eyes";[22] *trucs*, which showed transformations of bodies, objects and places; and a happy ending, called an apotheosis, which presented spectacular stagecraft and lighting effects in a state of ongoing change. While other genres such as melodrama also presented extraordinary transformations, such visual transformations of people, places and things were pivotal to the féerie. Revivified over the course of the century with new technologies and increasingly elaborate stage devices, spectacular transformations were central to the genre's form and its popular appeal. For example, a féerie like *Les sept châteaux du diable* (*The Devil's Seven Castles*) from 1844, despite a clearly moralistic structure revolving around the seven deadly sins, was a "spectacle *made perfectly for the pleasure of the eyes*".[23] Rather than a story, Gautier described it as a "complete féerie where the metamorphoses and the *changements à vue* follow one another without interruption…"

Transformation was a central feature of the most popular féerie from the time, *Les pilules du diable*, which had its premiere in 1839. This play would go on to be thought of, along with *Le pied de mouton*, as an archetypal féerie. The play begins in Madrid and ends in "The Empire of Folly", presenting the travails of Isabelle and Albert.[24] Isabelle's father, an apothecary named Seringuinos, is opposed to their wedding. He is insistent that Isabelle marry the pompous Sottinez, the godson of the grand inquisitor. Abetted by the fairy Sara, who creates the title's magical "devil's pills" which grant wishes, Isabelle and Albert run off together. Much of the play depicts the efforts of Seringuinos, Sottinez and their entourage to find and recapture them. As the play develops, Sara switches allegiances and another fairy, Folly, assists Isabelle and Albert with magical means. This conflict between good and bad fairies, and between young love and social obligations, serves largely as a pretext for a series of marvellous events, startling transformations and astonishing locales. Hippolyte Lucas in *L'Artiste* captured the effect, writing that "the eyes open as wide as they can… They are dazzled by all the marvels that they see, like a fireworks display…"[25]

Not surprisingly, Gautier was enchanted by *Les pilules du diable*. His review consists more of a discussion of particular marvels than a detailed description of the play, as "to make a summary of such madness is an impossible thing."[26] In this féerie, Gautier continues, "there is everything, except a play." Gautier's review focused on the ways in which the "féerique world"[27] is presented. Describing the comic effects, he devotes considerable attention to scenes where, during the search for Isabelle, Seringuinos tries to get some sleep and his valet tries to eat. In his simple desire for a place to rest, Seringuinos is repeatedly thwarted: "the chairs collapse under him or stretch into ladders; the beds become baths or wells; the walls retreat when he wants to lean against them…"[28] At one point, "the house goes upside down: which is to say, the roof becomes the ground floor…"[29] For his valet, a series of similarly extraordinary events denies him the chance to eat when, for example, "roast pigeons come to life, beat their wings, and go to devour a monstrous portrait of Gargantua on the wall…" The complex stage machinery that produced such tricks and transformations helped figure a world that shifts its coordinates, leaping from the dead to the living, the inanimate to the animate; the stage showed instability within everyday activities and the very ground upon which they unfold. Such spectacular transformations create a world of anxiety and frustration, thwarting desire and upending stability. Gautier situates the spectator viewing this play in a similar condition as he goes on to describe the effect:

> It's unimaginable: watching it, one suddenly loses all feeling for the possible or impossible; this world goes, comes, cuts, cries, sings, falls, rises, hits out and receives so much that troubles the eye and the head… Every object is suspect and contains some sort of trap; have faith in nothing…[30]

The spectator is drawn into this world, for it is both the character Seringuinos and the audience who are meant to "have faith in nothing", who experience a shared world of ongoing transformation.

Gautier would recount his fascination with these fantastic worlds of instability in his reviews of other féeries, for which he often offered detailed lists of transformations. For example, in *Bijou*, which premiered in 1838, after noting the plays dependence on showing transformations ("the *changements à vue*, the flights and the surprises"), Gautier then goes on to list some of them: "The settees become writing desks; the least suspect buildings change form like Proteus; the portraits yawn in their frames; the shop signs detach themselves and go for a walk…"[31]

With buildings, portraits and words all upended, basic sources of cultural signification are destabilized. Such a milieu creates a potential for random or ongoing change behind material of the most seemingly stable matter. Gautier concludes his description, writing that "the objects of the most innocent appearance all hide a trap or a pun." These are oneiric onstage worlds: "A féerie is a dream which everyone interprets in their own way. Indeed, what is more like a dream than these incoherent, impossible, ambulatory dramas…"[32] However, such dazzling visions of instability are not entirely immaterial and fantastic; they are, as Gautier writes, "a dream that we make wide awake".[33]

As well as an environment filled with dreamlike transformations, such plays also presented a rapidly changing series of locales that would be described as a type of visual voyage. Gautier characterized *Les pilules du diable* in terms of travel:

> over the course of several hours, all of creation passes in front of the eyes: you go from the earth to the sky, from the Plaza Mayor of Madrid to the railway of Saint-Germain; from the middle ages to nowadays; from the island of Genies to the Musard ball, it's a pell-mell more confused than chaos…[34]

Drawing the spectator, "*you* go", into the experience of voyage and ongoing movement uncoupled from narrative, progress or destination, the description situates the play as a bewildering journey that crosses spatial and temporal boundaries. Mixing historical and fantastic sites with contemporary ones, the play becomes a voyage through shifting landscapes. With references to dreams and nightmares alongside its depiction of travel, the play interweaves fantasy and travel with its visual transformations and spectacular events. Gautier elaborated on this in other reviews, such as his discussion of *La biche au bois* where "you leap from hell to sky, from Switzerland to China, from palace to cottage, without budging from your seat."[35] He describes the effect of this, drawing attention to the ways in which this resonated with the relatively novel experience of train travel: "These spectacles, purely ocular, are those which are best suited to worn-out and preoccupied civilizations like ours... the only necessary attention is watching, on the route of a railway, to the left and to the right, the vague silhouettes of the horizon flying by."[36] For Gautier, "What's charming in this type of play is the immense voyage that we make with our eyes... At each instant, the theatre changes..."[37] Through reviews and comments such as these, Gautier established a particular set of connotations surrounding the experience of viewing the féerie and its transformations: instead of concerns over character, narrative or moral lessons, a visual world of shifting forms akin to dreaming and travelling takes precedence. This develops an aesthetic sense of the féerie that pivots on its depiction of transformation.

This aesthetic of visual transformation was not limited to the French stage; it was also, for example, a central feature of pantomime, one of the most popular theatrical genres in England at the time. In this genre, metamorphosis and related tricks had long been evident.[38] In the middle of the nineteenth century, however, transformation took on a heightened significance as perhaps *the* central appeal of pantomime through the increasing importance of the "transformation scene". For the first half of the nineteenth century, pantomimes were typically divided into two distinct parts.[39] They would begin with a brief "opening" which would stage a fairy tale and then they would depict a more extended "harlequinade" which would place an emphasis on physicality and clowning. The shift from the world of the opening to the world of the harlequinade was called the transformation scene. In this scene, each of the main characters in the fairy-tale opening would be metamorphosed into the stock characters of the harlequinade. In the latter half of the nineteenth century, particularly on the London stage, the fairy-tale section of the pantomime became longer and more important, changing from a prelude to the main event. With only a brief harlequinade epilogue, the transformation scene was no longer a functional intermediary, but a spectacular climax to the evening's entertainment. The concluding scene of *The Island of Jewels* (1849), designed by William Beverley, was widely credited with the establishment of the transformation scene as a pivotal spectacular attraction.[40] J. R. Planché, who wrote the play, described the scene:

> No special tableau for the termination of the piece being suggested in the story, it was left to [Beverley's] taste and ingenuity to design one, and the novel yet exceedingly simple falling of the leaves of a palm tree, discovering six fairies supporting a coronet of jewels, produced such an effect that I scarcely remember having witnessed on any similar occasion up to that period.[41]

The scene employed typical imagery for later transformation scenes: nature, exotic places, enchanted women and enormous wealth. Moreover, the stage's gradual change, with leaves falling and fairies emerging, offered the kind of ongoing transformation that would become standard for these spectacles. Frustrated by the increasing prominence of these scenes, Planché wrote: "The *last* scene became the *first* in the estimation of the management. The most complicated machinery, the most costly materials, were annually put into requisition… As to me, I was positively painted out. Nothing was considered *brilliant* but the last scene."[42]

While such scenes would conclude the plot of the opening fairy tale, their emphasis was on spectacle, transformation and fantasy rather than narrative closure. Departing from their earlier function to show the metamorphosis of the play's characters, transformation scenes no longer focused on individuals; instead, they displayed an entire onstage world in a state of mutability. Typically, new places would be revealed, such as the "Palace of Jewels" at Princess's Theatre in 1858.[43] Another central characteristic was the presence of fairies, emerging from behind the mise-en-scène or appearing suspended from above. For example,

Figure 2. G. Webb and Co., Poster advertising *Ye Belle Alliance* at Covent Garden Theatre, 1855.

a poster advertising *Ye Belle Alliance* at Covent Garden Theatre in 1855 [Figure 2] shows a transformation scene above the main characters with different narrative episodes relegated to the corners of the image, highlighting the spectacular appeal of the play. Many transformation scenes also offered more abstract visual marvels. Some depicted metamorphoses of nature, such as "Fanciful Representation of the Apotheosis of the Chrysalis around the Fairy Ferns of Fancy", which apparently "astonished and dazzled" the audience at the Lyceum.[44] Relying upon new technologies and uses of stage lighting, they would also emphasize transformations of luminosity and colour. At the Adelphi in 1857, "The Realms of Light" offered an extraordinary vision in which "effect follows effect of increasing power, brighter and still brighter, till at length the stage is one blaze of dazzling colours... the admiration of the audience is raised to the highest degree by their eyes being feasted to the extreme on the utmost gorgeousness of hues."[45] The transformation scene at the Olympic in 1861 was described in *The Era* (December 29, 1861) as "in every respect a masterpiece of artistic beauty" due to "the lovely harmony of colour that fills the stage with a series of gorgeous rainbows that melt and re-form before the eye in a succession of exquisite tones of beauty." For some critics, the process of transformation itself was the central visual appeal; for instance, in *The Times*, a description of a transformation scene noted that "the change is of course effected as gradually as possible, the object of scenes of this description being not to startle the eye by the suddenness of the transformation, but to fascinate it by the slow evolution of one beauty out of another."[46] Pantomimes running for hours would end on such scenes, showing the enchantments of mutable places, shifting colours or simply transformation for its own sake.

A review in *The Times* noted that transformation scenes "may be said to have originated a new school of scenic decoration."[47] This "school" was international, extending, for example, to the United States. Premiering at Niblo's Theatre in New York in 1866, *The Black Crook* restaged – and reformulated – key aspects of the transformation scene and the féerie for American audiences. Based partly on the popular féerie *La biche au bois*, the play was an enormous success that would later be credited (falsely, as Raymond Knapp points out) with initiating the American musical.[48] A discussion of the play in *Frank Leslie's Illustrated Newspaper* notes that, in addition to the central attraction of the ballet with the "appearance of an unlimited number of pretty women with no clothes to speak of (in fact, very few to *see*)", two scenes stood out: "those of the 'Grotto of Stalecta', and the transformation scene of the *finale*".[49] Later plays, such as *The Twelve Temptations*, would mimic its spectacular appeals, so that "the transformation scenes of 'The Black Crook' are eclipsed in grandeur and wealth of material by those frequently displayed throughout the piece…"[50]

In addition to American theatre's incorporation of this spectacular form, the transformations of the féerie and pantomime were part of an exchange between English and French theatre.

Planché had drawn upon the féerie for his influential "fairy extravaganzas" on the English stage, crediting his viewing of *Riquet à la houppe* in 1821 with his development of the form.[51] This extended to include a later cross-pollination of approaches to staging spectacular fantasies and transformations, where the increasingly elaborate "apotheosis endings" of féeries – which presented spectacular stagecraft and lighting effects – were markedly similar to pantomime transformation scenes. Writing in *Le Constitutionnel* in 1865, Nestor Roqueplan suggested that such spectacles had national connotations, writing that "there exists, in matters of decor, two schools, the French and the English."[52] He goes on to point out that the French "are superior in all that asks for taste, style, historical science, architectural exactitude, ingenious and picturesque arrangements" and that the English, "formed in the school of Christmas pantomimes", are adept at manipulating stage machinery to create "a marvel of the surprises, the tricks, the effects which dazzle the eyes." This more industrial and technological approach, he continues, has influenced French stagecraft. Instead of valuing one over the other, he writes, "It's especially in a féerie, in *La biche au bois*, that the appropriate elements of the two systems can be most happily joined." Drawing upon similar associations of England with industry and France with artistry, Louis Ulbach also describes the implications of international exchange, using the apotheosis ending of *La biche au bois* as his example. He writes, "I don't think I'm making an error in attributing to English industry this decor of gilded paper, representing gemstones with women encased in diamonds."[53] Ulbach pointed out that in the scene "the effect is of a doubtful taste... which brings to mind the découpage of candy boxes rather than the illusions of dreams."

Often emphasizing the female form and the depiction of wealth, as well as exoticism and new stage technologies, the transformations of the féerie and pantomime were embedded within larger contexts of commodification and spectacle. Some accounts were ironic about the kinds of spectacle shown, as in one description of the floating fairies in a transformation scene as "some dozens of pretty ballet girls, dressed in some hundreds of yards of gold and silver tissue, and suspended in the air at Christmas time at each theatre, as regularly as the turkeys are hung up outside the poulterers' shops as high as the second-floor windows."[54] Despite these critical comments, the scene was still described as "resplendent and gorgeous", a spectacle of places and things in their desirable, luxurious and mutable wonder.

The visual transformations in the pantomime and the féerie played a significant role in an international field of nineteenth-century popular culture, part of changing approaches to the role of spectacle in mass entertainment, the relation between art and industry, and the place of narrative in fantasy genres. Through fairy tales and related forms of fantasy, the depiction of spectacular sights of change and mutability had become a central visual trope of popular entertainment.

"The Material Ideal": Modernism and Fantasy

For Gautier, the significance of the mutable worlds and transformations in the féerie went beyond their relation to a specific genre or form of popular entertainment, becoming central aspects of what he saw as the potential of theatre and art. This was reflected in the genre's influence on and relation to his writing. In the first of his regular theatrical feuilletons for *La Presse*, a review of the ballet *Les Mohicans*, Gautier wrote, "A ballet demands dazzling decor, sumptuous feasts, gallant and magnificent costumes; the world of the féerie is the milieu where the action of a ballet is most easily developed."[55] Gautier would go on to author (and co-author) plays and ballets, including *Giselle* (1841) and *La Péri* (1843), that elaborated on such an understanding of "the world of the féerie". In "The Theatre of Which We Dream", an article taken from his 1835 novel, *Mademoiselle de Maupin*, and republished in *La Presse* a few months before his review of *Les pilules du diable* in 1839, Gautier sets out an extraordinary vision of his dream theatre. He sets the scene: "a curtain made out of butterfly wings and thinner than the film inside an egg is slowly raised. The auditorium is filled with poetic souls sitting in stalls of mother-of-pearl and watching the play through drops of dew mounted on the golden pistil of lilies. Those are their lorgnettes." He then describes an imaginary play with a plot where "effects have no cause and causes have no effect", scenery where "everything is painted in strange, fantastic colours", characters who "belong to no time or place" and who "come and go without anyone knowing how or why", and spectacular sights such as "anemones like drops of blood shining on the grass and large daisies puffing themselves up like real duchesses wearing garlands of pearl on their heads".[56] Setting aside the intrigues of plot, the unity of setting and the details of characterization, Gautier offers a fantastic vision closely linked to his descriptions of the féerie.

Writing in 1874, the theatre critic for *Le Temps*, Francisque Sarcey, reflected on "The Theatre of Which We Dream", discussing how Gautier's predilection for a fantastic theatre was partly a critique of "bourgeois" theatre, particularly as it was established by the major author Eugène Scribe.[57] Much like the recurring images of spectacular events and visions of instability in the féerie, the theatre of which Gautier dreams breaks with elements associated with the "well-made play" such as a carefully structured narrative and an appeal to a certain kind of realism.[58] Writing decades later, Émile Zola, although propounding a naturalistic drama, would nevertheless celebrate the fantastic visions of the féerie in a similar manner: "between a king from a féerie and a prince of vaudevilles from Scribe, I make only one distinction: both are false, only the first delights me, while the second irritates me."[59] While clearly drawn to notions of realism, Zola's key distinction between these two kinds of plays is that the féerie is openly fantastic and marvellous while the well-made play has pretensions to realism and narrative coherence that belie its artificiality.

Gautier, however, goes further than simply approaching féer-ies as an unpretentious genre which offered an overt fantasy. Imagining a play made up of multiple and fragmentary images which need not follow the structure of narrative, Gautier situates the marvellous elements on a stage of fantasy as "facets reflecting different aspects by adding the colours of the prism."[60] Rather than the coherency of narrative or character, Gautier treasured the prismatic qualities of fantasy that could offer a spectrum of sights. Transformation functions as a key trope from which to evoke this kind of multiplicity, as it presents an unfixed and changing perspec-tive on the world. Gautier begins one of his feuilletons for *La Presse* lamenting the "singular prejudice" of the Théâtre-Français for not employing *changements à vue* (transformation scenes), writing that "life is mobile and changes at each instant. It is therefore necessary that the theatre be mobile like it, for risk of only representing a philosophical abstraction…"[61] Such an abstraction has a double meaning. In one respect, it refers to the need for theatre to adapt and change continually, and not to be stuck in traditional forms. In another respect, change is evident within the theatrical trope of the *changement à vue* itself. The transformations of the stage can be seen to resonate with a fantastic milieu as a state of flux. Rather than emphasizing a clear narrative structure which progresses towards a conclusion, spectacular transformation highlighted the ephemeral, the surprising and the mutable.

Such a theatre could offer an enlarged perspective; Gautier writes, "This chaos and this disorder appears to find itself, in the final analysis, accounting for real life more exactly under the allure of the fantastic than through the most minutely studied drama of mores."[62] Fantasy could be a means to show, through its very form, a reality not as something static or abstract, but as an experience of multiplicity, change and visuality. It could also be a means by which to show reality as something marked by subjectivity and shifting viewpoints. Gautier elaborated on this in a later discus-sion: "Art, we have too much forgotten today, should not repro-duce life itself, but only the image of life… Art is composed of images, of appearances, of evocations, of memories, of reflections.

The absolute truth is not its domain; when reality is produced, it disappears."[63] Discussing Gautier's approach, Sarcey noted that "what strikes me the most… is that there's not a shadow of fantasy in this criticism, which passes for fanciful; it is on the contrary from a philosopher."[64]

This philosophy that Gautier articulated in his discussions of theatre, and which was reflected in his writing on féeries, was part of a larger critical approach that engaged with art's relation to culture and society. The different potentials of a seemingly fantastic vision of theatre are offered by Gautier as an alternative to wider considerations of the role of art that had currency in French culture at the time. In his preface to *Mademoiselle de Maupin*, the book which contains the material reprinted in "The Theatre of Which We Dream", Gautier sardonically distanced art from considerations of morality and utility. James Kearns notes that this preface became "axiomatic for modernism" and "canonized in the histories of literary modernism as the manifesto of *l'art pour l'art*."[65] Kearns goes on to describe the aims of Gautier's preface:

> It attacked what Gautier saw as the philistinism and utilitarianism of the July Monarchy's dominant bourgeois ideology and, by arguing that the value of a work of art was quite distinct from that of the subject represented, it also attacked the subordination of art's formal means to any external system of ideas, be it moral, social, political, or philosophical…

Gautier derides conceptions of art that would link it to social progress or moral and spiritual values; in a frequently quoted passage, Gautier writes, "The only things that are really beautiful are those which have no use…"[66] Rather than subsuming the value of a work of art to its social or spiritual utility, Gautier approached the work itself as a potential instance of beauty all its own.

Gautier would extend such considerations to his understanding of the féerie. His approach to these plays, however, was not simply based on their aesthetic, aimless and meaningless beauty. For féeries "respond, just as well as tragedy, drama or vaudeville, to a postulation of the human spirit which it is right to satisfy."[67] Through their extraordinary spectacular fantasy, "they are like an azure gap in a pallid modern existence, and open perspectives of the ideal – the material ideal, if one can couple these two words…" As a breach in a muted and regulated modern life, the féerie's visual pleasures offer a sense of the ideal. But rather than an ideal based upon a notion of social values and spiritual meaning, or an ideal based on outcomes and usefulness, this is an ideal rooted in a fleeting moment of beauty.

In *Henrik Ibsen and the Birth of Modernism*, Toril Moi describes the central role that idealism played in nineteenth-century thought, relating to "the belief that the task of art (poetry, writing, literature, music) is to uplift us, to point the way to the Ideal. Idealists thought that beauty, truth and goodness were one."[68] Moi describes how modernism grew out of a challenge to such ideas, arguing that "modernism is the negation of idealism."[69] It is in the framework of idealism's relation to art that Gautier's reference to the féerie as "opening perspectives of the ideal" can be understood. With a "material ideal", connotations of an abstract notion of the ideal dissipate. Instead, the ideal appears as something seen. While major trends in nineteenth-century writing and criticism heralded the possibility for art to mobilize and enact an ideal which entwined beauty, truth and goodness, Gautier saw the potentials of art as much less prescriptive, offering a fleeting but vital sense of beauty. Zola picks up on this aspect of art in terms of the féerie, writing,

> You want us to leave our existence each day, you advance as an argument that the public is going to look to the theatre for consoling untruths, you support the thesis of the ideal in art, well then! Give us the féeries. That is honest, at least. We know we're going to dream wide awake.[70]

Zola's reference to dreaming wide awake and to consoling untruths suggest that he may have had Gautier's view in mind when writing this; elsewhere he further draws upon Gautier's approach, writing, "In our modern inquest, after dissecting the day, the féeries will be, in the evening, the waking dream of all human greatness and beauty."[71] Other writers in a modernist tradition shared this interest in féeries. For example, Marshall C. Olds describes how Gustave Flaubert was also drawn to the genre of the féerie, particularly in terms of the ways in which it visualized states of mind, presented animistic transformations, followed episodic structures and fashioned extraordinary apotheosis endings.[72] Writing and studying féeries, Flaubert was fascinated by the form.

Gautier's discussion of art, and the féerie, celebrates the beauty of an ideal world that is transitory and material, rather than stable and spiritual. In this respect, Paul Bénichou situates Gautier's writing on a cusp between Romanticism and modernism, part of a "School of Disenchantment"; drawing on Charles Baudelaire's article "Théophile Gautier" (1859), Bénichou describes how, for Gautier, art becomes a "consolation" of sorts, a last refuge for the ideal.[73] In Gautier's writing, the emphasis on situating art and the ideal within a passing moment of beauty also contributes to what Bénichou describes as a sense of melancholy.[74] This facet of Gautier's approach would have a significant influence on Charles Baudelaire, who dedicated Les fleurs du mal (The Flowers of Evil) (1857) to Gautier and described him as "the perfect magician of French letters".[75] Rosemary Lloyd writes, "for Baudelaire Gautier's melancholy derives from a constant awareness of decay in beauty and death in life, the transience of earthly things and the deception of sensuous pleasures…"[76]

Lois Cassandra Hamrick has explored how Gautier's use of the word and concept of "modernity" anticipates its influential discussion in Baudelaire's "The Painter of Modern Life" (1863). Hamrick points out that Gautier had engaged with a sense of "modernity" as connected to a passing contemporary moment, drawn in to broader themes of impermanence;

in Gautier's discussions of literature, for example, "the imagery adopted – that of the sun setting at the end of a long literary 'day' – accords a positive value to the notion of decadence."[77] For Gautier, Hamrick continues,

> In the absence of a model to emulate, one must take as parameters those of the moment in which one finds oneself. In other words, in a world having no absolute Ideal serving as an aesthetic standard, it is the particularities of modernity which have led to the development of the decadent style.[78]

In relation to the "material ideal" of the féerie, and the theatre of which he dreams, Gautier privileges spectacle, fantasy and transformation. These elements have a shared sense of instability; rather than suggesting an underlying ideal, moral, narrative or meaning, they present a stage that is in a state of ongoing transformation. In this respect, Gautier's vision of art and theatre closely relates to Baudelaire's description of modernity as "the transient, the fleeting, the contingent".[79] Through the féerie, a spectacular vision of a world *as* a state of instability is made into mass entertainment. Gesturing towards the marvellous and the beautiful, but showing them as an unattainable part of a constantly changing and visually spectacular world, the féerie was a perfectly modern form of fantasy.

Gautier would sometimes express this sense of fantasy and transience in other contexts through specific references to the féerie, fairy tales and fairylands. One of the most sustained examples of this occurs in Gautier's account of the Great Exhibition of 1851.[80] Lara Kriegel writes, "Historians, literary critics and nineteenth-century observers have all understood the Great Exhibition to be the culmination of early nineteenth-century practices of visual display and spectacle."[81] The importance of this world's fair in presenting a changing visual and commodity culture situated it in a context much like the féerie: a novel, spectacular way of showing the world. This was particularly evident in the two aspects upon which Gautier focused: the Crystal Palace and the Indian Court [Figure 3]. Gautier used the rhetoric of fairy tales and féeries to describe these important sites of nineteenth-century visual culture.

Thrilled by the possibility of finally satisfying a childhood dream of seeing India, Gautier arrives for the Exposition intent upon viewing the Indian Court. Of course, he is not really *seeing* India, but rather a contrived display of Indian goods. He is self-conscious about this, writing, "Happily, the English, knowing that we are too poor or too stay-at-home ever to make this féerique voyage, have put all of India in crates and have brought it to the Exposition…"[82] Pretending to accept blithely the modern means of display – characterized in terms of the féerie's spectacular decor – as substituting for the real India, Gautier plays along with the fantasy of the Exhibition. Gautier's account of the convenience of visiting India in this manner, such as his description of the display which is "placed very artistically and very methodically in cases and catalogued with the same phlegm as the cutlery of Sheffield or Birmingham", is clearly tinged with irony.[83] This extends to his discussion of the Crystal Palace.

Figure 3. Joseph Nash, "The Indian Court", 1854.

Within this "colossal cage of glass", "enormous greenhouse of global industry" and "extraordinary example of modern construction", Gautier writes that "one cannot misrecognize the genius of India, appropriated to the needs of English industry."[84] He writes of how the ephemeral and rootless characteristics of the Crystal Palace offer a suitable site for such a spectacle. Built with a skeletal iron armature and emphasizing glass, "[The Crystal Palace is] a marvelous construction that we would readily place in India... it is of a completely féerique lightness and holds its millions of mirrors, encased in the frame of a frail blue and white armature, valiantly in the air..."[85] As a seemingly fantastic and weightless display, the Crystal Palace offers an appropriate site for this journey through displaced wonders. Having used the word "féerique" to describe both a fantastic journey to India and the enchanting encasement of the display, Gautier links fantasy and travel with artificiality and spectacle. This is a voyage not to India, but to the modern spectacle of India, framed with iron and glass, uprooted and reordered.

Despite his awareness of the artificiality of the situation, Gautier immerses himself in the display. He is astonished and dazzled. His description is filled with a typically effusive and lengthy account of the sights. Amidst a characteristic wealth of descriptive terms, metaphors and comparisons, the sights continue to be described in the context of fairy tales and the féerie. Upon entering the Indian Court, he writes, "you believe that the jewellery box of *The Thousand and One Nights* is open in front of you."[86] He continues to elaborate on this fantasy of exoticism as he describes his memory of a travel album about India that he had often reread, continuing, "We see, in the Crystal Palace, the reality of these marvels, which seemed to us chimerical... It's not only in the mise en scène of féerique operas that such magnificence exists..." Later in the article, he describes how the subterranean wonders in Aladdin or the treasures of Haroun-el-Raschid contain fewer marvels.[87] Continuing to refer to the form and content of the féerie, he writes of the vision also in terms of luminosity: "If we don't leave the Crystal Palace blinded, it won't be the fault of

India; wear dark glasses like those for watching an eclipse, and plunge your eyes into these wardrobes, cloakrooms of fairies, péris and apsaras."[88] The various metaphors and comparisons used to characterize the experience of seeing "India" – a jewellery box, a theatrical setting, a cave and a wardrobe – suggest the containment of fantasy, the framing of an exotic fairyland. This extends Gautier's earlier discussions of the Crystal Palace; it also extends his discussions of the féerie, as India becomes staged as a spectacle of enchantment.

Despite his self-conscious descriptions of his absorption into the spectacle, he writes as if the site of wonder entirely engulfs him. In doing so, he takes a quite different approach from other accounts that would emphasize the supposedly edifying qualities of the Indian Court or would position themselves as objective commentators.[89] Falling into the spectacular sights on display, Gautier transposes visual spectacles of the féerie directly into his writing. He pauses at one point to reflect on his use of language, writing of "these luminous bombs of metaphors, these showers of silver and of gold, adjectives and comparisons which we are obliged to have recourse to in order to awaken in the mind of those who read us a faded and hazy image of the féeries that we see."[90] He continues his explanation of why he has described the display in such a manner through further reference to fairy tales:

> Despite not having given anything to drink to an old woman, we are in the position of the young girl in Perrault's tale; we cannot open our mouth without pieces of gold, diamonds, rubies and pearls immediately falling from it; we would really like from time to time to spit out a toad, a garden snake and a red mouse, if only for variety, but that is not in our power.[91]

This description refers to Charles Perrault's fairy tale "Les Fées" ("The Fairies"), where a young woman meets a fairy by a spring, provides her with a drink of water and is then given the gift of speaking in jewels. In referring to this tale, Gautier suggests that his rhetoric is not based upon any sense of actually reflecting on the sights or explaining their implications. Rather, he is powerless to resist the overwhelming enchantment that has been cast by this modern display. He writes as if he has no option but to reach for the most dazzling metaphors and rhetorical turns, which are to be found through reference to the visual imagery of fairy tales and the féerie. In some respects, it is as if he were a character within the féerie or dream play of the Exhibition; he is in a position much like one of the model characters he mentions in the "Theatre of Which We Dream" whose "main concern is to let pearls and bunches of roses fall from his lips and to disseminate the precious gems of poetry…"[92] While the tone is playful and humorous at times, it also carries a sense of threat and the dissolution of self. It is as if he has given himself over to the experience, and it has consumed him entirely with its artificial and dazzling beauties. It is as if the spectacular form of the féerie has been made real, and he is caught within its destabilizing marvels.

In the epigraph to the article he wrote about Gautier in 1859, Charles Baudelaire referred to this passage about speaking in jewels.[93] It would appear that Baudelaire was particularly interested in Gautier's account of visiting the Great Exhibition, as he would go on to evoke it in a poem that he would write soon after, "Parisian Dream", which appeared in the second edition of *Les fleurs du mal* in 1861. In this poem, Baudelaire extends the relation between spectacular beauty and the loss of self, further exploring the relationship between fantasy and sites of modernity. The poem describes a dream of "a marvellous landscape" and "a vast palace" which, through recurring references to metal, glass and crystal, provides an oneiric counterpart to the Crystal Palace. Amidst a range of fantastic imagery, the poem also depicts a site akin to the Indian Court, describing how a heavenly Ganges pours its treasures into this extraordinary place. After recounting this marvellous spectacle, the final two stanzas of the poem return to everyday reality as the narrator awakens to confront the actual squalor of his living conditions.

The narrator imagines a spectacular dreamlike landscape that he tames and controls. In order to articulate this fantastic dream, there are references to the sublime, the infinite and the marvellous; however, like the regulated fantasy of the Great Exhibition and Indian Court, such wonders are modified by references to symmetry, monotony and prohibitions. An ironic vision of fantasy builds throughout the poem, as descriptions of dazzling mirrors and a crystalline light become replaced by more ominous images of darkness by the end, in which the marvels on display are illuminated only by an inner light. The dream is brought to a close with the stanza:

> A silence like eternity
> Prevailed, there was no sound to hear;
> These marvels all were for the eye,
> And there was nothing for the ear.[94]

The stanza evokes the visual spectacle of the féerie in its emphasis on the "marvels" that "all were for the eye". The connection between the dream and the féerie is made directly: earlier in the poem, the narrator is described as an "architect of my féeries".[95] Linking the visual intoxication of the féerie with the Crystal Palace, the poem elaborates on a vision of spectacular and modern fantasy. Turning from such a spectacle to an "eternity" provides a reminder of the transience and superficiality of the wonders that the narrator has fashioned. This resonates with Baudelaire's description of modernity as "the transient, the fleeting, the contingent; it is one half of art, the other being the eternal and immovable."[96] Viewing the Great Exhibition in relation to the féerie, the poem provides an ambivalent image of modernity's enchantments: alongside their beauty and spectacle, one sees their relation to power, artificiality, constraint and ephemerality. Baudelaire sets out darker connotations of a modern world of fantasy and spectacle.

Gautier held on to instances of beauty and wonder in modernity, however fleeting, and the féerie would continue to provide a recurring example of this in his later writing. In a review of a restaging of *Les pilules du diable* in 1863, he describes the genre of the féerie as a "somewhat coarse form", writing that the play's authors "know very well that they are not making art, and that it is not art that the crowd asks of them…"[97] Nevertheless, this "type of spectacle corresponds to a secret desire of the human spirit, a desire made all the more lively as self-perfecting civilization makes the part of fantasy less large." In elucidating this experience of the fantastic in modern life, he refers to Baudelaire: "Happily the key to the *artificial paradises*, to borrow a characteristic expression of Charles Baudelaire, isn't found in all hands. The féeries, with their marvelous decors, innocently and soberly represent the mirages of the opium dream." The féerie's capacity to fashion fantasy in contemporary life is further discussed as he describes the play, adopting a similar structure and theme to Baudelaire's "Parisian Dream" where one witnesses overwhelming marvels and then awakens to confront reality. Gautier begins with a discussion of how "imaginations reduced by narrow reality" enjoy such plays for offering "brilliant and chimerical tableaux… which follow without more logic than the phantasmagorias of dream." He goes on to list the play's extraordinary marvels at length. This ends, though: "the dream finished, you find yourself in your room, contemplating with a sort of stupor the plumed drapes as if they were hiding from you, behind their banal curtains, magic tableaux which have disappeared." Destined to be artificial and transient, the visible marvels of the féerie could still offer fantasy in waking life, glimmers of the ideal produced by contemporary visual culture.

The Féerie and Visual Culture

Féeries themselves would sometimes be described as an array of modern technologies, luxurious goods and visual spectacles much like the Great Exhibition and other related exhibitions in the latter half of the nineteenth century. For example, in the 1860s, Ulbach described *La biche au bois* as an "exposition of painting, costumes, gilding and stage mechanics" and a review of *Rothomago* described the play's "triumph, quite foreign to literature, of magnificent and clever theatrical exhibitions, of decor, of machines, of tricks, of transformations."[98] In addition to such comparisons, the féerie's emphasis on spectacle, new technologies and transformation began to be situated and understood in terms of wider changes in visual culture.

One example of this was the comparison of féeries to illustrated books, reflecting a growing publishing market, new print technologies and the increasingly central role of images in contemporary storytelling. Writing about *Peau d'âne* (*Donkeyskin*) in 1863, B. Jouvin at *Le Figaro* noted, "In a féerie, the play counts for little or nothing; it's the text destined to frame and to explain the *illustrations*, and this text should be modestly placed in the anfractuosities of the drawing and, if need be, vanish."[99] Other critics drew attention to a specific comparison to illustrated fairy tales through reference to Gustave Doré; Roqueplan described a staging of *Cendrillon* (*Cinderella*) in 1866 as a "tale illustrated by the hand of a master, in the manner of Gustave Doré, with the resources of an ingenious, powerful and prodigious theatre…"[100] In his review of a performance of *Le pied de mouton* in 1860, Gautier focused on the broader sense of illustrations as forms of spectacle, writing that "the decors, the tricks, the transformations, the costumes, the dances, the prodigies, the apotheoses are the most important thing. The illustration of the tale gets the upper hand on the tale itself."[101] In his review of *Le pied de mouton*, Jouvin also described the play in terms of illustrations, suggesting that dialogue in féeries was analogous to the written text in "illustrated journals":

> Between two drawings, there exists a blank which the writer should fill; there are ten or fifteen lines of text, not less, not more. All the worse for the spiritual word which is enjambed on the eleventh or the sixteenth line: it is crossed out without pity… To pass, at the machinist's whistle, from a forest to a palace, or to replace an

effect of the moon with an effect of the sea, it's the
job of two puns; three if the counterweights are giving
some difficulty.[102]

Onstage dialogue, in this review, is approached as simply a pause
between new spectacles, part of a shift in importance from words
to images which was evident also in illustrated journals.

A similar description of the increased prominence of images
over words, but with reference to a different visual context, is
evident in a review of *Rothomago* from 1862; after summarizing
the story, Paul de Saint-Victor at *La Presse* noted, "The interest
isn't there: it is in the dazzling tableaux which are unwound by
the decorators, the costumiers and the machinists. When we
watch the magic lantern, we hardly hear the explanation of the
man who shows it to us."[103] In order to capture the centrality of
spectacle, Jouvin's review of *Le pied de mouton* also compares the
spectacle of the féerie to the projected images of the magic lantern,
writing how the play "lasts for twenty-one tableaux; it could last
forever: it's a matter for the magic lantern much more than that
of emotion."[104] Developing this connection to visual technologies
and optical devices, féeries were also compared to kaleidoscopes.
Describing the final scene of *Le pied de mouton*, the apotheosis
ending, Saint-Victor told his readers to "imagine a monstrous
kaleidoscope" and Gautier would extend this comparison to
encapsulate entire plays such as *Turlututu*: "The stage, like a kaleidoscope that one turns, changes and recomposes perpetually."[105]
Gautier would compare the féerie to the chromatrope as well in
his description of *Cendrillon*, which appears "like an immense
chromatrope [which] perpetually turns and decomposes itself in
front of you."[106] Such comparisons would highlight the ways in
which the féerie offered spectacles that resonated with optical
devices and new technologies of image production.

Developing the implications of this emphasis on spectacle,
some reviews would elaborate on how the authorship of féeries
was due to industry and technology rather than a playwright or
director. After noting some of the main actors in *Rothomago*,

Ulbach writes, "But, how to name everyone, and especially the true poets: the machinists who bring about all these surprises, the painters who open for us these enchanted perspectives, these profane paradises, these springs, these auroras, these nights, these palaces, these Alhambras of stunning light?"[107] Such a reference to the machinists and the painters suggests a decreasing importance for traditional notions of authorship, replacing the author of a play with its designer and with its technology. The theatre reviewer for *L'Année Littéraire et Dramatique* described how this should lead to a reconsideration of the ways in which authorship is valued, complaining that

> the theatres rich enough to go without talent require industry and applied science for their plays: they make themselves branches of Arts and Trades, of the Sorbonne, and largely exhibit engines and scientific experiments in the tricks. Gas, electricity and magnesium furnish them with streams of light which is enough for them; they inundate us with it.[108]

Ulbach at *Le Temps* offered a different perspective on the intersection of industry and spectacle. Referring to two of the most dazzling effects in *Aladin* (*Aladdin*), he suggests that a Legion of Honour should not only be awarded to literary authors, but also to "the great unknown artist who prepares these fabulous transformations, who creates an ingenious device with the aid of which a mushroom changes into a kiosk... and a ship suddenly transforms into a fantastic palace."[109] Although marked by a somewhat exaggerated tone, such accounts suggested that féeries, and their spectacular transformations, were being authored by industry and novel technologies.

The close association of the féerie with technology and visual transformation would result in it becoming associated with other contemporary spectacles. An article from 1889 titled "Fête de nuit" sets out what appears to be an account of a play: "It is getting late and the night has come. The féerie is going to begin, and nothing can describe it."[110] But rather than going on to discuss an actual theatrical féerie, it is quite a different spectacle to which the article is referring: the luminous fountains at the Universal Exposition of 1889 in Paris. The luminous fountains were among the most celebrated sights of the Exposition. In the *Journal des Débats*, Henri de Parville describes how "their success surpasses all that we could have imagined; they are running in competition with the Gallery of Machines, and even with the Eiffel Tower" and the prominent science writer, Louis Figuier, noted that they were, "along with the Eiffel Tower, the great attraction of the universal Exposition of 1889."[111] Luminous fountains drew upon scientific developments in manipulating the refraction of light to show colours projected onto the fountains as if they were captured in droplets and streams of water, in a state of ongoing movement and transformation. The luminous fountains would be written about in ways that drew upon their association with the féerie; for example, Figuier elaborated on their vision of spectacular transformation:

> Nothing can give the idea of the aspect of the fountain when the three hundred sheaves of water burst forth at the same time, in the midst of the night's obscurity. The streams of coloured water projected themselves in showers of fire, falling back down in a rain of sparks; then, brusquely, the decor changed: from a golden yellow it became red, green or blue. Finally, these diverse tints transformed themselves, falling into one another, going from ruby and from emerald to the most delicate opaline nuances. It was a féerique spectacle.[112]

Employing the term "decor", emphasizing the extraordinary transformations and describing them as féerique, this account situates the luminous fountains in the same kind of language used to describe the theatrical féerie's vision of spectacular mutability.

Descriptions of the luminous fountains also evoked changing notions of authorship, where an engineer or operator was responsible for their visual marvels, much like a féerie's basis in industry and technology. Describing the "infinite variety" of colours in the illuminated streams of water, Figuier noted how these are controlled by an operator like a painter at their palette or an organist at their instrument.[113] Offering a similar comparison between the operation of this machine and artistic creation, Eugène-Melchior de Vogüé described the engineer of the luminous fountains as "a poet, a poet in action".[114] Vogüé also drew attention to the labourers toiling at the bottom of the fountains: "I watched them at the base of their underground passage, these brave labourers, readying the féerie in the heat and in the darkness."[115] Such accounts indicate that the luminous fountains were drawn into the context of the féerie in multiple ways: through shared depictions of transformation, through a similar relation to contemporary industrial contexts and through the creative potential of new technologies.

Some accounts suggested that the luminous fountains went further than this, recasting the Exposition by bathing it in a transformative light: "Never has one seen reality enveloped in such a phantasmagoria. All the perspectives are changed and prodigiously enlarged…"[116] The shifting colours and lights of the luminous fountains bring about a substantial shift in perception, charging this emblematic site of modern life and commerce with fantastic potential, so that an "orgy of light seduces the gaze and transports the visitor into a land from *The Thousand and One Nights*. We are in fairyland."[117] Vogüé extended the implications of this comparison, suggesting that the luminous fountains offered an emergent visual language: "when the refined retina will distinguish, in the chromatic range of colours in movement, the vibrations that the ear perceives as sounds, there will be found perhaps a Chopin or a Liszt who will ravish souls with visual melodies."[118] This manipulation of colour and light might be, "for the painter and the thinker, the occasion for thoughts, fecund experiences."[119]

An extended discussion of the altered perspectives brought about by the luminous fountains provided the conclusion for a lengthy description of visiting the Exposition in the *Atlantic*

Monthly.[120] Near the end of the day, after having described numerous sights and spectacles, the reporter hurries out of the display of industrial might in the Gallery of Machines, writing, "I nearly forgot that I was there for enjoyment, and made haste to get into the open air."[121] Once outside, the Eiffel Tower at night becomes visible: "Then the vulgarity of the crowd, the trivial details, the clap-trap, the pasteboard aspect of huge temporary structures, were lost in a vaster and more comprehensive impression, at once more real and more fantastic."[122] The Eiffel Tower offers a comforting and substantial sight, a respite from the onslaught of overwhelming or fleeting images characteristic of the Exposition. But rather than lingering on this view, the correspondent's attention quickly shifts from this emblem of modern stability to an emblem of instability, the luminous fountains: "At a stated hour, the illumination of the fountains produced a marvelous transformation scene, beautiful enough for fairy-land…"[123] This spectacular image of transformation does more than offer a pleasing or astonishing sight; it seems to recast the environment into an enchanted world. The correspondent now walks among the "mysterious pavilions and strange gardens like Haroun Alraschid in search of adventure", seeing "a transcendent grandeur" in the outlines of the buildings which now belong to "precincts of enchantment".[124] While this description partly evokes the ways in which electric lighting created the effect of an extraordinary new visual world, it also draws attention to how the luminous fountains themselves became a metonym for such a world. The fountains offered an alternative to the display of the less poetic manifestations of industry and trade at the Exposition, while still offering a spectacular vision of the modern world as a sight of fantastic possibility and ongoing transformation.

The notion that the play of light and the figuration of transformation refigure the modern world was dramatized in the most prominent féerie produced in the year of the Exposition, *Le prince Soleil*. It was heralded as an apt theatrical spectacle, "a play for the Exposition".[125] Certain features may have contributed to this sense of the play's relevance to the Exposition. One central aspect of *Le prince Soleil* was its presentation of a journey through different nations, offering a veiled commentary on contemporary political subjects. Francisque Sarcey, in *Le Temps*, characterized it as a "scientific féerie, of which *Around the World in 80 Days* is the prototype."[126] As a variation on the more traditional féerie, the "scientific féerie" offered contemporary iconography and subject matter, often replacing the onstage display of fantastic wonders with technological wonders. With a journey that took the play's hero – and the audience – on a voyage through Sweden, Portugal, the Indian Ocean and the empire of the Sun, *Le prince Soleil* offered the international spectacle of the Universal Exposition in miniature, onstage.

Le prince Soleil also presented a visual correspondence with the Exposition's luminous fountains. Hector Pessard, writing for *Le Gaulois*, begins his review by describing the overall experience of watching the play in terms of a similar visual enchantment:

> I would never have believed that a human eye could contain so many things… Imagine an immense crucible, in which a fusion of turquoises, amethysts, rubies, sapphires mix their streams of light with waves of liquid gold, fringed by a silver foam… Conceive by a cerebral effort the rainbow's glimmerings, the aurora borealis's brightness, the desert's white lights shining upon this fire of metals and gemstones. It's done? You have imagined, supposed, conceived? Well, you have an idea, but an imperfect idea, of the bedazzlements of only one of the tableaux of *Le prince Soleil*.[127]

Marcel Fouquier in *La Nouvelle Revue* made a similar point, describing one particularly striking tableau as "an evanescent enchantment built on a foundation of fugitive light and féerique rays".[128] The scene takes place after a shipwreck, entwining visual wonders of luminosity with a dreamlike scenario: "Quite shaken by the incidents of his interrupted voyage, the prince imagines that he has been transported into the sun. He has hallucinations, and all that he thinks he sees, we see."[129] Linking it to the spectacular fantasies of *Le pied de mouton*, he described the scene as "an interlude of classical féerie, truly staggering, and even more dazzling" than the more contemporary scientific féerie of which it was a part.[130] Such accounts were indicative of the major role that the féerie and related spectacles of fantasy and transformation had come to play in contemporary visual culture. A century after the French Revolution, a new kind of royalty was envisaged on the French stage – no longer a sun king, but a sun prince, with a suitably dazzling visual form of instability for a modern age. Ephemeral and mutable, technological and enchanting, féeries such as this helped shape modern fantasy.

2 A CINEMA OF TRANSFORMATIONS
The Film Féerie and Georges Méliès

A CENTURY AFTER ITS THEATRICAL PREMIERE AT LA GAÎTÉ, the iconic theatrical féerie *Le pied de mouton* was transformed into a film. A single reel in length, running about fifteen minutes, *Le pied de mouton* (Capellani, 1907) presented the rapid unfolding of extraordinary imagery and bizarre situations. For example, in one of the film's early scenes, the main character, Gusman, rides a giant snail as he passes through a village.[1] The snail transforms into an enormous cello and then four women emerge from it, each holding a musical instrument. The cello disappears and the women join Gusman as he serenades his beloved Léonora. Soon after, the balcony upon which Léonora was standing lowers and Gusman embarks on this domestic chariot as it lifts him upwards into her home. Such marvellous voyages and transformations continue over the course of the film as it moves through a series of fantastic locales such as "The Brazen Towers" and "The Grotto of Sleep". The story is difficult to follow as the peregrinations of the narrative are dwarfed by the spectacle of vivid colours, extravagant design and startling trick effects.

This was one of many film féeries produced in the first decade of the twentieth century. These were among the lengthiest, most costly and most internationally popular films at the time. Richard Abel writes that they were "perhaps the most successful genre for French exhibitors" and the "real boon to vaudeville" in the United States.[2] Typically presenting a series of tableaux and events loosely based around a simple story, such films offered spectacular imagery set within a milieu of fantasy. Georges Méliès was the genre's most well-known and influential filmmaker, having produced both the first film féerie, *Cinderella* (1899), and the most well-known example, *A Trip to the Moon* (1902). Other major filmmakers, such as Edwin S. Porter, Cecil Hepworth and Ferdinand Zecca worked within this genre as well; Zecca would recall that "it's not in the dramas and the acrobatic films that I put my greatest hope. It was in the féeries."[3] These films presented cinema's first fairy tales, including "Bluebeard", "Little Red Riding Hood", "Sleeping Beauty" and "Aladdin", along with film versions of well-known theatrical féeries such as *Les sept châteaux du diable* and *La biche au bois*. Although dwindling in importance towards the end of the decade, the genre of the féerie established fairy tales and fantasy as subjects for cinema.[4]

The types of fantasies offered by the film féerie drew upon a range of source material. For example, in 1907, the year that *Le pied de mouton* was released, Pathé produced nine films that were categorized as "féeries and tales" in their catalogue.[5] These were divided equally between cinematic versions of theatrical féeries, other fantastic subjects and adaptations of fairy tales which had themselves often been staged. Cinematic féeries also incorporated material from other media, such as magic-lantern shows and illustrated books.[6] The connection between theatre's and cinema's féeries has been examined by theatre and film historians, including Georges Sadoul, A. Nicholas Vardac and Katherine Kovács.[7] More recently, in the work of scholars such as Tom Gunning and André Gaudreault, the film féerie has been taken as a key example of how early films negotiated tensions between presenting stories and offering a "cinema of attractions" that foregrounded spectacle.[8]

This chapter sets out a different way of approaching the uses of fantasy in this pivotal genre of early cinema by focusing on the implications and effects of transformation in the cinematic féerie. Compared to the theatrical féerie, the film féerie offered intensified transformations: rather than waiting for scene changes to be prepared, they happened in the instant of a cut; rather than unfolding over the course of hours, these films unfolded in a matter of minutes; rather than developing exclusively from stage effects, new cinematic ways of showing transformation emerged. This created new ways in which transformation could be understood, figured and negotiated. As the previous chapter examined, nineteenth-century observers of the theatrical féerie and its associated spectacles drew a host of different implications from the sight of transformation, ranging from enchantment to dislocation, from melancholy to consolation. Such reactions extended to changing notions of art, modern society, spectacle and technology. This engagement with the implications of transformation found new avenues through cinema in ways that continued to elaborate on the interrelation of fantasy, modernity and spectacle. By showing a filmic world where images were not simply representations of something fixed and stable, transformation could function to refigure meanings, disrupt stabilities, shift attention to unnoticed aspects of the material world and fashion a cinematic milieu alive to the possibilities of change.

Transformation and Visual Metaphor

As with its theatrical predecessor, the spectacle of trick effects and transformations in the cinematic féerie often took centre stage. In addition to rapidly editing different extraordinary settings together, other effects such as reverse motion, superimpositions and stage trickery could all contribute to the depiction of mutability in the féerie. But the most prominent trope of transformation was effected through the so-called "substitution splice": a cut, or series of cuts, that would show the appearance, disappearance or substitution of something onscreen. In this respect, the film féerie was described at the time as a longer and more elaborate version of the "transformation view", another popular genre which, rather like a magic show, would display the mutability of objects, people and places.[9] The short film *Metempsychosis* (Chomón, 1907) offers a typically elaborate example of how the substitution splice could refigure a filmic world. In a single tableau, a series of astonishing events take place: fairies suddenly appear; a costume metamorphoses into butterfly wings; a baby girl emerges from a rose and a baby boy emerges from a cabbage. The Pathé catalogue glosses the film as follows:

> These scenes unfold in a series of gracefully incoherent tableaux which truly appear to be the image of this changing, mutable diverse world where, if it is necessary to believe in certain metaphysics, the souls, brought from a perpetual swaying dance, transmigrate from one being to another through the stars.[10]

This description draws together visual incoherency and transformation with ancient beliefs in metempsychosis. The film offers a range of other allusions to mutability, such as a metamorphosing butterfly, magical beings and animate objects. Sights such as these would be extended over the course of an entire féerie, making images of mutability one of the genre's central visual tropes.

In 1907, the influential literary critic and essayist Remy de Gourmont discussed the potentials of transformation, cinema and the féerie in one of his regular columns in the *Mercure de France*. As a key figure in articulating and influencing Symbolist and Imagist approaches to art, Gourmont's discussion offers an important early instance of a major critic engaging with the relatively new form of cinema. Rather than striking the tone of a highbrow critic looking down upon a popular entertainment, Gourmont marvelled at cinema: "Only the churlish and uncurious scorn these spectacles. For intelligent people, they are a singular and sometimes stunning achievement."[11] Discussing a range of elements – such as film's use of settings that are filled with movement, rapid changes, extraordinary colour and dreamlike silence – Gourmont situated cinema in the kind of discourse circulating around the theatrical féerie. For example, he writes, in a description that recalls Gautier's accounts of the féerie, "the characters keep their customary nonsense to themselves. It's a great relief. The silent theatre is the ideal distraction, the best place to repose: the images borne aloft by light music. One need not even bother to dream."[12]

Gourmont also draws attention to the specific genre of the film féerie. Describing cinema's popular appeals, he notes the "féeries, ballets, transformations, apparitions, and sudden changes done by means of camera tricks…" Referring to the substitution splices in féeries as "sudden transformations", he goes on to write that this is a trope "whose secret I cannot fathom: this is a feature that belongs exclusively to the cinema." However, for Gourmont, the transformation in a "féerie of living characters… lacks the nuances that one can obtain through a fusion of images, through a shimmering rainbow of colors."[13] Fascinated by the féerie and its transformations, Gourmont nevertheless draws attention to the limitations of the genre's depiction of mutability.

While this might appear to be a minor and somewhat disparaging reference to a popular genre, his discussion of transformation in the féerie raises a much larger implication: the potential of the substitution splice to create new meanings through visual transformation. When he refers to "a fusion of images", he is alluding to how a combination of ideas or images through a single impression can become a way of revivifying language and perception, one of his central critical concerns. In "The Dissociation of Ideas" (1900), Gourmont writes, "There are two modes of thinking: one can accept ideas and associations of ideas in the manner they are commonly used or indulge oneself in new associations or – and this is rarer – in original dissociations of ideas."[14] The notion of ideas that are recombined is extended further, as Gourmont continues,

> The association and dissociation of ideas (or images, the idea being no more than a worn-out image) evolve according to indeterminate twists and turns whose general direction cannot readily be gathered. No ideas are so distant, no images so disparate that they cannot be joined in easy association at least for a moment.

Rather than seeing words and images as fixed, their potential instability is necessary for new ideas to be formed and for old ideas to be disrupted. In "The Funeral of Style" (1902), Gourmont articulated the potentials of metaphor to enact this instability by poetically combining words, images and ideas. He uses an extract from Gustave Flaubert's *Salammbô* (1862) as an example:

> Flaubert, who has a capacity for lying, and consequently an infinite capacity for artistic creation, is not exact when he writes: 'The elephants… their chests like ships' prows, cut through the ranks of Roman soldiers, leaving them flailing in armless swirls in their wake.' He succeeds in amalgamating the two images (elephants and soldiers, ships and waves) so effectively only because he has seen them in a single glance. What he gives us is no longer two drawings that can be superposed on one another symmetrically but the visually absurd and artistically admirable confusion of a double and troubled/triple [*troublé*] sensation.[15]

In this discussion of metaphor and language, Gourmont elaborates on a way of writing and perceiving where words, images and ideas become open to change and refiguration.

For Gourmont, this is a central feature of how language can create new meanings and engage with a changing world. In "The Dissociation of Ideas" (1900), he notes that "some associations are so durable that they seem to be eternal and so tightly linked that they resemble those double stars which the naked eye is incapable of differentiating."[16] He describes these as commonplaces, "the already seen, the already heard". For Gourmont, the commonplace "is at once more and less than a banality: it is a banality, but one that is sometimes ineluctable; it is a banality, but one that is so universally accepted it takes on the name of truth." He gives as an example of such a commonplace the association of honour and the military, going on to describe an event, likely the Dreyfus affair as Henri Dorra observes, in which the links between honour and militarism were disrupted: "it was unconscious, and it was temporary, but it did take place, and that is important for the observer."[17] Like an event that disrupts commonplace associations, the act of recombining words, as well as ideas and images, in order to establish new meanings and to disrupt seemingly stable categories is crucial to language's power to redescribe reality.

Such a conception of language is closely linked to the "fusion of images" that Gourmont describes as latent, but limited, in the transformations of the film féerie. The filmic trope of the substitution splice disrupts a fixed and readily comprehensible reality, helping form new continuities and potentials in a manner like metaphorical language. This way of approaching the effect of the substitution splice has been discussed by Paul Hammond, who notes its "metaphorical possibilities", and Elizabeth Ezra, who writes that it has "a poetic value, like any trope" and that "Méliès's use of filmic substitution is metaphor in motion."[18] Gourmont's approach provides a particular way of seeing this metaphorical quality, drawing our attention to how disrupting commonplaces and forging new connections can become a way to engage with the fluidity of language and meaning, and help refigure our understanding of the world.

The idea of new coherencies being formed through transformation can be seen in Méliès's own discussion of the substitution splice in his article "Cinematographic Views" (1907). Méliès describes how he discovered this cinematic trope when his camera temporarily jammed while filming a street scene at the Place de l'Opéra in Paris. He writes that

> a minute was needed to disengage the film and to make the camera work again. During this minute, the passersby, a horse trolley, and the vehicles had, of course, changed positions. In projecting the strip, rejoined at the point of the break, I suddenly saw a Madeleine-Bastille omnibus change into a hearse and men changed into women.[19]

In this anecdote, which was likely a fabrication, Méliès offers his apparently accidental realization that editing could be used to make things appear, disappear or transform – the central effect of the substitution splice.[20] This transformation of men into women and an omnibus into a hearse could be seen as an example of a surprising moment of discontinuity, a startling change.[21] Situating this filmic trope in its context of the urban environment at the turn of the century leads to other implications, however. The transformation of the omnibus and the men suggests the scope of changes wrought by modernity. By seeing a mode of public transportation, the omnibus, instantaneously transformed into an image of death, the hearse, Méliès draws out anxieties surrounding the perceived threat of modernity, urban life and technology that were prominent at the time.[22] The omnibus first appeared in France in the late 1820s, but as Masha Belenky writes, "Even though the real-life omnibus became a fact of urban life by the end of the nineteenth century, literary texts continued to use the powerful image of the omnibus to expose the underlying anxieties about the ever-changing modern world characterized by transformations, speed, and chaos."[23] In Méliès's anecdote, the omnibus becomes a hearse, capturing a sense of instability and danger around modernity. The transformation becomes further drawn into the effects of a changing society with the image of men metamorphosed into women. The public role of women in urban centres such as Paris had become significantly more visible by the turn of the century – men becoming women draws attention to changing conditions of the public sphere.[24] The transformation recombines images in order to disrupt the association of men with urban life, and casts this commonplace in a new light. Like Gourmont's discussion of metaphorical language, a destabilizing link is made between ideas and images; through this, different implications of social change are brought to the fore.

This coincides with certain key elements of metaphor. Discussing Aristotle's *Rhetoric*, Paul Ricoeur describes how metaphor can be conceived of as "a bringing-together of terms that first surprises, then bewilders, and finally uncovers a relationship hidden beneath the paradox." Such rhetoric draws upon both "the pleasure of understanding that follows surprise" and "the power of placing things before our eyes".[25] The examples in Méliès's anecdote suggest a similar kind of reformulation: a novel meaning is created through a visual surprise that reveals an underlying relationship between images. Shifting perspectives and disrupting commonplace associations – and making this strikingly visible to the eyes – the transformation offers a visual metaphor. Or, in Gourmont's terms, this substitution splice provides a "dissociation" and "recombination" of ideas. The links between modern transportation and liveliness, between men and public life, are shown as destabilized images.

Féeries offered diverse transformations, with specific examples of substitution splices only sometimes figuring a discernible metaphorical intent or effect: characters, places and things were all swept up in mutability. This wider sense of transformation, which would be extended through the longer féeries with their multiple settings and ongoing journeys, could still offer a similar effect of shifting categories and perceptions. In the same year that Méliès wrote "Cinematographic Views", he produced a major féerie, *The Merry Frolics of Satan* (1906), that showed the same concerns of technological threat and changing gender roles as his account of discovering the substitution splice. The premise of the film is that William Crackford, an English engineer who desires "to attain unknown speeds. 600 kilometers an hour!!!" makes a deal with the Devil for some magic pills that, when thrown on the ground, will apparently make his wishes come true.[26] After leaving the Devil's lair, Crackford throws one of the pills on the ground as his family is eating dinner. A cinematic vision of frustrated desire ensues, as his fantasy of travel proves to be comically nightmarish. Crackford's dream, as well as his trust in technology and magic, is ultimately punished: the film ends with him being roasted alive by Satan.

One of the most striking scenes of transformation occurs immediately after Crackford's visit to the Devil's lair. Returning home, Crackford enters his dining room, with his family seated at the dining table. Excited, he proceeds to throw one of the enchanted Devil's pills to the ground. A chest appears, out of which two attendants roll. They quickly return to the chest and pull another chest out, out of which two more attendants roll. Another box appears, and two more attendants come forth. They then proceed to open up more chests and pack away all the household furniture. Crackford's family dashes offscreen. Crackford, who has been helping the attendants pack his house into boxes, begins to assist them while they link a series of crates together. His family runs back into the room, now wearing their hats – ready to go on a trip, they are brought further into the turmoil as the attendants lift them (and Crackford's friend) into the crates, closing the lids. Joined together now, the attendants and Crackford dance around the crates as they are transformed into the carriages of a makeshift train. Crackford is given a locomotive, and he hops on, joyfully driving off despite the protests of his friend. Crackford's family members, all women, are not only passengers on his train: they strain against the bars of the carriages like animals in a cage. Once this devilish train has chugged offscreen, Satan appears and the attendants reveal their true selves as his servants.

The enchanted train leads Crackford and his family through pleasant locales which become transformed as if in a kind of diabolical Baedeker: "In the Streets of London" becomes "The Population Revolts" as the English throw things at them; the picturesque "The Torrent and the Ravine in the Alps" becomes "The Catastrophe" as a bridge breaks, sending Crackford's family down a chasm.[27] His friend wants to stop and help them, but, according to the catalogue description, Crackford explains that this is the work of rescue professionals and, besides, they should know how to swim. So, leaving his family behind, he enacts the tableau title: "Forward!!!"[28] Not only has Crackford's obsession with technology and travel obliterated his home, it has led to the death of his family. While Crackford is a caricature of (English) industrialism, these events are indicative of a larger concern that appears within Méliès's féeries: whether caused by diabolical magic, modern technologies or the speed of visual transformation, characters are swept up by movement and change. In many of Méliès's féeries, there are similar representations of female characters as bystanders or victims in a world of change: captured by imps in *The Kingdom of the Fairies* (Méliès, 1903) just after her engagement ceremony, Azurine is earlier swarmed by her attendants in her bedroom; blocked out by other guests at the party who make her virtually invisible in the mise-en-scène, Fatima is a visibly angry and reluctant bride in *Bluebeard* (1901); the assistant in *The Impossible Voyage* (1904) has a tray of food knocked out of her hands by a male scientist after she interrupts his work; even in *Cinderella*, the event of transformation leads to anxiety figured by the threatening image of a clock that strikes midnight. Unlike female characters in these films, male characters tend to become gleefully and naively engulfed in a momentum of change in which they are often powerless.

The Merry Frolics of Satan elaborates on this theme of transformation's force. With only the slightest narrative rationale, a series of trick effects shows a home transformed into a train and the destabilizing journey that follows, with dire consequences. An exaggerated image of domesticity – five women at the dining table – is metamorphosed into a scene of modern travel and masculine endeavour. Like Méliès's account of discovering the substitution splice when an omnibus becomes a hearse and men become women, transportation is recast as death and women are shown suddenly thrust into a world of dizzying movement. *The Merry Frolics of Satan* elaborates on this through a series of fantastic transformations and an extraordinary voyage, figuring an astonishing experience of dislocation and destruction. Whether in individual cuts or over the course of a film, the film féerie could offer a vision of ongoing transformation that thwarted commonplace ideas of cultural stability and the positive aspects of modern change.

Cinematographic Views

For Méliès, cinema has a special capacity to create transformations not only within a film, but also in its representation of the world. Méliès elaborated on the implications of transformation and film in "Cinematographic Views". The article explains the production of transformation views and féeries, recounting the discovery of the substitution splice as well broader ideas relating to the context of cinema at the time. A section of the article is devoted to outlining a miniature history of cinema through its characteristic "views", or genres, in the order in which they appeared. I want to examine this summary of cinema's brief history as it raises a set of implications regarding Méliès's conception of the potentials of film, fantasy and transformation.

The earliest cinematic view that Méliès describes is the "natural view", which is made up of "cinematographically reproducing scenes from ordinary life: views taken in the streets, in the squares, by the sea, on riverbanks, in boats, on trains; panoramic views, ceremonies, parades, funeral processions, etc."[29] Méliès suggests that the appeal of these natural views was originally based upon characteristics of cinema, particularly its capacity to register movement. This gradually changed so that the appeal of "natural views" was based upon their subject matter, such as exotic locales. The natural view is followed by the "scientific view". Here, Méliès draws attention to films which are taken through microscopes, presenting "enlargements of the workings of infinitely tiny creatures that are very curious to watch." He also includes other technological and scientific subjects: "surgical operations", "glass blowing", "steam or electric machine components in movement", "pottery-making" and "all sorts of diverse industries". The "scientific view" includes films created through special cinematic technologies that heighten perception as well as a broader array of films about industry. Méliès adds, "Strictly speaking, this special branch of cinematography could be placed in the category of natural views…" Yet, he continues, "One must not silently ignore this cinematographic specialty." While he may be referring to the popularity of these films at the time, there is an implicit distinction between the scientific view and the natural view: the scientific view shifts the perspective of the natural view by showing a hitherto unnoticed world of process, construction or movement.

The third view that Méliès sets out in his history of film is the "composed subject" where "action is readied as it is in the theater and performed by the actors in front of the camera…"[30] Although Méliès describes this view as theatrical, it goes beyond simply a fictional scene performed for the camera; it shows the performance of any event, whether scripted or not. The examples of this are "innumerable", including acrobatic acts, operas, religious scenes, newsreels and reenactments. This category would include most of the films produced at the time. The fourth and final view is the transformation view. This includes the briefest of trick films showing a transformation through a substitution splice or longer films which incorporate a series of different fantastic effects, like the féerie. Méliès writes that he "created this special area" and that it is the view to which he has "exclusively devoted [his] efforts".[31] He emphasizes that this view is not only characterized by its use of the transformations between images, noting that the "trade name" of "transformation views" is "unsuitable". Preferring the term "fantastic views", he elaborates on their other devices, including dissolves, the filming of elaborate stagecraft and the manipulation of properties of film for fantastic effects.

What is it about the introduction of fantastic effects – and particularly transformations – that marks this view as something categorically distinct from composed subjects? Clearly, part of the reason would be its centrality to Méliès's own film production; this outline of cinematographic views might be taken as a self-congratulatory gesture, placing his favoured genre at the height of creativity in cinema art and cinema history. Or perhaps the view's relation to fantasy distinguishes it from the other views which, although sometimes artificial, limit themselves to a representation of a more or less "real" world. In another respect, though, Méliès situates the "fantastic view" as a counterpart to the "scientific view". While they might seem at opposite ends of a spectrum of representation – one lifting high to fabricate a fantastic world of transformation and the other digging deep to reveal an unacknowledged world of animate life and creation – they both perform a related representational activity. They refigure a more static view (composed or natural) in terms of mutability. The fantastic view *adds* mutability and the scientific view *reveals* it.

The cinematic way of showing the world in the "fantastic view" and "scientific view", as Méliès describes them, resonates with certain features of metaphor.[32] Ricoeur draws a distinction between a *rhetoric* of metaphor and a *poetics* of metaphor. Rhetoric is based primarily on the word, using a figure of speech in order to cast it in a new light. Extending this to cinema, we can see how the substitution splice might, in specific cases, perform the same function with images. Poetics, however, takes this notion of refiguring the word and transposes it to an entire work. Examining the ways this is explored in the writing of Aristotle, Ricoeur describes how poetic language can enlarge a perspective on reality. Just as a metaphor can suddenly shift plain speech into a more dynamic expression, altering the ways we understand and use language, so can poetics lift the material of the world into a realm that is related to, but different from, the ways in which we might typically perceive it. This is not necessarily a distortion of the "real" world, but instead can be seen as an act of mimesis. Ricoeur writes that the context out of which Aristotle introduced his influential examination of mimesis was not one where nature was identified with "some inert 'given'".[33] Instead, "perhaps it is because, for [Aristotle], nature is itself living that mimesis can be not enslaving and that compositional and creative imitation of nature can be possible." In other words, Ricoeur concludes, "*Lively* expression is that which expresses existence as *alive*." In a similar vein, one can approach cinema's transformations not only in terms of the specific relations between images or the ongoing transformations that make up a film, but also in the broader sense of how all things are transformed by film. As Ricoeur argues, "To present [humankind] '*as acting*' and all things '*as in act*' – such could well be the *ontological* function of metaphorical discourse, in which every dormant potentiality of existence appears *as* blossoming forth, every latent capacity for action *as* actualized." In "Cinematographic Views", Méliès alludes to this kind of representation where certain cinematic views – the scientific and the fantastic – can reveal and project a different kind of world than we might usually imagine: an animate and mutable world.

Méliès concludes his description of "fantastic views" by describing filmmaking as "a profession in which everything, even the seemingly impossible, is realized, and the most fanciful dreams are given the semblance of reality. Finally, needless to say, one must absolutely realize the impossible, since one photographs it and renders it visible."[34] A similar idea of making the unreal real and the invisible visible is evident in the work and writing of the artist Odilon Redon, a contemporary of Méliès who was also working in Paris. Redon's drawings and paintings often depicted strange combinations of natural and fantastic images, as in a spider's grin (*Spider*, 1887) or an eye atop a balloon (*Eye-Balloon*, 1878). Much like Méliès, Redon described his "whole originality" as "making the most implausible beings live human lives according to the law of the plausible, placing the logic of the visible, insofar as is possible, at the service of the invisible."[35] Rather than the work of pure imagination, however, Redon writes of how his "most nourishing diet… is the direct copying of reality, the attentive reproduction of the objects of external nature in her tiniest, most particular and most accidental aspects." Both revealing transient aspects of a natural world and presenting fantastic combinations, Redon and Méliès share a similar perspective on the potentials of art.

Redon's drawings and paintings offered the same kind of sensation that Gourmont found in poetic metaphor. Although Gourmont includes "images" alongside "ideas" as something to be potentially recombined through metaphors, his understanding was primarily focused on language. However, Gourmont does draw attention to how Redon was able to capture a metaphorical effect through images: "Odilon Redon, who wanted to make visible certain images derived from Baudelaire and Flaubert, managed to do so, despite his genius for mystery, only by sacrificing visual logic to imaginative logic."[36] Redon referred to this passage in his journal: "[My drawings] are a kind of metaphor, as Remy de Gourmont put it; he placed them outside geometric art. He sees in them an imaginative logic. I believe that this writer has said in a few lines more than all that had been said earlier about my first works." Developing this idea, Redon describes how his work

> owes much to a combination of diverse elements that have been brought together, of forms transposed or transformed, independent of any contingencies, yet logical. All the critics' errors about my early work derive from their failure to see that they had to abstain from defining, understanding, or delimiting anything, from rendering anything more precise...

By combining images and creating new associations, visual art can operate metaphorically. Resonating with the "fusion of images" in cinematic transformations, such an approach depicts an unstable world: "My drawings *inspire* and cannot be defined. They do not determine anything. They place us, as music does, in the world of the ambiguous and the indeterminate."[37]

In *The Dark Side of Nature*, Barbara Larson explains how Redon's work engaged with changes in science, technology and culture in the late nineteenth century: "the ideas that man was a superior entity and part of a separate creation, that species were immutable, and that the laws of an ordered, regulated universe could easily be observed and understood... were being discredited by scientific theories that accepted continuous change and uncertainty of end product."[38] Through major scientific advancements, such as new technologies for studying microbes, developments in astronomy and the popularization of evolution (called "*transformisme*" in

Figure 4. Odilon Redon (1840–1916), *Le Soleil noir* (*The Black Sun*), c. 1900. New York, Museum of Modern Art (MoMA). Oil with incising on board, 12 ³/₄ x 9 ³/₈' (32.4 x 23.8 cm). Gift of The Ian Woodner Family Collection.

French), a different conception of the natural world was emerging. To take one example of how this can be seen in Redon's art, the anthropomorphized sun in *Le Soleil noir* (*The Black Sun*) (c. 1900) [Figure 4] could be linked to traditional iconographies of melancholy and solar imagery, but also to what Larson describes as a

Figure 5. *A Trip to the Moon*

context in which, due to improvements in telescopes, "stars could no longer be thought of as glittering ornaments pinned on the dark walls of the firmament, but had to be reconceived as changing, moving, dying, or originating in the ongoing panoramic drama of the cosmos."[39] This changing perspective of the natural world is treated in an iconographically similar manner in the most well-known image from a féerie, the lunar face in *A Trip to the Moon* [Figure 5]. Whereas Redon invests a similar visage with a haunting aura, Méliès is much more lighthearted. Moreover, this face is not static as in Redon's painting, but is exaggeratedly performed and moves towards the camera. Despite such apparent differences, both images are indebted to both a vision of science and a vision of fantasy as shared frameworks for seeing an animate reality.

A conception of the natural world as something alive and filled with tremulous potential has a longstanding resonance with traditions of fantasy. To take one prominent example, a passage from Wilhelm Grimm's introduction to the first edition of the Grimms' *Nursery and Household Tales* describes a similar idea:

As in myths that tell of a golden age, all of nature is alive [in fairy tales]; the sun, the moon, and the stars are approachable, give presents, and can even be woven into gowns; dwarves mine metals in the mountains; mermaids sleep in the water; birds (doves are the most beloved and the most helpful), plants, and stones all speak and know just how to express their sympathy; even blood can call out and say things. This poetry exercises certain rights that later storytelling can only strive to express through metaphors.[40]

This vision of an animate reality is not completely lost in a more modern and scientific era. As scholars such as Marina Warner and Simon During have described in different ways, refigurations of the phenomenal world continued to be prominent features in nineteenth-century visual culture, magic, spiritualism and science.[41] A similar fascination with an animate world was still evident in theatrical féeries at the time; writing about *Les 400 coups du diable*, the play which was the basis for *The Merry Frolics of Satan*, one reviewer noted:

We have rejuvenated [the theatrical féerie] with a bit of cinematography, we have infused it with a speck of telephone and aerial aviation, but it will always be the charm of the old fables which embellish the framework... It is always necessary to amuse us that the trees sing, that the water speaks, that the precious stones make love, that the flowers propose enigmas...[42]

While a perception of reality as something living and mutable could be linked to a certain kind of animistic, mystical, subjective or simply irrational perspective, it could also participate in a modern fascination with new ways of seeing and showing the world. In the case of Méliès's discussion of cinematographic

views, the projection of what is seemingly fantastic or impossible
– whether hidden processes or elevated worlds – entwines the
revealing and creative function of such a representation. Méliès
writes of how he is describing "the very particular kind of mimicry
in cinematographic views…"[43] While referring in part to the different kinds of representational forms that cinema's early history
offered, this mimicry or mimesis can also be seen as an activity
where a mutable world is projected.

Vital Objects, Mutable Tableaux and Elastic Spaces

While the metaphorical potentials of the substitution splice and
the filmic refiguration of the world are two frameworks in which
we can see transformation in Méliès's films, other tropes were
also used to highlight mutability. I turn now to examine three
recurring ways in which these films presented a cinematic vision
of transformation and mutability: vital objects, mutable tableaux
and elastic spaces.

VITAL OBJECTS

The first of these tropes, vital objects, refers to a central image in
several féeries where metamorphosis becomes linked to an object
that is spectacularly transformed, that creates transformation or
that leads to a spectacular journey. Showing an inanimate object's
potential to figure transformation is used to surprising effect in
the first of Méliès's féeries, *Cinderella*. Standing at the centre of
the film is not the transformation of Cinderella's plain surroundings, not the image of a resplendent Cinderella, not the motif of
the glass slipper and not the presence of a dreamy prince – all
aspects typically brought to the fore in retellings and restagings
of the tale. Rather, the clock that strikes midnight is presented

as the film's central image. Through this image, the film not only offers a renewed perspective on an object that might escape notice, but also projects the ambivalent potentials of transformation.

In the first of the film's four settings, after her sisters have departed for the ball, a disconsolate Cinderella buries her head in her hands. Suddenly, a fairy appears; she sets about enacting the well-known transformations: a pumpkin becomes a carriage, rats become assistants and Cinderella's outfit becomes a dazzling dress. While these transformations literally and figuratively carry Cinderella out of her home and into a world of fantasy, the fairy redirects attention to the limits of this transformation by pointing to a clock in the background, warning Cinderella of the deadline of midnight. In the next tableau, as Cinderella and other characters dance amidst luxurious trappings in the king's ballroom, a clock looms in the background on the edge of the frame. While dancing with the prince, Cinderella spins and at the turn she notices that it is almost midnight. Visibly upset, her anxieties are made tangible: a gnome suddenly leaps out of the face of the clock. Another clock materializes in his hands, he points to the hour, and then rolls off in a puff of smoke. The fairy godmother returns after these startling events to cast Cinderella a disapproving glare and transform her back into normal clothes.

Forced to return home, Cinderella sets her head down on the table of her bedroom in despair. She falls asleep, and the scene then depicts its most elaborate spectacle of fantasy. A large clock on the left side of the room (visually corresponding to its place in the previous setting) quickly slides towards her and bumps up against the table. Through a series of trick cuts, the clock leaps onto the table. The gnome emerges, clanging on a bell. Women then walk out from behind the clock, holding smaller clocks in their hands, bobbing from side to side like a swinging pendulum. They then kneel down and are transformed into four clocks which perform the same curious dance. Transformed back into the women, who gather together by the table, they become an enormous clock almost filling the room. The gnome reappears, perched within it, flailing his arms [Figure 6]. All is set right as

Figure 6. *Cinderella*

the clock disappears and the tale regains its narrative momentum with the arrival of the prince. But the strange embellishments of these animate clocks linger – a striking conflation of nightmarish trick effects and fantastic imagery. Through the transformation of the clock, *Cinderella* draws on earlier traditions of the theatrical féerie: as part of their extravagant mise-en-scène, these féeries would sometimes present enormous magical and animate objects onstage.[44] Due to the closer framing and smaller stage used in the film féeries, however, such objects could virtually fill the visual field, taking on an even more grandiose prominence. While partly an excuse for various spectacles and surprises, this image of time also enacts the ambivalence of change. For a tale so deeply associated with the satisfaction of dreams and desires, a curious emphasis is placed on the negative connotations of transformation. Unlike the earlier metamorphoses of the pumpkin, rats and Cinderella's clothes, the clock leads to a haunting vision of transformation – accentuating strictures of deadlines, nightmares of change and anxieties over transgression.

The use of animate objects to show the potentials and limits of transformation would be further developed in *Bluebeard*, released two years later. Despite the gulf between the dreamlike narrative of *Cinderella* and the nightmarish scenario in *Bluebeard*, the latter film also bases its fantasy and anxiety around an object. After an extravagant wedding and feast, Bluebeard hands his reluctant bride, Fatima, the key to the room which she is prohibited from entering. He departs, expecting that she has been tricked – the key is offered so that she will be tempted to enter his secret chamber; as punishment he will try to kill her, like his seven wives before who have each gone against this interdiction. As Fatima holds the key, wondering whether or not to enter the room, an imp suddenly appears from the rustling pages of a book. He entices her, through magical means, to enter the room – as she does this, the imp jumps for joy and then dives back into the book. In the next tableau, the darkened forbidden chamber, Fatima draws open the shutters of a window and the secret of Bluebeard's murdered wives is revealed. Having dropped the key in a pool of blood next to a

Figure 7. *Bluebeard*

chopping block, Fatima begins to try to wash the key and erase evidence of her transgression. The imp suddenly appears. Frustrated by the blood's indelible stain on the key, Fatima throws it to the ground and covers her face in despair. The imp casts an enchantment and, through a series of trick cuts, the key quickly enlarges almost to the size of a person [Figure 7]. At the key's final stage, a fairy appears next to it who scolds Fatima for her actions and, before disappearing, shrinks the key back down to size. The imp appears for the third and final time in the next setting where, while Fatima sleeps, he creates a dream vision of the seven murdered wives in ghostly shrouds, the punishing figure of Bluebeard and, finally, eight enlarged dancing keys. The good fairy appears once again, casting him out and dispelling the dream. Like *Cinderella*, two magical beings embodying different roles appear within the fairy tale, recalling the conflicts between good and bad fairies in the theatrical féerie. Moreover, an enlarged animate object – like a magical talisman – becomes a spectacular image of fantasy, while at the same time figuring the potentials and limits of change. The key becomes a sign of Fatima's anxiety in her new home, leading to independence and freedom but limited by her husband's power and threat.

As virtually all the scenes in these early féeries are filmed in a medium long shot, the images of animate and enlarging objects take on a central visual significance. Presenting a close-up of sorts, through trick effects, both films offer a renewed perspective on something that might escape notice. The view of the enlarged object destabilizes our perception. In this respect, it draws upon a prominent antecedent in the visual culture of fairy tales: Gustave Doré's illustrations to *Les contes de Perrault* (*The Tales of Perrault*) in 1862, which accompanied well-known stories such as "Cinderella" and "Bluebeard" drawn from Charles Perrault's canonical fairy tales.[45] The connections between Doré's illustration and Méliès's films are evident not just in a similar style and iconography, but also in the ways that objects and moments of indeterminacy are used to punctuate the tale visually. In Doré's dozens of illustrations, including panoramic images of imposing landscapes and tableaux of important situations, several have a closer framing. These include the illustrations of Little Red Riding Hood hesitantly gazing at the wolf, of Sleeping Beauty reaching out to the cursed spindle, and of Fatima holding her hands near the key to the forbidden chamber. These illustrations depict a character gazing at something in order to underline its immense potential to offer a turning point. In the two films I have been discussing, Méliès is similarly attentive to the centrality of objects in articulating the potentials of change. However, rather than singling out a particularly important detail to communicate a narrative, such materialized visions of transformation come to dominate the world of the film. Like a view through a microscope, an unnoticed and seemingly static object begins to seethe with potential.

In *Cinderella*, one could include another object alongside the clock as a thing enlarged before our eyes and filled with transformative potential: the magnificent carriage transformed from a pumpkin. Both *A Trip to the Moon* and *The Impossible Voyage* shift the fantastic creation of a wondrous vehicle into a modern frame of industry and science. After the gathering of scientists that begins *A Trip to the Moon*, the next tableau shows the fabrication of a rocket – the scientists observe its construction, as riveters and blacksmiths are hard at work. In the next tableau, the scientists gaze out over the city as smoke rises from the factory. Similarly, in *The Impossible Voyage*, after the meeting in the "Institute of Incoherent Geography", the next tableau shows an enormous workshop – metal is being forged, calculations are made, experiments are carried out and the construction of vehicles is shown. The next tableau offers a counterpart to the view of the factories from above in *A Trip to the Moon* – here, there is a view from below as the foundry is shown with its enormous furnace. As films titled and constructed around fantasies of travel, the means of transportation take on a special significance not only in terms of where they go, but also in terms of how they are produced. Recalling Méliès's discussion of the scientific view, a central aspect of such films was the cinematic revealing of unnoticed details of how things are made or how technological processes work. In *A Trip to the Moon* and

The Impossible Voyage, a similar vision of the underlying processes at work in constructing modern technologies is made into a spectacle. Whether showing the construction of transportation or the animate potentials of an object, transformation is fantastically revealed. In some respects, this is a vision of mutability that appears unbounded. The unpredictable transformations revealed through the close view and embellishment of an object are ambivalent and multifaceted. Similarly, the vehicles whose fabrication is shown onscreen lead to imaginary and unexpected realms, as well as to catastrophe and chaos.

One of Méliès's earlier féeries, *The Christmas Dream* (1900), gestures towards a more comforting vision. Midway through the film, after two children have dreamt of Christmas gifts, the setting shifts to the public sphere at Christmastime. In a church, where an elderly man leads a group of children pulling on the cords of a bell, several people arrive out of the snowy evening. The setting then shifts to the belfry, filled with a pasteboard bell clanging from side to side. Like the enormous clock in *Cinderella* or the enlarged key in *Bluebeard*, the bell takes up most of the frame. However, unlike the clock and key, which undergo a series of transformations, this is a simple and direct image that lasts as long as earlier scenes filled with detailed mise-en-scène and characters. Moreover, the bell signals an hour of social and religious cohesion. This is a time of community and tradition, embodied in the old bell-ringer inviting the children of the village to assist him. The nostalgic reverie offered by the close view of the bell and the situation surrounding it – at a time when the social significance of bells in community life had been radically transformed[46] – is expressed through a single enlarged image of an object in motion. Compared to the frenzied journeys, sudden transformations and ambivalent changes shown elsewhere in the earliest fairy-tale féeries produced by Méliès, this is an atypical moment. It is a respite from the extraordinary and unpredictable transformative objects that fill the frames of the féerie.

MUTABLE TABLEAUX

Another important way in which mutability was foregrounded over the course of an entire féerie was through the catalogue descriptions that would accompany the films.[47] These were a central feature of how these films were described and marketed at the time of their release; circulated internationally, these descriptions would provide a listing of the tableaux of longer films, and particularly féeries, as well as sometimes being accompanied by further explanation of the events in the film or images of different tableaux. Méliès took the tableau listings very seriously, and wrote them himself.[48] He explains his approach to them in a handwritten note about *A Trip to the Moon*:

> The scenario being entirely composed for the cinema, *exclusively*, only the poster carried the nomenclature of the tableaux. In the projection, the film passed without any subtitles and it was perfectly understood in all the countries.[49]

In some cases, the circulation of the list of tableaux, along with more detailed descriptions, was itself a selling point; for example, the 1902 Edison catalogue description for *Little Red Riding Hood* (Méliès, 1901) notes, "A complete description and lecture will accompany each film."[50] This suggests that such material would be used both to advertise the film for the theatre and perhaps to guide a lecturer's commentary during the projection of the film.[51] The listing of tableaux was a crucial extratextual facet that was part of how the féeries were conceived by their producers, sold to exhibitors, marketed to audiences and accompanied by lecturers.

In the American catalogue description of *Cinderella*, 20 tableaux are listed.[52] These include places (such as "Cinderella in Her Kitchen" and "The Ball at the King's Palace"), events (such as "The Wedding" and "The Bride's Ballet") and characters (such as "The Godmother of Cinderella" and "The King, Queen and Lords").

About a quarter of these descriptions focused on an object or a transformation, including "The Dance of the Clocks", "The Hour of Midnight", "The Transformation of the Rat", "The Pumpkin change to a Carriage" and, simply, "The Transformation". As part of a multifaceted emphasis on different aspects of the film, such descriptions suggest the range of appeals on offer in such films, highlighting visions of transformation alongside settings and events.

As féeries became increasingly elaborate and lengthy, such listings of tableaux became more extensive. For example, *The Kingdom of the Fairies* is given a full page of coverage in Charles Urban's 1905 catalogue.[53] The film, a major follow-up to *A Trip to the Moon* and a partial adaptation of the féerie *La biche au bois*, depicts the kidnapping of Princess Azurine by a spiteful witch, and Prince Bel-Azor's travels through different fantastic places in an attempt to rescue her. It all ends happily, of course. But the story would seem to be secondary to other features in the catalogue: the availability of a colour version, which doubles the price; the elaborate staging, with "gorgeous scenes and costumes"; performers "engaged from 17 Parisian Theatres"; the film's thrilling elements such as the "introduction of new fire, element and cyclonic effects"; and the sheer scope of the film, noted in feet, as well as minutes. These various elements emphasized the film's tremendous spectacle. This is supported by a lengthy enumeration of the tableaux:

1. Betrothal of Prince Bel-Azor
2. The Gifts of the Fairies
3. The Witch's Curse
4. The Boudoir of Princess Azurine
5. Abduction of the Princess by the Demons – The Chariot of Fire
6. The Top of the Tower – The Castle in Alarm
7. Flight through the Skies in the Chariot of Fire
8. The Armoury of the Castle
9. The Vision in the Haunted Castle

10. The Genius bestows upon the Prince the Armour
11. The Impenetrable Armour – the Prince Knighted
12. Embarkation on the Royal Gallery
13. Encountering a Tempest at Sea (New Effects) – Thunder and Lightning and Torrents of Rain – The horizon overcast by angry clouds – The heaving seas, mountainous waves and rain produced by real water.
14. The Ship Wrecked on the Rocks
15. Sinking to the Ocean Bed – Real Fishes and Sea Monsters
16. The Prince Rescued by the Mermaid Queen
17. The Submarine Caves – Encounter with a Cuttle Fish
18. Review of the Habitues of the Deep – Father Neptune's Car
19. The Palace of the Lobsters
20. The Azure Grotto – the Flowers of the Sea
21. In Neptune's Empire – Great Submarine Spectacle
22. The Whale – the "Omnibus of the Deep"
23. On Land Once More – the Entrance to the Cave
24. Escape from the Cavern – On the Edge of the Precipice
25. The Plunge of a Hundred Yards
26. The Castle of the Devil – the Witch in League
27. The Castle on Fire – Rescue of the Princess
28. The Death of the Witch – (Enclosed in a Cask and cast from the Cliffs into the Sea)
29. The Palace of the King – the Wedding Procession
30. Apotheosis – The Kingdom of the Fairies

This list makes up most of the advertisement, highlighting a range of different images and events within the film.

Rather than providing a straightforward description, such lists cast the films in a new light. One of the refigurations offered by this list is that it almost doubles the amount of tableaux in the film. Notwithstanding some moments where the stage is quickly transformed, there are 19 different settings in the film. Increasing the number of tableaux was a practice used in virtually all of the catalogue descriptions of féeries. Part of the reason for this discrepancy was likely to embellish the film and to allude to the scope of spectacle.[54] This was also a continuation of a feature of the theatrical féerie that had been operative for over half a century. As Roxane Martin describes, in the listings of tableaux, several might be noted within a single decor, each offering a new fantastic sight or extraordinary scenic effect.[55] Individual instances of spectacle became foregrounded, in some respects structuring the play rather than different settings, acts or narrative events. This practice was standard in theatrical féeries by the time the cinematic féerie arrived on the scene.

In a similar way to the tableau descriptions of theatrical féeries, the enumeration of tableaux for *The Kingdom of the Fairies* draws attention to different objects, places, characters and events, offering punctuating moments in the flow of images. Most of these tableaux draw attention to new places, presenting a world which can shift instantaneously between, for example, "The Palace of the Lobsters" and "The Azure Grotto – the Flowers of the Sea". Some of these tableaux stress a movement or encounter rather than a new setting, as in the plunge, the embarkation, the betrothal and the encounter with a cuttlefish. There are also many tableaux which do not correspond to a change in setting. These describe various transformative events. There are magical curses, bursts of action and steps on a journey. Despite the difference in visual prominence, narrative relevance and spectacular importance of various tableaux, each takes on a significant place in the film's rapid unfolding of images. Made up of objects, places and movements, only the most rudimentary chronicle of events is offered. Rather than a narrative, the film becomes a continually changing world of things, places and movements. Renegotiating the categories of what is significant, the listing of tableaux resists a rigidly predefined structure. Aspects that might escape notice or that might be seen as minor elements of the frame are figuratively enlarged, situated as central features of the film. The listing of tableaux signals how this film and other féeries were attuned to disruptions and sudden shifts in perspective. Scene changes, trick shots and new images present an unpredictable onscreen world. The ground of transformation is vast, drawing in spaces of mutability, things with immense potential, characters who offer undreamt-of possibilities and voyages where the act of departing can be as important as the journey itself. The catalogue descriptions of tableaux do not follow a set structure, but instead emphasize a film that is grounded in diverse types of images and events unfolding in a world of instability.

ELASTIC SPACES

Despite the fragmentary qualities of féeries, they would sometimes be described in terms which emphasized their continuity. The review of *The Kingdom of the Fairies* in the *Los Angeles Times*, for example, situates the linking of separate tableaux through dissolves as a central feature of the film: "There are no curtains or changes of scene. Although there are numerous sets, all fade into each other, just as the fairyland scene is supposed to do."[56] As an ongoing world of mutable places and objects, *The Kingdom of the Fairies* is described in the Charles Urban catalogue as a "continuance of marvelous surprises, startling visions".[57] The film partly offers such a "continuance" through its rapid unfolding which moves fluidly between different sights, but it also invites connections between different tableaux and spaces both visually and discursively. For example, near the end of the film, the tableau "The Palace of the King – The Wedding Procession" dissolves to reveal "Apotheosis – The Kingdom of the Fairies". Rather than simply presenting one place and then the next, the tableau descriptions indicate a connection between the two places. Their similar phrasing, separating two places with a dash, suggests a resonance between "The Palace of the King" and the "Apotheosis", as well as linking "The Wedding Procession" with "The Kingdom of the Fairies".[58] This transforms royalty and marriage into more celestial fantasies. This is not only a feature of the extratextual tableau listings; it is elaborated visually, as a slow dissolve situates the group of celebratory characters within a heavenly cloud, immersing them in an ethereal light.

A similar kind of visual connection between tableaux occurs throughout the first part of the film, which shows the kidnapping of Azurine and the prince's preparations to save her. After the first setting, the next four decors [Figures 8–11] are visually connected: a similar site of instability is shown in the upper-left corner of each of the settings. This begins with an image of seeming stability, "The Boudoir of Princess Azurine", which is transformed into "Abduction of the Princess by the Demons – The Chariot of Fire" in the tableau listing. Compositionally, the image of Azurine's bed becomes linked to a chariot, the vehicle for her abduction. This transforms an image of domestic comfort into a diabolical mode of transportation. The combination of images metaphorically draws out the latent potential of the bed as a site of nightmares and dreams. Moreover, the design of the bed, decorated with aquatic motifs, foreshadows the underwater journey that will soon form the centerpiece of the film. Like *The Merry Frolics of Satan*, the home is not simply a place of stability, but might be suddenly transformed. Connections between the

Figures 8–11. *The Kingdom of the Fairies*

tableaux continue as a new setting is revealed: "The Armoury of the Castle". The armoury is visually rhymed with the boudoir by placing a hallway of weapons in the upper left of the frame, in the same place as the bed. Steps lead up to this hallway, just as steps lead up to the bed. Taken together, these two images combine to offer similar vistas – one of dreams and one of adventure. The next setting of "The Vision in the Haunted Castle" shows Azurine being hoisted up a tower by her assailants. As in the "Abduction" tableau, the upper left of the frame becomes a focal point of danger. The dissolve from the armoury to the tower suggests a shared site of militarism; much like Azurine's bed being transformed into a chariot, Bel-Azor's armoury is transformed into something nightmarish. By visually linking these various scenes and events, the film draws continuities between elements of each setting. Built upon a shifting visual ground, the sequence invites connections and alters perspectives.

As well as such temporal connections between tableaux, the film plays with perceptions of space. The introductory and concluding scenes within the kingdom are set alongside a lengthy underwater excursion, a contrast emphasized in the Charles Urban catalogue which titled the film both *The Kingdom of the Fairies* and "Wonders of the Deep". Much like the sequences on the moon and within a crater in *A Trip to the Moon* or on the sun and within the sea in *The Impossible Voyage*, *The Kingdom of the Fairies* demonstrates cinema's capacity to traverse boundaries and combine depths and heights. Like a scientific view and a transformation view, the film shows both the depths of an animate world (an underwater kingdom) and the heights of fantasy (a royal kingdom). In *The Kingdom of the Fairies*, the traversal of boundaries from heights to depths is caused by a shipwreck. This leads to the strange underwater world in the film, where various denizens of the deep provide a series of visual marvels. The reemergence from this underwater world is brought about by a fanciful image of movement: a gigantic pasteboard whale, an "omnibus of the deep", which appears and carries the adventurers to shore. The catalogue describes the tableau:

This omnibus is no other than a whale of natural propor-
tions. The Prince and his suite shrink back astounded.
But Neptune tells them not to hesitate. So they permit
themselves to be swallowed one by one without a pro-
test. The whale makes several motions with his fins and
glides up to the surface of the ocean.[59]

Playfully linking the fantastic journey that the film has shown
with a more modern and urban context, this "omnibus" carries
the characters onwards in their dizzying journey.

This play with depths extends also to the film's use of space. At
certain points, tableaux reveal new worlds from within the frame,
displaying depths emerging in the background of the image. For
example, the description for the tableau titled "The Flora of the
Sea. The Azure Grotto" indicates the effect of a series of flyaway
flats revealing new sights:

(This tableau forms with the preceding a series of
charming transformations.) The submarine flowers,
algae, corals, madreporas gradually settle down beneath
the ocean bed and finally reveal an azure grotto of dazzling beauty. The grotto, in turn, fades away and discloses
the magnificent tableau which follows.

In her analysis of haptic space, Antonia Lant describes a similar
scene from *Palace of the Arabian Nights* (Méliès, 1905) in which
painted flats separate to reveal a depth of space, explaining that
"Méliès chose motifs that probed or highlighted the alluring yet
illusory depths of the cinema, the impossible compressions and
expansions of far and near, the unclear identities of figure and
ground."[60] Through such elaborations of depth, as well as through
the dissolves, visual links and compositional overlaps noted earlier,
Méliès used elements of film form to elaborate on a fantastic world
of new perspectives and shifting continuities.

CONCLUSION

Drawing on traditions of fantasy, Méliès's féeries and other examples of the genre offered a multifaceted engagement with the potential of cinema to show a mutable world. These films emphasize something distinct from a plot, which, as Ricoeur describes, "'grasps together' and integrates into one whole and complete story multiple and scattered events…"[61] But that does not mean that the féerie should mainly be understood as presenting a series of more or less discrete spectacles. As this chapter has explored, the féerie can be seen in a different light by focusing on its transformations, particularly in relation to ideas of metaphor. As Ricoeur argues, metaphor, like narrative, participates in the configuration of new meanings and continuities. Unlike narrative, metaphor does this through a trope rather than through temporality. Joining seemingly disparate words together becomes "a creation of language that comes to be at that moment, a *semantic innovation* without status in the language as something already established with respect to either designation or connotation."[62] Similarly, the transformations that course through Méliès's films – and that can be seen to function as part of a larger understanding of film as a form of fantasy – create meanings by bringing to light new figurations, disrupting seemingly stable categories and offering novel perspectives on the world.

3 FAIRY-TALE AESTHETICS
Early Film Theory and *The Blue Bird* (1918)

WITH THE POPULAR SPECTACLES OF FAIRY TALES ON THE French stage and in early cinema having largely faded from view by the 1910s, more narratively structured forms of fantasy appeared in cinema. Fairy tales were used as familiar and popular source material to fill a need for stories. In this respect, a wide range of different adaptations of fairy-tale subjects appeared over the course of the decade; these included various versions of "Cinderella" and *Alice in Wonderland*, and film cycles, such as L. Frank Baum's *Oz* series and the Fox Kiddies. While such films often relied upon marvellous effects and mise-en-scène for their spectacular attractions, they might be seen to manifest a relatively straightforward set of concerns: an address to an audience of children, the use of well-known tales and the appeal of escapism. However, these uses of fairy tales were by no means the only ways in which such films were understood, discussed and presented. By way of introduction, I want briefly to examine how one of the decade's most prominent fairy-tale cycles, the Fox Kiddies, was seen to offer a familiar context of escapist childhood fantasy while also negotiating wider issues circulating around fairy tales and film in the 1910s.

Directed by Chester M. Franklin and Sidney Franklin, and produced by William Fox, the Fox Kiddies were planned as an ongoing series of major productions starring children that would adapt "a veritable library of fairy tales and folklore".[1] This led to a cycle of films including *Jack and the Beanstalk* (1917), *The Babes in the Woods* (1917), *Aladdin and the Wonderful Lamp* (1917) and *Ali Baba and the Forty Thieves* (1918) which starred child actors in the main roles. Given their subjects and stars, they would seem to have been part of a major strategy by Fox to appeal to children cinemagoers. An article in the *New York Times* on *Jack and the Beanstalk* noted that children's films are "a development entirely along natural lines" as "it is obvious that children should have films which are within their understanding, and about which there can be no doubt regarding the desirability of their seeing. William Fox has begun the creation of moving pictures based on fairy tales and other familiar pieces of juvenile literature that have gained immortality."[2] The article places an emphasis on important elements of fairy-tale films, coupling an address to children with reference to their timeless quality.

But this was not enough. The article also notes that such tales are conducive to cinematic qualities of spectacle and wonder: "only limited by flights of the imagination, they give wonderful scope for the making of beautiful and attractive pictures." Such "unlimited vistas" are presented "not only for young, but for older folks as well." As another discussion of *Jack and the Beanstalk* explained, just as an adult might enjoy the circus, "Jack's adventure is a simple and marvelous tale that appeals to childhood, and to the 'second childhood' latent in all of us."[3] An expanded audience that included adults seems to also have been a central concern for Fox. The trade paper *Motion Picture News* described how, "In an effort to discover how large a proportion of the audiences at the Globe have been youngsters, William Fox directed that an actual count be taken of those who attend at several successive performances."[4] Rather than aiming to discover its appeal to children, the article continued, "It will then be possible to prove statistically the assertion of the Globe's box-office that 'Jack and the Beanstalk' has been exercising as great an appeal to grown-ups as to kiddies." This tension between films addressed to children and those with a wider appeal had been a subject of some concern over the previous few years. For example, in a poll of important issues facing film exhibitors published almost a year earlier, opinion was split, with roughly half responding that there was demand for children's pictures and half responding that there was not.[5]

Reviews of the Fox Kiddies discussed similar issues. In *Variety*, the review of *Aladdin and the Wonderful Lamp* noted that "whether the antics of precocious children 'playing theatre' will entertain those old enough to vote is the only question at issue."[6] An editorial in *Photoplay* weighed in on the issue rather directly; titled "Children's Shows a Failure", it explained the situation:

> We believe that every effort on the part of exhibi-
> tors to provide specific entertainment for children
> has failed... The truth is that children do not provide
> a sufficient percentage of the patronage of a picture
> house to warrant special performances designed for
> their entertainment. Furthermore, most children don't
> want to be entertained as such. And still furthermore,
> most parents like to take their children with them to
> the movies...[7]

With such considerations in mind, fairy-tale films were not the exclusive province of children. They were at least partly addressed to adults, continuing the tradition of earlier theatrical and cinematic fairy tales.

Also, like these earlier forms, spectacular visualisations of fantasy were often among the most important attractions of film fairy tales in the 1910s. Summing up the appeals of *Aladdin and the Wonderful Lamp*, a review in *Variety* noted, "As a spectacular production it is little short of stupendous, the mammoth scenes following in rapid succession with almost bewildering frequency... the scenic investiture represents a wealth of time, thought and expenditure of coin of the realm."[8] Such an emphasis on spectacle would shift the focus away from timeless children's tales to visual marvels; for example, an "Editorial Note" in a movie-magazine retelling of *Jack and the Beanstalk* fabricated a curious visual origin for the story: "'Jack' was first illustrated on slate-rock and the trunks of trees; thereafter by the crude wood-cuts of German foresters, but the breathing images of the real characters remained for the modern camera-man."[9] The visual appeal of these films became directly linked to earlier traditions of the féerie in an article in *La Cinématographie Française* anticipating the release of the Fox Kiddies. It noted, "For many years, one of the most attractive forms of spectacle, that which best amuses the public, the Féerie, has been neglected. Resuscitating this unjustly forgotten genre, the 'Fox Film Corporation' has just published something entirely new in this genre..." Possibly drawn from marketing material, the article goes on to note the success of American féeries in New York at sites such as the Winter Garden and the Ziegfeld Follies, going on to suggest, "Before deciding to produce féeries for the screen, William Fox made a very serious study of this genre of entertainment which he desired to adapt to cinema, which allows for the production of incredible scenic effects..." Such féeries were "among the greatest attractions in the history of theatre": "Immense ensembles, strange scenes with luminous and fantastic effects, these are the forms of the féerie one finds suitable, adapting themselves marvellously to the cinematographic art."[10] Altered, modified, updated – the extraordinary depictions of fantasy in the féeries examined in the previous chapters continued to inform an understanding of cinema's fairy tales.

Rather than simply harking back to a cinema of transformations or displaying cinema's reliance upon theatrical models, new ways of using and understanding an assemblage of transformation, spectacle and modern fantasy emerged. This chapter examines how fairy tales related to the discourse surrounding cinema, its specificity as a medium, its aesthetic potentials and its social role. Cinema's status as a relatively new and quickly expanding institution meant that it had to draw upon a range of more established cultural and artistic forms to forge its identity. In this respect, this chapter also draws out some of the ways in which a fairy-tale cinema was linked to the presentation of fantasy in other artistic and cultural forms. However, the prominent examples that I examine cast such uses of fantasy in a new cinematic light.

Writing in the 1910s, some of the earliest film theorists, including Vachel Lindsay, Hugo Münsterberg and Émile Vuillermoz, were fascinated by cinema's relation to fairy tales and fantasy. This was not restricted to the more rarefied heights of theoretical and critical writing, as it was also evident in the fan-magazine and newspaper discourse circulating around cinema. A continued interest in how fairy tales might integrate with cinema in surprising and imaginative ways also extended to individual films, whose aesthetic and narrative strategies used fairy tales and fairy-tale tropes in their elaboration of the fantastic possibilities of cinema. This chapter aims to illuminate these various strands of fairy tales in cinema in the 1910s. In particular, by looking closely at the writing of film theorists and one of the decade's most prominent fairy-tale films, *The Blue Bird* (Tourneur, 1918), I examine how fairy tales contributed to an understanding of cinema's aesthetic and social potential.

Fairy Tales and Film Theory

In *The Art of the Moving Picture*, Vachel Lindsay devoted considerable attention to fairy tales; in the revised edition of the book in 1922, he writes, "Fairy-tales are inherent in the genius of the motion picture…"[11] Hugo Münsterberg's sustained analysis of the medium of film in *The Photoplay: A Psychological Study* (1916) also situated fairy tales and fantastic forms as integral to cinema's "aesthetic idea".[12] Émile Vuillermoz, writing in one the first regular newspaper columns of film criticism in France, beginning in 1916, was similarly fascinated by the fantastic qualities of cinema, describing it as a "marvellous domain" akin to "that of the féerie".[13] Working from different backgrounds – Lindsay was a prominent poet, Münsterberg was a major scholar and writer on psychology, and Vuillermoz was a music critic – they shared a vision of fairy tales as central to the potentials of cinema. Why were they so interested in fairy tales? Although Münsterberg knew Lindsay's writing on cinema, and Vuillermoz could have possibly been familiar with the work of either author, their diverse reference points and different approaches suggest that there was no single determining influence on this aspect of their writing.[14] Their interest in fairy tales likely does not derive from nostalgia for the film féeries discussed in the previous chapter either – these films are almost never mentioned in their writing. These authors may have been interested in fairy tales partly due to associations with childhood; fairy tales may have been seen as a suitable rhetorical trope through which to express some of the novelty and primal appeal of the infant art of cinema. However, their writing develops another avenue for exploring how cinema resonated with fairy tales: they saw that the fantastic mutability in fairy tales related closely to cinema's potential, and that this was what could make film a distinctive art.

HUGO MÜNSTERBERG

Münsterberg recounts how he became fascinated by film after seeing *Neptune's Daughter* (Brenon, 1914). He writes, "Until a year ago I had never seen a real photoplay. Although I was always a passionate lover of the theater, I should have felt it as undignified for a Harvard professor to attend a moving-picture show..."[15] After watching *Neptune's Daughter*, he continues, "my conversion was rapid. I recognized at once that here marvelous possibilities were open, and I began to explore with eagerness that world which was new to me." This exploration would result in *The Photoplay*, one of the earliest works of film theory. *Neptune's Daughter* was a telling choice of inspiration: the "marvelous possibilities" of cinema were opened up for Münsterberg – "probably the most famous academic in the United States" at the time – by one of the earliest feature-length fairy-tale films.[16] A showcase for the popular swimming and stage star, Annette Kellerman, the success of *Neptune's Daughter* led to a cycle of extravagant underwater fantasies which centered on the travails of mermaids. These included later Kellerman star vehicles, such as *Daughter of the Gods* (Brenon, 1916) and *Queen of the Sea* (Adolfi, 1918), and other films which immersed their viewers in a similar aquatic milieu of fantasy, such as *Undine* (Otto, 1916) and *Sirens of the*

Sea (Holubar, 1917). A review in the *Los Angeles Times* described *Neptune's Daughter* as "boasting a plot in which fact and fancy are deftly blended" before going on to summarize the story of King Neptune's daughter, Annette (Annette Kellerman), becoming involved in various court intrigues; along the way, she metamorphoses from a mermaid into a mortal, falls in love with a king, turns back into a mermaid, and then undergoes a final transformation into a human being. Whatever charms this scenario may have had, accounts from the time placed the emphasis, not surprisingly, on spectacle.[17] In particular, the display of Kellerman's body, her extraordinary swimming skills, the exotic locale and the fantastic subject matter were discussed prominently. Münsterberg may have been drawn to *Neptune's Daughter* film for these reasons.[18] But as he develops his understanding of film in *The Photoplay*, *Neptune's Daughter* comes to stand for something more, emblematizing cinematic qualities.

Münsterberg begins his chapter on "The Inner Development of the Moving Pictures", writing, "It was indeed not an external technical advance only which led from Edison's half-minute show of the little boy who turns on the hose to *The Daughter of Neptune* [*Neptune's Daughter*], or *Quo Vadis*, or *Cabiria*, and many another performance which fills an evening."[19] Rather, "The advance was first of all internal; it was an aesthetic idea." He goes on to describe how cinema developed its "aesthetic idea" by drawing upon theatrical practice, while also diverging from it in cinematic ways. He singles out several key distinctions between theatre and film, making references to fairy tales along the way. First, cinema's capacity to show "the real background of nature and culture" goes far beyond theatre.[20] While he discusses the example of street scenes, he gives as his first example, with *Neptune's Daughter* perhaps in mind: "The stage manager of the theater can paint the ocean and, if need be, can move some colored cloth to look like rolling waves; and yet how far is his effect surpassed by the superb ocean pictures when the scene is played on the real cliffs, and the waves are thundering at their foot, and the surf is foaming about the actors." Second, films are marked by a "rapidity with which the whole background can be changed". Here, he notes Max Reinhardt's revolving stage, but suggests that cinema is quicker and more seamless – able to depict a series of locations and to interconnect them. He goes on to describe how cinema can speed up, reverse or substitute images. Through such effects, "Every dream becomes real, uncanny ghosts appear from nothing and disappear into nothing, mermaids swim through the waves, and little elves climb out of the Easter lilies."[21] The last cinematic quality he singles out is the close-up, which "leaves all stagecraft behind".[22] While marvellous scenes could be shown in theatre, such as "the great historical plays where thousands fill the battlefields or the most fantastic caprices where fairies fly over the stage",[23] the close-up is a specifically cinematic wonder. These various characteristics indicate that cinema is an art form independent from what has come before: "A new aesthetic cocoon is broken; where will the butterfly's wings carry him?"[24]

While noting a range of examples, Münsterberg's discussion of cinematic tropes consistently returns to different elements drawn from filmic and theatrical fairy tales. With allusions to *Neptune's Daughter* and references to other fantasy films, Münsterberg develops an image of cinema aesthetics that is linked to imagination and transformation. From the scope of animate nature and shifting settings to the more limited purview of metamorphoses and close-ups, cinema has a retinue of seemingly fantastic devices that can help distinguish it from theatre. Later in the book, he notes,

> Writers who have the unlimited possibilities of trick pictures and film illusions in mind have proclaimed that the fairy tale with its magic wonders ought to be its chief domain, as no theatre stage could enter into rivalry. How many have enjoyed *Neptune's Daughter* – the mermaids in the surf and the sudden change of the witch into the octopus on the shore and joyful play of the watersprites![25]

He goes on to list other kinds of film that might be seen as especially cinematic, concluding that no single kind of film should be seen as the essence of cinema. Nevertheless, his emphasis on a series of tropes that show a mutable and animate world closely related to fantasy was pivotal to his larger concerns. It allowed him to shift attention away from cinema as narrative or realist towards other artistic possibilities.[26]

This becomes crucial as Münsterberg develops his argument. Part I of *The Photoplay* focuses on how cinema evokes mental processes: depth and movement are created through mental activities rather than actually being shown to us through a flat screen and succession of static images; the close-up focuses perception in a manner like the mental act of attention; emotions are shaped by cinematic means; with editing's power to show memories or fantasies, "*It is as if reality has lost its own continuous connection and become shaped by the demands of our soul.*" Such concerns regarding the "psychological factors" of watching cinema then lead on to the second part of the book, which traces the aesthetic elements. Here, Münsterberg argues for an understanding of film as operating in a sphere separate from any kind of imitation of reality; film "*becomes art just in so far as it overcomes reality, stops imitating it and leaves the imitated reality behind it.*" He continues, "To imitate the world is a mechanical process; to transform the world so that it becomes a thing of beauty is the purpose of art. The highest art may be furthest removed from reality." In this conceptualization, art "does not lead beyond itself, but contains in its own midst everything which answers the questions, which brings the desires to rest." Given its potential place in a realm distinct from narrative, the art of cinema might be compared to "musical tones" which "unfold our inner life, our mental play, with its feelings and emotions, its memories and fancies, in a material which seems exempt from the laws of the world of substance and material, tones which are fluttering and fleeting like our own mental states." Münsterberg then draws together this notion of film creating a distinct aesthetic world with his understanding of film's relation to mental processes, writing "*the photoplay tells us the human story by overcoming the forms of the outer world, namely, space, time, and causality, and by adjusting the events to the forms of the inner world, namely, attention, memory, imagination, and emotion.*"[27]

Münsterberg largely sets aside considerations of fairy tales and fantasy as he develops this argument. However, having drawn attention to cinematic tropes that evoke fairy tales at the start of his discussion of cinema's "aesthetic idea", they provide an important aspect of his larger argument. The instability brought on by editing, the marvels of the close-up, the disruptions to the image created by trick effects and the vision of an animate natural world all resonate with the shifting viewpoints of cinematic and mental forms. While some of these tropes can be seen to be part of cinema's capacity to copy reality, their fantastic qualities and effects can be further seen as part of cinema's capacity to transform the world, mirror our mental processes and establish a site of aesthetic wonder.

ÉMILE VUILLERMOZ

While Münsterberg tends to avoid a narrative or realist understanding of cinema, his contemporary in France, Émile Vuillermoz, directly attacked such a way of approaching film. Writing for the newspaper *Le Temps*, Vuillermoz would elaborate on a range of facets of cinema, treating pragmatic issues such as film exhibition alongside discussions of the possible directions that the French film industry might take.[28] Vuillermoz also explored film aesthetics with reference to a wide range of non-cinematic reference points such as the philosophy of Henri Bergson, the poetry of Paul Verlaine and the music of Claude Debussy. Within this wide-ranging examination of cinema, Vuillermoz consistently emphasized cinema's capacity to show the world in a new light, celebrating the fantastic qualities of cinema rather than its narrative possibilities. A poetic and animistic potential, often characterized in terms of the féerie, was especially cinematic for Vuillermoz.

Taking Münsterberg's interest in the cinematic qualities of natural settings further into realms of the fantastic, Vuillermoz saw film settings as having a féerique quality. For example, to return to the ocean milieu of *Neptune's Daughter*, Vuillermoz's review of *Ocean* (Andréani, 1916) ends by describing the implications of its extraordinary "visions of nature" and "nocturnal landscapes":

> In these fugitive apparitions, all the nobility of an art being born is revealed. And the true victory of the cinema is to hold captive the sirens of the stream and the fairies of the land who are magnificently disinterested in the human comedy, but play among themselves in such dazzling féeries![29]

Narrative only disrupts this marvellous quality: "To tell the truth, there is a somewhat worrying subtitle: *The Ocean* or *the Children of the Sea!…* What are we to make of these children of the sea?" Rather than wanting to follow "their little personal affairs", he continues, "the light and waves, the dialogues of the wind and of the foam, and the disputes between the storm and the rocks interest us far more!" This is related both to a poetic sensibility and to a departure from "theatrical business", with Vuillermoz observing that "if [cinema] continues to be only a clandestine dramatic agent, it will be reduced to poverty." For Vuillermoz, French filmmakers should focus on this féerique potential of cinema rather than attempting to mimic American cinema's banal stories and expensive spectacles. Noting the marvellous scenes of nature in *Déserteuse* (Feuillade, 1917), he writes, "The day when all these admirable elements of dream and of féerie will be put to the disposition of a poet rather than being wasted by librettists, the French cinematographic art will be able to defy all the foreign competition."[30] A vision of a poetic perspective coupled with an attention to animate nature informs this vision of cinema: "Let's divine in the stream, the prairie or the shrub, the invisible and present naiad, nymph or dryad… A good *metteur en scène* should convert to pantheism."[31]

In addition to this fascination with the fairylands of cinematic settings, Vuillermoz drew attention to another potentially fantastic effect of film: editing. Rather than simply filming a living natural world in order "to capture the mystery of life", filmmakers "ought to have higher ambitions. All the forces of the universe are at their fingertips. If only they produce a féerique synthesis."[32] Such a synthesis could be fashioned through editing's capacity to shift perspectives, cross distances and join together distant times. For example, the use of parallel editing in *Intolerance* (Griffith, 1916) to move from place to place and from era to era is described as "transport[ing] us like a féerie through the centuries", and the film itself is described as a "tumultuous féerie".[33]

Like Münsterberg's discussion of cinema's "aesthetic idea", the animate environments and shifting visions of the féerie coincide with Vuillermoz's understanding of cinema and its potentials. However, Vuillermoz's approach to cinema was more closely concerned with the material of the phenomenal world than Münsterberg's psychological and aesthetic focus. Richard Abel points out that this approach elaborated on "cinema's mission of discovering and revealing 'the spirit of things'."[34] Informing this vision of cinema was what Abel characterizes as Vuillermoz's "training in Symbolist aesthetics".[35] In particular, Vuillermoz consistently returns to describe cinema through reference to Baudelaire: film is an "artificial paradise" and an "invitation to the voyage" that can be particularly meaningful for "a public inquisitive for dream and fantasy."[36] These are key elements of cinema's poetic possibilities for Vuillermoz, who shared with Münsterberg an interest in how cinema was linked to fairy tales and the féerie through an aesthetic that functioned outside of narrative and realism. Like Münsterberg's aesthetic realm, Vuillermoz saw cinema as a place "which doesn't make the weight of matter heavy, the kingdom where everything is limitless and imponderable, and where all dreams are realisable."[37] Able to project fantastic worlds of unstable forms, cinema could fashion artistic marvels. Coupling a poetic and fantastic perspective on film, Vuillermoz writes in the conclusion to his first article, which attempts to justify and explain his role as a film critic, "It is time to see that the luminous screen on which we so curiously fix our gazes is a magnificent window open on to life and dream."[38]

VACHEL LINDSAY

Like Münsterberg and Vuillermoz, Vachel Lindsay saw fairy tales as central to film aesthetics. In *The Art of the Moving Picture* (1915), Lindsay's discussion of film and fairy tales examined similar ideas of how cinema could realize mutable worlds of fantasy.[39] The book is divided into chapters which, in Lindsay's poetic and heterodox style, trace different types of film and emphasize different facets of cinema's potential place in contemporary American society. Fairy-tale films are part of the general category of "splendor pictures", marked by cinema's epic scope; this type of film "is based on the fact that the kinetoscope can take in the most varied out-of-door landscapes. It can reproduce fairy dells. It can give every ripple of the lily-pond."[40] Other "splendor pictures" have their own kinds of settings and subjects: crowd pictures show "great impersonal mobs of men", patriotic films project "tremendous armies, moving as oceans move", and films of religious splendor "can show us cathedrals within and without". While each type of film relies upon images of grandiose movements, the depiction of an animate world of enchanted possibilities characterizes the fairy-tale film. Within this realm of fairy-tale splendor, Lindsay focuses on animate objects, fairy-tale settings and tropes of fantasy. Rather than a straightforward description of how such elements have been used in specific films, Lindsay offers a wide-ranging discussion of their cinematic and social possibilities.

Early in his chapter on "The Motion Picture of Fairy Splendor" he recounts a Mother Goose rhyme in which a series of different things take on a life of their own, describing it as "perhaps the world's oldest motion-picture plot".[41] The importance of the animate potential of objects in Lindsay's approach to cinema is part of his conception of how film functions in a manner related to hieroglyphs, built from images. For Lindsay, cinema's "opportunity to magnify persons and things instantly, to interweave them as actors on one level, to alternate scenes at the slightest whim, are the big substitutes for dialogue."[42] This expressive use of images is cinematic: "By alternating the picture of a man and the check he is forging, we have his soliloquy. When two people talk to each other, it is by lifting and lowering objects rather than their voices... The boy plucks a rose: the girl accepts it." Summarizing this type of filmic expression, he writes, "Moving objects, not moving lips, make the words of the photoplay." In one respect, Lindsay is describing how filmmaking at the time used objects to articulate narrative and communicate character.[43] But Lindsay takes this idea further, suggesting that the image of objects can dominate a film: "the mechanical or non-human object... is apt to be the hero in most any sort of photoplay while the producer remains utterly unconscious of the fact. Why not face this idiosyncrasy of the camera and make the non-human object the hero indeed?"[44] Lindsay connects this central role of objects to the imaginative resources and animate realms of trick films and fairy tales, describing such wonders as furniture which moves itself in a Pathé trick film and the central role that could be given to Cinderella's slipper or Puss-in-Boots's footwear.[45]

This animate potential should extend beyond objects to include also buildings and environments because, in film, "non-human tones, textures, lines, and spaces take on a vitality like that of flesh and blood." This suggests a life within the mise-en-scène, similar to Vuillermoz's vision of féerique settings. No longer a background for characters and narrative, the sites shown on film can take on a magic all their own:

> The normal fairy-tale is a sort of tiny informal child's religion, the baby's secular temple, and it should have for the most part that touch of delicate sublimity that

we see in the mountain chapel or grotto, or fancy in the dwellings of Aucassin and Nicolette. When such lines are drawn by the truly sophisticated producer, there lies in them the secret of a more than ritualistic power. Good fairy architecture amounts to an incantation in itself.

Film itself draws out these animate potentials within places, as "the camera has a kind of Hallowe'en witch-power" so that long-standing metaphors and myths of enchanted environments can be visualized: "the fairy wand can do its work, the little dryad can come from the tree."[46] As places teeming with fantastic potential, offering a kind of instability or transformative power in place of inert objects and settings, fairy tales can become part of cinema's magic.

This cinematic potential of animate objects and environments should be seized upon by filmmakers. Lindsay writes that "after the purely trick-picture is disciplined till it has fewer tricks, and those more human and yet more fanciful, the producer can move on up into the higher realms of the fairy-tale, carrying with him this riper workmanship." One facet of how such fantasies can be "disciplined" is through a careful construction of meaning: "The possible charm in a so-called trick picture is in eliminating the tricks, giving them dignity till they are no longer such, but thoughts in motion and made visible." Anticipating Münsterberg's discussion of cinema's relation to thought, Lindsay sees transformations as a kind of mental imagining. This is not a matter of embellishing the world with fantastic properties; it is revealing different latent facets of the world by making it animate or by transforming it in a manner much like metaphor, discussed in the previous chapter. Rather than the simple replacement of one thing by another, a process of meaningful change should be made visible. Describing the effects of such transformations, using a statue transfigured into a person as an example, he writes, "The actor cannot logically take on more personality than the statue has. He can only give that personality expression in a new channel."[47] Giving expressive potential to objects and settings, Lindsay sees a vast creative and revelatory potential within cinema's fairy-tale tropes.

Writing just a few years after Lindsay, in *The Uncanny* (1919), Freud would explore the place of fantasy in daily life in similar terms of childhood fantasies of omnipotence and animism.[48] While such concerns resonate with aspects of *The Art of the Moving Picture*, Lindsay had little interest in the relation between such fantasies and the subconscious. Instead, he would emphasize the ways in which the fantastic potential of film could extend outwards in order to recast contemporary life. Describing action films as sculpture-in-motion and dramatic films as painting-in-motion, he writes that "the Fairy Pageant, along with the rest of the Splendor Pictures, may be described as architecture-in-motion."[49] Developing this idea in terms of reimagining America, he outlines a rather fanciful project in which the architecture of the nation is rebuilt along the lines of a "permanent" World's Fair, with cinema as its inspiration and guide.[50] He writes that "for many years this America, founded on the psychology of the Splendor Photoplay, will be evolving." Shifting between references to changes to the material structures of American cities and the immaterial visions of animate potential offered by cinema, Lindsay combines the literal and metaphorical procedures of transformation: "America is in the state of mind where she must visualize herself again."[51] A fairy-tale cinema, especially conducive to showing the animate and transforming potentials of places and things, resonated with a vision of America as a site of ongoing change and possibility.

FAIRY-TALE AESTHETICS

The entwinement of fairy tales with cinema, as a way of understanding film's aesthetic form, was not just evident in theoretical approaches. Lindsay wrote that although such fairy tales were rarely shown in cinema, certain common cinematic devices drew upon their enchantments:

Note how easily memories are called up, and appear in the midst of the room. In any plays whatever, you will find these apparitions and recollections. The dullest hero is given glorious visualizing power. Note the "fadeaway" at the beginning and the end of the reel, whereby all things emerge from the twilight and sink back into the twilight at last. These are some of the indestructible least common denominators of folk stories old and new.[52]

Drawing attention to the almost magical properties of the flashback and the fade, Lindsay traces the potential for basic cinematic tropes to shift time and space, inviting us to see a world transformed. The same year, an editorial from *Photoplay* lamenting the relative scarcity of fairy-tale films and calling for their return defined their form in a markedly similar manner: "Cut-backs, fade-aways, double-exposures and startling close-ups were the only things which ever realized a fairy story, or a tale of witchcraft, or anything involving the supernatural in stage narration."[53]

Such references to the magical possibilities of film were part of a wider discourse circulating around cinema at the time. Poems in fan magazines would invoke a language of fairy tales and fantasy to express cinema's enchantments. Minna Irving's "The True Wonderland" (1911) recounts a series of extraordinary sights, including:

> A woman with a tongue so long
> She wore it for a sash,
> A lobster playing on a flute,
> A starfish eating hash.[54]

To see such things, the poem concludes, is simply a matter of attending "A moving picture show!" This sense of film's extraordinary possibilities is taken further in Sam J. Schlappich's "The Fairies of the Screen" (1915), which recounts how the enchanted figures of fairies that used to be seen to wander the world have now, through cinema, become visible once again.[55] In "The Magic

Film" (1911), Irving describes film editing's ability to transcend space and time in terms of fantasy; she begins by describing a series of enchanted objects, including Aladdin's lamp, the seven-league boots that cross enormous distances, and magic items with power over life and death.[56] Cinema, though, is "greater far" than all of these things: it is "the wonder of the age" which transports viewers to "fairylands", "summons back the past", "shows to us the ocean floor" and "calls the mighty dead to life". As we will see later in this chapter in the analysis of *The Blue Bird*, cinema's capacity to enact such fairy-tale wonders could shape a film's aesthetic strategies. In a wider sense, poems like these contributed to a popular discourse that associated fairy tales with cinema through their marvellous transformations, animate worlds and magical leaps through space and time.

To return to the analyses of Lindsay, Münsterberg and Vuillermoz, while they each offered different views in their visions of cinema's social and artistic possibilities, they saw cinema's relation to fairy tales in similar terms as integral to film, part of its potential as a medium. Setting aside considerations of narrative traditions and escapist entertainments, they situated fairy tales and the féerie as coinciding with cinema through a series of interrelated tropes: an animate world of mise-en-scène, the dynamic shift of space and time effected by film editing, and the marvel of visual transformation. Underpinning these considerations was a sense in which cinema's artistic potentials were not yoked to established forms, but able to offer new realms of enchantment and marvellous images of instability. Rather than a retreat into realms of fantasy or idealism, evoking a premodern past or childhood, this notion of film aesthetics was situated in contemporary contexts of aesthetics, psychology and society. These early forays into film theory fastened onto fairy tales, finding a form that was particularly conducive to exploring cinema's future.

The Blue Bird and Cinematic Fantasy

The connection of fairy tales with the aesthetics of film found perhaps its fullest expression in American cinema of the 1910s with *The Blue Bird* (Tourneur, 1918). The film adapts Maurice Maeterlinck's play of the same name, first performed in 1907 at the Moscow Art Theatre. Drawing together fairy-tale tropes, a series of fantastic events and philosophical concerns, the play had been a popular success in its printed form and in various restagings in London (1909), New York (1910), Paris (1911) and Berlin (1912). Beginning inside a cottage in the midst of winter, it shows the voyage of a girl and a boy, Mytyl and Tyltyl, as they search for an elusive bluebird, a symbol of happiness. Much of the play is made up of the children exploring and marvelling at a series of extraordinary locales, including "The Land of Memory", "The Palace of Night" and "The Kingdom of the Future".[57] Relating to different aspects of temporality, consciousness and life, their fairy-tale journey allows them entrance into an enchanting world of being. It ultimately culminates in the realization that happiness had, all along, been present within their home. An account of its production in New York describes how "Maeterlinck says in his 'Wisdom and Destiny', the book that gives the key to his philosophy of life, 'The intimate happiness of every human being is in exact proportion to his sense of the universe.'"[58] Rather than presenting happiness as an attainable goal, the play situates it as an awareness of oneself and the world. Even the children's quest is one of perception rather than action: their voyage is initiated when they are granted the ability to see the soul of things by the kindly fairy Berylune, so that their pets and household goods come to life, and the children are made aware of a fantastic world underneath the surface of reality. While partly sentimental and moralistic, the play is also witty and ironic, using secondary characters and strange situations to fashion an atmosphere of enchantment. Its tone is also quite dark at points, as the children encounter death in a sometimes threatening world of fantasy.

As well as being indebted to and inspired by *Peter Pan*, *The Blue Bird* was categorized as "a féerie" or "a fairy play", though seen as a distinctly poetic one. A review of the London staging in the *New York Daily Tribune* noted how, unlike *Peter Pan* where "fairyland is seen as it is refracted through the mind of a child", in *The Blue Bird* "fairyland appears as a mirage illumined by the imagination of a poet."[59] While the author, Maeterlinck, was mocked in some accounts as "a philosopher who proposes to deliver a message of importance through the medium of a play addressed to children",[60] reviewers saw a philosophical and poetic quality in the play that was directly addressed to adults. One account, for example, described it as "based on the endless search for happiness, and it reaches great heights and depths which only those who have grown old in the search can fully understand."[61] The review in *Journal des Débats* linked this to the form of the féerie; after first noting that "nothing is more rare than a féerie which is not an absurd mixture of ridiculous adventures and burlesque inventions and which consists otherwise only as an exhibition of tricks, costumes and decors", the review goes on to remark that "nevertheless what resources are offered by the féerie to the poetic imagination!"[62] Adolphe Brisson in *Le Temps* also situated the play in relation to the poetic and artistic potentials of the féerie, writing, "It's exquisite; go and see this masterpiece. And bring your children... It's not the noisy and vain féerie of *Le Châtelet*. It's an intelligent féerie, and not at all boring, I assure you... *The Blue Bird* has the radiance and the mystery of a tale of Andersen."[63] The play was linked to some of the key implications of the féerie discussed earlier, in Chapter 1, with one article describing it as a "philosophical féerie, which recalls the theatrical dream of Théophile Gautier."[64]

When it was made into a film several years after its theatrical premiere, *The Blue Bird* was still situated in a context that coupled poetic and cultural value with its fairy-tale quality. The critic for the *Chicago Daily Tribune* described it as "a delicate and beautiful portrayal of Maeterlinck's exquisite fantasy."[65] It had "an atmosphere of fairy land", which some earlier critics had seen as difficult to achieve in the stage production.[66] The *Los Angeles Times* developed the notion of its poetic fairy tale through a tautology: "The drama of Maurice Maeterlinck is always poetry. Sometimes it is a fairy tale. And as all fairy tales are nothing but poetry, my first statement remains true."[67] The review in the *New York Times* adopted a similar tone, drawing attention to its marvellous fantasy tropes by describing how its director, Maurice Tourneur, "used the art of magic to make the souls appear and act their parts, to cause instantaneous transformations, to show the flight of people and Father Time's ship through the air, to make all sorts of mysteries take place before one's eyes."[68] Such a retinue of fantastic imagery was also part of the film's advertising, as in one example from *The Janesville Daily Gazette* (June 15, 1918) that placed the emphasis on the "Thousand Beautiful Scenes" in the film and listed its wondrous sights at length, including: "The Soul of Fire", " The Soul of Light", "The Soul of Sugar", "The Palace of Night", "The Joy of Thinking", "The Happiness of Pure Air", "The Kingdom of the Future" and "The Transformation of the Home of the Happy Dead". Referring to the visual marvels of objects, characters, settings, states of mind and transformations, such a list evoked the kinds of tableaux that were evident in both film and theatrical féeries. Further recalling the féerie, and its characteristic trope of the *changement à vue*, one review noted how "one scene of exquisite loveliness melts into another just as lovely."[69] The film was explicitly linked to the féerie in one account: "The 'Blue Bird' is a fairy play, or feerie, as the French critics classify it."[70] The description goes on to point out how "the 'Blue Bird' is distinguished… by being written by a philosopher and a poet instead of a hack playwright, and by having meaning and a moral sustaining and underlying its spectacular effects; it has the imagination and philosophy of a great poet and thinker."

In 1918, the same year that the film version of *The Blue Bird* was released, Victor O. Freeburg's *The Art of Photoplay Making* drew attention to the play's cinematic qualities.[71] In a chapter titled "Symbolism and Allegory", Freeburg wrote that "fundamentally

[*The Blue Bird*] is a cinematographic conception." Setting aside its "familiar Sunday School moral that true happiness consists in being unselfish", he draws attention to what he sees as its specifically cinematic qualities:

> Its dreams and visions, its many settings and fanciful wanderings, its transformations of things into human beings, its dramatization of animals and natural settings, its symbols in action, all constitute the very effects which can be produced more successfully on the screen than anywhere else in art.[72]

In this list, Freeburg draws out many features of a fairy-tale aesthetic that earlier writers, such as Lindsay and Vuillermoz, had discussed in terms of film. Through its use of transformation, animate objects and an enchanted world, the play resonated with cinema's tropes and devices of fantasy.

Keeping within the framework of cinema's specificity, Freeburg goes on to note, "We firmly believe that new opportunities will discover new genius. If Maeterlinck still prefers to express himself in words, some new Maeterlinck will arise and express himself masterfully in the motion picture." It is little wonder that Freeburg called for a Maeterlinck of the movies. In the 1910s, Maeterlinck's reputation had extended beyond his considerable influence on artistic and theatrical practice decades earlier through plays such as *The Blind* (1890) and *Pelléas and Mélisande* (1892), as well as poetry and essays. By the 1910s, he had become established as a public figure with the status as one of Europe's best-known and respected intellectuals. He had won the Nobel Prize in 1911, with an article in the *New York Times* noting that he was "recognized as the greatest literary figure of the present day" and concurring with the *Evening Post* that "he is without question the most prominent figure in European literature to-day, holding a place similar to that occupied in succession by Ibsen, Tolstoy, and Bjørnson."[73]

To return to the early theorists of film discussed previously, Vuillermoz saw Maeterlinck's writing as cinematic. Describing film's "ubiquity and its enlarged retina" that can take in the multiple facets of nature, space and time, he wrote,

> To reconstitute the mystery of life, to give it all its troubling splendour and miracle, the piety and cares of a poet are necessary. A naturalist would only accomplish half the task and wouldn't know how to move us. It's necessary for a Maeterlinck of film to sing for us the poem of *The Life of the Bee* or *The Intelligence of Flowers!*[74]

Similarly, writing in *The Art of the Moving Picture*, Lindsay described Maeterlinck as a "prophet-wizard", situating him alongside other artists who have offered an enlarged vision of the world, including Rembrandt, William Blake, Samuel Taylor Coleridge and Edgar Allan Poe. Lindsay goes on to explain that these "prophet-wizards… have a common tendency and character in bringing forth a type of art primarily at war with the realistic civilization science has evolved… when it comes to a clash between the two forces, the wizards should rule, and the realists should serve them." Later in the discussion, he mentions Maeterlinck's authorship of *The Blue Bird* "and many another dream", continuing, "I devoutly hope I will never see in the films an attempt to paraphrase this master. But some disciple of his should conquer the photoplay medium, giving us great original works."[75]

The director of the film version of *The Blue Bird*, Maurice Tourneur, was well positioned to take on this role. By the late 1910s, Tourneur had become established as one of the most prominent directors in American cinema through major films in a range of genres, such as *The Wishing Ring* (1914), *Alias Jimmy Valentine* (1915), *The Whip* (1917) and, a film that will be discussed in the next chapter, *The Poor Little Rich Girl* (1917). An article in *Photoplay* in 1918 noted that he was "accurately called 'the poet of the screen'".[76] After recounting that Tourneur had earlier worked with Auguste Rodin, the article goes on to quote from Rodin describing the need for "a director with vision, imagination, a grasp of all the arts, a keen sense of symbolic values, to carry the cinema to the point where it can express the evasive values of Maeterlinck, the twilight harmonies of Debussy, the subtle evocations of Verlaine."[77] It then asks, somewhat rhetorically, "Is [Tourneur] the fulfillment of Rodin's prophecy?" While situating Tourneur in a context of cultural and artistic value might be seen as a gesture to align film with high art, the mention of Verlaine, a major Symbolist poet, and Debussy, a composer who had written the score for Maeterlinck's *Pelléas and Mélisande*, indicates a specific association with modernism. The film version of *The Blue Bird* elaborates on this, as I will go on to examine, through its allusions to the paintings and murals of the nineteenth-century artist Pierre Puvis de Chavannes and Maeterlinck's writing on theatre in "The Tragedy of Everyday Life" (1897). Drawing on such influential works in a modernist tradition, and elaborating on the aesthetics of film fairy tales, *The Blue Bird* engaged with an intermedial milieu of fantasy in order to fashion cinema as a site of modern fantasy.

PUBLIC ART

At the beginning of *The Blue Bird*, an intertitle sets the scene: "One Winter's Eve, No Matter Where Or When, There Lived A Little Boy, Tyltyl, And His Little Sister, Mytyl." The film fades in on a medium shot of Tyltyl, outside the family cottage, eating a piece of bread. The scene cuts to a medium shot of his sister, Mytyl, licking her lips and gazing at the food. They exchange glances, and Tyltyl tears off a piece of bread and passes it to his sister. The film then introduces their mother and father: "Daddy Tyl" is chopping wood in a forest and "Mummy Tyl" is cooking, lit by the light of the stove. After establishing the family, the sequence then shifts to show the community in which they live. We first see the home of their wealthy neighbours and then "the humble hut of poor Neighbor Berlingot". In condensed fashion, these images introduce labour within an inhospitable milieu, where there is a generosity within family and disparities of wealth in the larger community. The film elaborates on this in its next sequence, which begins by showing Berlingot's ill daughter in medium close-up, gazing out her window at Tyltyl's and Mytyl's home. Watching Mytyl feed her pet bird, she tells her mother, "You told me about the bird that brings happiness... Perhaps if I had Tyltyl's little bird, I'd be well and happy, too..." When Berlingot goes to her neighbours to ask for the bird in order to satisfy her daughter's desire, she is immediately refused. This minor incident will set in motion the dreamlike narrative that follows in which Berlingot, transformed into the Fairy Berylune, sends Mytyl and her brother on a quest for the bluebird of happiness.

In these introductory scenes, the film is elaborating on a thematics where the kindness within families does not extend to a wider community. This introductory sequence is not taken from the text or stagings of the play; instead, it can be seen to draw upon Puvis de Chavannes's *Winter* (1889–93), one of two murals that he painted for the Hôtel de Ville in Paris. (The version of the mural as an oil painting is reproduced below [Figure 12].) *Winter* shows a scene of labour and community in a bleak wintry environment. In the midground and background, it depicts a

Figure 12. Pierre Puvis de Chavannes (1824–98), *Winter*, 1896. Oil on canvas, 93.3 x 146.5 cm.

Figure 13. *The Blue Bird*

hunt, a woodcutter and several men working together to pull down a tree; in the foreground, there is an image of shelter and group solidarity, with a man warming a child's feet by a fire and another sharing bread with a woman. This foreground subject presents a similar iconography of warmth and community to the opening scenes of *The Blue Bird*, where we see the image of the mother at the stove and the children sharing a piece of bread. Further entwining the film and the mural, the woodcutter who stands alone in the midground, framed by the barren trees, is evoked by the introductory image of the father in *The Blue Bird* [Figure 13]. Jennifer L. Shaw draws attention to the painting's ambiguous details that nevertheless offered a powerful sense of "community solidarity" and "the distribution of charity in times of want" that "incit[ed] the viewer to think about duty."[78] The opening sequence of *The Blue Bird* establishes a similar environment of wintry cold and scarcity, as well as raising issues surrounding the actions and meanings of community. However, depicting the family as separating themselves from their neighbour, social responsibility is shown to be limited. As the film goes on, one of the moral lessons that it develops is that such a narrow scope of kindness stems from a flawed understanding of one's place within the world. This is ultimately overcome when, after their voyage through fantasy, the children offer to give the bluebird of happiness to their neighbour.

While the film's thematics and moral lessons are partly introduced through visual reference to *Winter*, *The Blue Bird* draws upon Puvis's murals in broader ways. As noted earlier, an extended journey that makes up much of *The Blue Bird* presents a series of allegorical sites that allow the characters better to understand their place in the world. The film slightly reorders – and abbreviates – the play's presentation of this voyage in order to show a clear movement from age to youth: beginning in the deathly embrace of the "Palace of Night", it moves through the home of the children's grandparents in "The Land of Memory" to the adult environment of the luxuries in the "Palace of Happiness", and then to more benign springtime fantasies of youth, ultimately concluding in the infancy of "The Land of the Future". Such an episodic structure highlights allegorical and symbolic implications, situating a narrative of cause and effect as a secondary concern. This becomes a visual and thematic focus in individual sequences, with many scenes of the children and their cohort being shown different kinds of experiences, places and states of being. In the "Palace of Night", for instance, Tyltyl encounters "Wan Sicknesses" and "War" behind locked doors. The director of *The Blue Bird*, Tourneur, had worked as an assistant for Puvis earlier in his career; much like the murals Puvis had painted for such public sites as the Boston Public Library, *The Blue Bird* displays a series of interrelated symbolic visions. The images are also presented in a similar manner to these murals: in the children's visit to the "Palace of Happiness", where they are shown such marvels as "The Happiness of Pure Air" and "The Joy of Pure Thoughts", the images are masked with a curvature at the top like Puvis's murals at the Boston Public Library. The critic for the *Chicago Daily Tribune* observed: "I have a suspicion that the person who really should review this picture is the art editor, for it is six reels of what might be described as living etchings in color."[79]

Presenting an ongoing sequence of symbolic images, *The Blue Bird* resonated with the form of the mural, and particularly Puvis's influential examples. In doing so, it participated in a well-established context of fantasy as allegorical public art. Shaw draws out the implications of this for Puvis's murals:

> The enthusiasm for Puvis's work – the belief that his murals provided the best hope for a continuing tradition of high art in public decoration – derived from the ways his paintings mobilized individual subjectivity and personal fantasy for the purpose of public edification. In his murals Puvis de Chavannes used large flat areas of color, rhythmic composition, and suggestive subject matter to appeal as if in a dream to the individual subjectivities and feelings of viewers. He attempted to teach by appealing to the unconscious – to the deepest levels of subjectivity – rather than to convince on an intellectual level using the language of conventional tropes. By commissioning work from Puvis de Chavannes, the state attempted to forge a new aesthetic for public decoration that would instill, through individual fantasy, a sense of collective identity in the viewing public – an aesthetic that would draw people together by encouraging simultaneous dreams of France.[80]

Rather than resorting to "old paradigms of representation that valued idealization and clarity", Puvis offered a public dream through art.[81] *The Blue Bird* elaborated on this through cinema and an aesthetic of fantasy.

THE TRAGEDY OF EVERYDAY LIFE

The shifts in perception and awareness so central to the film become vividly realized when the children are introduced to an enchanted figuration of their everyday lives. After the introductory scenes, the film shifts to within Mytyl's and Tyltyl's cramped home as the family prepares dinner and the children then get ready for bed. The scene emphasizes naturalistic and seemingly minor details of the home. The first cut-in is not of a character or a significant event, but rather a milk jug set upon the dinner table. This does lead to a narrative event, of sorts, as the family cat prowls around the table and takes a surreptitious sip. Tyltyl's dog notices this and becomes rather agitated – a series of shots alternate between the cat and the dog as they face off. Using the close shot not to highlight a human drama, but rather to show the animals (as well as the table settings), helps establish a sense of naturalistic detail. The scene continues to develop with other examples of everyday activities – Tyltyl drops his scarf and is told by his mother to hang it up properly, Mytyl takes the bread out of the oven, the children wash their hands and Mytyl takes a loaf of sugar to the table.

Rather than emphasizing an attention to naturalistic detail in order to develop the background out of which the narrative and characters will emerge, the film turns to give this environment a drama all its own. As the children sleep, they are visited by, as an intertitle tells us, the "Fabric of moonbeams". This takes the form of two angels who hover atop their bed. The children are then awoken by the noise of their neighbour's Christmas party, gazing with wonder at the celebrations, shown as silhouettes of dancers and musicians. Berlingot suddenly knocks on the door to their home, interrupting this reverie at the window and mysteriously asking for "the Bird that is Blue". After the children gesture towards their bird, Berlingot replies, "It's not blue enough. You will have to go at once and find me the one I want." As the baffled and somewhat frightened children stare at her, she explains, "You think I look like your Neighbor Berlingot, eh?… There's not the least resemblance. I am the Fairy Berylune!" A series of transformations suddenly follows. The children's clothing becomes enchanted, with Mytyl's nightgown changing into her daytime outfit and Tyltyl becoming magically dressed when he sits upon the bed and, in reverse motion, his clothes spring onto him. The furniture also takes on an animate life, rearranging itself in a dance of objects. The room itself appears to have enlarged, with geometrical precision in place of its clutter.

This is a transformation of perception. Explaining that their home is no less beautiful than the home of their wealthy neighbours, only they "don't know how to see it", Berlingot presents them with a magical cap. Transformed into the Fairy Berylune, resplendent in a white gown and butterfly wings, she explains, "When you wear this enchanted hat, and turn the diamond, you will see the inside of Things... the soul of Bread, of Water, of Fire..." The fairy Berylune shows them a transfigured vision of the things around them. The fire in their oven is revealed as a figure in billowing robes who performs a dance [Figure 14]. As Ben Carré, who was responsible for the production design of the film, points out, this image of metamorphosing motion and light alludes to Loïe Fuller's dances [Figure 15], a figuration of the féerique noted in Chapter 1.[82] The dance of fire is framed

Figure 14. *The Blue Bird*

Figure 15. Jules Chéret (1836–1932), *Folies-Bergère. Loïe Fuller*, 1897. Colour lithograph, 120 x 80 cm.

by Berylune and the two children watching; the film then cuts to a full shot of the spotlit performance, and then a reaction shot of the two children. The children are situated as spectators, peering in on the revelation of an animate world, with the film inviting the viewer to share their perspective. The children are then shown "The Pure Spirit of Water" with the tap on the water tank producing glittering light which dissolves into a figure shrouded in bundles of white, who turns to them and reveals her smiling face. As they watch fire and water engage in a dance-like struggle, their dog, now an actor in a canine costume, then joins them, excitedly explaining, "At last we can talk, my little deities! I had so much to tell you, and you wouldn't understand my bark and my tail-wag…" Their cat, also an actor in costume, then appears, and sips from the milk jug. After showing a brief fight between the cat and the dog, the film goes on to present more anthropomorphized things, including sugar, milk, bread and light. This is a display of cinematic marvels partly seen through the eyes of the children, and partly directly addressed to the film's audience. Fantasy is woven into the fabric of naturalism, emerging from within a material world. The dormant world of mise-en-scène has come alive.

While this display of fantasy shows the possibilities of filmic transformation, it was, of course, not uniquely cinematic. Drawn from the play, it presents an animate world which had been staged in different ways in theatrical productions of the play. However, in its attention to the animated and fantastic potential in objects and environments, *The Blue Bird* presents the kind of visual fantasy that film theorists at the time saw as particularly cinematic. Just as Lindsay heralded the transformations of furniture and architecture in film, *The Blue Bird* visualizes the children's home as a mutable environment. Just as Münsterberg marvelled at the cinematic possibilities of tropes such as the close-up and trick shot, the film shows objects and things taking on a new kind of life through cinema. Just as Vuillermoz saw film as projecting a fascinating animistic world, so does the film draw out enchantment from within the everyday.

This was both an extension and playful elaboration of Maeterlinck's influential discussion of theatre in "The Tragedy of Everyday Life" (also translated as "The Tragical in Daily Life"). The essay, appearing in the late 1890s, argues for the reawakening of an artistic and philosophical concern for moments in theatre which would seem non-dramatic or secondary to the narrative action. Stillness, silence, eventlessness, inwardness, waiting and indeterminacy emerge as elements of the tragedy of everyday life, a world filled with possible meanings that is seen to exist outside of certain notions of dramatic narrative structure. In foregrounding these elements, the essay traces an understanding of life that calls for a deep attentiveness to moments, words, experiences and things that might escape notice as they can contain a more profound significance than the narrative events. In a well-known passage, Maeterlinck writes:

> I have grown to believe that an old man, seated in his armchair, waiting patiently, with his lamp beside him; giving unconscious ear to all the eternal laws that reign about his house, interpreting, without comprehending, the silence of doors and windows and the quivering voice of the light, submitting with bent head to the presence of his soul and destiny – an old man, who conceives not that all the powers of this world, like so many heedful servants, are mingling and keeping vigil in his room, who suspects not that the very sun itself is supporting in space the little table against which he leans, or that every star in heaven and every fibre of the soul are directly concerned in the movement of an eyelid that closes, or a thought that springs to birth – I have grown to believe that he, motionless as he is, does yet live in reality a deeper, more human and more universal life than the lover who strangles his mistress, the captain who conquers in battle, or "the husband who avenges his honour".[83]

The Blue Bird offers a similar kind of vision, taking objects and environments away from a function tied to narrative and character, imbuing them with a life of their own and reconnecting them to a larger whole of which they are a part.

One expression of this expansive vision is closely aligned with a specific object that was introduced in the milieu of the home, when Tyltyl drops his scarf. After he drops the scarf, it is shown through a close-up. Told by his mother to pick it up and to be careful not to hurt it because his grandmother knitted it for him, Tyltyl teases his mother, "Hurt it?... Can it feel things?... Has it got a soul?" Tyltyl is blind to the object's significance, but will soon be shown its "soul" after his world is fantastically transformed and he has set out on his journey. Rather than showing the scarf's animate life immediately, it becomes figured in a later scene when the children visit the "land of memory". As they wait disconsolately in a clearing, the dim space behind them is gradually illuminated to reveal the home of their deceased grandparents, emerging like a memory from the darkness. Once the children have joyously greeted their grandparents sitting outside, now alive in this enchanted realm, they are led into their home. As they pass through the door, the camera slowly tracks forward into the cottage while panning slightly to the left, opening up the space to view. Lasting over 20 seconds, it is a striking filmic effect, all the more pronounced by being a rare instance of moving camera in the film. Crossing a threshold not just of space but also of time, it turns the filmic device of the moving camera into a metaphor for temporality, crossing from the present into the past, into memory. Inside the space of the past, Tyltyl and Mytyl encounter seven children who are, as the intertitle explains, their "little dead brothers and sisters". This matter-of-fact presentation of mortality and lost memories contributes to an uncanny vision of the past, one that is both homely and unsettling. The trope of the moving camera is repeated as they leave, tracking out of the cottage with Mytyl and Tyltyl as they bid farewell to their memories.

Vuillermoz wrote that "one of the most noble and most thrilling missions of the cinematographic art is to express the soul of things."[84] This scene answers Tyltyl's earlier question of whether the scarf has a "soul"; it extends the scarf's association with his grandparents and with the past into an actualized realm of family and memory, expressing the "soul" of the object by drawing it into a different frame of reference and meaning. In so doing, the scene offers an example of what Gilles Deleuze describes as "attentive recognition". Drawing on Bergson, Deleuze contrasts attentive recognition with automatic or habitual recognition where perception situates an object as part of a definite sphere of action. In attentive recognition, "My movements – which are more subtle and of another kind – revert to the object, return to the object, so as to emphasize certain contours and take 'a few characteristic features' from it." Unlike a "sensory-motor image" which "retains from the thing only what interests us, or what extends into the reaction of a character", attentive recognition no longer fits the object into a sphere of use. Instead, such an image "enters into relation with a 'recollection image' that it calls up."[85] This is a central feature of what Deleuze will describe as the "time image", pivotal to his larger argument about the shift from an action image to a time image in cinema. In *The Blue Bird*, Tyltyl's mother shifts the scarf's meaning away from an item of clothing towards the material of memory; this becomes actualized and dramatized when the children visit their grandparents. While clear in its implications, and lacking "the disturbances of memory and the failures of recognition" that ultimately result from such images for Deleuze, the scarf nevertheless develops a shifting perspective on temporality through an object. The film develops such effects throughout, dislodging the home from its plane of naturalistic verisimilitude towards landscapes of dream and temporal disjuncture. In doing so, it offers similar kinds of optical images related to both fantasy and recollection that Deleuze sees in later examples, such as German expressionism and the French avant-garde, where "it is a whole temporal 'panorama', an unstable set of floating memories, images of a past in general which move past at dizzying speed, as if time were achieving a profound freedom."[86]

Deleuze extends such considerations further, finding in what he describes as "the crystal image" a kind of cinema that merges actual and virtual images, further disrupting a sense of movement and unified perception. Jacques Rancière points out that the metaphor of the crystal image, a key concept for Deleuze, was to be found in Maeterlinck's writing, quoting from "The Tragedy of Everyday Life": "Let but the chemist pour a few mysterious drops into a vessel that seems to contain the purest water, and at once masses of crystal will rise to the surface, thus revealing to us all that lay in abeyance there where nothing was visible to our incomplete eyes."[87] Maeterlinck situates the poet as a chemist, able to create a "sudden revelation of life in its stupendous grandeur" akin to new formation of multifaceted crystals. Recalling the previous chapter's discussion of Méliès and metaphor, Remy de Gourmont extends this process further, likening it to the activity of poetic metaphor. Dissociating the conjoined ideas in a commonplace and creating new ideas is similarly linked to a crystallization of liquid:

> If one were to use words only according to their absolute and unique meaning, connections would become elusive in ordinary speech; so one must leave them some of the vagueness and flexibility with which past usage has endowed them and, in particular, not insist on the abyss that separates the abstract from the concrete. There is an intermediary stage between ice and fluid water, when needles start to form, when the ice cracks and gives way to the hand immersing itself.[88]

This sense of a poetic or metaphorical process that can transform one state to another, producing a word or image of shifting meanings, is evident in *The Blue Bird*. The magical diamond upon the cap which Berlingot gives to the children, and which opens up their vision to the enchanted world of animate forms and living memories, functions as a materialization of the crystal image. This shared use of the trope of the crystal in Maeterlinck, Gourmont and Deleuze, as well as the play and film version of *The Blue Bird*, is no coincidence; it is a privileged image of poetic creation that figures an enlarged perception, a prismatic trope that recalls the shifting forms of Gautier's dream theatre discussed in Chapter 1. The crystal and the diamond are metonyms for *The Blue Bird*'s attempts to show a multifaceted world and mutable perspective through cinema.

In "The International Exploration of Cinematic Expressivity", Kristin Thompson traces the expressive use of film form in the 1910s. She writes of how tropes that had been used "in order to ensure narrative clarity", such as the cut-in or shot/reverse shots, began to be used expressively as "functions of cinematic devices that go beyond presenting basic narrative information and add some quality to the scene that would not be strictly necessary to our comprehension of it."[89] Thompson describes different ways in which filmmakers (including Tourneur) manipulated elements such as lighting, editing, framing and the moving camera to create expressive effects. In the example of *The Blue Bird*, however, a more thorough renegotiation of film form is at stake – there are frequent and pronounced examples of tropes such as the insert shot, setting, lighting and the moving camera that resituate what these very tropes *do*, what meanings they might have and how they might participate in a novel way of showing the world.

An advertisement appearing in *Variety* on March 29, 1918 described *The Blue Bird* as addressed to "an army" of women "eager to see" this "mighty message of cheer from the great Belgian author to this war-torn nation". However odd this advertisement might appear, it indicates that the film's avant-garde tendencies were, at least in part, presented in terms of the concerns and experiences of a mass audience during the First World War, offering solace and comfort through a novel perspective on themes of mortality, community and suffering. Beginning with a situation of scarcity in its wintry environment, *The Blue Bird* elaborates on an expansive vision of the world, presented through fantasy and allegory. Moving beyond individual desires and the limits of verisimilitude, the film emphasizes a poetic cinema of communal visions and memories. Tropes, themes and aesthetic forms drawn from fairy tales and fantasy provide the basis for such an ambitious and poetic vision of cinema's possibilities.

CONCLUSION

In an analysis of Münsterberg's writing, Laura Marcus observes that "he engaged with the question of 'modern beauty', in his assertion that film 'is a new form of true beauty in the turmoil of a modern age, created by its very technique and yet more than any other art destined to overcome outer nature by the free and joyful play of the mind.'"[90] In a call for the government to assist the French film industry during wartime shortages, Vuillermoz argues for the value of cinema in similar terms: "The screen procures a sort of imperious and beneficial hallucination which lightens the burden, for several hours, of sorrowful minds and hearts... it is, after the prosaic labour of the day, the precious nocturnal escapade into the gardens of dream!"[91] A similar sense of fantasy's capacity to offer a shift in perspective and a space of visual enchantment is evident in Constantin Stanislavski's speech to the Moscow Art Theatre Company in 1907 about staging the play of *The Blue Bird*, in which he noted that "the smoke from factories veils the beauty of the world from us; the abundance of manufactured luxury blinds us, and plaster ceilings keep from us the stars and the sky."[92] Such hope that beauty and art could emerge from within a fatiguing, constraining or destructive modernity found expression through film's fairy tales. Their visions of transformation, drawing upon fantasy in a wider visual and theatrical culture, were entwined with film aesthetics in an attempt to fashion a distinctive form for cinema. Rather than simply a retreat into the premodern, the Romantic idealization of childhood or realms of otherworldly fantasy, film fairy tales helped negotiate the shifting potentials of cinema in contemporary life as a public art of community, memory, perception and mutability.

4 MARY PICKFORD AND THE FANTASIES OF STARDOM

A SENSE THAT PERSONAL IDENTITIES, SOCIAL ROLES AND
life situations were not static, but could be open to sudden change,
became one of the most important fantasies in cinema, as well as
in the larger context of modernity. Dramatized in countless ways
and imbricated in the discourse circulating around film, such a
notion of mutable personhood was integral to film's fairy tales.
Films sometimes offered a dreamlike depiction of such fantasies,
with enchanted environments and magical transformations effect-
ing marvellous change. This was also taken up by narrative, with
the story arc of "Cinderella", for example, offering a culturally
powerful tale of individual transformation from poverty and loneliness into wealth and marriage. But perhaps the most prominent
figuration of fairy-tale transformation in the 1910s was through
the emergent star system.

One of the most important tropes of stardom in this period
was the fantastic tale of how a regular person – typically a young
woman – could become magically transformed by the film
industry. An article in *Motion Picture Magazine* from 1917 titled
"The Enchanted Threshold" begins with a fairy-tale invocation:
"Once upon a time there lived a great magician."[1] It goes on to
describe the "strange metamorphoses" of extras and stars alike in
Hollywood, recounting how cinema "does a wondrous magic work,
this wizard, 'Moving Pictures', and at turning lives topsy-turvy
he has no equal in the world."[2] There were certain features that
recurred in such accounts of film's transformative power, particularly in relation to stars: the transformation from everyday life to
stardom is described as if it were instantaneous; references to fairy

tales, and particularly "Cinderella", would be used to characterize stardom; the star would have a propensity for daydreaming or fantasizing, ultimately leading to their success; offscreen identities and onscreen roles would be entwined in a shared context of fantastic possibility. Such a rhetoric of stardom would continue to play a major role in imaginaries of Hollywood for decades. This "fairyhood of the twentieth century", as an article in *Movie Weekly* described it, was pivotal to the fantasies of cinema.[3]

Examining how such fantasies were projected through one of the most significant stars of the 1910s, this chapter examines three films starring Mary Pickford: *Cinderella* (Kirkwood, 1914), *The Poor Little Rich Girl* (Tourneur, 1916) and *The Little Princess* (Neilan, 1917). Pickford's role in each of these films dramatized transformation in ways that interrelated cinema, fantasy and stardom. Pickford was "the decade's leading star", demanding an extraordinarily high salary and, by the second half of the decade, wielding considerable influence over her projects.[4] While she acted in genres ranging from melodrama to comedy, her roles in these three films situated her in a realm of fantasy and fairy tales. Pickford performed a complex and sometimes contradictory persona. She was closely associated with roles as children or young adolescents, performing what Gaylyn Studlar refers to as a "kind of cultural pedophilia that looked to the innocent child-woman to personify nostalgic ideals of femininity."[5] For Studlar, this served to mediate Pickford's evident power offscreen as an independent businesswoman, with its "distinctively New Woman elements".[6] Pickford's persona also drew upon features of nineteenth- and early-twentieth-century children's literature where, as Peter Stoneley describes, the character type of the girl or young woman was "instrumental to articulating and assuaging the fear of social change. Her growing up can naturalize change and make it seem more manageable."[7]

Both Studlar's emphasis on the infantilization of Pickford and Stoneley's analysis of children's literature draw out important implications of Pickford's persona. This chapter extends these concerns to consider how Pickford's roles within fantasy films used an image of childhood and a narrative trajectory of growing up, while also navigating broader concerns circulating around cinema, modernity and stardom. Situated within a milieu of transformative fantasy, Pickford played out the promises – and restrictions – of modern life. While the decade's most prominent example, she was not unique in doing this; this chapter also explores other expressions of stardom and fantasy, ending with a discussion of how Marguerite Clark, another enormously popular star in the 1910s, played a similar role. Through the intersection of stardom and enchantment, cinema developed a culturally resonant form through which to display a modern world of mutable identities and transformative play; this was underpinned by fantasy and fairy tales.

Cinderella Stories

Cinderella offered an iconic role for Pickford. Along with numerous versions in other media and the prominence of the general narrative arc, several film versions of "Cinderella" had appeared in the early 1910s, making it one of the most frequently adapted film subjects of the time. Just a few months before *Cinderella*, Pickford had starred in "The Famous Modern Fairy Play", *A Good Little Devil* (Porter, 1914). This was an adaptation of the play which Pickford had starred in on Broadway in 1912, itself a version of a French féerie produced earlier in the decade. Neither an innovative film subject nor a novel departure into fantasy for Pickford, *Cinderella* was likely seen as a safe project. Fittingly, the role would emblematize Pickford's star persona. In the 1920s, Pickford was attached to a new film version of "Cinderella" in fan magazines, quoted as saying, "I've done it in every other guise."[8] She offered her ideas on why the tale is so appealing:

> All people are Cinderellas at heart… They like to imagine that some day they will be rich and have every conceivable luxury, no matter how poor their present

circumstance may be. I think that this is the biggest and most popular theme in pictures. I have used it any number of times.[9]

Such a scenario of wish-fulfilment, based upon social mobility, offers an important appeal of the tale. But rather than circulating only around this narrative, the various tropes of fantasy in *Cinderella* evoke a range of different implications. In some respects, the film is an exploration of fantasy, with a sometimes conflicting treatment of its potentials and limitations.

Cinderella begins in a milieu of fantastic possibility. This is largely motivated by the appearance of a fairy who, early in the film, rewards Cinderella for an act of kindness. The fairy transforms a forest into a fairyland, as beneficent fairies emerge from the landscape to assist Cinderella in her chores, gathering wood for her while she sleeps. The fairy also enacts the pivotal scene of transformation when she metamorphoses a pumpkin, a rat and a mouse into the carriage, coachmen and horses that will take Cinderella to the ball. The mouse had been shown in an insert shot earlier in the film in an unrelated scene, establishing a sense of an everyday environment, like the forest in which Cinderella gathers wood, that is swept up in transformative possibility. In addition to these enchantments, the fantasy of love is also presented through fantastic tropes. After encountering Cinderella in the forest, Prince Charming's daydream of her being transformed into a princess is shown through a superimposed image. Cinderella also fantasizes about Prince Charming, shown through a superimposed image, as she sits alone on the side of her bed, dreamily gazing forward and recalling her earlier encounter with him. These various manifestations of fantasy embellish the original tale with the tropes of fairy-tale and fantasy films: the elaboration of an animate environment, spectacular transformations, and shifts of space and time through memory and desire.

After Cinderella has been transformed so that she can attend the ball, in the second half of the film, the proliferation of different kinds of fantasy begins to subside. An earlier world of fantastic environments, things and visions becomes focused around a progression towards marriage. No longer is the natural environment of the forest central; it is replaced by a luxurious palace with the rituals of romance and courtly behaviour. As the film becomes more focused on detailing the narrative, Cinderella's relationship to fantasy also becomes more ambivalent. Returning home after the ball, she dreams of an enormous clock about to strike midnight, a figuration of the fairy godmother's interdiction that Cinderella not stay out past midnight. The image of the clock is superimposed in the top of the frame, hovering over Cinderella as she sleeps. The scene then cuts to the clock, filling the frame, as its hands spin and it begins shaking. Intercut with medium close-ups of Cinderella and her fitful sleep, the image of anxiety intensifies as the clock's hands and numbers take on an animate life, moving, dancing and rearranging themselves in abstract patterns. Visual enchantment takes on a negative hue and becomes relegated to nightmares. Much like Méliès's version of "Cinderella", discussed in Chapter 2, anxiety is situated around the image of the clock as an animate object which emblematizes change. Of course, the film ends happily, with a kiss – but not before Cinderella and the prince are interrupted by the tolling of a clock.

The two parts of the film, a proliferation of fantasy and a narrative progression, establish a contrast between childhood and adulthood. *Cinderella* offers narrative coherence in place of its initial enchantments. This division allowed the film both to display fairy-tale wonders and then to move into a realm more conducive to narrative, establishing a more realist sense of cause and effect as well as a certain level of character psychology. The shift from a magical fantasy world into a social world also captures a tension in cinema's use of transformations. Without a narrative through line, fantasy in *Cinderella* was a site of playfulness – both in terms of character and film aesthetics – that could show a mutable world with unexpected wonders. With a more focused desire, this polyphony becomes muted.

When the Cinderella story was transposed into a contemporary context in *The Golden Chance* (DeMille, 1915), released a year later, the emphasis was on the fairy-tale narrative rather than a filmic fairyland. In the film, living in a tenement and married to an abusive alcoholic thief, Mary (Cleo Ridgely) gets a job as a seamstress for a wealthy couple. Her employers ask her to pretend to be their guest in order to keep a wealthy businessman in town. In this unexpected new role, she participates in a milieu of extravagance and luxury, charming the businessman Roger (Wallace Reid), who falls in love with her and proposes. While she sleeps that evening, her husband coincidentally breaks into the house and stumbles upon her. Waking her up with a violent reminder of her real-life circumstances, she is cast out of this milieu of fantasy. But Roger does return, finding her in her apartment later in the film; a fight between Roger and her husband ensues, and her husband is killed. The film ends on an ambiguous note as Mary and Roger stand awkwardly, turning away from one another, lost in their thoughts. The film combines a melodramatic narrative with a fairy tale; Sumiko Higashi aptly characterizes it as "Cinderella on the lower East Side".[10] The connections of the film's scenario to the Cinderella story are evident: a young woman is transformed and allowed to enter a world of wealth and romantic love in which her desires are satisfied; this dreamworld is taken away from her, but then re-established.

In addition to narrative similarities, *The Golden Chance* recasts many of *Cinderella*'s images of fantasy. As well as motifs such as the stairway and the luxurious home, shared visual tropes connect the two films. Like Cinderella, who gazes down at her new dress after the fairy has transformed her [Figure 16], Mary is shown fantasizing about wearing the clothes she is sewing [Figure 17]. Just as Cinderella's fantasy of the prince is superimposed beside her while she sits alone, Mary's fantasy of Roger appears superimposed in a mirror in her room. Both films also use similar images of a nightmarish scenario to highlight the limits of transformation – the clock that strikes midnight which emerges from above a sleeping Cinderella [Figure 18] is visually echoed in a scene in which Mary's vicious husband looms behind her while she sleeps [Figure 19]. While *The Golden Chance* situates fantasy within a more ironic and realist frame than *Cinderella*, the differences between the two films go beyond their tone or treatment of the subject matter. In *The Golden Chance*, fantasy is closely bound up with the narrative. An early scene, where Mary sits alone outside her home on the stairwell balcony tending to a plant, provides a hint of escape from her life that corresponds to the extended scenes of Cinderella's dreamy fantasies in a forest. But in *The Golden Chance* dreams are situated, almost exclusively, in terms of the story arc. By contrast, *Cinderella*'s early scenes take time to elaborate on a fantastic and enchanted world of possibility. Both films suggest that part of growing up is finding a path for desire, confining fantasy to dreams or nightmares. But *Cinderella* takes time to show a pre- or non-narrative world of fantasy.

Cinderella reflexively shows different perspectives on cinema fantasy in a scene which precedes Cinderella's transformation by the fairy. After saying her prayers and going to sleep, she is awoken by a sound from outside her home; she looks out from the window to see fairies dancing in the moonlight. This vision of a marvellous fairyland is contrasted with her stepsisters who, after having visited a fortune-telling witch to discover their romantic destinies, are also awoken by mysterious noises, only to see the night-time activities of the witch and her retinue outside their window. Setting Cinderella alongside her sisters, the film contrasts two approaches to fantasy: one based on innocence and one based on desire. While the stepsisters seek romance and wealth, and are greeted by a diabolical scene, Cinderella's childlike relation to fantasy leads to a vision of bucolic enchantment. The scene also sets out two scenarios of film spectatorship, with the window evoking a film screen. Cinderella's viewpoint becomes akin to what Vuillermoz saw as cinema's potential: "the modern miracle placed within everyone's means. This luminous picture window opened in the wall is the will-o'-the-wisp, the clearing in which fairies dance. It is the place of dreams in a prosaic existence; it is a refreshment of the eyes after the fatigue of withering labour."[11] The images from the window, and from cinema, are situated as a rewarding and enchanting glimpse of a marvellous world for

Figure 16. *Cinderella*

Figure 17. *The Golden Chance*

Figure 18. *Cinderella*

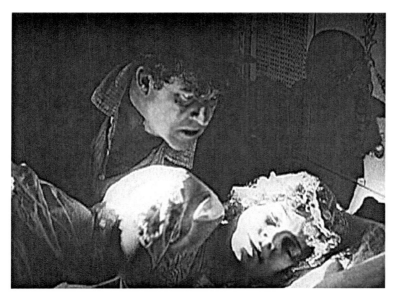

Figure 19. *The Golden Chance*

Pickford/Cinderella, whose relation to fantasy is shown to be natural and unaffected.

A similar depiction of fantasy was evident in an article on *Cinderella* in *Photoplay*.[12] It shows four stills from the film, accompanied by an up-to-date Cinderella story that tells of a naive young actress, appropriately named "Marie", who ends up marrying a dashing male lead. The most prominent image is drawn from the scene of Cinderella's vision of fairyland, showing Pickford/Cinderella gazing out the window, her face tilted upwards and illuminated by the moonlight.[13] Not coincidentally, it is as if she were watching a movie screen, suggesting a kinship with the moviegoing reader. Displaying both the star's beauty and the longing intensity of her gaze, the image interrelates the Cinderella story, the fan magazine's tale of stardom, the act of fantasizing and watching a movie. Moreover, mixing onscreen and offscreen worlds, the image alludes to Pickford's transformation into a star and, perhaps, the filmgoer's or film fan's sense of their own possibilities of self-transformation.

This was related to a wider conception of stardom as offering the possibility of a sudden shift from the everyday into a realm of fantasy. To take two of many examples, both June Caprice and Lila Lee were linked to the fantastic potentials of stardom in fan-magazine articles. A profile of Caprice describes how "little Cinderella came to New York" after being "discovered on her way from school one day, and captured for screen purposes by the Fox Film Company".[14] A similar article on Lee, noting how she was twice singled out for stardom, explains that "it is such a romance as occurs hardly anywhere but in that world of romance, the realm of the theatre and the movies. Many a Cinderella has found her way to fame and fortune thus unexpectedly in the world of make-believe."[15] The article goes on to fabricate a fantasy of sudden transformation for other stars: "Mae Marsh, Mabel Normand, Norma Talmadge, Mary Pickford – girls who were never, or hardly ever, heard of became famous overnight when their good fairies led them into the magic light of the Kliegs." Such accounts helped market both the stars and their films: the profile of Caprice was written to accompany her role in *A Modern Cinderella* (Adolfi, 1917) and Lee was starring in *The Cruise of the Make-Believes* (Melford, 1918) when her "Do You Believe in Fairies?" profile was published.

Profiles of stars would also link their personalities to fantasy. For instance, an article about Mary Fuller introduces her with the typical reference to fairy tales, "once upon a time", before going on to recount her association with fantasy: "'I began acting,' she said, 'when I was a very little girl. I lived in a land of make-believe... I loved fairy-tales, and when I could find no one to tell me stories, I made them up myself.'"[16] This childhood fascination with fantasy apparently carried her to New York in search of work, where she wrote for a living, and then ultimately to Hollywood. It was as if stardom had been latent, part of a relationship to fantasy that would then become realized by cinema. *Cinderella* presents a similar scenario to these accounts of stardom, showing Cinderella undergoing an extraordinary transformation that rewards both her innate connection to fantasy and her propensity to dream. Pickford is central to this as well, as the film's Cinderella narrative echoes her own magical "transformation" into a film star.

The Little Princess (1917): Sites of Transformation and Fairy-Tale Interludes

While *Cinderella* establishes a milieu of fantasy and then turns to a more narrative focus, *The Little Princess*, released three years later, situates realms of enchantment throughout the film. The film was based upon Frances Hodgson Burnett's short story "Sara Crewe or What Happened at Miss Minchin's" (1887), as well as its later versions as a successful play (1902) and children's book (1905).[17] The film begins in India, with the intertitle "Bombay – the city of temples where dreams are magically woven into the fabric of real life." In this milieu of ornate pillars, palm trees and spacious foyers, Sara Crewe (Pickford) is introduced hiding, anticipating her impending move away from "India's flaming skies of cobalt and crimson to the grey masked streets of London". Relocated to London, where she is separated from her father and enters a boarding school, Sara is immersed in a more regimented world. But she demonstrates a continued proximity to fantasy, related to her childhood experience in India, despite her constrained circumstances. Soon after, she learns that her father has died, and she must work as a servant. Sara holds on to her relation to imagination and fantasy, and the film presents the remuneration for this when it is revealed that her father has left her an enormous inheritance. This sudden change from poverty to wealth is shown as a surprise when two of her father's colleagues discover who she is and secretly transform her decrepit attic lodgings into a dazzling banquet room.

In the early parts of the film, before her father's death and before she becomes impoverished, various episodes show Sara in a milieu of fantasy. As well as a fast-paced carriage ride through a park, a garden party projects a beautiful world, with light streaming through the foliage with a fountain, a lake and swans in the background. After learning of her father's death, sorrowful and alone, Sara finds comfort with her friend, the servant Becky. And fantasy, despite this sad situation, doesn't end. The two girls forge a bond, reading, imagining and fantasizing together. For example, at one point, Sara and Becky pause at the door to the attic, imagining wonders in their daily life, as Sara explains, "Never open a door too quickly, Becky. We might surprise the dolls at play." They listen at the door and then there is a cut to the attic room where their dolls are shown to be playing, animated through stop motion. While such scenes indicate a childlike fantasy materialized through filmic effects, the final scenes of the film in which her room is transformed show that such dreaming has not been misplaced.

Sara's relationship to fantasy is expressed most overtly in a scene where she tells the other children in the school a fairy tale. Backlit by the light of the fire, Sara takes the children on an imaginative journey, explaining, "You can see fairy tales so much better in the dark!" Behind them, a superimposed image gradually emerges from the darkness: framed by an ornate proscenium, we see a boat on water, with the balustrades of a palace and palm trees behind it. As the scene dissolves to a shot of Sara in an elegant dress, lying on cushions, surrounded by water and swans, she then becomes the actor in her own fantasy, playing Morgiana in a retelling of "Ali Baba and the Forty Thieves". The interlude shows the entire fairy tale, elaborating on a romantic plot where Morgiana is in love with the vizier's brother who is too poor to marry her. Casting herself in a role that allows for luxurious costumes, a milieu of fantasy, grotesque caricatures, romance, dance and heroic exploits, Sara imaginatively returns to a landscape of fantasy that had been taken from her when she departed from India. Her role as storyteller is emphasized, with several interruptions that return to her recounting the tale. The interlude provides an opportunity for a different kind of fantasy narrative than the one in the film, with adult desires, a more sexualized appearance and quick-witted activities projected for Sara's (and Pickford's) adoring and absorbed audience. The fairy-tale interlude, shown in the darkness, offers a cinematic reflexivity that situates Sara/Pickford as storyteller and star.

This sequence was met with different reactions in the reception of the film. The review in the *New York Times* (November 12, 1917) described it as "a long and useless Oriental interlude". The fan magazine *Photoplay*, however, singled it out for positive comment: "One of the most delightful passages in it is the story of Ali Baba, an interlude describing pictorially how the Little Princess told the tale to her friends in a boarding school. It is deliciously fantastic."[18] These responses indicate a tension between narrative coherency and spectacular fantasy that would be a central concern in the *Variety* review:

> Artcraft's production is exceptionally effective, but somehow one gains the impression that the scenario is not all it should be. A great deal of the footage is

taken up with a visualization of an Arabian Nights story related by little Sara... The director has gone to no end of trouble and expense in securing tremendous sets for this, which has no direct bearing upon the story of Sara, which forms the basis of the feature picture.

Describing the scene as "very lavish... both in footage and in expenditure for scenic and sartorial display", the narrative fulfilment of fantasy – where her life is transformed at the end – is seen as comparatively muted, as the director "seems to have stinted himself in dwelling upon the gradual fitting up of Sarah's attic room". These various reactions to the interlude draw distinctions between fantasy that is part of a narrative arc and fantasy that appears as a spectacular detour into the realms of enchantment.

With an increasingly narrativized and, arguably, realistic emphasis in feature films of the 1910s, the aesthetics of fantasy was sometimes marginalized. Fairy-tale and fantasy interludes, which were also called "inserts", such as this retelling of Ali Baba, became a recurring trope for the depiction of fantasy. Looking back on the decade's fairy-tale films, an article in *Picturegoer* first mentions prominent feature films such as *Cinderella* (Kirkwood, 1914), *Snow White* (Dawley, 1916), *A Daughter of the Gods* (Brenon, 1916) and *Prunella* (Tourneur, 1918).[19] The article goes on to note, "either the public or the directors grew a little tired of them, and the fairy tale disappeared for a while, only to creep into filmland again in the form of inserts".[20] Examples of these include "scenes in a fairy grotto" in *Sirens of the Sea* (Holubar, 1917) and "a pretty fairy story told by the heroine" in *Merely Mrs. Stubbs* (Edwards, 1917). Suddenly shifting a filmic world into a milieu of fantasy, visualizing a story or dream, this trope became a way to introduce marvels in the midst of the everyday.

Sometimes fairy-tale interludes would seem to be quite removed from narrative concerns, leaping into spectacular worlds. For example, a review of *Peggy* (Ince, 1916) in the *New York Times* describes how "a clever interlude is introduced in the picture" as Peggy (Billie Burke) tells a group of neighbourhood children a fairy tale.[21] Abandoning the diegetic world, "this interpolated fairy story" shows the main character "making an excursion into Bugland." Although "one of the most delightful parts of the picture", the article suggests that this interlude is "perfectly irrelevant" and that "the fairy tale has nothing to do with the development of the main story". While this elaboration of the fantastic may have had little narrative rationale, it did highlight the film's star, showing "Miss Burke in her most beguiling aspect, tripping lightly through bizarre scenes, her famous hair radiant even in its screen reflection, the incarnation of girlish grace and beauty." In other films, a fairy-tale interlude might relate more closely to the film's narrative. In *Children in the House* (Franklin and Franklin, 1916), for example, a fairy tale told by one of the characters offers a chance to sketch out the narrative dynamics, providing an insight into character desire and motivation. But at the same time, the interlude transforms the melodramatic narrative into a realm of symbolic abstractions and visual enchantments. It also allows the film's star, Norma Talmadge, to display a freedom of movement and a scarcity of costume, within a realm of fantasy, that contrasts with her more restrained role throughout the rest of the film. The interlude becomes a kind of magical site set against contemporary spectacles, as the telling of the tale is contrasted with a performance in a nightclub. These examples resonate with the use of the interlude in *The Little Princess*, indicating how such visual transformations could cast a narrative, a star or a setting into a realm of fantasy.

Functioning as a kind of transformation within a film, fairy-tale interludes became one of the most prominent sites for fantasy in cinema of the 1910s. Whereas other cinematic tropes, such as flashbacks or close-ups, tended to be drawn into a continuity of storytelling that effaced transformative and magical effects, the fairy-tale interlude elaborated on cinema's capacity to shift worlds and perspectives. Such interludes showed a fluid interchange between spectacular fairy tales and narrative coherency, fantasy and verisimilitude, enchantment and everyday life. Several films directed by Cecil B. DeMille offer similar interludes, from the more psychological exploration in *The Whispering Chorus* (1918) to the spectacular Babylonian interlude in *Male and Female* (1919). *Forbidden Fruit* (1921), a remake of *The Golden Chance*, offers one particularly extravagant example of an interlude; Higashi notes that "DeMille escalates the level of conspicuous consumption... so that historical flashbacks are required for more ostentatious spectacle than those afforded by contemporary life."[22] In a *Photoplay* pictorial, this fantastic interlude is shown in a two-page spread; the caption at the bottom of the image links it to earlier traditions of spectacular fairy tales:

> "Cinderella's Ball" a beautiful scene from Cecil B. DeMille's production "Forbidden Fruit"... the ballroom with its floor of plateglass mirrors provides one of the most striking effects ever scene on the silver-sheet. How crude and inartistic the transformation scene of the old-fashioned stage pantomime would seem in comparison with this setting.[23]

Further connecting such interludes to theatrical fairy tales, an article on the film féerie in *La Semaine à Paris* described *Forbidden Fruit* (along with *The Kid* (Chaplin, 1921)) as an example where "the féerie is only a passage, an attraction in the film".[24]

Although *The Little Princess* employs such an interlude as a central scene of spectacle rather than a key narrative event, it is nevertheless integrated into the film's larger thematic and aesthetic concerns. Developing a vision of the world where fantasy is integrated with real life, the interlude functions as an extension of the stardom of Pickford, the imagination of Sara and the film's own celebration of the transformative powers of fantasy. These various aspects of the film establish a milieu in which fantasy remains near, despite the fears that it has vanished. Pickford's restricted role in the school, where she is reduced to poverty and punished for any attempt to go beyond her social role, finds a release in such images of fantasy, as well as in the concluding scenes of the film. Moreover, torn from a position of safety due to her father's sudden death, fantasy allows Sara to overcome emotional suffering that might be seen to resonate with the wartime context in which the film was made, with her father shown in uniform throughout. The "loss" of India in Sara's life might also be seen as part of a wider context, with the imperial role of Britain under threat but ultimately cast as something benign and mutually beneficial as her father's exoticized associate, Ram Dass, helps Sara. Channelling fantasy around the figure of Pickford as a girl in order to engage with transformations in individual identity, social class, the experience of the war and colonialism, the film hints at various larger social and political issues in its elaboration of fantasy. Like *The Blue Bird*, film fantasy becomes public art. In this respect, though, the emphasis is less on the poetic and disruptive transformations of *The Blue Bird* and more upon the coherence of an individual embodiment of transformation through Pickford. Her engagement with the potentials of storytelling, fantasizing and transformation offers a culturally resonant image of fantasy as a means to overcome loss, projected through and as cinema.

The Poor Little Rich Girl (1916) and the Confines of Modernity

In one of Pickford's most important star vehicles from the decade, *The Poor Little Rich Girl*, fantasy is closely entwined with film aesthetics and film viewing.[25] The film is based on Eleanor Gates's book of the same name, which she adapted into a play. The story focuses on Gwen, a lonely and imaginative girl in the midst of wealth and a constricting adult environment. Due to an overdose of medication, she almost dies. The play presents her entering a fevered dream in which she imagines a world of fantasy outside of, but related to, her constrained life. Much of the play depicts this fantastic milieu, which becomes a journey through different allegorical and expressive visions. The original source material was likely influenced by the theatrical version of *The Blue Bird*, presenting a similarly poetic fairy-tale voyage that both transforms the everyday and reveals a novel perspective on the world. The prominent critic George Jean Nathan noted this relationship in the foreword to the 1916 book of the play version of *The Poor Little Rich Girl*, which he contrasts with "the not inhollow symbolic strut and gasconade of such over-paeaned pieces as let us for example say 'The Blue Bird' of Maeterlinck..."[26] Deanna M. Toten Beard points out that this was likely a defence of American writing for the stage as *The Poor Little Rich Girl* was particularly significant and innovative in that context, "perhaps the earliest American experimentalist drama".[27] The dream scenes near the end of the film, in particular, offered its director, Tourneur, and art director, Carré, a foray into cinematic fantasy that preceded the more extended visions of enchantment in *The Blue Bird*. The film reduced the scope of the extended fantasy scenes, however, instead adding scenes that developed Pickford's star performance; Pickford explained that these were added with the help of Frances Marion, so that "where there was not enough comedy we invented little slapstick scenes of our own."[28] This helped create a film that entwined a comedic star performance with extended sequences of fantasy.

The film begins by setting out a contrast between Pickford's playful persona and her oppressive, though affluent, living conditions. After an establishing shot of an enormous mansion, *The Poor Little Rich Girl* introduces Gwen (Pickford) walking down a staircase in the background of a large hall, and then skipping joyfully forward. She pauses before entering her room, framed by two rigid servants who tower over her. Once past them, she immediately goes to look out her window. Large bars in the window suggest the oppressive environment she lives in, but she smiles excitedly before the scene cuts to her point-of-view: an insert shot of children ice skating. Despite this image of freedom and play, bars are still visible in the foreground – such images of restriction are part of a recurring motif of barriers and framed images in the film. After watching the children skating, Gwen quickly glances back to make sure that she is alone, and then turns again to the window and shouts out at those below; but she has been noticed by her attendants, and an offscreen figure closes the blind. In this opening scene, the film establishes a contrast between the youthful playfulness of Gwen and the constraints of her environment.

Episodes of Gwen struggling against her repressive environment make up much of the film. In the opening scene, watching other children play through the window, she sees a world of movement, joy and youthful abandon open up to view. A similar situation is shown in a later scene by the window of her room, with a caged bird emblematizing her entrapment, when she hears an organ grinder playing a song for the neighbourhood children. This leads her to invite the organ grinder in. When he does agree, hesitantly, Gwen fabricates a makeshift party with his music, joined by a plumber working in the home. While brought to a close by one of the servants, the scene offers another instance of Gwen attempting to cross the threshold of her restrictive life, calling to those outside her window, transgressing barriers of social class and creatively transforming her surroundings. She also disrupts restrictions through masquerade. At one point, as punishment for throwing her clothes out of the window in a fit of frustration, she is forced to wear boys' clothes rather than her frilly dresses. Crying, Gwen catches her reflection in a mirror. She suddenly brightens up, admiring her new boyish clothes and proudly donning a cap to hide her hair. This leads to a scene in which, after having met a neighbourhood gang of boys, she engages in a playful mud fight. A similar episode of freedom from a restrictive environment is shown later in the film when Gwen, who is supposed to take a bath, stands on the sink and accidentally breaks it. As water pours out, she indulges in play, dancing under it like a fountain. These activities of transgression, play and dance provide the opportunity for Gwen to disrupt her regimented life. They project a childlike fluidity in images of gender, with Gwen's resistance to the image of doll-like perfection imposed by her parents. They also allow Gwen to move between class demarcations, figured particularly in the separation between her home and her less wealthy neighbours.

Gwen's confined life is partly equated with modernity. This is immediately made evident as the film introduces her "family": her father ignores her as she enters his room and continues to discuss business matters; the numerous servants, "Tyrants of Modern Civilization" as the intertitle describes them, engage in their duties with military precision; her mother is shown preparing for a birthday party for Gwen, to which Gwen is not invited. With images of capitalism, the assembly line and the "social butterfly",[29] the film establishes a basic situation of a neglected and lonely child who is repressed by modern types. The film elaborates on this in other ways, showing a series of images of modern life that restrict or contain the exuberance of Gwen. There are scenes of her being whisked away in an elevator, taking a joyless ride in a car when she would rather walk, and further encountering her mother's focus on social appearance and her father's financial concerns. Contrasted with a more romanticized experience of freedom and nature that she longs for, modernity is situated as restrictive and confining.

As well as a release for the character, fantasy becomes associated with the potential of cinema to offer a similar alternative to everyday life. Gwen's episodes of play and fantasy are sometimes structured around images that evoke a cinema screen – her gaze out the window and at her new outfit in the mirror become spurs for creativity and imagination. Cinema, as a space of transformative possibility, becomes entwined with fantasy through one of the film's most striking tropes where Gwen's misunderstanding of language is materialized onscreen. After one of the servants tells Gwen that her father's office is full of "bears", referring to the state of the market, there is a transition to a fantastical scenario in which her father, walking along a city street, is attacked by a group of bears. A similar scene of Gwen's subjectivity occurs when one of the characters refers to the governess as a "snake in the grass". This is followed by a transition to a bizarre scene of the character's head attached to a snake's body, writhing underneath a tree. Taking language and recasting it visually, these scenes evoke not only Gwen's subjective misunderstanding, but words themselves as material for filmic play.

Fantasy fully refigures the world in the film's concluding scenes, which entwine the star performance of Pickford at play with cinema's fairy-tale aesthetics. Two of the servants entrusted with looking after Gwen during her "birthday party" – which, as noted earlier, is her mother's opportunity to put on a social gathering – eagerly want to see a show at the theatre. In order to ensure that they can sneak out, despite their responsibilities, they give Gwen a drug so that she will sleep. Mistakenly giving her a double dose, the maid leaves and Gwen becomes very ill. The film then shifts into Gwen's subjective world of fantastic dreams and nightmar- ish events. Returning to the space at the start of the film, she tumbles down the staircase and falls unconscious. In her dream, the room is transformed into a place of neoclassical splendor. A group of superimposed fairies emerges from offscreen, join hands and dance around Gwen. There is a brief return to the "real" world when the plumber – who has heard the noise of her fall – arrives to discover her lying unconscious. He too is transformed, as the intertitle explains: "every character in her actual life is borne into her delirium." In this visualized dream state, the plumber wakes her and explains: "You are in the Garden of Lonely Children, in The Tell-tale Forest of Dreams. Here, things appear as they really are." Hearing the organ grinder, she imagines him next to her. She then asks to set out: "I wish I could find the Land of Happy Children. Let us go hunt for it." A car appears, but quickly sets off – rather than being taken by this emblem of modern life, their journey is on foot.

As they explore the world, they encounter various extraordinary creatures and enchanted realms. Characters introduced earlier in the film appear as literal figurations of their metaphorical descrip- tions so that, for example, a two-faced character is shown as having two faces, her head rotating in order to display them. Events are also captured and refracted in the dream state, so that a struggle between a donkey ("a silly ass") and a serpent ("a snake-in-the- grass") in her dream state is revealed as the butler's attempts to get her governess away from her. When Gwen's father appears in the diegetic world, he is similarly transformed within Gwen's dream. She approaches Wall Street, represented by a building so huge that she has to climb the steps one at a time; once inside, she sees her father working at an enormous machine, pulling a lever and adjusting a wheel – like an assembly-line labourer – as it churns out money.[30] After encountering her mother, who is literally burning candles at both ends, the journey nears its conclusion. In the diegetic world, her parents and her doctor fear that she might soon die. In the realm of delirium, this is made tangible, as a shrouded woman offers her "eternal sleep" and she looks upon a graveyard. About to embrace death, an alternative vision appears, with a woman dancing in a brightly lit glade beside a body of water. Here, Gwen dances with the woman and, as the intertitle explains, "The hopes of dreamland lure the little soul from the Shadows of Death to the Joys of Life." As she continues to dance, the background is transformed into her childhood home, and she is reunited with her parents. She awakens in the "real" world, and the transformations of the dream are partially actualized in real life – her mother now tends to her, her father has decided to abandon Wall Street and move back to their country home, and Gwen is encouraged to "go barefoot, and make mud pies".

In some respects, the film offers a resolution to the constraints of modern life through a Romantic return to nature. However, its images of fantasy offer something more than simply an escape from contemporary concerns. The climactic sequence extends the tropes of mutability, play and dance that course throughout the film. The elements of reflexivity in scenes at the window and the mirror alongside the visual metaphors and the extended dream all become part of cinema's capacity to refigure a static world. Gwen/Pickford embodies this kind of mutability, presenting a figure able to overcome the strictures of a modern environment. From the movement of the ice skaters at the start of the film to that of the organ grinder winding the instrument, from Gwen's participation in the earthiness of a mud fight to the water of indoor plumbing, from the dream's depiction of fairies gathering around her to the turn away from death brought on by dance, the film uses images of movement to fashion a lively cinematic world.

Arriving at purer forms of experience by showing a world in a state of flux, the film recasts cinema and its star as embodiments of fantastic potential.

Like *Cinderella* and *The Little Princess*, *The Poor Little Rich Girl* uses the tropes of fairy tales and fantasy to renegotiate imaginatively everyday experiences and modern life. In each of these films, this is presented reflexively, with scenes in which Pickford gazes out of windows or dreams of wonders evoking the act of cinemagoing or watching a film. Working through scenarios that corresponded to the daily lives of moviegoers, gazing at film screens and dreaming of their fantastic possibilities, Pickford and her fantasy films helped establish an idea of film as fantasy: a site of marvellous potential for transformation and play, fluidly bridging the everyday and the extraordinary.

Marguerite Clark and the Discourse of Stardom

As Richard deCordova and others have examined, the star system depended upon both a star's roles in individual films and a network of discourse circulating around a star. DeCordova writes, "The star's identity is intertextual, and the star system is made up in part of those ongoing practices that produce the intertextual field within which that identity may be seized by curious fans."[31] While Pickford's extratextual identity only sometimes alluded to fairy tales, another of the decade's most popular stars, Marguerite Clark, was often linked to a language of fantasy. Clark was described as "one of the 'Big Four' of movie stars", along with Pickford, Charlie Chaplin and Douglas Fairbanks, in a *New York Times* article in 1916, and named as the third most popular star, after Mary Pickford and Francis X. Bushman, in a *Motion Picture Magazine* fan poll in 1917.[32] Beginning in the theatre, Clark had performed in plays for adults, including *The Affairs of Anatol* (1912), but had established herself in fantasy-themed plays such as *Peter Pan* (1909), *Snow White* (1912) and *Prunella* (1913).[33] Just a few weeks before its American premiere, she was scheduled to play a starring role in *The Blue Bird*.[34] This relation to fantasy would continue in Clark's film roles as she starred in a series of prominent fantasy and fairy-tale films, including *Snow White* (Dawley, 1916), *The Seven Swans* (Dawley, 1917) and *Prunella* (Tourneur, 1918). By the latter part of the decade, she was perhaps the film star most closely associated with onscreen fairy tales.

Clark elaborated on this connection in an article titled "Filming Fairy Plays" to coincide with her role in *The Seven Swans*, based on the Brothers Grimm tale "The Six Swans". Linking her own personal interest in fairy tales with her film role, Clark situates herself as dwelling in a realm of fantasy that would become projected onscreen:

> I really grew up with the fairies. I used to live in a place with a fine garden and I'm sure that if fairies ever really existed they would have delighted in it... I think I got, perhaps, more than the average out of my dreams. And it seems like a fulfilment of those dreams that I am now able, in the picture, to depict fairy rôles to delight the hearts of other small people, such as I was, and to make their dreams come true.[35]

Through such comments, Clark associated her onscreen roles with her own engagement with fantasy. While this drew upon conservative associations of women with fantasy and childhood, Clark negotiated some of the more retrograde implications of her fairy-tale stardom in profiles and interviews. A condescending tone is evident in a *Photoplay* article titled "Little Miss Practicality" in which the author characterizes her as a "winsome, whimsome little lady" and "just a charming, fascinatingly pretty girl, whose charm is such a strange, wayward, elusively and delightfully feminine thing".[36] The actual interview establishes a rather different picture of a modern independent woman, with Clark noting her preference for the stage over films, unwilling to answer questions about her love life, emphasizing the discrepancy between gender roles in terms of financial independence and driving off rather abruptly in her new car.

In *Photoplay* two years later, another profile on Clark begins with an emphasis on her "winsome sweetness" and the editor's insistence that the interviewer "find out something about her home life. Does she live with her mother? Can she cook and does she, and can she sew?"[37] The profile takes a much different direction, with Clark begrudgingly agreeing to an interview. Clark goes on to discuss her films, noting certain cinematic qualities: "A photoplay is not handicapped by stage limitations. It has a field all its own and should exploit that field. Take my picture *Wildflower* for instance. It was a light little story but the setting was enchanting." Clark's insight into both her own roles and film aesthetics extended to her status as a star. The article describes how her work leaves little time for play, and she discusses her status as a wealthy film star; asked how she could afford "a $100,000 Liberty Bond", her forthright response, which the interviewer misconstrues as naive, was that "my admirers think I earned it". The contrast between her fantasy screen roles and her apparent real life is summarized: "My impression of Miss Clark, formed by viewing her pictures, was that she was a happy-hearted little elf smiling her way through the sour old world. She is all of that and something more. She is a serious-minded little person intent on doing her work well."[38] Unable or unwilling fully to take into account the gulf between his perception of her onscreen appearance and his encounter with her in real life, the author of the piece still concludes by situating Clark's independence in limited terms, continuing to infantilize her.

Judging by interviews with her at the time, Clark was resistant to such accounts. In her article "Filming Fairy Plays", Clark refused to abandon herself to some kind of essentialized notion of her relation to fairy tales or childhood, presenting herself as both working at and playing at fantasy: "I try to go back and imagine myself in such a position, as I seemed so capable of doing in my very youthful days." As well as depicting an active role, she describes how her performances in fairy-tale films offer playful escape from the trappings of her modern roles: "I forgot all about long frocks and having my hair done up… and became a childish princess…"[39] Several years earlier, while performing as Snow White on the stage, Clark similarly explained how the fairy tale offered a welcome break from her roles in "naughty farces", and although she might have wished for something with "a great deal of thought in it", she still had "never enjoyed playing any-thing so much…"[40] She explained how the play may open up an avenue for future roles, such as "Strindberg's 'Swan White'". This extended also to her discussion of having some creative control over her films; describing herself as "something of an authority on fairy tales",[41] she recounts how she had given the director, J. Searle Dawley, a stack of fairy tales including works by Andersen, the Brothers Grimm and d'Aulnoy, to consider filming.[42] Such accounts indicate that rather than playing a passive role as a fairy-tale star, she engaged creatively with fantasy. Moreover, her conception of the roles themselves highlighted their independence:

> I think that the self-reliant type of girl is much more popular than the weeping heroine, tho tears are effective at times. It seems to me that the public prefers the kind of heroine who takes matters into her own hands rather than one who is simply dissolved into liquid brine upon the slightest provocation. Surely we admire the active type more than the lachrymose individual in real life…[43]

She concludes, "I am sure that what is true to life is true of the screen; for, after all, the screen is nothing but a reflection of our-selves". In such accounts, Clark situated herself as actively using the imagination, artistry and potential of seemingly constricting fairy-tale roles.

This extended to wider considerations of cinema's fairy tales. The effect of working on fairy-tale films in a wartime context is described as "something of a relief to find oneself suddenly

translated into another atmosphere, a veritable land of enchantment, like a corner of Fairyland dropped from the clouds into the
heart of the world's greatest metropolis." In addition to providing
a space for her own playfulness, enchantment and imagination,
such roles might offer a productive and beneficial site of fantasy
for others: "perhaps sometimes a poor little kiddie with only a
sordid tenement room as a playground is having a chance to dream
some of the dreams that were part and parcel of my childhood."
Moreover, this has a wider applicability to adult experiences:

> I sometimes think it's a pity to ever grow up and forget
> those dreams. I think if a lot of us could remember
> them, and occasionally, when things seem to go a bit
> hard and we are all tangled up in the skein of life, evoke
> them from the past, it would help us to be a little kinder,
> perhaps, and relieve us of the strain that comes from
> living in a hustling, bustling age, when people feel they
> haven't time to dream.[44]

These irruptions of fantasy within contexts of war, deprivation
and modernity cast stardom and cinema as interrelated sites
that could offer a space of dreaming potential within modern
life. However artificial and constrained such dreams were in a
wider social context, they nevertheless offered what was perhaps
the most culturally significant expression of fantasy in the early
twentieth century.

5 SITES OF ENCHANTMENT AND *The Thief of Bagdad* (1924)

THE THIEF OF BAGDAD (WALSH, 1924) WAS THE MOST extravagant American fairy-tale film of the 1920s. Filled with marvellous mise-en-scène, elaborate action sequences and fantastic trick effects, the film presented a milieu of exotic Arabian fantasy alongside the acrobatic performance of its star, Douglas Fairbanks. Writers on film who had earlier emphasized the cinematic possibilities of fairy tales, such as Vachel Lindsay and Émile Vuillermoz, were astonished. The film was, for Lindsay, the realization of his approach to cinema and fairy tales; he described it as "the greatest movie so far in movie history" and "a text for motion picture philosophy".[1] Vuillermoz began his review of the film in *Le Temps* writing, "For the first time, the Americans have managed to intelligently and skilfully use the precious resources of their studios and their stars in choosing a truly cinematic scenario."[2] He continued his appraisal of the film's subject: "The féerie is the true domain of cinema."

The Thief of Bagdad situated its star, Fairbanks, in a context of fantasy similar to the star vehicles of Mary Pickford (to whom Fairbanks was married at the time) and Marguerite Clark, among others, discussed in the previous chapter. However, partly due to his star persona and partly due to connotations of gender, Fairbanks was seen to be more active and dynamic in his fashioning of cinema fantasy. For example, referring to both his role within the film and his role as its producer, the review in *Motion Picture Classic* notes: "It is time the public was guided to loftier ideas – and [Fairbanks] guides them – and by guiding them he stakes everything on its intelligence to appreciate this fantasy."[3]

As such an account suggests, and as this chapter will go on to examine, *The Thief of Bagdad* entwined fantasy with the potentials of cinema and its place in a wider modern culture.

While the review in *Motion Picture Classic* notes that Douglas Fairbanks "scoffs at traditions and conventions" and that "one can make no comparisons with anything ever projected past or present",[4] *The Thief of Bagdad* was immersed within trends in cinema at the time.[5] It was another in a series of spectacular costume films starring Fairbanks, which included *The Mark of Zorro* (Niblo, 1920) and *Robin Hood* (Dwan, 1922). Describing the experience of viewing this latter film, René Clair used a rhetoric of fantasy which anticipated later descriptions of *The Thief of Bagdad*: "Judge *Robin Hood* as you would judge a ballet, a féerie. Watch, for an instant, with simple eyes."[6] *The Thief of Bagdad* also drew upon the iconography and subject matter of an exotic "Oriental" milieu that had been evident in earlier spectacular fantasies such as *Aladdin and the Wonderful Lamp* (Franklin, 1917) and the fairy-tale interlude in *The Little Princess* (Neilan, 1917). In this respect, *The Thief of Bagdad* offered a fashionable exoticism which had recently caused a stir with the success of American films such as *The Sheik* (Melford, 1921), as well as German films such as *Sumurun* (Lubitsch, 1920), *Destiny* (Lang, 1921) and *Waxworks* (Leni, 1924).[7] Major European films of the 1920s also used other kinds of fairy-tale fantasies in ways that resonated with *The Thief of Bagdad*: for example, the German film *Siegfried* (Lang, 1924) presented a fantastic quasi-mythical world that anticipated elements of *The Thief of Bagdad*, and in France a year later *L'Inhumaine* (L'Herbier, 1925), advertised as a "féerique story", situated modernist design in a framework of fantasy.[8]

Within this context, the novelty of *The Thief of Bagdad* was due less to an entirely unique depiction of fantasy and more to its specific place in Hollywood filmmaking and American culture. This led some reviewers to cast it in terms of a new kind of cinema; as the *New York Times* noted, the word "film" "hardly seems to fit such a wonderful picture."[9] In an editorial in *Motion Picture News*, the editor William A. Johnston praised the film, writing,

"We are inclined to view it apart from purely trade considerations – the fact that it will not reach the picture theatres for a long time, its box-office value as compared with other big pictures, including Fairbanks' own previous successes, etc., etc."[10] Instead, he suggested that the film will "prove a spur to the public interest in motion pictures" due partly to its innovative exploration of cinema's potential: "There are pictures now and then that greatly broaden our mental horizon as picture people – and this is one of the greatest of all these uplooking pictures."

This chapter focuses on how *The Thief of Bagdad* attempted to carve out such an enlarged vision of cinema as an aesthetic and institutional form of fantasy. I examine how the film presented fantasy in ways that resonated with wider contexts of spectacular fairy tales, the cinema experience and the enticements of a burgeoning consumer culture. I then conclude this chapter by exploring the continued prominence and the shifting treatment of such issues in several of the most popular and critically lauded American films of the late 1920s. Focusing particularly on those films which were recipients of major awards at the first Academy Awards ceremony in 1929, I trace some of the ways in which other major films from the time negotiated the relation between fantasy and cinema, drawing on the tropes of stardom, spectacle and transformation that were central to earlier fairy-tale films. While used to much different effect, the elaboration of fantasy in films such as *Wings* (Wellman, 1927), *Sunrise* (Murnau, 1927) and *Seventh Heaven* (Borzage, 1928) also projected an experience of cinema and modernity underpinned by a sensibility of fantasy.

A Fairy-Tale Atmosphere

The Thief of Bagdad begins in an elaborately designed world of extraordinary places and tempting goods. Our guide through this fantastic landscape is the thief, Ahmed (Douglas Fairbanks), who spends the early part of the film bounding through the space in search of whatever he desires. During one particularly ambitious robbery attempt, he climbs into the palace of the Caliph and is struck by the beauty of a sleeping princess (Julanne Johnston). Sneaking into her room the next night, he quickly realizes that he cannot steal her, and instead sets about to win her love. He masquerades as a prince, but this proves unsuccessful and he is reduced to melancholy. Things are set right after the princess, who has become enamoured of Ahmed, arranges a competition between her suitors to gather the greatest treasure in the world – with the help of the local "Holy Man", as well as others along the way, Ahmed sets out on a lengthy quest on which he encounters a series of wondrous creatures and places. Returning to Bagdad with magical items, he liberates the city from the nefarious schemes of one of the princess's suitors and finally wins the love of the princess, setting out with her upon a magic carpet. The list of the "Best Films of the Month" in the November 1924 *Pictures and the Picturegoer* begins, "There are a dozen reasons why *Thief of Bagdad* should head the Honours List for this month", going on to note that its appeals include "lovely settings" and a "new grace which has crept into the movements of Douglas Fairbanks".[11] But the article emphasizes the novelty of the film in terms of fairy tales: "at last a producer has had the courage to turn the camera's cunning to good account, and has given us a real fairy tale on celluloid. *Thief of Bagdad* is prodigal in fairy stuff."[12]

In some respects, the film's introductory scenes would seem to allude to fairy tales in order to situate it as a moralistic and traditional tale for children. A framing narrative set in a desert introduces the film. A man tells a child a story and, pointing to the night sky, the stars spell out the ostensible moral of the film: "Happiness must be earned." This is followed by two title cards, with the second describing how "the works of those gone before us have become instances and examples to men of our modern day." Despite the serious tone, there are hints in these first few moments that something other than a moral lesson is being introduced. This title card quotes from the preface of Richard Burton's translation of *The Arabian Nights*, though modifying it slightly;

Burton's original reads "Verily *the words* and works of those gone before us" might offer lessons for today.[13] Omitting "words" in the opening intertitle sets a tone of visibility and activity, rather than storytelling. Moreover, the scene, set atop a hill in a desert landscape, evokes the start of Burton's preface where he wrote of telling the tales that he had collected to local townspeople in "Arabia" and "Somali-land":

> The women and children stand motionless as silhouettes outside the ring; and all are breathless with attention; they seem to drink in the words with eyes and mouths as well as with ears. The most fantastic flights of fancy, the wildest improbabilities, the most impossible of impossibilities, appear to them utterly natural, mere matters of every-day occurrence.[14]

The atmosphere sets the stage for storytelling, with "the after-glow transfiguring and transforming, as by magic, the homely and rugged features of the scene into a fairyland lit with a light which never shines on other soils or seas."[15] While the opening scene of the man telling a story to a child in *The Thief of Bagdad* establishes a didactic purpose where the film itself might offer a contemporary lesson, it also offers a milieu of dreaming distances, exoticism and enchantment.

Reviews at the time emphasized these fantastic qualities. An article in *The Film Daily* noted that newspaper reviews offered "Praise galore" in two respects: "Practically every critic raves over its pictorial appeal. Practically all of them refer to its fairy tale atmosphere."[16] Minimizing the importance of its story, described as a "trifle long in the telling", the review in the *Los Angeles Times* heralded the film as, among other things, a "pictorially flashing extravaganza", "a great feast for the epicures" and a film that "sweeps and carries you away with it, but as a spectator not touched to the heart but rather conquered by the spell of some great undreamed of achievement, by some marble-white East Indian temple and ivory palace in far Cathay".[17] While this review is thrilled by this experience, such accounts were not always positive. *Time* magazine uses a similar rhetoric with a very different implication, noting that "Going through miles and miles of glowing pictures in an art museum gets to be rather wearisome... So boredom sets in eventually as Douglas Fairbanks takes one on a personally conducted tour of ancient Bagdad... It is all a studied beauty, like a florid poster in action."[18] Adopting a similar tone, the reviewer in *Motion Picture Magazine* writes, "We believe that 'The Thief of Bagdad' is the beginning of new motion pictures, but it failed to thrill us or inspire us except for slight esthetic thrills born of its sheer beauty."[19] Such reviews drew upon intermedial comparisons to different sites of visual culture, consumption, display and travel, stretching the limits of the cinematic experience in order to express the novelty of the film's spectacular fantasies.

When attention shifted to the film's fairy-tale qualities, descriptions continued to emphasize spectacle over narrative through a recurring intermedial comparison to the illustrated fairy-tale book. The *Los Angeles Times* reviewer wrote that the film gives you the feeling of being "a child reading a wonderful and superlatively illustrated story book. Unless you can accomplish this point of view you may not enjoy it to the fullest. You may marvel at its beauty of photography, but you will not get the full value of its enchanting fascination."[20] Similar comparisons were made in *Motion Picture Magazine*, which noted that the film's imagery "might readily be one of the lovely Rackham or Dulac illustrations come to life", and *Film Daily*, which wrote that "it is just as though some one was turning over a book of a thousand pages of Maxfield Parrish drawings illustrating The Arabian Nights."[21] By relating the film to the experience of looking at illustrated storybooks, these reviews shifted fairy tales away from their associations with morality, narrative and tradition towards an experience of wonder based upon visual spectacle. The review in *Classic Screen and Stage Pictorial* noted that "if you can imagine a rich compilation of Maxfield Parrish drawings – these inviting the spectator on a fanciful cruise – you will have some conception of its quality and appeal."[22] The reference to a "fanciful cruise" suggests an abandonment to visual enchantment. *Variety* phrased it simply: "the picture carries its audience along."[23]

These reviews described the film's spectacular fantasy in a similar tone to earlier prefaces for illustrated versions of the *Arabian Nights*. In the reviews quoted above, the references to fairy tales note two particular illustrators, Edmund Dulac and Maxfield Parrish. Produced in the early flourishing of high-quality colour illustrated books, versions of the *Arabian Nights* with illustrations by Dulac (1907) and Parrish (1909) offered abridged versions of the tales accompanied by colourful illustrations of key scenes and sights.[24] The prefaces to the books emphasized the experience of wonder that can be drawn from such images. Introducing the version illustrated by Dulac, Laurence Housman's preface noted that "the expression of so much life, habit and custom, so many coloured and secluded interiors, so quaint a commingling of crowds, so brilliant and moving a pageantry of Eastern mediævalism" provides the tales with "their perennial charm".[25] The perspective of a reader when confronted by these spectacular marvels and exotic details was one of voyaging, as "those of us who read are all travellers; and never is our travelling sense so awakened perhaps, as when we dip into a book such as this".[26] Kate Douglas Wiggin offered a similar account of the pleasures of the tales in her preface to the version illustrated by Maxfield Parrish, but she invited readers to immerse themselves more fully in its fantastic milieu: "Enter into this 'treasure house of pleasant things', then, and make yourself at home in the golden palaces, the gem-studded caves, the bewildering gardens. Sit by its mysterious fountains, hear the plash of its gleaming cascades, unearth its magic lamps and talismans, behold its ensorcelled princes and princesses."[27] In these introductions, fairy tales were presented as visual marvels, with their imagery drawing a reader – or viewer – into an enchanted world. Reviews of *The Thief of Bagdad* linked a similar experience of looking through and being carried away by the wonders of an illustrated fairy-tale book with watching the film.

Such an immersion within spectacular fantasy was elicited by the film's exhibition. Premiering at the Liberty Theatre in New

York on March 18, 1924, the film was accompanied not just by a buzz of anticipation for the new Douglas Fairbanks costume film and crowds eager to catch a glimpse of the star, but also by an extraordinary arranged scene in the lobby:

> Undoubtedly what added to the eagerness of the throng were the beating of drums, the droning of voices in dirgelike songs and the odor of incense that emanated from the theatre, where no stone had been left unturned to give the place the Oriental atmosphere for the picture...[28]

The lobby presented eager spectators with "perfume from Bagdad, magic carpets and ushers in Arabian attire..."[29] At the intermission, the ushers "made a brave effort to bear cups of Turkish coffee to the women in the audience." Not only did this "thoroughly Oriental atmosphere" remain in place for the run of the film in New York, but as a road show picture, the lobby (along with an orchestra) accompanied the film as it played in different theatres across the United States; advertisements of the travelling exhibition made this one of the film's main attractions. For example, an advertisement in *The Charleston Daily Mail* (September 28, 1924) drew attention to the "car load of gorgeous oriental stage settings" and an advertisement in *The Davenport Democrat and Leader* (November 23, 1924) claimed that the film "will be presented... as it was for one year at the Liberty Theatre, New York, and six months at the Woods Theatre, Chicago." The exhibition was significant as both an advertising ploy and as part of the experience of viewing the film at the time, offering exoticism with a hint of cosmopolitan excess. The lobby set a mood of sensual fantasy, establishing an environment of sight, sound, smell and taste that corresponded with the film.

The importance of this lobby was demonstrated by the participation of the New York theatre producer Morris Gest. The role of Gest in the exhibition of the film was widely reported, often accompanied by the staggering figures he would be paid for orchestrating it; for example, *Variety* reported that it was "some-what of a startler to Broadway. It makes a unique combination of the greatest showman and the greatest single picture, if not also the greatest film male drawing card."[30] Gest had a consid-erable reputation, having been responsible for both producing lauded Broadway spectacles and bringing European stage plays and directors to New York. His most recent success, premiering just several months earlier, was the Broadway production of *The Miracle*, directed by Max Reinhardt. Kenneth Macgowan, writing for *Motion Picture Classic*, describes the presentation of *The Miracle* at the Century Theatre:

> ...the Century Theatre is no more. [Otto] Kahn, who founded it, and Gest, who put Aphrodite and [Eleonora] Duse and the Chauve-Souris into various portions of its capacious interior, have called to their assistance Max Reinhardt and Norman Bel Geddes and made the place over into a cathedral... Once you are inside the auditorium doors, there isn't a square inch of the Century left. Geddes has seen to that in a very extraordinary way.[31]

This refiguring of the site of exhibition had a simple effect: "You are in the atmosphere of a cathedral." Using a similar phrasing, typical in reviews at the time, *Motion Picture News* described the milieu of *The Thief of Bagdad* as an "atmospheric treat", going on to note that it was "a part of Morris Gest's scheme to provide a per-fect harmonious setting for Fairbanks' opulent Oriental canvas."[32]

While *The Thief of Bagdad*, like *The Miracle*, used a particularly spectacular exhibition to heighten its fantasy, the "atmosphere" that was created was part of a wider trend in cinema exhibition in the 1920s. Picture palaces, which offered an environment that evoked a sense of fantasy, romance or exoticism, were becoming a major feature of the cinema landscape.[33] In "Theater Entrances and Lobbies", published in 1925, E. C. A. Bullock begins by situating the design of cinema theatres in such a context:

The people of today's hurly-burly, commercialized world go to the theater to live an hour or two in the land of romance. So it is that the sophisticated playgoer must be taken up, on the architect's magic carpet, and set down suddenly in a celestial city of gorgeous stage settings, luxurious hangings and enchanting music. The atmosphere of a king's palace must prevail to stimulate the imagination of those who come within its doors.[34]

For Bullock, this extends outward so that "even before the patron enters the theater, the architect must stress first impressions through one of the most important architectural problems, – entrance and lobby appeal." Similarly, John F. Barry and Epes W. Sargent note how, in the design of motion picture theatres, "All the decorative details are elements that make up the atmosphere of a palace, to stimulate the imagination of tired minds and re-create the strength of weary hearts."[35] Fashioning a space of enchantment, such sites took an element that might be seen as secondary to the films themselves – the "atmosphere" – and situated it as central to the overall experience of cinemagoing.

Giuliana Bruno writes of how John Eberson, "the master architect of atmospheric theaters", may have developed his notion of atmosphere through his knowledge of "the concept of *stimmung*, which encompassed atmosphere, sentiment, state of mind, mood, and tonality, and which had its roots in nineteenth-century discourse."[36] Another possible lineage for such "atmospheric theaters" comes from the language of advertising. Stephen R. Fox describes how "atmosphere advertising" which "made its pitch obliquely, by suggestion or association", emerged as a major form of advertising in the 1910s.[37] T. J. Jackson Lears describes how the "the triumph of 'atmosphere' in automobile advertising involved the incorporation of fantasy into the emerging distribution system."[38] The atmosphere in the exhibition of a film was used in a similar way: it was a means to elaborate on fantasy as a feature of cinemagoing that could itself be a pleasure outside the experience of viewing a specific film. Writing several years later, in 1932, the French film critic Léon Moussinac, quoting from Eberson, discussed the introduction of "atmospheric theatres" in Paris.[39] He describes, among other things, the "atrocious vulgarity" this brings to the "doors of the cinema", going on to write, "What becomes of the film in all that? Exactly what it has become for the shopkeepers of cinema, no longer the essential object of the cinematographic spectacle, but the accessory." Years earlier, the reception and exhibition of *The Thief of Bagdad* indicates how cinema fantasy could extend beyond the boundaries of an individual film, drawing the cinema experience into a wider milieu of fantasy.

Fantasies of Consumer Culture

The elaboration of a fairy-tale atmosphere in *The Thief of Bagdad* linked it to a wider cultural and social context of fantasy: in the first decades of twentieth century America, the fantasies of fairy tales were closely linked to the fantasies of consumer culture. Spectacular visions of magical objects which seemed to reverberate with potential, environments which seemed to contain immense possibilities of transformation and narratives that portrayed bodies and worlds as mutable were the stuff of fairy tales. They were also the material for an emerging consumer culture. Through such sights and spaces as advertisements, department stores and window displays, fairy tales were integrated into a commercial aesthetic, what William Leach describes as "a new set of commercial enticements… to sell goods in volume" and "the core aesthetic of American capitalist culture, offering a vision of the good life and of paradise."[40] This would include "the visual materials of desire – color, glass, and light"[41] as well as the places, images and narratives that spectacularly displayed the magical potential of consumer culture and its myriad goods. A visual and rhetorical langue of exoticism would become similarly entwined with the commercial aesthetic.[42] Films and film culture in the 1910s and 1920s would sometimes elaborate on the context of consumer culture directly, displaying its sites, projecting its allure and narrating its potentials (and dangers) to a mass audience. The fantasies of consumer culture and cinema were also linked in more fundamental ways, presenting similar attractions circulating around transformation, desire and spectacle. In *The Thief of Bagdad*, fairy-tale tropes are deeply entwined with fantasies of self-transformation, extraordinary sites of possibility and visions of enchanted commodities; fairy-tale fantasies are used to engage with some of the experiences, both real and imagined, of consumer culture.

Depicting a dreamworld of adventure and a milieu of ongoing desire, the scene which introduces us to the setting of *The Thief of Bagdad* is prefaced by an intertitle: "A street in Bagdad, dream city of the ancient East –". The establishing shot sets the stage for this fantastic Orientalist world [Figure 20]. Most of the frame is filled with a long shot of an enormous wall, establishing the scope of the set; dwarfed by the setting, people carrying various goods walk through the street. Barely visible, near the bottom of

Figure 20. *The Thief of Bagdad*

the frame, there is the tiny figure of Ahmed (Douglas Fairbanks) lying on a ledge. The scene dissolves to a shot of him, apparently sleeping, and then shows his face in close-up. By focusing upon a dreaming Fairbanks, the scene might suggest that the film itself is the outward manifestation of inward desires, a fantasy made real. But this effect is quickly shattered. A man walks by and stoops down to drink from a water fountain. Ahmed twitches, and when the man walks away, Ahmed displays the wallet he has just stolen, and quickly hides it in his trousers. Ahmed/Fairbanks has not been asleep; his dreaming innocence was a deception. Rather than a "dream city", this is an environment of waking dreams.

The first part of the film elaborates on this by presenting a material world of fantastic possibility and a series of thrillingly satisfied desires: Ahmed steals freshly baked bread by climbing a wall; he escapes with a stolen magic rope, leaping past people at prayer; he steals a valuable ring by clinging to the underside of a carriage. In the mise-en-scène, figures and objects are set in relief against the richly detailed environment of this dream city. In one scene, after having fled with the magic rope, Ahmed finds himself suddenly brought still. Standing in the window of a mosque, looking down, he overhears the Holy Man speaking to a group of men: "Toil – for by toil the sweets of human life are found." Ahmed bellows with laughter, "Thou liest," and leaps down. Gesturing with a grabbing hand, he tells them, "What I want – I take. My reward is *here*." He has a point. In this city, where Ahmed thieves in the midst of a world filled with spectacles, baubles, smells, sounds and objects of desire, his reward is right in front of him.

These opening scenes in *The Thief of Bagdad* depicted "the excitement, the sensory stimulation, the profusion of goods, the crowds, the unnerving, often illusory, ambience" that Elaine Abelson describes as typical facets of the department store.[43] As well as its general tone and atmosphere, the film also evokes consumer spaces through specific means. For example, one of the most important elements of interior design in department stores – creating a space that invites the free movement of customers – is central to the film's early scenes.[44] Vachel Lindsay, whose lengthy analysis of *The Thief of Bagdad* in *Progress and Poetry of the Movies* will be discussed in more detail later, drew attention to how the stairway in the Caliph's palace is "a sort of sublime metaphor of all the escalators going up and down in department stores, or in some of the gigantic subway stations in New York."[45] It is not just the stairways that offer this expansive circulation – Ahmed bounds across this space, making it a giant playground, a tableau displaying his gymnastic skill. The director, Raoul Walsh, describes the effect: "all I did was keep my eyes open and marvel at the ease with which Fairbanks turned into a human fly and went up city and palace walls without apparent effort."[46] Ahmed's traversal of space and boundary-crossing vitality displays not only his athletic prowess, but also an environment suited to the free movement of desire.

Polished and reflective surfaces provide a visually enticing grounding for this world of fantasy. Lindsay writes, "The hard-edged quality of photography was overcome by building glazed floors by the acre… till the tall princess seemed to be walking upon still water in fairyland."[47] Accounts of the film's production described Fairbanks's reaction to initial design plans:

> "They have not the light and airy quality we want," he said. "We must lift them off the earth." Then he asked for acres of polished pavement, capable of exquisite reflection. Around this the high walls, the minarets and domes, the balconies and ledges and the long stairways of our dream city of Bagdad were built.[48]

The creation of such fantastic and theatrical environments was, as William Leach discusses, key to the creation of children's departments, model showrooms, bargain basements and display cases in department stores: "Merchants worked on an imaginative canvas, relying on color, glass, and light and on theatrical strategies – or on what they called 'central decorative ideas' – to transform interior spaces."[49] The evocation of consumer spaces was a recurring element within films of the 1920s. For example, in *Cecil B. DeMille and American Culture*, Sumiko Higashi draws out various implications of these strategies of commercial display in the films of one the era's most prominent directors, Cecil B. DeMille. But whereas DeMille's films from the period would typically include extravagant sights as fantastic interludes within a more realistic world or as contemporary spectacles of consumer culture, *The Thief of Bagdad* establishes a distinctive kind of display by using them throughout the film, *as* the film. Fairbanks, in a November 1924 publicity article, was quoted as saying, "I care not that DeMille gives his bulging bathrooms to a soiled world so long as I give its romance."[50] This aesthetic grounded in fantasy was pivotal to the "dream city" in *The Thief of Bagdad*, with its "central decorative idea" of marvellous exoticism.[51]

While presenting a cinematic vision that resonated with the visual aesthetic of consumerism and fantasy, *The Thief of Bagdad* also presented a more didactic moral lesson. As noted earlier, the opening intertitle shows a moral: "Happiness Must Be Earned". This is, in some respects, reflected in the film itself; a key turning point finds Ahmed embarking on a lone quest for magical treasures which takes up much of the latter half of the film. Somewhat like the shift in earlier fairy-tale films, such as *Cinderella*, from playful fantastic worlds to more adult narratives, Ahmed's turning point suggests a transformation of the character from irresponsible youth to mature self-sacrifice. Gaylyn Studlar writes,

> In the maturation of the "bad boy" of Bagdad, moral and masculine certainty – even the certainty of the American work ethic – are rearticulated out of the potential disorder of oriental fantasy dominated by sensual scenic opulence and the virtuosic display of the male body.[52]

In Studlar's argument, the dream city – as well as the erotic overtones of Fairbanks's performance and the fantastic milieu in which the film is set – is ultimately overcome and replaced with an ethos of work. This is evident within the film's narrative and certain instances of overt moralism.

However, the increasingly extravagant depictions of fantasy in *The Thief of Bagdad*, once Ahmed is engaged in his quest, can also be seen as an intensification of its fantasies of consumer culture. Searching out magical treasures to compete with other men for the hand of the princess, Ahmed takes on characteristics of the collector, a type of consumer which had often been associated with apparently more worthy, and masculine, pursuits. Discussing manifestations of the figure of the collector in the previous century, Leora Auslander writes,

> Appropriate consumption for bourgeois men was deemed to be highly individual, often authenticity-based, creative, self-producing, order-making activity – all best enacted in collecting... In Balzac's and others' fantasies, rather than shopping in the banal department stores and specialty or custom shops frequented by female consumers, collectors were – with great ingenuity and intrepidness – to hunt down and uncover unexpected, unrecognized treasures at auctions, flea markets, and in antique stores... Buying at auction required persistence, guile, quickness, and a willingness to take risks, as did sifting through flea markets, characterized as exotic and dangerous places, to uncover treasures amidst heaps of junk, stolen objects, and dubious characters.[53]

Ahmed's quest connotes – and enacts – such a journey of masculine consumption. The quest's apparent moral value stems partly from a series of tropes related to gendered pursuits: "One could be a manly consumer if in consuming one was really hunting (as in Balzac), liberating captive princesses (and putting them in one's own cave); creating an immortal chef d'oeuvre; creating oneself; competing with other men for the love of women."[54] Auslander's description reads like a virtual summary of Ahmed's quest, where the search for magical items is characterized as a journey of consumerist endeavour. Rather than turning away from the proliferation of spectacular fantasy through Ahmed's quest, the film heightens its central role in identity and desire.

As the values attached to consumerism and labour had been undergoing a substantial transformation in American culture, such an emphasis on the productive possibilities of fantasy was not a radical departure from social norms. In an analysis of advertising and consumer culture in the first decades of the twentieth century, Lears writes that "the crucial moral change was the beginning of a shift from a Protestant ethos of salvation through self-denial toward a therapeutic ethos stressing self-realization in this world – an ethos characterized by an almost obsessive concern with psychic and physical health."[55] Ahmed's quest entwines such a display of physical and mental strength with an expansive sense of individual self-realization through fantasy and desire.

A similar approach to the possibilities of fantasy was connected to the discourse circulating around Fairbanks and the production of the film. In advertising, articles and reviews, Fairbanks is presented as actively creating a fairy tale, using his own relationship to fantasy to his best advantage. For example, an article in a press book for the film noted that Fairbanks drew the inspiration for his construction of the "beauty city" of Bagdad from the vivid childhood memories of reading the "Thousand and One Nights" and dreaming of it, "with his fertile imagination picturing the wonders of far-distant lands when life and romance went hand in hand."[56] An article in the *New York Times* about Fairbanks's production of the film linked his creativity with military precision; its subheading was: "First Like a Philosopher He Ponders the Idea and Then Like a General He Plans and Executes the Film Play".[57] Discussions of Fairbanks's vision extended to publicity surrounding the film's production. The title of a pre-release publicity article, "Doug Rubs the Magic Lamp", captures the sense that the production of the film drew upon a kind of active relationship to enchantment.[58]

By contrast, accounts of Julanne Johnston, Fairbanks's co-star who played the princess, would sometimes situate her as passively embodying fantasy. One article refers to her as "assuredly 'such stuff as dreams are made on,' this fairy princess of *The Thief of*

Bagdad…"[59] Johnston is quoted as saying, playing the role(s) nicely, "'It was all like a fairy tale,' she said. 'My being chosen I mean.'"[60] Needing to clarify the distinction between her life and the film's story, Johnston suggests the conflation of fantastic transformation with becoming a star. Her connections with the role extend into a kind of innate relationship to fantasy: "You feel that she wanders, always and always in a dream world of her own, where she really belongs, and that you in common with other ordinary mortals are condemned to stay forever outside its gates."[61] One article notes that her success is like magic: "Julanne's success simply proves that it doesn't pay to worry, work, or strive too mightily… A career has been a casual affair in her scheme of things."[62] Unlike the ways in which Johnston's relationship to fantasy is described, Fairbanks takes on and develops the active role of imaginative producer and enchanted character, as well as star.

In addition to situating Fairbanks as a productive figure of fantasy, the film's elaboration of enchantment was associated with a wider cultural value attached to consumerism and its relation to fantasy and desire. Through an emphasis on elements such as the educational qualities of advertising, the virtues of adjustment to consumer culture and the establishment of public morale, the institution of advertising helped create an elaborate field of political and social value for commercial culture. Kathleen G. Donohue writes that "By the second decade of the twentieth century the consumer had become a legitimate economic identity… And policy makers were coming to believe that the economic interests of the nation's citizens included a consuming as well as a producing interest."[63] Calvin Coolidge's speech to the American Association of Advertising Agencies in 1926 suggests the currency and centrality of such ideas in the mid-1920s.[64] In the speech, Coolidge emphasized the role that advertising plays in American society, and the responsibilities that it has. He noted that advertising "informs its readers of the existence and nature of commodities by explaining the advantages to be derived from their use and creates for them a wider demand. It makes new thoughts, new desires, and new actions. By changing the attitude of mind it changes the material condition of the people."[65] Granting an enormous power to the field of advertising, Coolidge went on to say that "the uncivilized make little progress because they have few desires. The inhabitants of our country are stimulated to new wants in all directions."[66] *The Thief of Bagdad* offered a similar world in which fantasy provides both a milieu of wonders and a spur to desire, offering a seemingly limitless world of fantasy that is both a dreamlike consumerist vision and a social necessity for its protagonist.

One example of this context of productive consumerism offers a direct link between this turn towards the citizen-as-consumer and the iconography and subject matter of *The Thief of Bagdad*. Appearing in newspapers such as the *Oakland Tribune* (September 17, 1921) and the *Republican and Times* from Cedar Rapids (December 15, 1921), a large advertisement titled "The Genie of Your Lamp" carried the copy:

> Aladdin rubbed his wonderful lamp and the treasures of the Orient were showered at his feet. So advertising spreads before your eyes the wares of the world.
>
> It is the genie that crowds your life with so many comforts and conveniences.
>
> It is the magic carpet upon which you may stand and, in the twinkling of an eye, review the merchandise of Bagdad, the products of Europe or the varied output of humming American factories.
>
> It is your "open sesame" to economy and satisfaction in every day buying.
>
> Don't rob yourself of the benefits that come from regular and systematic reading of our advertising columns.
>
> Advertising is too important to be missed. Read it every day.
>
> You will find it a profitable practice.

This advertisement was part of a series in newspapers and magazines (including film fan magazines) that would rhetorically link fantasy with consumerism. A similar format and aim would be picked up a year later, in an advertisement printed in newspapers including the *Newark Advocate* (April 25, 1922) and the *Modesto Evening News* (April 24, 1922), with the title "The Magic Carpet": "You could sit on the fabled carpet of Bagdad and view the world. In the whisk of an eyelash it would carry you any place you wanted to go. All you had to do was wish." This transporting fantasy offers more than simple escape from the day to day – it offers a means to make sense of the world: "Advertising is a sort of magic carpet. Read it and in the twinkling of an eye you can review the merchandise of the world, pictured and displayed for your benefit." These advertisements marketed advertising itself as a means to present a modern world of fantastic possibility that was both pleasurable and valuable: attending to spectacular images and desiring them was part of what it meant to be a modern citizen.

Vachel Lindsay wrote a manuscript in the mid-1920s, focusing on *The Thief of Bagdad* and its relation to American culture, that developed the aesthetic implications of such a vision of fantasy. In many respects, *The Thief of Bagdad* exemplified Lindsay's key concerns in *The Art of the Moving Picture*, discussed in Chapter 3, regarding the potentials of cinema to show animate objects, mutable environments and metamorphoses in the elaboration of a transforming American society. In this later analysis, Lindsay focuses on how the elaborate landscape of spectacular fantasy in *The Thief of Bagdad* could extend into wider considerations of contemporary American culture. Part of Lindsay's argument is that cinema itself was closely linked to other forms of modern experience; he describes a range of activities, including reading the newspaper, eating breakfast, reading a novel, visiting an art gallery, touring a national park, going on a trip and walking down the street, as "nearer to motion picture psychology than is the normal theater, though there are still people who do not know this."[67] Like some of the reviews of the film noted earlier, Lindsay went outside the specific frame of reference to film in order to account for the experience of viewing *The Thief of Bagdad*. In doing so, the film itself could emblematize a changing society and culture.

Earlier I noted some comparisons that Lindsay drew between *The Thief of Bagdad* and the department store. But for Lindsay, the film offers something much more coherent and well-ordered than this space of desire. He writes that Fairbanks's earlier star vehicle, *Robin Hood*, "was on the borders of department-store splendor… The thing seemed to fall apart of its own weight…" *The Thief of Bagdad* avoids such excesses largely through its adept handling of objects and spaces. Lindsay first outlines the film's aesthetic presentation of objects, and the ways in which it gives them an almost animate force: "certainly the most important is the ability to make something small, like a ring, a crystal, a dagger, not only instantly large, but instantly alive, moving, and suggestive." The depiction of such objects is not simply a formal quality of cinema itself, as he had argued in earlier writing, but is also a feature of the film's design:

> It is one of the triumphs of *The Thief of Bagdad* that, from first to last, every scene that is a principal scene has for its central actor what would be a minute and inanimate thing upon the stage, and pretty generally an inanimate and ineffective symbol in fiction or verse. There is no doubt that a fairy tale gives a special opportunity for dramatic activity on the part of things which are supposed to keep still.

He gives, as one example of many over the course of the film, the magic apple: "The very motion of the apple, quivering in the hand, makes it, as it were, a part of the hand and not an inanimate thing. One feels that it has a living potency. It is a hieroglyphic of promise, of hope…"[68]

Such animate objects – or hieroglyphs as Lindsay characterizes them – are set alongside the film's depiction of spaces, or what he describes as the "Vista". Much like his earlier discussion of "fairy-tale architecture", these are images which offer opportunities for the creation of mutable environments and dreamlike vantage points: "Over and over, long streets are shown in the magical City of Bagdad, the dream city of our Arabian Nights childhood, and these are not stage vistas… They are vistas made magical, vistas made into gigantic actors, as definitely as the minute objects we have named have been made into actors. Many times the vistas are streets, but not necessarily so." For Lindsay, it is the careful handling of such vistas counterpointed with animate objects that offers *The Thief of Bagdad* its coherence and structure. Noting a range of forms of visual culture – from circuses and parades to political cartoons and magazines – he writes,

> This way of thinking from picture to picture, of leaping from vision to vision, without sound, without gesture, without the use of English, with as little use of type as possible, this tendency increasing every hour must be ruled by the motion picture, if it is to have any direction and leading, because the film art is so much more powerful than all the rest, by reason of the occult elements of motion and light.

The fantastic promise of animate objects and vistas in *The Thief of Bagdad* is structured in such a way as to allow for a meaningful and organized vision: "We cannot outlaw our pictures. We can only master our pictures, and set them in some sort of reasoning succession." He writes, "The contrast is the unreasoning 'show', the distorted and merely expensive smear, the lavish department-store basement gone wrong, the heaped-up material bought and paid for, the loot of a robbed civilization, rather than the well-organized splendor of a growing culture."[69] On the other hand, for Lindsay, immersing oneself in the visual delights of a carefully constructed film like *The Thief of Bagdad* becomes an opportunity to perceive a coherent world of fantastic objects, movement, spectacle and light – a cinematic vision of a new America.

The ordering of images to fashion a new visual world was closely related to a language of advertising and consumer culture which was undergoing a substantial shift during the first decades of the twentieth century, what Lears describes as a "containment of the carnivalesque".[70] Lears writes that "the recurring motif in the cultural history of American advertising could be characterized as the attempt to conjure up the magic of self-transformation through purchase while at the same time containing the subversive implications of such a trick."[71] Rather than celebrating an excess of possibilities in consumer goods, as in earlier contexts, a culture was emerging that would structure and restrain the commercial aesthetic without entirely abandoning its relation to fantasy and its promises of transformation. This kind of fantasy also helped create a space for cinema as a site that was both fantastic and socially valued. The review in *Motion Picture Classic* described *The Thief of Bagdad* as "a perfect excursion into the realm of fancy", going on to note the beneficial effects of this: "we have looked upon a wealth of magic – which stimulates the imagination."[72] Similarly, one of the British press book's "interviews"with Fairbanks quoted him requesting that the studio "promise them [your readers] for me that it will take them to the Land of Heart's Desire. That it will encourage them not to be ashamed of their secret longings, because the strain of fantasy that makes a child like a Fairy Tale is but a longing for higher and more beautiful things which remain with most of us until the end."[73] Fairy-tale fantasies, rather than a silly waste of time or a retreat from the world, were characterized as both a spur to desire and a starting point for creativity. This rhetoric did not meet or stoke any single desire, but a broader sense of modern fantasy as potentially transformative and culturally valuable.

Wings (1927) and the Modern Fairyland

Whereas *The Thief of Bagdad* was set entirely within the realm of fairy tales, many films in the decade would use elements of fairy tales and fantasy within other generic and narrative frameworks. *Wings*, which won the first Academy Award for best picture – described as "outstanding picture of the year" at the time[74] – is a particularly prominent example of how fairy-tale elements were incorporated within a more realist mode in order to negotiate the role of fantasy in cinema and modern life. Unlike *The Thief of Bagdad*, which presented an expansive vision of marvellous fantasy as a key feature of cinema that could be culturally valuable, *Wings* limited the scope of fantasy and demarcated its place in cinema.

Telling the story of two pilots during the First World War, Jack (Charles "Buddy" Rogers) and David (Richard Arlen), *Wings* weaves a narrative of adventure and masculine rivalry around the spectacles of aerial manoeuvres and combat. Midway through the film, a sequence set in Paris while Jack is on a short furlough presents an interlude of fantasy in the midst of the war. Learning that Jack has been called back to the front, Mary (Clara Bow) seeks him out and finds him drunkenly flirting with another woman in the ostentatious surroundings of the Folies-Bergère. Up until this point, Mary has appeared as a secondary character, mainly in early scenes before the war where we see her falling in unrequited love with Jack and in a subplot where she joins the Women's Motor Corps in France. In the milieu of a Parisian nightclub, Mary undergoes a sudden transformation from small-town sweetheart and military servicewoman to flapper.

The scene begins with Mary trying to get Jack's attention in order to tell him that he must return to duty, but he is too drunk to recognize her and too absorbed by his female companion to care. He tells Mary, "Run 'way, li'l uniform. No bubbles in uniform." His state of mind is accentuated by a playful use of film form: Jack sees animated bubbles emerging from his drink and from musical instruments as a band plays, and when he looks at Mary, all we see is a blurred image of her from his point of view. Disconsolate and swept away by the crowd, Mary walks into the washroom; the attendant notices her sadness and asks, "What's the matter... lost your man?" Mary, startled, first says nothing, but then explains her predicament: "He's just a boy. He doesn't realize—" The attendant walks up to her, gestures at her clothes and tells her, "If you would catch the fly, do you set the vinegar? No, *ma cherie*! But the sugar, yes!" She then leads Mary to a backstage dressing room, and tells her to put on one of the dancer's dresses. Mary, surprised and hesitant, is drawn in. Wearing a slinky dress rather than a military uniform, and undulating her body rather than expressing her concerns, she finally grabs Jack's attention. Her loving gaze leads Jack to say, "She has bubbles even in 'er eyes – she wins." Taking him up to his hotel room, where Jack passes out, she saves him from forgoing his duty. But Mary has sacrificed her military career – she is discovered by two leering military policemen, and is dismissed from her duties.

As well as drawing upon motifs of the Cinderella story, with a helpful fairy godmother in the figure of the washroom attendant and the sudden transformation that ensures that Mary can attend "the ball", Mary's metamorphosis presents an abbreviated star turn for Bow; Jeanine Basinger writes, "Right in the middle of a war movie, Clara Bow steps out in a low-cut, dazzling gown with spangles, earrings, high heels, and diamond bracelets. After all, a star is a star."[75] The Cinderella story provides a fitting framework for this, as associations with Cinderella would feature prominently in Bow's film roles and in the extratextual material related to her star identity. Cynthia Felando writes of how Bow's star vehicle *It* (1927), released the same year as *Wings*, contains a "number of references to Cinderella", noting a review in *Variety* that described it as "one of those pretty little Cinderella stories".[76] *It* couples playful romance and comedy with the narrative transformation of Betty Lou (Bow), who begins as a salesgirl in a department store and ends up with its wealthy owner. In addition to the story's resonance with Cinderella, specific scenes and motifs emphasized the film's fairy-tale basis; Felando singles out a scene in the film where Betty recuts her regular clothes to turn them into an evening dress, describing this modern transformation scene as an "especially compelling reworking of a crucial moment in the Cinderella story…" The trope of fairy-tale transformation extends beyond Bow's film roles and into the story of her ascent into Hollywood – she apparently got her break after winning a fan-magazine contest for aspiring stars. Marsha Orgeron describes how "the language of the contest promised fans a chance – however remote – to transform themselves into the images they gazed at in the pages of the magazine and, more important, on the so-called silver screen; the language was of the cinema-age fairy tale, and the reader was the imagined princess."[77] This account echoes earlier descriptions of the fairy-tale wonders of being discovered and becoming a star, discussed in the previous chapter.

Such associations between stardom and fairy tales in the 1920s found an even more extensive link to another prominent flapper star, Colleen Moore. Her star vehicle *Ella Cinders* (Green, 1926) playfully retells the Cinderella fantasy as Ella (Moore) wins a star-search contest, arrives in Hollywood, becomes a star and finds a Prince Charming husband. The film makes fun of the clichés and contradictions of this type of transformation throughout. The pompous "Pollyanna Club" meets at Ella's home, the star search turns out to be a fraud and Hollywood itself is a guarded, and makeshift, land of fantasy. This association between stardom and fairy tales extended, in a rather unique way, into Moore's construction of an oversized doll's house, her Fairy Castle. As Amelie Hastie describes, filled with extraordinary images and specially manufactured miniature models that evoked fairy-tale fantasies, Moore's Fairy Castle toured the United States and Canada in the 1930s, and was displayed at various department stores.[78] Entwined with Moore's star persona and her reflections on the fantasies of Hollywood, the Fairy Castle presents itself as a condensed image of the fairy tales circulating around stardom and cinema in the 1920s.

Drawing upon such links between fantasy and stardom, particularly through the image of the flapper, *Wings* presents Clara Bow's star turn as a fairy-tale interlude. The setting of the Folies-Bergère entwines this fantasy with a visual spectacle of dynamism, movement and urban life, presenting a counterpart to the aerial combats that had so far constituted the main elements of the film's spectacle. The sequence takes place in a modern Paris, which is introduced with the name of the entertainment venue growing in size against the background of an animated image of flickering lights, a wine bottle and glasses, and the silhouetted figure of a woman. Immediately setting the tone of release from wartime duties, the image coalesces the abstractions of modernist visual art with drink, sexuality, luminosity and movement. This becomes figured aesthetically when the film introduces the Folies-Bergère: crowds stream past a sign for the bar depicting a woman on a swing wearing a see-through chemise and stockings, done in the style of a Jules Chéret poster. Camera movement accentuates the liveliness of this environment, with one particularly striking tracking shot that glides over the tables and past the customers to arrive at Jack, drinking champagne.

The dynamism of the aesthetics and the setting provide a space for the expression of Bow's star identity as a flapper. Lori Landay writes of how the flapper film's "iconography centers on the flapper, modern styles of dress and décor, jazz parties and nightlife, dancing, drinking, smoking, and the erotic possibilities of everyday life."[79] But more than simply a modern subject – as Mary's work with the Motor Corps was also part of a modern identity – the scenes shows a kind of modernity entwined with fantasy. This is presented vividly in an extreme close-up of Mary's sequined dress, glittering and reflecting light, as she shakes her body in an attempt to draw Jack's attention. The image of her dress, which lasts for a few seconds, appears as a play of shifting light, with barely discernible images of Bow herself as if in a multifaceted mirror. Landay describes how Bow "embodied the kinaesthetic power of dance and movement" so crucial to the flapper film, and this scene provides an abstract figuration of this: showing her body in movement, multiplied in the reflection of her glimmering dress.[80] The shot functions as a metonym for both Bow and modern urban life, presenting a dynamic environment of aesthetic playfulness and transformation. However delightful or enticing, this is ultimately dismissed as a transient dream. Paris is earlier described in intertitles as a place of "forgetfulness" and a place for those soldiers "trying to forget"; the sequence is brought to a close with the intertitle, "Vanished, the fairyland of Paris". Like the bubbles which a drunken Jack imagined emanating from champagne, music and a shimmering dress, this landscape of modern fantasy is shown as ephemeral, insubstantial froth.

For part of the film, however, fantasies of a different sort play a prominent role. Leslie Midkiff DeBauche notes that the intertitle which "moved its audience into the diegetic world of the film" has as its background "a low-angle view of a castle on a hill – a metaphor for the realm of the imagination as well as a visual equivalent of the medieval rhetoric associated with flyers and World War I's air war."[81] As the film shows Jack's journey from innocence to maturity, it consistently uses a similar rhetoric of fantasy. Intertitles draw attention to the legendary qualities of the experience, describing the planes as "these knights of the air", an enemy airship as "the great dragon" and gunfire as "a stream of fire into the belly of the monster". Through such allusions, Jack's narrative journey is entwined with fantasy. Situated within this historical context and functioning as part of a process of maturation and male adventure, however, Jack's tale is presented quite differently from the enchanting possibilities figured in the urban milieu and the image of female transformation.

Showing the dazzling superficialities of a modern fairyland and quickly dismissing them is part of the film's strategy to deal with the memory of the war. After the interlude, the film's fantasy ends altogether. The pilots lose their innocence, becoming a lone man wandering in the wilderness (David behind enemy lines) and a lone man seeking vengeance (Jack behind enemy lines). The folk motifs of metamorphosis and celebration become tragic motifs of blindness and fate. The future shifts from a place of excitement to one that anticipates doom. Women no longer have an active role: Mary is sent home, only to reappear at the end of the film in the very different role of a sedate small-town sweetheart; a mother holding a child appears in the film's climactic moments, a witness to the melodramatic horrors of the story; Sylvia, a character from Jack and Mary's home town who was introduced on a swing through a dynamic moving camera, is shown near the end of the film immobile, still upon the swing, crying at hearing of her sweetheart's death. These images of stasis place women within melodramatic tableaux, and are quite unlike the transformation, visual spectacle and fairy-tale motifs in the Paris interlude. As such, the interlude is rhetorically characterized as outside of the *real* story, as a place of forgetting – something that, however enchanting, simply cannot be taken seriously in a reflection on history. Visually associating Paris with crowds, movement and spectacle, the film channels the energy of modernity into a foreign space. The transformative play of a fantastic modernity and a cinema of fantasy is placed on the margins, and then set aside for a more restrained and solemn vision of the past.

As noted earlier, *Wings* was the recipient of the first Academy Award for outstanding production. Most of the films to win major awards also drew upon a language of fantasy and fairy tales. For example, *Two Arabian Knights* (Milestone, 1927), which won for best director of a comedy, situated a comedic adventure set during the First World War within an exoticized Arabian setting. The title of the film highlighted this milieu with its allusion to *A Thousand and One Nights*; this was echoed in reviews such as the *New York Times*, which described it as "a comedy of a thousand and one laughs".[82] Other winners at the Academy Awards were less overt in their presentation of fantasy, but nevertheless elaborated on an interconnected sense of transformation, spectacle and modernity in ways that were similar to *Wings*, though with very different implications.

Seventh Heaven, for which Frank Borzage won the award for director of a dramatic film and which was one of three films for which Janet Gaynor won best performance by an actress, entwined romance and melodrama with elements of fantasy and fairy tales. Set in Paris around the time of the First World War, the film tells the love story of Chico (Charles Farrell) and Diane (Janet Gaynor). Chico works in a sewer underneath the streets, and he aspires to be a street cleaner one day; Diane is an orphan who lives with her abusive sister. Chico assists Diane, sheltering her from imprisonment by reluctantly pretending that he is married to her. From this rather bleak and melodramatic starting point, they gradually fall in love. After Chico enlists as a soldier, they are separated; however, their romantic union survives intact at the end of the film despite the suffering brought about by the war.

Figure 21. *Seventh Heaven*

Alongside its narrative relation to fairy tales, with the Cinderella story of an orphan mistreated by a wicked sister who moves from loneliness and poverty to social acceptance and love, the film presents images and tropes redolent with fairy-tale fantasies.

Summarizing the overall effect, a review in *The Times* (October 14, 1927) wrote of how the film "plays continuously on a note of religiosity which, outside the theatre, would doubtless make one shudder, and winds up in much the same ecstasy of spirit as that in which a child might witness a transformation scene at a Drury Lane pantomime." The reference to the transformation scene is apt, as the film visualizes a world open to mutability. This is figured in a scene early in the film, when Chico first brings Diane to his loft. They climb the stairs together and the camera, in what the *Variety* review (May 11, 1927) described as a "new trick shot", slowly rises with them, passing through floor after floor until they reach the seventh floor of the building. When they finally enter the loft, we see that it is spacious, with a large window that looks out onto Paris. Chico, proudly says, "Not bad, eh? I work in the sewer – but I live near the stars." Crossing fluidly from depths to heights, both visually and in its rhetoric, the scene recalls earlier fantasy films such as Méliès's féeries in its display of cinema's capacity to traverse spatial boundaries. This extends to surfaces and depths in a later scene in the film which takes place just after Chico has volunteered for the war, without having told Diane. Preparing for his departure, Chico notices something in the mirror – in the background, Diane suddenly appears in the window that overlooks Paris, wearing her wedding dress [Figure 21]. She quickly walks towards the window and gracefully climbs through it into the apartment. Crossing thresholds and displaying her sudden emergence within the frame, the scene plays with the boundary of the window as a site of transformation and fantastic possibility. An article in *Picturegoer* drew attention to the film's fairy-tale qualities, describing the "Cinderella change of the little street waif… into the radiant vision in the bridal dress", noting that the film's "chief charm and attraction" was its "fairy tale quality" rather than its "sordid realism".[83] Moreover, with the ascent up the stairs alluding to an elevator and the apartment window suggesting a shop display, the film evokes a milieu of fantastic modernity.

Fantasy becomes central near the end of the film when Chico and Diane overcome their separation brought about by the war: every day, at 11 o'clock, they both stand in silence, saying one another's names, with their proximity in spirit emphasized by their shared gaze upon a clock, the intertitle "heaven" and a dissolve between them. In this crossing of distances, film aesthetics transfigures a situation of loneliness to show a unity of souls. The film entwines an aesthetics of fantasy with dreaming, praying and remembering. Whereas *Wings* situates fantasy as an interlude, *Seventh Heaven* interweaves fantasy with setting, character and narrative, establishing a sense of romanticized hope within a context of poverty, suffering and war.

The integration of fantasy with the experience of modern life is also evident in *Sunrise*, the film that won the Academy Award for best artistic production. The film begins in a village, where The Man (George O'Brien), a farmer, is having an affair with The Woman from the City (Margaret Livingston) who embodies and projects a vibrant modern life. Almost as if in a trance, The Man plans to kill his wife (Janet Gaynor) so that he can be with the city woman; however, just before following through with a violent attack, he is suddenly stricken with remorse. Marshall Berman summarizes the journey that follows in a passage that draws attention to the film's themes of transformation, modernity and fantasy:

> Just then, like a spirit in a fairy tale, a trolley car suddenly materializes in the depths of the forest. Magically yet realistically, it transports the shaken couple to a real city. They spend a tourist day exploring the city, and Murnau makes the trip transform them both. It is the wife, played by Janet Gaynor, in whose changes we really believe. She begins the story totally absorbed in farm work and care of her baby and emotionally dead. In the city, she comes to life, and grows into an animated, vibrant, radiantly sexual person. Now the husband no longer needs a city girl: by plunging into the city, his wife has become that girl. Murnau's surreal Times Square is the medium of her metamorphosis.[84]

The film's vision of an urban environment is one of the decade's most striking depictions of a fantastic modernity, overtly entwining modern experiences with enchantment and transformation. In some scenes, as Lucy Fischer and other have pointed out, this extends to a reflection on cinema itself – the temptations of the woman from the city lead to the moon dissolving into an image of urban frenzy projected as if on a cinema screen and later settings within the city, such as a photographer's studio and the fairground of Luna Park, allude to cinema.[85] The city and cinema become two interconnected sites of modern fantasy, overlapping not only in their links to desire, movement and spectacle, but also in their transformative power. And rather than situating this as an interlude to be set aside, it becomes central to the film – a fantastic modernity recasts the perspectives and perceptions of the film's protagonists.

Hollywood itself is a site of fantasy in *The Last Command* (von Sternberg, 1928), one of two films for which Emil Jannings won the award for best actor. The film tells the story of a traumatized Russian general (Jannings) who loses his position of power and gets a job as an extra in a film about the Russian Revolution; most of *The Last Command* is told through a flashback which recounts his fall from power, framed by him coming to terms with his past by performing his role as a general once again in the film-within-a-film. An introductory title card sets out the fantastic possibilities of cinema, describing Hollywood as "The Magic Empire of the Twentieth Century! The Mecca of the World!" *The Last Command* reflexively elaborates on this power of cinema; despite its emphasis on the artificiality of Hollywood, evident in its reflexivity and its scenes of film production, cinema nevertheless provides a space in which its exiled protagonist is able to re-experience and work through his past. By extension, cinema's capacity to bring the past to life and to draw distances near becomes part of its power, its allure and its value. Unlike *Wings*, which sets fantasy off from its main narrative, situating it as a fairy tale that is soon forgotten, *Seventh Heaven*, *Sunrise* and *The Last Command* – like *The Thief of Bagdad* – all elaborated on the central role of fantasy in figuring a modern experience.

6 DELIMITING FAIRY TALES
Snow White and the Seven Dwarfs (1937)

SNOW WHITE AND THE SEVEN DWARFS (HAND, 1937) WAS
both the first feature-length animation produced in Hollywood
and the most financially successful fairy-tale film of the twentieth
century. Its story is well known: based on the Brothers Grimm
fairy tale, it tells of a young princess, Snow White, who is forced
to flee her castle due to the jealousy of her stepmother, the wicked
queen. After journeying through a nightmarish forest and being
granted a reprieve by a sympathetic huntsman who had been
sent to kill her, Snow White finds a cottage inhabited by seven
dwarfs; she soon befriends them, settling in and keeping house.
With the help of a magic mirror, the wicked queen discovers
where Snow White lives and, donning a disguise, tricks her into
eating a poisoned apple. Thinking her dead, the dwarfs encase
her in a glass coffin and watch over her; the film ends happily,
though, when the prince – who Snow White had encountered
earlier in the film – arrives from the forest and wakes her with
a kiss. Incorporating elements of different fairy tales, such as
"Cinderella" in its presentation of Snow White and "Sleeping
Beauty" in its concluding kiss of awakening, as well as being influenced by elements of fantasy drawn from other films and a wider
visual culture, *Snow White and the Seven Dwarfs* was immersed in
a tradition of fairy tales and fantasy.[1] At the same time, though,
it renegotiated key aspects of this tradition. Through certain
tropes, imagery and narrative events, *Snow White and the Seven
Dwarfs* reflexively attempted to define itself as a stable, timeless
and enduring vision of fantasy, setting out its fairy-tale form in
terms of both cultural and commercial value. In doing so, as this

chapter examines, it was part of a wider ongoing negotiation of the place of fairy tales in cinema and film culture.

One of the most important ways in which *Snow White and the Seven Dwarfs* offered a distinctive vision of fairy-tale fantasies was through its relationship to earlier animated films, produced by Disney as well as others. In the 1930s, fairy tales were a rich source of material for animated films, which often entwined narratives and images of fantasy with the visual fluidity afforded by animation. For example, a markedly different vision of "Snow White" can be seen in *Snow White* (Fleischer, 1933), with Betty Boop as the main character. This was one of several animated adaptations – or, rather, mutations – of fairy-tale subjects directed by Dave Fleischer and "starring" Betty Boop, including *Jack and the Beanstalk* (1931), *Dizzy Red Riding Hood* (1931) and *Mother Goose Land* (1933). *Snow White* transforms basic incidents and iconography from the tale – including the wicked queen, the magic mirror and the glass coffin (turned into a block of ice) – to fashion a world alive to the possibility of animated transformations, with objects and characters undergoing a series of fluid changes over the course of the film. Paul Wells writes that "metamorphosis is the guiding and necessary principle" in the film, showcasing "the ambiguities and magical distortions of ancient fairytales".[2] Alongside this play with animated form, the film included references to urban settings and contemporary music, with a performance of "St. James Infirmary Blues" by Cab Calloway during Betty Boop's oneiric funeral procession. In "Animation and Animorphs", Norman M. Klein elaborates on *Snow White*'s references to modern life, writing of how it "turns a Mystery Cave ride into a blend of Coney Island and Manhattan."[3] As Wells points out, the film's "images are a long way from the safe ideological dislocations of the later Disney version and foreground the dark agendas which define the Fleischer output as a genuine contemporisation of the fairytale form."[4]

While more restrained than the Betty Boop series, a similar approach to the form of animated fairy tales – and particularly their relation to visual transformation – was evident in the Silly

Symphonies, a series of short animations produced by Disney alongside the popular Mickey Mouse films. The Silly Symphonies, which began in 1929 and continued to be produced until 1939, adapted a wide range of fairy tales, fables and nursery rhymes, including *The Ugly Duckling* (Jackson, 1931), *Babes in the Woods* (Gillett, 1932), *The Three Little Pigs* (Gillett, 1933), *The Pied Piper* (Jackson, 1933) and *Water Babies* (Jackson, 1935). Such films showed an anthropomorphic world, magical transformations and spectacular metamorphoses. Visions of mutability were prominent in other Silly Symphonies as well, often through depictions of an animate and fantastic natural world. *The Goddess of Spring* (Jackson, 1934) offers a particularly striking example of this. The film begins in a brilliantly colourful world of nature, showing a procession of elves playing musical instruments and a dancing goddess, Persephone. Seating herself upon her throne, she watches a ballet of flowers. Émile Vuillermoz described this dance as "a minute of intoxicating lightness" and "a manifestation of childlike naivety" that offered "a ceaselessly renewed pleasure".[5] In this account, Vuillermoz was drawing upon the same kind of rhetoric used to describe the transformation scene and the féerie decades earlier: *The Goddess of Spring* "dazzles us like a revelation" with its "freshness, ingenuity and féerique poetry".[6] A scene midway through the film, after Persephone has been kidnapped by Hades and brought down to hell, displays a particularly striking spectacle of mutability. In a playful vision of hell, with what J. Michael Barrier describes as a "Cotton Club flavour",[7] demons perform a dance around an enormous flame which spews forth fireworks and changes colour like a luminous fountain. Through such spectacular imagery, *The Goddess of Spring* presented the same kinds of visual marvels as those seen almost a century earlier in pantomimes and féeries.

Spectacular transformation was pivotal to the attractions and forms of many Disney films from the 1930s, entwined with shifting colours and synchronized music to showcase new film technologies. Filmmakers and writers who were exploring the nature and potentials of cinema were fascinated. For example,

Sergei Eisenstein wrote extensive notes on these films in the 1940s, collected in *On Disney*, which focused on the attractions of their mutability, describing them as a "triumph over the fetters of form".[8] The art historian Erwin Panofsky, in an article published in 1934, was similarly astonished by animation's visual transformations: "The very virtue of the animated cartoon is to animate, that is to say, endow lifeless things with life, or living things with a different kind of life. It effects a metamorphosis, and such metamorphosis is wonderfully present in Disney's animals, plants, thunderclouds, and railroad trains."[9]

While visual transformation can be seen in *Snow White and the Seven Dwarfs*, particularly in scenes showing the queen's magic and the anthropomorphism of the natural world, it was largely muted by more classical norms of verisimilitude and story structure. Offering a romantic tale about a female protagonist, with musical numbers, a large budget, and interludes of comedy and terror, it drew upon key production trends in the 1930s such as the woman's film, the musical, the prestige picture, the comedy and the horror film.[10] As well as participating in this contemporaneous context of popular film, *Snow White and the Seven Dwarfs* also presented itself in a seemingly more timeless frame. For example, an article in *Time* magazine, which featured prominently in advertisements, drew attention to its combination of film trends and seemingly timeless qualities:

> Skeptical Hollywood, that had wondered whether a fairy story could have enough suspense to hold an audience through seven reels, and whether, even if the plot held up, an audience would care about the fate of the characters who were just drawings, was convinced that Walt Disney had done it again. Snow White is as exciting as a Western, as funny as a haywire comedy. It combines the classic idiom of folklore drama with rollicking comic-strip humor. A combination of Hollywood, the Grimm Brothers, and the sad, searching fantasy of universal childhood, it is an authentic masterpiece, to

be shown in theatres and beloved by new generations long after the current crop of Hollywood stars, writers and directors are sleeping where no Prince's kiss can wake them.[11]

As such an account indicates, *Snow White and the Seven Dwarfs* incorporated contemporary forms while also invoking a sense of enduring cultural value circulating around fairy tales. Rather than material for visual marvels, spectacular transformations and dreamlike fantasies, fairy tales were seen in relation to timelessness.

This association was not due to the film simply drawing upon a wider cultural connotation of fairy tales; as earlier animated films and feature films indicate, the relationship between fairy tales and the distant past was by no means secure, and often marginal or altogether irrelevant. Instead, the film itself – as well as the discourse surrounding it – actively sought to limit the fantastic marvels of fairy tales in an effort to present them as stable, timeless and valuable. This drew in wider concerns of how fantasy should be produced, distributed and consumed, concerns that were evident in other films from the 1930s, including *The Scarlet Empress* (von Sternberg, 1934), *The Good Fairy* (Wyler, 1935) and *Ball of Fire* (Hawks, 1941). As this chapter will go on to examine, they also elaborated on the potentials of fantasy in modern life, though to much different effect.

"The Home of Both Thought and Vision": Metaphors of the Book

In the 1910s, a period in which there was considerable interest in both filmic and theatrical fairy tales, two adaptations of "Snow White" appeared, both starring Marguerite Clark: a prominent play which premiered in 1912 and a film, *Snow White* (Dawley, 1916). Karen Merritt has examined similarities between these versions of the story and the Disney film, which include presenting Snow White in ways that evoked Cinderella and presenting the dwarfs as childlike.[12] There were also substantial differences, some due to animation's formal potentials (such as highlighting the role of the animals) and others due to narrative economy (such as conflating a queen and a witch into one character).[13] In terms of the two films, one of the most immediately apparent distinctions is that they begin quite differently. The version starring Marguerite Clark starts with a brief prelude set at Christmas which shows the characters, as dolls, transform into the characters of the film. Entwining childhood fantasy with an actualisation of cinema's anthropomorphic potential, the scene resonated with Vachel Lindsay's observation that "it is a quality, not a defect, of all photoplays that human beings tend to become dolls and mechanisms, and dolls and mechanisms tend to become human."[14] After the opening credits, the Disney version begins quite differently: there is a close-up of a large, finely bound, gilt-edged book with seven dwarfs embossed in gold upon its cover. The book opens to reveal an intricately designed page, brilliantly coloured with luminous reds, golds and blues, which introduces Snow White. The page then turns to introduce the queen. Unlike the figuration of fantastic transformation in the earlier *Snow White*, the book offers a very different perspective on the starting point of the film fairy tale. Rather than cinema making the inanimate objects come alive, it is a book which marks the entrance into the filmic world. My aim in this section is to examine how the book which begins *Snow White and the Seven Dwarfs* both borrows from and diverges from a fairy-tale tradition, fashioning a certain way of inviting its film audience into a space of fantasy.

In some respects, the opening of *Snow White and the Seven Dwarfs* draws upon associations between fairy-tale films and illustrated children's books evident in the previous chapter's discussion of *The Thief of Bagdad*, where the fairy-tale picture book became closely associated with the film's atmosphere of fantasy. Beginning the film with the image of a book also echoes the theatrical version of the 1910s where, asked about the play's design, its producer Winthrop Ames (who had produced the first American stage version of *The Blue Bird* two years earlier) described how "we wanted to get the real picture-book idea; we wanted the stage pictures to look exactly like the pictures a child will find in a well-illustrated child's book."[15] This trope is picked up in the *New York Times* review (January 14, 1938) of *Snow White and the Seven Dwarfs*: "You can visualize it best if you imagine a child, with a wondrous, Puckish imagination, nodding over his favorite fairy tale and dreaming a dream in which his story would come true."

But more than just another example of this association with illustrated books, particularly well suited to drawn animation, the opening images of Disney's version help recast the status of the fairy tale by connecting it to literary adaptations. For example, *David Copperfield* (Cukor, 1935) similarly begins with the title page from a book, followed by a turn of the page to show the first chapter, and then a fade to black and a fade up on the story world.[16] The beginning of *Snow White and the Seven Dwarfs* embellishes this association with a literary past in an appeal to timelessness, encasing the film itself in a book that would seem to be outside of history: at the end of the film, the book reappears, closes shut and then drifts off into blackness. In its initial presentation, the book is similarly abstract: its pages are not accompanied by a voice-over and the pages turn on their own. Although set upon a table with a candle beside it, the book is not part of a story world, unlike the similar beginning of *Pinocchio* (Sharpsteen and Luske, 1940) in which a spotlight shifts from the book version of "Pinocchio" to Jiminy Cricket singing "When You Wish upon a Star". Serving little narrative purpose, as its contents are soon dramatized in the narrative, the book is there largely to offer an instance of self-definition for the film's novel mode of feature-length cinematic storytelling.

Drawing upon the well-established trope of beginning a film with a book, while also heightening its timeless and iconic qualities, *Snow White and the Seven Dwarfs* substantially associates fairy tales with literature and the written word rather than the visual spectacles of theatre or the transformative marvels of cinema. It also distances its fairy tale from the spoken word of the storyteller. It was commonplace for fairy-tale books to situate themselves within this tradition of oral storytelling. Maria Tatar describes how the

> frontispiece to Perrault's *Histoires ou Contes du temps passé*... appears to have stood model for countless frontispieces to nineteenth-century collections of fairy tales: an elderly, careworn peasant woman with a spindle or spinning wheel by her side and a cluster of attentive youngsters at her feet becomes the visual entry point to the world of printed fairy tales.[17]

Variations on this tableau of storytelling are evident in different fairy-tale films, from the children gathered around Sara Crewe in *The Little Princess* to the opening scene of *The Thief of Bagdad* where a child is told a tale. Tatar goes on to note that this evocation of storytelling is also evident in the fairy tales of the Brothers Grimm, which "further propagated the myth of a hardy peasant woman [as the storyteller] by including a portrait of Dorothea Viehmann in the second edition of the *Nursery and Household Tales*."[18] The opening to *Snow White and the Seven Dwarfs* avoids this allusion to the storyteller and its association with women's voices, folkloric origins and the spoken word.

The shift away from metaphorical or figurative allusions to a storyteller – often a female in the iconography of fairy tales – recasts certain associations that had been built up around fairy tales. No longer rooted in the transmission of oral culture, the book at the start of *Snow White and the Seven Dwarfs* institutes a different form and place for the tale. This is not a complete turn away from a tradition of fairy-tale storytelling; there had long been an important link between the distribution of books and the circulation of fairy tales. Ruth Bottigheimer has described the notion that a fairy-tale genre emerged through oral storytelling as "an outmoded theory" in an essay titled "The Ultimate Fairy Tale: Oral Transmission in a Literary World".[19] Fairy tales had circulated alongside other books and commodities for centuries; Roger Chartier's study of reading practices in early modern France emphasizes the place of the written word, present in iconic situations of fairy-tale storytelling such as the *veillée*.[20] Dissatisfied with an historical opposition between traditional oral culture and writing, he writes that "this basic opposition fails to account adequately for the culture of the sixteenth to eighteenth century, when, typically, different media and multiple practices almost always intermingled in complex ways."[21] While the film's inclusion of a book as the site of the tale may neglect a substantial tradition of female storytelling associated with fairy tales, it does more than simply distort this tradition. It participates in another strain of fairy tales, engaging with the diverse implications of what it means to offer fairy tales as a book.

For some works in the fairy-tale tradition, the image of a book provides an opportunity for wonders by opening up a world of fantastic images and places. For example, an illustration of an open book appears on top of the "Table of Contents" for Wanda Gág's illustrated retellings of *Tales from Grimm* (1936).[22] Fascinating and mysterious creatures from the fairy tales inside the book flow from its pages. Within films, the associations between a book and the enchantments of fairy tales is a recurring trope as well – for example, the imp that leaps out of the pages of a book in *Bluebeard* (Méliès, 1901) or the various animated creatures that visually pop out of the book which begins *The Tale of the Fox* (Starewicz, 1930). The explosive potential of the fairy-tale book is the subject of an early Disney film, *Mother Goose Melodies* (Disney, 1931). The film begins with Old King Cole demanding his pipe, his slippers and his book. Various dignitaries fulfil this last request by delivering a massive tome, titled "Mother Goose". This book – the king's entertainment – is then opened, and characters from nursery rhymes perform routines, spilling out of the pages. The film ends with the book falling to the ground due to its uncontainable fantasies, with its characters dancing upon it. A similar scenario is reworked in *Mother Goose Land* (Fleischer, 1933), with a book of nursery rhymes providing bedtime reading for Betty Boop, and coming to life in the process. In these and other examples, a children's book functions not as the beginning of a tale, but the tale itself, not as a framing device, but as a container of wonders that itself cannot be contained.

Rather than associating itself with such images of play, dreams and visual spectacle, *Snow White and the Seven Dwarfs* adopts a more restrained vision of fantasy. With its neomedieval aesthetic, its elaborate and weighty binding, and its associations with a time-less realm, the book evokes a distant past [Figures 22 and 23]. This reflects broad trends in the marketing and advertising of goods in the 1930s. T. J. Jackson Lears writes of how "advertisers began an unprecedented effort to associate their products with the past... dissolv[ing] the tension between past and present in the soothing syrup of traditionalism."[23] In addition to the book's iconography, a sense of tradition is further developed by its content; it presents conservative and simple oppositions of good and evil women by contrasting the introductory page of Snow White, emblematized by images of nature (a bird) and work (a broom and dustpan), with the queen, who is embellished with imagery of vanity (a peacock) and violence (a dagger).

Figure 22. *Snow White and the Seven Dwarfs*

While the book functions on one level to give a sense of historical distance and moral clarity to the film, it also participates in a specifically modern context. Megan L. Benton describes the "'craze' for finely made, physically distinctive books in the fifteen or so years that followed the First World War…"[24] The "seemingly insatiable market for fine books", such as the Macy subscriber series, led to a major trend in publishing where high-quality books were made into objects of exclusivity, quality and value. Adding to their allure, they were presented as alternatives to mass publishing, with "stable and enduring value – in contrast to the volatile world of goods that one merely consumed, or used and gradually depleted."[25] One of the most important inspirations and antecedents for this trend was the Arts and Crafts movement, particularly in the way it invited a reflection on the conditions of production in an industrial context; Benton writes, "To Morris, fine printing defied the industrialized capitalist structure of modern English society by recreating instead a medieval unity of labor and craft, of production and purpose, not profit."[26]

Figure 23. *Snow White and the Seven Dwarfs*

Through the image of the book, *Snow White and the Seven Dwarfs* associated itself with this resonant notion of a premodern, artisanal and communal mode of production. While Disney's studio was often presented as a new model of production that combined collaborative effort with joyful creativity, a "fun factory", it was also associated with preindustrial modes of production.[27] For example, Lewis Jacobs, writing in 1939, described Disney as "first and last a craftsman", going on to note that "in article after article he has stressed that, unlike most Hollywood producers, he is not interested in what money he can make at the moment. His is a far-seeing policy that is based on group co-operation…"[28] As Benton points out, "By adapting Morris's practices, postwar fine publishers preserved at least the appearance of cultural and artistic integrity while engaging in a patently for-profit enterprise."[29] In the case of Disney, a similar set of associations was being generated. In addition to the advertising and stories about the production of *Snow White and the Seven Dwarfs*, the film's credit sequence also drew attention to the collaborative nature of the labour that produced the film; the review of the film in *Variety* (December 29, 1937), for example, barely mentions the literary or folkloric sources, but includes a rather detailed account of the credits that precede the introduction of the book:

> More than two years and $1 million were required by the Disney staff, under David Hand's supervision, to complete the film. In a foreword Disney pays a neat compliment to animators, designers and musical composers whose united efforts have produced a work of art. No less than 62 staff names are flashed in the credit titles as being responsible for various divisions of the job.

As the first image to evoke the product of this labour, the book functions as an emblem of workmanship.

By opening with this image of the book, *Snow White and the Seven Dwarfs* grounds its fairy tale by associating it with the past and with the value of artisanal production. Rather than evoking the living presence of the storyteller or the wondrous potentials of the illustrated book, *Snow White and the Seven Dwarfs* contains and limits the marvels of fantasy. Moreover, unlike the instabilities of transformation or the space of consumerist "atmosphere" evident in earlier fairy-tale films, *Snow White and the Seven Dwarfs* uses the image of the book to enfold its fantasies and make its novelty into something seemingly more stable and valuable in a modern age.

In some respects, the book situates the film itself as a site of safety within an age of change and uncertainty. One further facet of this can be seen in descriptions which envisaged books as miniature cathedrals or homes, as in Edward Burne-Jones's "comparison of [William Morris's] Kelmscott Chaucer to a 'pocket cathedral'".[30] Douglas E. Schoenherr writes of how John Ruskin described "his very first Mediaeval illuminated manuscript": "a well-illuminated missal is a fairy cathedral full of painted windows, bound together to carry in one's pocket, with the music and the blessing of all its prayers besides."[31] The metaphor of the book as a home or a cathedral with spiritual or fantastic connotations was developed by Walter Crane, a leading figure in the Arts and Crafts movement as well as an influential maker of fairy-tale books. The frontispiece to Crane's illustrated book of the Brothers Grimm fairy tales actualizes the metaphorical link between the book and the home by depicting a large house, seemingly filled with the tales. He elaborated on this idea, in a passage which also draws attention to the book and home as places filled with potential for comfort, beauty and fantasy:

> A book may be the home of both thought and vision. Speaking figuratively, in regard to book decoration, some are content with a rough shanty in the woods… Others would surround their house with a garden indeed, but they demand something like an architectural plan. They would look at a frontispiece like a façade;

they would take hospitable encouragement from the title-page as from a friendly inscription over the porch; they would hang a votive wreath at the dedication, and so pass on into the hall of welcome, take the author by the hand and be led by him and his artist from room to room, as page after page is turned, fairly decked and adorned with picture, and ornament, and device; and, perhaps, finding it a dwelling after his desire, the guest is content to rest in the inglenook in the firelight of the spirit of the author or the play of fancy of the artist; and, weaving dreams in the changing lights and shadows, to forget life's rough way and the tempestuous world outside.[32]

The book which begins *Snow White and the Seven Dwarfs* can be seen to extend this, elaborating on the connection between the book and the space of a home (or cathedral) to include cinema as a similar site of architectural passage and comforting dwelling.[33] Within the film itself, Snow White's search for and discovery of a safe place is the central narrative concern.[34] Interweaving a theme of dwelling with its own form, partly through the image of the book, the film presents fantasy as a comforting place in which one might reside.

Consuming Fantasy

Before *Snow White and the Seven Dwarfs* was given a wide release in 1938, a book adaptation had been distributed for the Christmas market. This was a cause of some concern to Anne Carroll Moore. As the head of the New York Public Library's children's division, Moore was one of the most influential figures in children's literature in the 1930s. Seeing a copy of the book before seeing the film, she described it as "the saddest publication of 1937", going on to write, "It smelt quite as bad as it looked… I feel unutterably sad for the children who received the Hollywood Snow White for Christmas."[35] Moore's antipathy towards the book was due to more than simply a matter of taste – for Moore, the type of commodification of the book and the way in which it was presented went against her principles of what children's books could and should be. Returning to a critique of *Snow White and the Seven Dwarfs* several months later, this time presumably having seen the film, Moore develops her concerns. She wonders whether the film and its book versions will, on their release in Germany,

> be looked upon as a presentment of a well-loved folk tale with American variations so at variance with the atmosphere and main characters of the tale as to call for clear recognition of its incongruities, its lack of integration and of that essential unity which belongs to the fairy tale.[36]

This suggests that what disturbed Moore so greatly had to do with the form that the Disney versions of the tale took, departing from what she saw as constitutive features of fairy tales. The film and its book became a threat: "Not in my memory has there been a sharper challenge to libraries, schools, and homes to sustain integrity as works of art tales which have formed the bedrock of literature for children during the 19th and 20th centuries."[37] Recasting fairy tales and drawing them away from an already established network of circulation, what horrified Moore may have been her fear that films such as *Snow White and the Seven Dwarfs* would overpower the institutions of publishing and distribution for fairy tales and children's literature that she had helped develop. Moreover, such films might refigure the ways in which fairy tales were used in these contexts, abandoning apparently traditional qualities through "the easy acceptance of sophisticated characters and settings with interpretations which derive from comic strip and music hall rather than from the natural environment of old tales and the simplicity of the characters."

Fantasy, and its place in a network of distribution, was central to the magazine in which Moore was writing, *The Horn Book*. *The Horn Book* attempted to assess, develop and advertise children's literature. Emerging from a bookshop's suggested reading list, the magazine began in October 1924. It presented monthly listings of quality books alongside articles and commentaries about the traditions of and future directions for children's literature. In 1938, Bertha Mahony Miller, the editor of *The Horn Book*, cast a backwards glance over two decades of children's book publishing. She wrote that, as a result of children's book departments and an emerging network including libraries, book reviews and her own magazine, there had been a "steadily enlarging stream of good books, beautifully illustrated and well made".[38] But this is not her concern; rather, the pressing issue is how these books are to be distributed: "the production of the books is far ahead of their distribution at the moment. The books are not yet reaching the children." And they are not even reaching upper- and middle-class children: "I don't mean just that they are not reaching the children in those sections of the country where poverty is rife. They are not reaching the children in those sections where the standard of living is high."[39] She goes on to outline a series of suggestions for remedying this situation, such as better children's sections in libraries, more programmes on radio, an increase in book clubs, exhibitions and school storytelling, and a greater effort by bookshops. Such suggestions and concerns were indicative of a growing awareness that however lovely or valuable a children's book may be, it nevertheless required a network of distribution. A central concern was how children's stories and fairy tales might circulate, and be consumed.

Through scenes of reflexivity and self-definition, *Snow White and the Seven Dwarfs* takes up this issue, offering a vision of the place of fantasy, its potential uses and its commodification. In this respect, the film participates in what Arjun Appadurai describes as "culturally formed mythologies about commodity flow..."[40] Appadurai writes that as the distance between consumers and producers is shrunk, so the issue of *exclusivity* gives way to the issue of *authenticity*. That is, under premodern conditions, the long-distance movement of precious commodities entailed costs that made the acquisition of them *in itself* a marker of exclusivity and an instrument of sumptuary distinction… As technology changes, the reproduction of these objects on a mass basis becomes possible, the dialogue between consumers and the original source becomes more direct, and middle-class consumers become capable (legally and economically) of vying for these objects. The only way to preserve the function of these commodities in the prestige economies of the modern West is to complicate the criteria of authenticity.[41]

Snow White and the Seven Dwarfs reflexively engages in the process of attributing value to fairy tales at key moments within its narrative through scenes that depict – in often moralistic terms – what kinds of fantasy are valuable and what kinds of fantasy are artificial. Through its imagery and narrative, it presents a vision of what fairy tales should be, how they should be produced and how they should be circulated in consumer culture. The book at the start of *Snow White and the Seven Dwarfs* had already invited certain ways of valuing and experiencing the film to follow, fashioning a sense of authenticity, timelessness and dwelling. Similar concerns are developed and extended within the film itself.

The book which begins *Snow White and the Seven Dwarfs* reappears midway through the film. At this point, Snow White has fled the castle of the wicked queen, and the queen has sent out her huntsman to kill her. But, taking pity on her, he has spared her life and brought back the heart of a pig rather than Snow White's heart. Realizing that she has been tricked by the huntsman, the queen races down to her underground chamber to take matters into her own hands. She takes a book of spells titled

"Disguises" from her bookcase and looks over the formula for a "Peddler's Disguise". As she examines the spell, the page of the book is shown in close-up. It is, as Robin Allan notes, "an ironic mockery of the opening story book title."[42] Although similar in typography and appearance, it is unlike the book which begins the film as it is tattered, and set upon a table with a candle which has dripped down almost to the bottom; it evokes a ruined and used version of the book which began the film. The queen mixes her potion of disguise as she villainously declaims the ingredients, reading from the book, "A thunderbolt to mix it well, now begin thy magic spell." Once she finishes her incantation, she takes a sip of the potion that she has created and undergoes a nightmarish transformation – the scene blurs, devolving into a swirling whirlpool and a flurry of bubbles. She clings to her throat as she transforms into an aged woman. As her body changes, she cries out, "Look! My hands! My voice, my voice! A perfect disguise." She then sets about realizing another enchantment, creating the poisonous apple that will eventually cause Snow White's death-like sleep. This spell book has caused extraordinary and sudden transformations built upon material goods and dark magic.

In a parody of the abstract and benign book seen at the beginning, we enter a world of horrors rather than a world of animated wonders. By refiguring the image of the book, the narrative contrasts two perspectives on storytelling. There is the storytelling of the film itself, presented in the introductory images of the book, with connotations of cultural value, group workmanship and stability. And there is the storytelling of the queen, individually transforming her body with old, dark magic. Clinging to her throat, crying of how her voice and hands have transformed, how she has adopted another self, the queen makes the gestural and vocal aspects of storytelling appear wicked and unnatural. Compared to fashioning a book or a film, the traditions which root storytelling in the performing body of the storyteller are made to seem demonic.

These scenes of transformative storytelling are interrupted by an interlude in the cottage of the dwarfs. Here, by contrast, storytelling takes on a lovely hue. The scene begins with "The Silly Song" in which "the words don't mean a thing" and where rather than using mysterious potions, the dwarfs perform with carved wooden instruments. The scene also has a transformation of sorts, when Dopey climbs upon Sneezy's shoulders and puts on an enormous overcoat. After the song, the dwarfs ask Snow White to tell them a "true story, a love story". Snow White hesitates, and then begins her tale with a traditional beginning of fairy tales: "Once there was a princess." Although her story is a song, "Some Day My Prince Will Come", and the scene follows certain conventions borrowed from the genre of the musical, the situation is marked as specifically that of telling a fairy tale. It begins with Snow White in medium shot, casting a thoughtful glance upwards, and then cuts to a communal scene: in the foreground, along the bottom of the frame, the dwarfs form an attentive audience. Adding to the connotations of storytelling, we see the fireplace behind them. The scene expands Snow White's social role as storyteller to include her being a mother of sorts to the dwarfs, as she takes them up to bed when her "story" has finished and the clock has chimed. The contrasts between the scenes of storytelling in the dungeon and the scenes of storytelling in the cottage are striking. The queen's wicked storytelling is individual, immediately transforming her body to fulfil a vindictive desire. It is also a key turning point in the plot, setting the elements of the film's climactic scenes in motion. Snow White's storytelling is sentimental, taking place in a community with overtones of maternal care and a young girl's simple desires. Unlike the instantaneous and embodied changes of the queen, this is an expression of patient and passive fantasy.

The act of transformative storytelling is not the only kind of fantasy that the film presents as distorted; the consumption of fantasy can be dangerous as well. Donning her peddler's disguise, the queen sets out to kill Snow White. Oblivious to this impending danger, Snow White reprises the motif of "Some Day My Prince Will Come", safely ensconced in the dwarfs' cottage, baking a pie. Suddenly, a shadow looms over her. But rather than the prince, the queen has found her. Finding out that the dwarfs, as expected, have departed for the day, the queen begins a deadly sales pitch: "Making pies?" Snow White replies politely, "Yes, gooseberry pie." "It's apple pies that make the menfolk's mouths water. Pie made from apples like these…" And the queen takes the poisonous red apple out of her basket, holding it out for Snow White to admire. Inveigling her way into Snow White's home, the queen continues to sell the apple: "This is no ordinary apple, it is a magic wishing apple." "A wishing apple?" "Yes… one bite and all your dreams come true… there must be something that your little heart desires." The promise of a desire fulfilled proves to be too much for Snow White, and she offers her wish "that he will carry me away to his castle, where we will live happily ever after…" The queen hurries her, "Fine, fine, now take a bite." With the queen looking triumphantly on, Snow White takes a bite of the apple, and dies.

This incident, contained in altered form in the original tale, speaks to many psychological and archetypal implications. But, in a more explicit sense, the scene demonstrates that Snow White will die for believing in the immediacy of transformation, in the magical power of fantastic goods and in the words that emerge from the mouths of old women and anonymous peddlers. Lears writes that, in mid-nineteenth century America, "Unlike the shopkeeper, who sought a place at the center of the village community, the peddler represented the enticements and threats posed by the world beyond local boundaries… In the common view, the peddler became a modern trickster, a confidence man who gained his goal through guile rather than strength – particularly through a skillful theatricality."[43] Having been "relegated to the backwaters of commercial culture" decades earlier, the image of the peddler had come to emblematize "an older, preindustrial version of market exchange…"[44] Bringing temptations from afar, coupled with promises of satisfied desires, the peddler queen takes on these connotations, selling an untrustworthy fantasy.

These perspectives on the relationship between fantasy and commodification are picked up again at the end of the film. The seasons have passed and the dwarfs, unwilling to bury someone "so beautiful, even in death" have built a glass coffin for Snow White, and laid it in a forest grotto upon a bier of gold. Birds, deer and rabbits come to pay their respects, bringing bouquets of flowers. The dwarfs arrive, remove the lid of the coffin so that they can place flowers in Snow White's dead hands, and gather around mournfully. A beam of light shines through the trees above, illuminating Snow White. The prince has been watching this touching scene. He has, the title card tells us, been searching for Snow White. Upon seeing her, lying there, he sings a mournful song. Entering the clearing, he kisses the corpse of Snow White upon the lips. This kiss brings her to life. She departs her glass coffin, alights upon the prince's horse and they head off together to gaze upon a castle in the sky.

Like Snow White's consumption of the apple, the prince is tempted by an object. For him, it is Snow White within the glass coffin, sanctified by connotations of purity: feminine, youthful, immobile, encased, with a radiant beam of light shining upon her in what Roland Marchand describes as the "popular visual cliché" of advertising at the time.[45] Clearly labelled, with her name on the bottom of the coffin, Snow White is presented as an object quite unlike the mysterious and untrustworthy material of desire that the wicked queen brings from afar. While the peddler's selling of the apple can be seen as a negative and outdated emblem of commodity exchange, the body of Snow White is presented in a peculiarly modern way, like a mannequin behind a shop window or an expensive product in a display case. William Leach writes of how such commercial displays presented "a mingling of refusal and desire that must have greatly intensified desire… Perhaps more than any other medium, glass democratized desire even as it democratized access to goods. There it is, you see it as big as life – you see it amplified everywhere, you see everything revealed – but you cannot reach it."[46] Of course, the prince reaches *it*: Snow

White. The apotheosis of such a desire, deep in the bosom of nature, gives life back to Snow White and results in a happy ending. This concluding incident of *Snow White and the Seven Dwarfs* binds modern forms of consumer culture with life, love and nature.

These scenes of consumption play an important narrative role, presenting modified events and situations from the original tale. But at the same time, they also present the ways in which desire should or should not work. Like the image of the book which begins *Snow White and the Seven Dwarfs*, scenes that evoke fantasy in the film value stability rather than metamorphosis, comforting daydreams rather than imaginative transformations, and the regulated movement of goods rather than the dangers of material desire. The negotiation of these concerns is central to the film's self-definition; as a new form of visual entertainment in American culture, a film which "pioneered a great new entertainment field for the motion picture cartoon",[47] as it was described upon receiving its special Academy Award, it is little wonder that *Snow White and the Seven Dwarfs* marked out, thematized and displayed a relationship to fantasy that would coalesce with its imagined – or wished for – place in a wider cinematic and cultural context. In doing so, it shifted the emphasis away from potentially disruptive or mutable forms, asserting a relation to authority, tradition and cultural value that could offer a different, firmer foundation for fantasy.

Traps of Transformation

Disney was, of course, not unique in such attempts to resituate the place of fairy tales in film culture. Turning now to other examples from the 1930s, we can see that a range of films had a similar concern with containing or dismissing the potentials of film fantasy. Among the most prominent figures in such a renegotiation was Shirley Temple, the star who presented Walt Disney with his honorary Academy Award, along with seven little ones for each of the dwarfs. Charles Eckert summarizes Temple's impact as one of the decade's most popular stars:

> Through the mid-depression years of 1934 to 1938 Shirley Temple was a phenomenon of the first magnitude: she led in box-office grosses, single-handedly revived Fox and influenced its merger with 20th Century, had more products named after her than any other star and became as intimately experienced at home and abroad as President Franklin Roosevelt.[48]

Slightly later in her career, two years after *Snow White and the Seven Dwarfs* was released, Temple starred in a new version of *The Little Princess* (Lang, 1939). Unlike the film from 20 years earlier with Mary Pickford discussed in Chapter 4, fantasy takes on a limited role within this film. In addition to relying on Temple's established star persona of precocious childhood cuteness, the film alters key elements of the narrative so that its themes of fantasy and loss become considerably muted; for example, the beneficent Ram Dass is introduced early on so that his appearance later in the film lacks the sudden transformation of the earlier version and, at the end, rather than fantasy being a means to deal with and work through the loss of a loved one, Sara's father is alive after all. Like the earlier version, the film presents a fairy-tale interlude; however, rather than showing its star as a storyteller projecting herself into a land of exotic and transformative fantasy, it is a childlike dream where Temple is a queen in a nursery-rhyme world of fantasy, adjudicating over a stolen kiss and performing in a ballet. Through alterations such as these, the film elaborated on a constrained scope of fantasy in cinema and modern life.

The following year, Temple starred in another remake of a pivotal fairy-tale film from the 1910s, *The Blue Bird* (Lang, 1940). Clearly influenced by *The Wizard of Oz* (Fleming, 1939), the film begins in black and white before shifting into colour, once the children are awoken by the Fairy Berylune and introduced to a fantastic world. Unlike *The Wizard of Oz*, which frames its beginning and ending in black and white, *The Blue Bird* retains its colour after the adventures of the children, suggesting that the world has been given a fantastic hue – at least in the children's minds – due to their experiences. However, other than this interesting use of colour, the sensibility of fantasy so crucial to earlier versions of the tale is substantially limited. While still presenting extraordinary landscapes of fantasy, it avoids the more abstract allegorical figurations, it omits the magic crystal which alters perspectives, and it introduces suspense and deadlines into different sequences to heighten the narrative drive. It also adds a subplot about the children's father going to war; released in 1940, the reference to current events is obvious. In the film, though, a truce is declared to make for a rather forced happy ending. Introducing a more narratively focused tale and uncomplicated fantasy world, the film offered a very different kind of *Blue Bird*. It frames itself in a different manner as well: drawing upon *Snow White and the Seven Dwarfs*, it begins with the image of a book version of "The Blue Bird", overtly shifting its origins from a stage play to a work of literature. Rather than the expansion of perception through cinema's fairy-tale tropes, the film participates in what Eckert describes as "the mitigation of reality through fantasy" so central to Temple's star vehicles.[49]

A very different play with the potentials of storytelling and fantasy was evident in a major production a few years earlier, *The Scarlet Empress*. The film shows young Sophia (Marlene Dietrich) taken away from her family and transformed into Catherine, tsarina of Russia. Particularly well known for its presentation of Dietrich's star persona and its baroque visual style, the film alludes to fairy tales at certain key points in the narrative. The film begins with a doctor visiting Sophia as a young girl; following the doctor's departure, Sophia's attendant comments that the doctor is also a hangman. Inquisitive, Sophia asks, "What's a hangman? Can I be a hangman some day?" and her attendant tells her in a relaxed, teacherly tone, "Your highness, a hangman is an executioner, a man who takes heads off skilfully. Sometimes that curious profession becomes the sport of tyrants. As a matter of fact, I was about to read to you of Peter the Great, and Ivan the Terrible, and other Russian tsars and tsarinas who were hangmen." As Sophia lies in bed, her attendant reads to her the story of these well-known tyrants – this is figured in a terrifying montage where the optical effect of a turning page separates scenes of murder, sadism and torture. Probably the decade's strangest example of a storybook beginning, images of terror emerge as if from an illustrated book, preparing Sophia for her life to follow and parodying a child's bedtime stories.

This ironic use of fantasy extends throughout the film. Sophia's entrance into courtly life and marriage is presented as a nightmarish rite of passage, an experience that has already been shaped by the machinations of the court. The enormous sets, densely packed framings and looming sculptures in the background all contribute to a sense of a deadening and constricting environment. The film also offers what Gaylyn Studlar describes as an "Alice in Wonderland world complete with spatial distortions, confusing temporal gaps, an abundance of grotesques, and a wicked 'Red Queen'."[50] This skewed vision of fairy-tale fantasies is also articulated through the film's intertitles which, as Marcia Landy points out, "'direct' the narration".[51] The first one, for example, reads: "About two centuries ago, in a corner of the Kingdom of Prussia, lived a little princess – chosen by destiny to become the greatest Monarch of her time – Tsarina of all the Russians – the ill-famed Messalina of the North." Studlar notes that this title "takes its cue from the beginning of all good fairy tales to foreshadow the action as already enacted, known, closed to any phantom possibilities of pretended here-and-now existence."[52] This becomes so overwrought that it tends towards self-parody at points, with the authority of history and narration creating a fatalistic tone; for example, one intertitle sets out the narrative before it has even begun: "On March the fifteenth, 1744, Princess Sophia Frederica departed for Russia, full of innocent dreams for the future, and completely unaware of the fate which was to transform her into the most famous woman of her day."

Late in the film, after her enforced marriage, Sophia (now renamed Catherine) resists. She exits her home and finds herself in a shadowy forest at night [Figure 24]. Here, she undergoes a decisive turn towards power when she encounters, and seduces, a soldier. The scene interweaves typical fairy-tale motifs of metamorphosis, an enchanted forest and cast-out royalty. This will quickly become part of a narrative chain of events where Catherine inhabits the throne on her own, rather brutal, terms. Rather than her metamorphosis into the kingdom's new leader opening up the possibility of a straightforward happy ending, Catherine's attainment of her new role relies upon power struggles and manipulation. Landy observes that the film presents the metamorphosis of Catherine into a queen in ways that resonate with Dietrich's own process of becoming a star.[53] Showing a transformation that is both constrained and self-destructive, the film has also been approached more broadly in terms of representing social mobility; Landy quotes Peter Baxter, who writes, "It is finally – for all its make-believe – nothing less than a nightmare version of the American dream as Sternberg had lived it, the dream quite literally of 'upward mobility' that overtakes its subjects, inflates them with limitless ambition, and gives them everything they want in return for everything they are."[54] Entwining fairy-tale tropes with images of violence, control and entrapment, the film shows horrors, rather than fantasies, of transformation.

A similarly ironic sense of fairy tales and fantasy is evident in the cycle variously described as the "Gothic romance", "paranoid woman's film" and the "Bluebeard cycle" that emerged several years later.[55] Circulating around a narrative of a woman's marriage to a man who has a secret past or a murderous intent, examples include *Rebecca* (Hitchcock, 1940) and *The Secret Beyond the Door* (Lang, 1948), both of which directly reference fairy tales at several points in their narratives, as well as using the overarching structure of the fairy tale "Bluebeard". Maria Tatar writes, "In the 1940s Hollywood produced more than a dozen films modeled on the

Figure 24. *The Scarlet Empress*

Bluebeard plot."[56] Rather than drawing on fairy tales to evoke the marvels of transformation, these films present them as dangerous stories to inhabit or believe in. This is not only brought about by using the darker material of the Bluebeard narrative, but also by inverting and parodying the more benign transformations of Cinderella and other similar fairy tales. For instance, Hitchcock described the protagonist of *Rebecca* as Cinderella (encountering her wealthy husband-to-be at the Princess Hotel), but whatever connotations of fantasy and potential this tale may have held are soon overturned.[57] Tania Modleski describes one example of how the tale is inverted:

> The night of the ball, the heroine descends the great staircase radiantly dressed in a lavish white gown, only to be greeted by her horror-stricken husband, who, in a cruel reversal of the Cinderella myth, orders her back to her room to change her dress.[58]

Films such as these, as Tatar notes, "explicitly disavow fairy tales such as 'Cinderella' and 'Sleeping Beauty' as paradigms for romance."[59]

While such a vision of fairy tales may seem to be far removed from *Snow White and the Seven Dwarfs*, the Bluebeard cycle can be seen to be following a similar conception of the form of fairy tales in contemporary culture. Whether associated with enduring works of literature and stable narrative trajectories, as in the case of *Snow White and the Seven Dwarfs*, or with dangerously naive fantasies and constricting artificial roles, as in the case of many films in the Bluebeard cycle, fairy tales were used as forms of limitation rather than potential, evoking traps rather than transformations. This was, of course, not entirely new. *The Golden Chance*, discussed in Chapter 4, provides one example of an ironic fairy tale from decades earlier, and fairy-tale narratives had long been reworked to highlight their excesses, naivety or threats to identity – one sees this as early as the films of Méliès and, on stage, in the nineteenth-century féerie. But what became increasingly visible in the 1930s and into the 1940s were films that restrained or derided fairy tales, fantasy and transformation. Much like *Wings*, discussed in the previous chapter, the potential of fairy tales was limited, if not dismissed altogether.

The Good Fairy, for example, situates a language of fairy tales against a background of business and labour in order to demonstrate the commercialization of fantasy. The film was based on a play written by Ferenc Molnár; adapted by Preston Sturges, it anticipates his later satires on fantasy in modern life in films such as *Christmas in July* (1940) and *Sullivan's Travels* (1941). The opening credits to *The Good Fairy* are shown over an illustration of a looming silhouette of a tree and a castle on a hilltop. This sets a mood of fantasy for the film, a sense that seems to continue with its opening shots of a group of young children dancing and singing a nursery rhyme in a playground. Once they have finished, their attendant tells them, "Once more girls, and with more *life*, more *feeling*." As they go through their nursery routine once more, the camera tracks back slowly to reveal a barred gate through which the main view of the playground has been shot, and then cranes up to a sign atop the gate, "Municipal Orphanage for Girls". Rehearsing nursery rhymes within a walled institution, the film immediately establishes an ironic depiction of childhood fantasy. Later scenes in the orphanage continue this parody, with a scene of fairy-tale storytelling beginning with a long tracking shot of the young women in the orphanage at work, glumly and mechanistically washing plates at a seemingly endless sink. Stacking dishes in the cupboards, Luisa (Margaret Sullavan) is telling a story from borrowed motifs of princes, princesses and ogres to a group of children scouring potatoes. At the climax of the story – the good fairy's attempts to rescue an imprisoned prince and princess – Luisa acts out her role, climbing up a ladder; rather than a marvellous finale to her tale, the ladder crashes, plates smash and she falls. Contrasting the fantasies of Luisa with the everyday realities of life, the film sets a tone that becomes increasingly satiric of fairy-tale fantasies.

After falling to the ground, Luisa is "discovered" by Maurice Schlapkohl (Alan Hale). He is intent on finding "sweet" usherettes for his cinema, the "Dream Palace", and thinks of the orphanage as a perfect place to look. He quickly recruits Luisa, pleased with her simplicity; she is a perfect usherette, dwelling in a world of childlike and naive fantasy that resonates with the fantasies offered by cinema. As Luisa is about to embark on this career in the outside world, the director of the orphanage asks her if she will still do her good deed each day. She replies, "Yes ma'am," and then recites, as if it were a mantra, the motto of the orphanage: "Each day a good deed I place to my account in heavenly grace, a bank whose customers are blessed with peace of heart for interest." The language of commercial transactions overwhelms moral and religious values in this contemporary context. After hearing this recital, Schlapkohl is pleased: "Sold," he says, "I'll take her." In her new role as an usherette, she works in the modern fantasy world of a cinema, directing customers to their seats with an illuminated wand. The relationship between fantasy and commerce extends to other aspects of Luisa's experience outside the orphanage. For example, she meets a wealthy businessman named Konrad (Frank Morgan) who tries to seduce her by awkwardly tempting her through fantasy and with money. He presents a fantastic scenario: "Suppose that you are walking through the woods one day and all of a sudden you met a wizard who stopped you and said, 'Little girl, what do you want, because I'm terribly terribly rich and I want to throw some of it your way.'" Interested, Luisa asks, "Is this the story of the enchanted woods?" He replies, "Uh, no, no, no, the enchanted bankroll." When Konrad finally gives up hope, due to Luisa pretending that she is married, he offers to help her make someone else rich in order to retain some of his pride at having power and wealth. Luisa responds, "I was thinking of my making somebody rich... like the good fairy – just one wave of the wand." "One wave of the chequebook," he appropriately adds. As the film continues, it develops a story where Luisa plays the role of a good fairy by transforming the life of a random stranger, with the help of Konrad's money. *The Good Fairy* playfully mocks the conditions of transformation and fantasy in contemporary life, dispelling the power and meaning of fairy-tale marvels by showing them to be based in commercial transactions and modern deceits.

The link between fairy tales and the sudden turns of fate in capitalism is also a recurring theme in comedies written by Charles Brackett and Billy Wilder from the period. Fairy tales are interconnected with commerce in both *Bluebeard's Eighth Wife* (Lubitsch, 1938) and *Midnight* (Leisen, 1939). These films situate their star, Claudette Colbert, in a fantastic world of wealth that threatens to consume her. In *Midnight*, Eve Peabody (Colbert), described as a "streamlined Cinderella" in one trailer for the film, arrives from a train onto the rainy streets of Paris. Penniless, she convinces a cab driver (Don Ameche) to take her job hunting. When he suggests that she should stay at his place, she dashes away and stumbles into an extravagant party, posing as an invited guest. She catches the attention of one guest (John Barrymore), who first notices her removing her shoe – with a close-up of her foot, for added Cinderellaesque measure. A wealthy man, he soon convinces her not to be his Cinderella, but to play the role of a society woman in a convoluted plot of jealousy and infidelity. In this guise, Eve does take on the characteristics of Cinderella, living in an extravagant mansion. The move from the rainy city streets to a mansion was, of course, a film cliché at the time, and *Midnight* makes knowing reference to its artificiality. This extends into minor comments in the film, where Eve misconstrues the fairy tale she has become immersed in, describing the cab driver who is in love with her as a "fairy godmother", although he turns out to be her Prince Charming, and characterizing her benefactor as the wolf in "Little Red Riding Hood", although he plays the role of her fairy godmother. Eventually, after falling in love with the cab driver, she departs her phony "happily ever after" for real love.

In one extraordinary scene, the film also displays the ambivalent power of fairy-tale transformations tied in with consumerist fantasies. Unaware that she has already been installed in the lap of luxury by her "fairy godfather", as the trailer describes him, she awakens nervously at the Ritz, where she has spent the night. She thinks that she has snuck into the room, but porters arrive to bring new clothes to her. Astonished, she covers up under the sheets, as they bring in a series of suitcases and a large portable closet. In the midground, Eve lies in bed with an expression shifting between wonder and terror – in the foreground, there is the image of the key in the porter's hand, as he asks her if he should open the closet. Alluding to the enchanted key in "Bluebeard" which would open the secret chamber, the scene casts this closet of expensive clothes as something both tempting and dangerous. The porter swings the closet around so that it dwarfs Eve in the frame, and then begins to pull out the various clothes as she gazes in amazement. These clothes are the material of her transformation, and they appear as something both oppressive and filled with potential in this scene: unexpected, enticing and overpowering.

Bluebeard's Eighth Wife, released the previous year, is similarly suspicious of fairy tales and transformation. The film tells the story of Nicole (Colbert) marrying a rich businessman, Michael Brandon (Gary Cooper) who, as she puts it, buys "wives just like shirts". Frustrated at her knowledge that she is a disposable eighth wife, she resists his sexual advances and refuses to play the role of wifely commodity. The film's fantasy is not that of the Cinderella story and sudden wealth, but that of "Bluebeard" being overturned. *Bluebeard's Eighth Wife* thematizes the traps of transformation offered by the Cinderella/Bluebeard narrative through its references to pre-structured and financially arranged relationships. In these films, fairy-tale transformations are still visible, but mediated by a reflexive and ironic treatment of their implications. In such films, fantasy is presented as something pre-packaged, constructed by oppressive tradition, naive belief, male power or capitalist society. Indicating fatigue or doubt with earlier fantasies of modern life, these films speak to a different experience of modernity than an immersion in transformative possibility. Such reflexive uses of fairy tales suggest just how interwoven their fantasies had become with modernity. Anthony Giddens writes that it is a characteristic element of modernity that "social practices are constantly examined and reformed in the light of incoming information about those very practices."[60] Giddens contrasts the reflexivity of modernity with traditional cultures, where "the past is honoured and symbols are valued because they contain and perpetuate the experience of generations."[61] Miriam Hansen extends these concerns into the context of American films in the so-called classical period, describing how they were reflexive of modernity, "and that reflexivity does not always have to be critical or unequivocal; on the contrary, the reflexive dimension of these films may consist precisely in the ways in which they allow their viewers to confront the constitutive ambivalence of modernity."[62] Rather than simply perpetuating earlier uses of fairy tales, films of the 1930s and 1940s explored ideas of tradition, storytelling and fantasy in ways that questioned the place of fairy tales in modernity.

While often casting doubt on the potentials of fantasy in modern life, not all films shared this perspective. For example, *Ball of Fire* (Hawks, 1941), another in the series of fairy-tale comedies written by Brackett and Wilder in this period, offers a different approach to fairy tales. The film begins with the title card, "Once upon a time – in 1941 to be exact – there lived in a great, tall forest – called New York – eight men who were writing an ency-clopedia." The title card immediately signifies the fairy-tale basis of the film, with its "once upon a time"; but rather than remain-ing in this timeless realm, it goes on to note the year, offering the specificity of an historical moment. The film is a modern updating of *Snow White and the Seven Dwarfs* in which Professor Potts (Gary Cooper), along with seven other encyclopedists who stand in for the seven dwarfs, give shelter to a nightclub performer, Sugarpuss O'Shea (Barbara Stanwyck) who is running from the mob. Potts plays the role of the prince to O'Shea's Snow White, with the film loosely following the narrative trajectory of the fairy tale.

As well as alluding to *Snow White and the Seven Dwarfs* through its narrative, *Ball of Fire* reworks a scene from the Disney film to elaborate on a vision of a dynamic modern world: Potts's first meeting with O'Shea refigures the scene where Snow White meets the prince. In the Disney film, we first see Snow White washing steps, surrounded by white birds. Humming a song to herself, she walks to a well and draws up a pail. Addressing the birds, she whispers in a sing-song voice, "Want to know a secret? Promise not to tell? We are standing by a wishing well." And she begins her song: "I'm Wishing". As she sings into the well, the scene cuts to the prince, atop a white horse. He is just outside of the castle, intrigued by the dreamy voice he hears. The scene cuts back to Snow White. Reworking the preceding scene, where the queen gazes into her mirror, Snow White gazes at her reflection in the well [Figure 25]. As she sings, the water of the well echoes her words in an animated "echo song", with ripples enlarging in the water. Raymond Knapp points out that "in some tradi-tions of echo songs, the echoes seem to respond as answers to questions rather than as simple repetitions… here, however, the echo simply repeats obediently…"[63] Along with the responsively anthropomorphized well, Snow White's labour and the attendant animals help characterize this as an expression of benign fantasy set in contrast to the queen's dark magic in front of the mirror. Snow White is rewarded for the purity of her fantasy as the prince joins her in song.

Figure 25. *Snow White and the Seven Dwarfs*

Ball of Fire offers a similar scene, but with quite different implications. Arriving at a nightclub for the last of his stops in a busy
day researching slang, Potts watches O'Shea and Gene Krupa
performing "Drum Boogie". Exposed to something radically different from his daily life, his attention is fixed on the energy of
the performance, the excitement of the environment and O'Shea's
midriff-baring costume. When O'Shea and Krupa return for an
encore and ask everyone to gather around, Potts nervously joins
the crowd. O'Shea takes control of the scene, rearranging tables
and asking for a spotlight, while Krupa settles down on a chair.
Singing the song in a whisper, accompanied by Krupa on matchsticks, O'Shea captivates the audience who are asked to join in
with parts of the song. The song nears its end, and Krupa suddenly
strikes the matchsticks alight; the crowd erupts in applause after
O'Shea blows them out. Like Snow White, O'Shea is engaged in
work while singing an "echo song"; further alluding to the scene
from *Snow White and the Seven Dwarfs*, O'Shea's face is shown on
a reflective surface (the table) [Figure 26] with the prince (Potts)

waiting on the periphery. But the scene presents a radically different vision of fantasy. Unlike Snow White's song of wishing for future happiness through marriage, O'Shea's song is lyrically about nothing, simply repeating the lines "drum boogie, drum boogie" over and over again; instead of the ripples in the well speaking back, it is the audience; instead of the white doves on the lip of the well peering in, it is the matchsticks, about to burn up. No prince steps in. A scene of sentimental fantasy becomes recast in terms of community, performance and ephemerality. Returning to the tenor of earlier cinematic fairy tales, fantasy is drawn into a contemporary filmic frame of dynamism and energy. While this was becoming increasingly occluded in the 1930s and the 1940s, *Ball of Fire* indicates the ongoing negotiation of the place of fantasy in modern life.

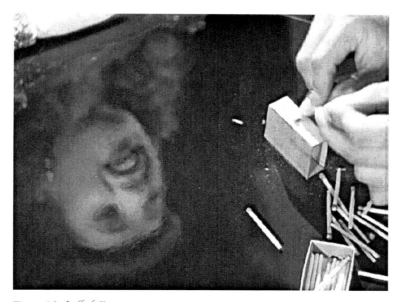

Figure 26. *Ball of Fire*

Afterword

MUTABILITY LESSONS

AN ETHEREAL LIGHT SHINES DOWN UPON A BOOK. THE cover opens, and the slowly turning pages reveal an illustrated fairy tale. A voice-over reads the tale aloud, telling of a princess trapped in a castle who waited "for her true love and true love's first kiss". This is the opening scene of *Shrek* (Adamson and Jenson, 2001), overtly referencing the beginning of *Snow White and the Seven Dwarfs*, as well as a larger context of conservatism, nostalgia and escapism associated with fairy tales, and particularly Disney's use of the form. But, coming to the end of the story, the narrator Shrek (voiced by Mike Myers) mockingly interjects: "Like that's ever gonna happen. What a load of..." and he tears a page from the storybook to use as toilet paper. Rather than subtly undermining an old-fashioned fairy tale, Shrek, who has been narrating the story, simply flushes all that crap down the toilet. Smash Mouth's "All Star" replaces the insipid score, the medieval style of the picture book gives way to computer animation, and instead of a princely figure, we are introduced to the lovable ogre merrily bathing in mud and getting ready for his day. *Shrek* celebrates an earthy, folkloric set of fantasies, such as the pleasures of the grotesque body, the bonds of friendship and high spirits. A certain idea of the old-fashioned and sentimental fairy tale becomes the subject of parody and ridicule: iconic fairy-tale characters are rounded up and exiled from their magic kingdom by an evil lord, the archetypal plot of a prince saving a princess is made to seem less a rite of passage and more an unwelcome task, and the climactic scene of transformation celebrates beastliness over beauty.

Shrek is part of a resurgence of interest in the multiple potentials of the fairy-tale form, a trend that had begun decades earlier. This is evident in a wide range of novels, short stories, poems, plays, paintings and critical works employing fairy tales as a site of social and cultural critique, particularly associated with issues of gender and desire; works of Angela Carter and Margaret Atwood provide two of the most dynamic and influential examples.[1] As Cristina Bacchilega points out, fairy tales offer writers "well-known material pliable to political, erotic, or narrative manipulation... Thinking of the fairy tale predominantly as children's literature, or even as 'literature of childhood', cannot accommodate this proliferation of uses and meanings."[2] In addition to the parodies and revisions of the psychological, narrative and archetypal implications of fairy tales that reinforce conservative tropes of femininity, fairy tales have been influenced by wider stylistic contexts such as magic realism and postmodernism. By the 1990s, many fairy tales had been taken to realms far removed from sentimentality, becoming what Tom Shippey describes as "a contested site, viewed by many as an actual or potential means of social comment, social control, or social change."[3]

Many films over the past few decades have reworked the narratives, tropes and situations of fairy tales to engage with such possibilities, from the incorporation of "Little Red Riding Hood" as an iconic tale of sexuality in *The Company of Wolves* (Jordan, 1984) and *Cape Fear* (Scorsese, 1991) to the explorations of storytelling in *The Piano* (Campion, 1993) and *Pan's Labyrinth* (del Toro, 2006) to the reworkings of "The Wizard of Oz" in *Wild at Heart* (Lynch, 1990) and *Twister* (de Bont, 1996). This is not entirely new; fairy tales had continued to play a diverse and sometimes prominent role in cinema following the 1940s, where the previous chapter left off, in genre films ranging from musicals to horror and in different modes of film production such as art cinema and animation. That said, fairy tales have become increasingly central to contemporary film, often in multifaceted and complex ways.

Fairy tales have also become prominent material for big-budget Hollywood productions. Although not always as overt as the red pill that leads to an awareness of the "Wonderland" in *The Matrix*, the narratives and tropes of fairy tales have been central to popular cinema for decades, informing the work of filmmakers such as George Lucas and Steven Spielberg.

I conclude this book by looking at a specific aspect of the form that fairy tales have taken in contemporary cinema, where films draw upon fairy tales to reflect on the institution of cinema or the medium of film. I examine three films: *Sleepy Hollow* (Burton, 1999), *Shrek 2* (Adamson, Asbury and Vernon, 2004) and *Harry Potter and the Prisoner of Azkaban* (Cuarón, 2004). The first of these films is directed by Tim Burton, the most financially successful filmmaker to return consistently to fairy tales for subject matter, and the latter two examples are part of the most popular film series to draw upon fairy tales. While major popular and critical successes, I have not selected them specifically as representative of the wider realm of contemporary fairy-tale films. In this respect, I could have chosen other films by the same directors, such as *The Chronicles of Narnia: The Lion, the Witch and the Wardrobe* (Adamson, 2005) with its entrance into a quasi-Christian fantasy world, *Alice in Wonderland* (Burton, 2010), which employs an extravagant fairy-tale vision as material for a 3D blockbuster and a young woman's rite of passage, or *A Little Princess* (Cuarón, 1995), which revisits a canonical tale of fantasy that I have discussed in previous chapters. Examples of fairy tales inscribed within contemporary films abound; instead of attempting to summarize this diversity, I focus on *Sleepy Hollow*, *Shrek 2* and *Harry Potter and the Prisoner of Azkaban* in order to trace some of the ways in which cinema's social and technological context continues to be seen through the optic of fairy tales. What emerges is that key elements of the relationship between film and fairy tales that were being developed a century earlier, such as the depiction of visual transformation and the entwinement of fantasy with modernity, remain central to understanding and expressing the potentials of cinema itself.

Shrek 2

Shrek parodies the stock characters, situations and tropes of fairy tales, particularly as they have been associated with Disney. *Shrek 2* further elaborates on themes of transformation and consumer culture. The film begins with the happily married ogre couple, Shrek and Fiona, on their honeymoon – trapping fairies to make fairy lights and tossing mermaids back in the sea. Leaving this idyll to visit Fiona's parents, they arrive in the kingdom of Far Far Away, a fantastic Hollywood with its own sign set in the side of a hill. Its royalty are fairy-tale stars such as Cinderella and Rapunzel who live in gated mansions. This kingdom is founded on transformation, for Fiona's father, the king, is also a fairy-tale star: the frog who was transformed into a prince. The narrative is motivated by his attempts to hold on to his status by placating the villainous fairy godmother, who was responsible for his metamorphosis (and success). The king attempts to disrupt Fiona's marriage to Shrek so that she can marry the fairy godmother's son, the handsome and shallow Prince Charming. Pushing Fiona into a canonical fairy-tale role, the father attempts to enforce a constricting "fantasy" for his daughter.

The fairy godmother, characterized as both a Hollywood agent and a no longer youthful career woman, first appears upon a billboard announcing "For all your happily ever afters" in a negligee and matching slippers, lying in a provocative pose. Shrek mutters, "We are definitely not in the swamp any more." And much like *The Wizard of Oz*, the narrative progresses towards return, towards the lessons that there is no place like homely, that the desire for transformation is both unnecessary and self-destructive. This is shown vividly in a scene early in the film where Fiona, at home with her parents, worries about her less than fairy-tale marriage. After all, her husband is literally an ogre, though a kind-hearted one. Alone in her childhood bedroom, she pauses to look at her prince and princess dolls, and sheds a tear. Bubbles suddenly appear in the sky, out of which the fairy godmother emerges, her little wings fluttering furiously. She tells Fiona, "I'm here to make it all better," and begins a musical number. Zinging around the room, waving her wand and magically investing the furniture with animate life, she sings how "with just a wave of my magic wand your troubles will soon be gone; with a flick of the wrist and just a flash you'll land a prince with a ton of cash." Her song extends to the transformative fantasies of consumer culture that she can supply: "a high-priced dress made by mice no less, some crystal-glass pumps and no more stress", "nip and tuck, here and there, to land the prince with the perfect hair". The absurdity of the whole scene, with the fairy godmother's frenzied promises of fairy-tale transformation and the creepy sight of the furniture dancing, becomes increasingly horrific as the song's list of changes increases in tempo, as flying chairs, cosmetics and bottles of perfume swarm around Fiona in a maelstrom of purchasing power. Fiona shouts, "Stop!" She then explains, "I really don't need all of this," to the collective gasp of the assembled living furniture and the fairy godmother.

While Fiona is characterized as too self-assured to buy into this bombardment of transformation, Shrek's desire to be transformed into a handsome prince leads him to the fairy godmother's enchanted cottage, nestled at the foot of a giant factory. Making his way through the evil lair, accompanied by Donkey and Puss in Boots, Shrek spies the fairy godmother in the process of creating a potion. She circles around a frothing cauldron, adding a "pinch of passion" and "just a hint of lust" with an evil laugh. Like the wicked queen in *Snow White and the Seven Dwarfs*, the fairy godmother is engaged in the dark magic of desire. She sees Shrek and shouts out, "What in Grimm's name are you doing here?" Shrek replies, "Fiona's not exactly happy." The fairy godmother teaches him a lesson in fairy tales: "Is there some question as to why that is? Well, let's explore that shall we?" She flies up to her bookshelf, tossing a series of books on her desk: "Cinderella", "Snow White", "The Handsome Prince" and, fittingly, "Pretty Woman". Noting "no ogres" again and again, her lesson concludes, "You see, ogres don't live happily ever after." Shrek and his companions do not give up, though; they later sneak in to the chamber and, in a rush, grab a "happily ever after potion". Dashing out, they spill a cauldron of potion in the factory, transforming swans into dancers, two workers into an anthropomorphic clock and candelabra, and the rest of the labourers into doves. Drinking the potion, Shrek is transformed into a handsome man – but this transformation, after various peregrinations, is shown to be unnecessary.

In *Shrek 2*, the potentials of transformations are overturned, made to seem ridiculous, duplicitous and dangerous. While it is a certain kind of consumerist transformation that is being parodied, the pastiches of the visual spectacle of metamorphosis that I have singled out reach back to earlier fairy-tale films. The spilled potion that transforms various characters, as well as Shrek, alludes to *Babes in the Woods* (Gillett, 1932), where the witch's potion is used to transform a child into a spider, and then animals into children, in a stunning display of animation's fluidity. With the appearance of a candelabra and clock, the scene also recalls *Beauty and the Beast* (Trousdale and Wise, 1991); this link is developed in the earlier encounter between Fiona and her anthropomorphic furniture. In this investment of living qualities in inanimate objects, *Beauty and the Beast* drew upon the earlier *La Belle et la Bête* (Cocteau, 1946). Such marvels go back to early fairy-tale films – as discussed in Chapter 3, *The Blue Bird* (Tourneur, 1918) had a similar scene of furniture rearranging itself through magical means, and Vachel Lindsay's exploration of film fairy tales in *The Art of the Moving Picture* in the 1910s focused on an early trick film where furniture took on a life of its own, describing this investment of animate qualities in the inanimate as something "fundamental in the destinies of the art" of cinema.[4] While *Shrek 2* situates metamorphosis at the core of both Hollywood and fairy tales, it parodies such visions of mutability, showing fantastic transformation as unnecessary and infantilizing – a trap of consumer culture. In this respect, despite its attempt to distance itself from a Disney model of fairy tales, *Shrek 2* is quite similar to *Snow White and the Seven Dwarfs* in the negative connotations it builds around the possibilities of transformation.

Sleepy Hollow

While *Shrek 2* offers one prominent approach to fairy tales in contemporary cinema, other recent films have drawn upon fairy tales to show a world of mutability and fantasy as central to both a modern experience and an understanding of the potentials of cinema. This is a central conceit of *Sleepy Hollow*, which situates fairy tales and other visions of mutability at its core. Near the start of the film, Ichabod Crane (Johnny Depp) is sent away from his home in New York to investigate a series of murders in a small village, Sleepy Hollow. Ichabod applies quasi-scientific techniques of investigation to find the killer, thinking that the townspeople are simply being superstitious by attributing the murders to the legendary Headless Horseman. Despite Ichabod's best efforts at a rational explanation, he is forced to contend with curious local customs, a particularly knotty history, magic, witches and the fairy-tale basis of the crimes. He is also forced to contend with his own relation to the fantastic, discovering through dream sequences that his mother was a witch, murdered by his religious father. Understanding the magical foundations of both his past and the town's past, and accepting that his newfound love, Katrina Van Tassel (Christina Ricci), uses magic, Ichabod ultimately emerges content, stepping out to face a burgeoning New York City at the beginning of the nineteenth century.

Alison McMahan characterizes *Sleepy Hollow* as "a hybrid genre film that combines two structures – fairy tale and horror – and the fairy-tale structure is the dominant".[5] In addition to this broad framework of fairy tales, various fairy-tale motifs are interwoven with key characters and narrative events. The opening shot of the film is an extreme close-up of bright red drops of sealing wax falling on parchment, alluding to the beginning of the Brothers Grimm's "Snow White", where the queen pricks her fingers and three drops of blood fall on the white snow. This link to "Snow

White" is developed through the character of Mary Van Tassel (Miranda Richardson). She is the murderer, it is revealed at the end, who has been controlling the Headless Horseman through magic. As the jealous stepmother of Katrina Van Tassel, she plays a similar role to the wicked queen from *Snow White and the Seven Dwarfs*: slicing apples, telling Ichabod that it is Katrina's "turn to sleep", asking rhetorically, "was it wicked of me?" Her past – as well as the origin of the Headless Horseman – is shown early in the film as a fantastic tale. Standing by a fireplace, Baltus Van Tassel (Michael Gambon) tells Ichabod a story: a vicious Hessian mercenary, pursued by soldiers near Sleepy Hollow, runs into the woods to hide and stumbles across two young girls gathering twigs; although he gestures for them to be quiet, one girl defiantly snaps a twig and watches attentively as he is caught and decapitated. It will later be revealed that the girl was Mary Van Tassel, and that she dug up the grave of the mercenary and magically recreated him to be her servant, the Headless Horseman. This story, told by a superstitious villager beside a roaring fire, roots the origins of the narrative and the town's history in a fairy-tale event: two girls in the woods encountering a monstrous character.

When Ichabod is told the story of the Headless Horseman, the camera tracks forward towards the roaring fireplace, from which the fairy tale visually emerges. This connection between the shifting forms of fire and the visualization of fantasy occurs again, midway through the film, as a little boy watches the projections from a shadow lantern: witches, goblins, ghouls and dragons dance along the walls of his room. This vision of projected nightmares provides a visual background for the scene to follow, in which the boy's parents are murdered by the Headless Horseman. Before his arrival, there is a sudden flare-up in the fireplace which, for a flickering instant, takes his shape. The idea of fire as a site of prophecy and nightmarish images is evident in Washington Irving's original "Legend of Sleepy Hollow" where Ichabod

> was to pass long winter evenings with the old Dutch wives as they sat spinning by the fire, with a row of

apples roasting and spluttering along the hearth, and listen to their marvelous tales of ghosts and goblins, and haunted fields, and haunted brooks, and haunted bridges, and haunted houses, and particularly of the headless horseman...[6]

As well as being closely associated with storytelling and fantastic shifting forms, the image of fire has also been linked to film. In the notes collected in *On Disney*, Sergei Eisenstein explores this in detail, writing of how fire's "attractiveness", much like the metamorphoses of animated film, is due to "its omnipotence in the realm of the creation of plastic shapes and forms".[7] He elaborates on this in relation to *Snow White and the Seven Dwarfs*, writing, "The ghostly mask which prophesies to the witch in Snow White, appears in... fire. And what, if not fire, is capable of most fully conveying the dream of a flowing diversity of forms?!"[8] Connected to prophecy, storytelling, fairy tales and mutable and shifting forms, fire comes to function as an important motif of fantasy – and cinematic reflexivity – in *Sleepy Hollow*.

While the story of the Headless Horseman is associated with fairy tales and the image of fire, Ichabod is associated with the thaumatrope, or "wonder turner" [Figure 27]. This is a

Figure 27. *Sleepy Hollow*

nineteenth-century optical device made up of a circular piece of paper with a piece of string attached to either side. On one side of the thaumatrope, there is an image such as a bird or a man's face and on the other there is another image such as a cage or a hat. Spinning the thaumatrope blends the images together, making a single picture. Ichabod carries one around with him, spinning it at important moments in the film. He will dream of it as well, remembering his mother and himself as a child; working magic and then spinning a thaumatrope for his "bedtime story", Ichabod's mother offers him solace while a storm rages outside. The thaumatrope ultimately provides Ichabod's bridge between science and magic, motivating his return to Sleepy Hollow near the end of the film after he has mistakenly believed that he had solved the crimes – reflecting upon the unstable image of his thaumatrope, he realizes that Katrina's magic was a form of protection rather than a curse. In a scene midway through the film, Ichabod demonstrates this thaumatrope to Katrina who responds, "You can do magic, teach me." Still spinning the device, he tells her, "It is no magic. It is what we call optics. Separate pictures which become one when they're spinning." Drawing attention to this optical illusion where a series of images create an artificial sense of continuity, Ichabod provides a commentary not just on the thaumatrope but also on the nature of cinema and its creation of a new kind of image created through movement. In *Techniques of the Observer*, Jonathan Crary writes of the thaumatrope's significance in the history of visual culture:

> Similar phenomena had been observed in earlier centuries merely by spinning a coin and seeing both sides at the same time, but this was the first time the phenomenon was given a scientific explanation *and* a device was produced to be sold as popular entertainment. The simplicity of this "philosophical toy" made unequivocally clear both the fabricated and hallucinatory nature of its image and the rupture between perception and the object.[9]

Such a "rupture" between "perception and the object" is explained in Ichabod's concluding line in the scene: "It is truth, but truth is not always appearance." Entwining this reflection on the thaumatrope with cinema and the production of artificial images, *Sleepy Hollow* engages with the relation between film and fantasy.

As well as providing a means for Ichabod to realize the limitations of his vision and understanding, no longer to be someone "bewitched by reason" as one character describes him, the thaumatrope is part of a network of interrelated motifs that signal the limits of rationality and perception in the film. This is emphasized in the setting for his demonstration of the thaumatrope, which takes place in the ruins of Katrina's childhood home. Turning away from Katrina, who has carved a magical symbol in what remains of the fireplace, Ichabod looks out of the remnants of a window where he sees a bird. Switching from an "actual" bird to the image of one when he turns to his thaumatrope, Ichabod enters into a world of artificial and unstable images, a different world from his framed vantage point through a window. Early in his influential discussion of perspective in art, Erwin Panofsky discusses the idea of framing and watching as if through a window: "We shall speak of a fully 'perspectival' view of space… only when the entire picture has been transformed… into a 'window', and when we are meant to believe we are looking through this window into a space."[10] Panofsky sees perspectival art as creating a fundamentally different mode of relating to the work of art from what had come before:

> Through this peculiar carrying over of artistic objectivity into the domain of the phenomenal, perspective seals off religious art from the domain of the magical, where the work of art itself works the miracle, and from the realm of the dogmatic and symbolic, where the work bears witness to, or foretells, the miraculous.[11]

Viewing from the window, Ichabod holds on to vision as a comforting and stable framed view. But, as the mise-en-scène reminds us, he is clinging to a mode of vision that is in ruins. Ichabod's vantage point in realism and objectivity cannot account for the truth of Sleepy Hollow's fantasy. The film's motifs of fairy tales, fire and the illusionary optics of the thaumatrope suggest an alternative vision, one which resonates with cinema's basis in metamorphosis and magic.

Harry Potter

Almost midway through *Harry Potter and the Prisoner of Azkaban*, Professor Snape (Alan Rickman) quickly enters the classroom where Harry Potter (Daniel Radcliffe) and the other students are awaiting a lesson. He loudly shuts the door behind him and, with a wave of his wand, closes all the windows to darken the room. He pulls down a projector screen and then tells the students: "Turn to page 394." He is about to teach them about magical metamorphosis, which relates to the most recent threat to Hogwarts. Perhaps coincidentally, considering the various editions of the novel on which the film is based, page 394 in the Bloomsbury edition from 2004 contains an account of mutability; the page ends with a description of two characters casting a spell that transforms a rat into a man: "It was like watching a speeded-up film of a growing tree. A head was shooting upwards from the ground; limbs were sprouting; next moment, a man was standing where Scabbers had been, cringing and wringing his hands."[12] Comparing a metamorphosis to a time-lapse film of natural processes, J. K. Rowling draws attention to the ways in which transformation is, in some respects, cinematic.

This is developed throughout the film. From the natural form of the Whomping Willow, a tree which violently shakes off its leaves as the season changes, to the written form of the Monster Book of Monsters, which comes alive and attacks Harry Potter, objects and things in *The Prisoner of Azkaban* take on a magical animate life. Narratively motivated by the fantastic milieu in which the film is set and spectacularly motivated by the visual appeal of novel uses of computer generated imagery, the film present a world alive to change. The theme of transformation is also central to the plot of the story which, like both *Shrek 2* and *Sleepy Hollow*, has as its key narrative revelation a secret based upon mutability and magic, where two central characters turn out to be metamorphic beings.

In addition to the centrality of visual and narrative transformation, the film also shows a temporal mutability. Garrett Stewart describes how one might expect that "movies relying on computer electronics for their graphic tropes, even in the new mongrel status of a partly digitized cinema, would tend to gravitate toward themes of a more radical transmutation, or even transmogrification."[13] Stewart goes on to note that one outcome of this is evident in fantasy films that play with temporality, "spectacles in which morphing, not so much of human agents but of whole captured spaces, tends to replace superimposition as the reigning time-lapse function."[14] This trope of mutable time is central to *The Prisoner of Azkaban*; as well as depicting images of temporality, such as an enormous swinging pendulum, it also shows Harry and Hermione (Emma Watson) revisiting and changing past events with the aid of a magical necklace pendant that, when spun like a thaumatrope, rewinds time.

These engagements with mutability extend to the form of representation itself. Professor Snape's slide show uses a magic lantern with multiple slides that magically rotate; with this device, he shows a series of canonical works of art – a cave painting, a Greek vase, an Egyptian wall painting and a drawing by Leonardo da Vinci – refigured as images of lycanthropy. These reworking of well-known artworks indicate that werewolves have long existed, an important element of the plot. More than that, though, refiguring iconic works of art and then projecting them, the film shows that once static images of human bodies are actually images of metamorphosis within this cinematic world of fantasy. The magic lantern, a precinematic optical technology like the thaumatrope in *Sleepy Hollow*, is used to reveal instability and provide a lesson in mutability.

Figure 28. *Harry Potter and the Deathly Hallows Part 1*

A later film in the Harry Potter series, *Harry Potter and the Deathly Hallows Part 1* (Yates, 2010), similarly returns to earlier modes of visual presentation, telling a fairy tale called "The Tale of the Three Brothers". The tale provides a pivotal plot point, as well as an interlude of fantastic transformation. Read aloud by Hermione, the tale is shown through an animated sequence with silhouetted figures; it depicts a world made up largely of light and shadow, displaying a fluidity of forms such as Death's appearance from a pile of leaves, his creation of magical items (the "Deathly Hallows" of the film's title) and the shifting settings which imperceptibly emerge from the background [Figure 28]. Ben Hibon, the film's animation director, describes the scene, referring to the Brothers Grimm, and discusses the visual style: "The work of artist Lotte Reiniger... was another early reference. Her silhouette-style stop-motion animations are beautifully handcrafted and captured the naïve visual tone we were after."[15] Lotte Reiniger was a pivotal figure in the history of animation; beginning in the 1910s, she created silhouette animations for more than half a century with the feature-length film *The Adventures of Prince Achmed* (1926) among her most well-known works [Figure 29]. In the 1970s, she wrote about the influence of various traditions of shadow plays on her artistic practice and how she was "perpetually entertained by [their] richness of gesture, the rustic simplicity of the figures and their colouring, and the ceaseless flow of their coming and going."[16] Describing the influences for the sequence of "The Tale of the Three Brothers", Hibon draws attention to a similar context and aesthetic effect:

> We also looked at Asian shadow-play, which is visually striking, very intricate and yet so beautifully simple. The technique is basic, but the end result is particularly charming and engaging. There's something so ingenious about projecting shadows onto a simple cloth... A shadow play evokes a sense of wonder and enchantment.[17]

Like Reiniger's incorporation of earlier forms of visual culture into the modern frameworks of animated film and modernist aesthetics, *Harry Potter and the Deathly Hallows Part 1* employs the resources of digital animation to show a world of mutability

Figure 29. *The Adventures of Prince Achmed*

through reference to past animators (Reiniger) and earlier kinds of popular entertainment and fantasy. In some respects, the narrative and visual basis of the film emerges from this striking sequence. The reworking of earlier kinds of images also occurs in *Harry Potter and the Prisoner of Azkaban*, which invests animated life and mutable potential in media that once were static. For example, Sirius Black's moving face, in a "Wanted" poster and in a newspaper, is prominently displayed in the mise-en-scène in the early parts of the film. Through a series of repeated motions, his image is given an animate life, what Lev Manovich describes as a "loop" found in early devices of sequential movement or later digital manifestations.[18] Throughout the film, the paintings on the walls of Hogwarts also depict movement, with their characters watching and sometimes interacting with the world around them. At one point in the film, the animate subject within one of the paintings – the opera singer who guards the hallway – has disappeared. The students gather around this painting's torn canvas, with three gashes and an absent figure. The represented body has been, impossibly, torn from the ground of its image. The scene continues to play with perception when it cuts to a shot from behind the painting, as Dumbledore runs his hands along the torn canvas. Unlocking the figure from the ground of representation, the film plays with a transforming space in a manner that recalls trick films and féeries from more than a century earlier in a contemporary, digitally fitted cinema of transformations.

Much like *Sleepy Hollow*, the ability to confront and accept change becomes central to the lesson in mutability offered by *Harry Potter and the Prisoner of Azkaban*. In the film, metamorphosis is figured perhaps most strikingly in the sequence of images in which the nightmarish Dementors attempt to tear Harry's soul from him: through digital effects, his face is smeared, his teeth becoming clearly visible in his cries of agony and his flesh appearing as if it were lifting off his head. These images recall Francis Bacon's well-known images of the human face at points of its dissolution. They form the film's ultimate visual threat of metamorphosis and transformation – the erasure of Harry Potter.

While Harry, of course, ultimately does survive, the final image of the film visually returns to his experience of transformation by showing him at full speed upon his Quidditch broom, as he flies through the open air, his face digitally distorted and stretched in a cry of joy. The mutability lesson is clear: rather than a threat to identity and stability, metamorphosis and change can be a cause of celebration. Like more than a century of fairy-tale films, through tropes and visual motifs of transformation, the film presents a cinematic world of mutability and a cinematic world as mutability. It is little wonder that in a wider context of rapid social and technological change, films such as the ones examined in this afterword – alongside even more overtly cinephilic examples like *Hugo* (Scorsese, 2012) – are reaching back to cinema's powerful and lasting tradition of visual fantasy that expressed and imagined an experience of transformation.

Notes

Introduction

1   Miriam Hansen, "The Mass Production of the Senses: Classical Cinema as Vernacular Modernism", in *Reinventing Film Studies*, ed. Christine Gledhill and Linda Williams (London: Arnold, 2000), 333.

2   Émile Vuillermoz, "Devant l'écran: Lueurs", *Le Temps*, June 4, 1919. Unless otherwise noted, all translations from the French are my own.

3   Marie-Louise von Franz, *Shadow and Evil in Fairy Tales* (Dallas: Spring Publications Inc., 1974), 3.

4   Bruno Bettelheim, *The Uses of Enchantment: The Meaning and Importance of Fairy Tales* (London: Penguin, 1976), 27.

5   Marshall Berman, *All That Is Solid Melts into Air: The Experience of Modernity* (New York: Penguin, 1988), 15.

6   Marina Warner, *From the Beast to the Blonde: On Fairy Tales and Their Tellers* (London: Vintage, 1995), xv–xvi.

7   Jack Zipes, introduction to *The Oxford Companion to Fairy Tales*, ed. Jack Zipes (Oxford: Oxford University Press, 2000), xvii. Zipes goes on to note, "It is this sense of wondrous change that distinguished the wonder tales from other oral tales as the chronicle, the legend, the fable, the anecdote, and the myth; it is clearly the sense of wondrous change that distinguishes the *literary* fairy tale from the moral story, novella, sentimental tale, and other modern short literary genres" (xviii).

8   Neil Philip, "Creativity and Tradition in the Fairy Tale", in *A Companion to the Fairy Tale*, ed. Hilda Ellis Davidson and Anna Chaudhri (Cambridge: D.S. Brewer, 2003), 41.

9   Vachel Lindsay, *The Art of the Moving Picture* (1915, rev. ed. 1922; repr., New York: The Modern Library, 2000), 40, 87.

10 Hansen, "Mass Production of the Senses", 333.

11 Ibid., 341–42.

12 Steven Watts, *The Magic Kingdom: Walt Disney and the American Way of Life* (Columbia: University of Missouri Press, 1997), 104.

13 Ibid., 104–5.

14 Jack Zipes, *The Enchanted Screen* (London: Routledge, 2011).

15   Christine Gledhill, "Rethinking Genre", in *Reinventing Film Studies*, ed.
       Christine Gledhill and Linda Williams (London: Arnold, 2000), 229.

16   I am basing my description on the following accounts: Émile Abraham,
       "Chronique théâtrale", *Le Petit Journal*, August 17, 1863 and B. Jouvin,
       "Théâtres", *Le Figaro*, August 20, 1863.

Chapter 1

1   Théophile Gautier, *Histoire de l'art dramatique en France depuis vingt-cinq
      ans* (Brussels: Hetzel, 1858–59), 2:175.

2   This review is quoted at length in the Larousse encyclopedia's definition
      of the term "féerie": Pierre Larousse, *Grand dictionnaire universel du XIXe
      siècle* (Paris: Administration du grand dictionnaire universel, 1866–77),
      8:189. Germain Bapst quotes the same review at length in *Essai sur
      l'histoire du théâtre: la mise en scène, le décor, le costume, l'architecture, l'éclairage,
      l'hygiène* (Paris: Hachette, 1893), 568. The review was initially printed
      in "Revue de théâtres", *Journal Officiel de l'Empire Français*, August 18,
      1869.

3   Émile Abraham, "Théâtres", *Le Petit Journal*, August 16, 1869.

4   Francisque Sarcey, "Chronique théâtrale", *Le Temps*, August 23, 1869.

5   Nestor Roqueplan, "Théâtres", *Le Constitutionnel*, August 21, 1869.

6   For histories of the féerie, see especially Paul Ginisty, *La Féerie* (Paris:
      L. Michaud, [1910]); Katherine Kovács, "A History of the Féerie in
      France", *Theatre Quarterly* 8, no. 29 (Spring 1978): 29–38; Roxane Martin,
      La féerie romantique sur les scènes parisiennes, 1791–1864 (Paris: Honoré
      Champion Éditeur, 2007).

7   Other forms that fairy tales took in the nineteenth century included
      major collections and translations, new literary fairy tales, children's
      theatre, fairy paintings and illustrated works. For example, well-known
      collections of fairy tales were published in the early part of the century,
      with the Brothers Grimm publishing their first collections of fairy
      tales in the 1810s alongside literary fairy tales such as Hans Christian
      Andersen's in the 1830s. Major artists, such as George Cruikshank,
      Gustave Doré and Walter Crane, contributed to the visual culture of
      fairy tales, along with a fashion for paintings of fairies, fairylands and
      other related subjects. The scholarship on nineteenth-century fairy
      tales is large; for some excellent introductions to the field, not all
      of which focus exclusively on the nineteenth century, see especially
      Warner, *From the Beast to the Blonde*; Jack Zipes, *When Dreams Came
      True* (London: Routledge, 1999); Maria Tatar, *The Hard Facts of the
      Grimms' Fairy Tales*, 2nd ed. (Princeton: Princeton University Press,
      2003); Jane Martineau, ed., *Victorian Fairy Painting* (London: Royal
      Academy of Arts, 1997).

8   See F. W. J. Hemmings, *The Theatre Industry in Nineteenth-Century France*
      (Cambridge: Cambridge University Press, 1993).

9 An account of the most successful new plays in Paris from 1870 to 1890 placed several féeries at the top of its list while also singling out féerie revivals as among the most profitable plays ("The Drama in Paris", *The Era*, August 29, 1891).

10 Paul de Saint-Victor, "Théâtres", *La Presse*, March 11, 1862.

11 Charles Rearick, *Pleasures of the Belle Époque: Entertainment and Festivity in Turn-of-the-Century France* (New Haven: Yale University Press, 1985), 121.

12 Tom Gunning, "The Birth of Film Out of the Spirit of Modernity", in *Masterpieces of Modernist Cinema*, ed. Ted Perry (Bloomington: Indiana University Press, 2006), 27.

13 Vivian Sobchack, in the introduction to *Meta-Morphing*, discusses some of the implications of mutability. She notes, for instance, mutability's relation to: ideas of dispersed power, technoculture, the instability of identity, consumerism, the challenge to metaphysics and the uncanny (Vivian Sobchack, introduction to *Meta-Morphing: Visual Transformation and the Culture of Quick-Change*, ed. Vivian Sobchack (Minneapolis: University of Minnesota Press, 2000), xii). In *Fantastic Metamorphoses, Other Worlds*, Marina Warner explores a history of mutability in culture and art, elaborating on implications such as: "Metamorphosis as divine fantasy, as vital principle of nature, as punishment, as reprieve, as miracle, as cultural dynamic, as effect of historical meetings and clashes, as the difference that lures, as the lost idyll, as time out of time, as a producer of stories and meanings…" (Marina Warner, *Fantastic Metamorphoses, Other Worlds: Ways of Telling the Self* (Oxford: Oxford University Press, 2002), 74). These diverse implications indicate the power and complexity of the idea of metamorphosis.

14 Ginsty, *La Féerie*, 66.

15 See Peter Brooks, *The Melodramatic Imagination: Balzac, Henry James, Melodrama, and the Mode of Excess* (New Haven: Yale University Press, 1976).

16 Martin, *La féerie romantique*, 233.

17 Ibid., 233–34.

18 For reference works that refer to Gautier, see Louis Dochez, *Nouveau dictionnaire de la langue française* (Paris: C. Fouraut, 1859), 609 and Larousse, *Grand dictionnaire*, 189; for reviewers who refer to Gautier, see Auguste Vitu, *Les mille et une nuits du théâtre* (Paris: P. Ollendorff, 1888), 5:297 and Francisque Sarcey, "Théophile Gautier", in *Quarante ans de théâtre: feuilletons dramatiques* (Paris: Bibliothèque des "Annales politiques et littéraires", 1900–2), 1:91–100.

19 Gautier is referring to, respectively: *Bijou* (1838) (*Histoire de l'art dramatique* 1:101), *Les sept châteaux du diable* (1844) (ibid., 3:254) and *La corde de pendu* (1844) (ibid., 3:281).

20 Théophile Gautier, "Revue dramatique", *Le Moniteur Universel*, August 17, 1858.

21 Gautier, *Histoire de l'art dramatique*, 1:256.

22 Kovács, "History of the Féerie", 37.

23 Gautier, *Histoire de l'art dramatique*, 3:253.

24 Ferdinand Laloue, Anicet Bourgeois and Laurent, "Les pilules du diable", *Magasin théâtral: choix de pièces nouvelles jouées sur tous les théâtres de Paris* 33, 1842.

25 Hippolyte Lucas, "Théâtres", *L'Artiste* 2, no. 2 (1839): 223. Lucas goes on to mention how the play resonated with a recent work by Gautier, *Une larme du Diable*, by revelling in diabolic pleasures.

26 Gautier, *Histoire de l'art dramatique*, 1:225.

27 Ibid., 228.

28 Ibid., 226.

29 Ibid., 227.

30 Ibid.

31 Ibid., 102.

32 Gautier, *Histoire de l'art dramatique*, 3:281.

33 Ibid., 225. Gautier is rephrasing a line from the play: Sottinez says at one point, "I dream wide awake." (Laloue, Bourgeois and Laurent, "Les pilules du diable", 15).

34 Gautier, *Histoire de l'art dramatique*, 1:225.

35 Gautier, *Histoire de l'art dramatique*, 4:67.

36 Théophile Gautier, "Théâtres", *La Presse*, March 31, 1845. (This passage is omitted from the reprinted version of the review in Gautier, *Histoire de l'art dramatique*, vol. 4.)

37 Gautier, *Histoire de l'art dramatique*, 1:228.

38 See Ray Johnson, "Tricks, Traps and Transformations: Illusion in Victorian Spectacular Theatre", *Early Popular Visual Culture* 5, no. 2 (July 2007): 151–65.

39 See Erroll Sherson, *London's Lost Theatres of the Nineteenth Century* (London: John Lane the Bodley Head Ltd, 1925), 30.

40 In 1885, Augustus Harris, the manager of Drury Lane, recalled how "Mr William Beverley... invented transformation scenes, and his beautiful effects made the annual pantomime the sheet anchor of the new manager" (Augustus Harris, "'The National Theatre', 1885", in *Victorian Theatre: The Theatre in its Time*, ed. Russell Jackson (New York: New Amsterdam Books, 1989), 276).

41 Quoted in *English Plays of the Nineteenth Century. V. Pantomimes, Extravaganzas and Burlesques*, ed. Michael R. Booth (Oxford: Oxford University Press, 1976), 205.

42 J. R. Planché, *The Recollections and Reflections of J. R. Planché*, (London: Tinsley Brothers, 1872), 2:135.

43 "The Christmas Pantomimes, Burlesques, &c", *The Times*, December 28, 1858.

44 "The Christmas Pantomimes and Burlesques", *The Times*, December 27, 1859.

45 "Christmas Holiday Amusements", *Morning Chronicle*, December 28, 1857.

46 "The Christmas Pantomimes and Entertainments", *The Times*, December 28, 1857.

47 "Christmas Pantomimes, Burlesques, &c", *The Times*, December 28, 1858.

48 Raymond Knapp, *The American Musical and the Formation of National Identity* (Princeton: Princeton University Press, 2005), 20–29.

49 "Paris in New York", *Frank Leslie's Illustrated Newspaper*, October 6, 1866.

50 "Musical and Dramatic", *Frank Leslie's Illustrated Newspaper*, February 26, 1870.

51 See Paul Buczkowski, "J. R. Planché, Frederick Robson, and the Fairy Extravaganza", *Marvels & Tales: Journal of Fairy-Tale Studies* 15, no. 1 (2001): 42–65.

52 Nestor Roqueplan, "Théâtres", *Le Constitutionnel*, March 27, 1865.

53 Louis Ulbach, "Revue théâtrale", *Le Temps*, March 27, 1865.

54 "Holiday Amusements", *The Times*, December 27, 1859.

55 Gautier, *Histoire de l'art dramatique*, 1:6.

56 Théophile Gautier, *Mademoiselle de Maupin*, trans. Helen Constantine (London: Penguin, 2005), 211–13.

57 Sarcey, "Théophile Gautier", 97.

58 See Douglas Cardwell, "The Well-Made Play of Eugène Scribe", *The French Review* 56, no. 6 (May 1983): 876–84.

59 Émile Zola, *Le naturalisme au théâtre* (Paris: G. Charpentier, 1881), 358.

60 Gautier, *Histoire de l'art dramatique*, 1:215.

61 Théophile Gautier, "Théâtres", *La Presse*, June 16, 1851.

62 Gautier, *Histoire de l'art dramatique*, 1:215.

63 Théophile Gautier, "Revue dramatique", *Le Moniteur Universel*, November 21, 1859.

64 Sarcey, "Théophile Gautier", 92.

65 James Kearns, *Théophile Gautier, Orator to the Artists: Art Journalism in the Second Republic* (London: Legenda, 2007), 24.

66 Gautier, *Mademoiselle de Maupin*, 23.

67 Gautier, quoted in Larousse, *Grand dictionnaire*, 189.

68 Toril Moi, *Henrik Ibsen and the Birth of Modernism* (Oxford: Oxford University Press, 2006), 4.

69 Ibid., 67.

70 Zola, *Le naturalisme au théâtre*, 358–59.

71 Ibid., 356.

72 Marshall C. Olds, *Au pays des perroquets: Féerie théâtrale et narration chez Flaubert* (Amsterdam: Rodopi, 2001).

73 Paul Bénichou, *Romantismes français*, vol. 2 (Paris: Gallimard, 2004), 1980.

74 Ibid., 1965.

75 Charles Baudelaire, *The Flowers of Evil*, ed. Marthiel Mathews and Jackson Mathews (New York: New Directions, 1989), xxiii.

76 Rosemary Lloyd, *Baudelaire's Literary Criticism* (Cambridge: Cambridge University Press, 1981), 137. Lloyd also notes how, in Baudelaire's view, Gautier's "[m]elancholy... is counterbalanced by the skilful and harmonious evocation of plastic beauty" (138).

77 Lois Cassandra Hamrick, "Gautier as 'Seer' of the Origins of Modernity in Baudelaire", in *Baudelaire and the Poetics of Modernity*, ed. Patricia A. Ward (Nashville: Vanderbilt University Press, 2001), 36.

78 Ibid., 36–37.

79 Charles Baudelaire, "The Painter of Modern Life", in *Selected Writings on Art and Literature*, trans. P. E. Charvet (London: Penguin, 2006), 403.

80 Three feuilletons that Gautier wrote for *La Presse* about visiting the Great Exhibition of 1851 were published in September 1851 and reprinted as "L'Inde", in *Caprices et Zigzags* (Paris: V. Lecou, 1852), 232–71.

81 Lara Kriegel, "Narrating the Subcontinent in 1851: India at the Crystal Palace", in *The Great Exhibition of 1851: New Interdisciplinary Essays*, ed. Louise Purbrick (Manchester: Manchester University Press, 2001), 147.

82 Gautier, "L'Inde", 233.

83 Ibid.

84 Ibid., 239–40.

85 Ibid., 239.

86 Ibid., 240.

87 Ibid., 254.

88 Ibid., 250. Gautier also describes the display of clothes with an allusion to the multicoloured robes in *Peau d'âne:* "it realizes the marvels of the fairy tales, it makes dresses from the colour of the weather, the colour of the sun, the colour of the moon" (Ibid., 252).

89 See Kriegel, "Narrating the Subcontinent in 1851". Gautier's viewpoint is also different from the vantage point from above, as in Queen Victoria's description of the Exhibition: "We went up into the Gallery, and the sight of it from there into all the Courts, full of all sorts of objects of art, manufacture etc. had quite the effect of fairyland." (Quoted in C. R. Fay, *Palace of Industry, 1851* (London: Cambridge University Press, 1951), 146.)

90 Gautier, "L'Inde", 254.

91 Ibid.

92 Gautier, *Mademoiselle de Maupin*, 213.

93 Charles Baudelaire, "Théophile Gautier", in *Selected Writings on Art and Literature*, trans. P. E. Charvet (London: Penguin, 2006), 256. Rosemary Lloyd notes that it is "one of the very few [works] in Baudelaire's literary criticism… to open with an epigraph" (Lloyd, *Baudelaire's Literary Criticism*, 116).

94 Charles Baudelaire, "Parisian Dream", trans. Edna St. Vincent Millay, in *The Flowers of Evil*, ed. Marthiel Mathews and Jackson Mathews (New York: New Directions, 1989), 129, 131.

95 Although usually translated differently, the word "féeries" is from the original French.

96 Baudelaire, "The Painter of Modern Life", 403. Baudelaire wrote this article at around the same period as writing "Parisian Dream"; the poem is dedicated to Constantin Guys, who is one of the main subjects of "The Painter of Modern Life".

97   Théophile Gautier, "Revue dramatique", *Le Moniteur Universel*, June 1, 1863.

98   Ulbach, "Revue théâtrale", March 27, 1865; G. Vapereau, *L'année littéraire et dramatique* (Paris: L. Hachette, 1863), 5:233.

99   Jouvin, "Théâtres", August 20, 1863.

100   Nestor Roqueplan, "Théâtres", *Le Constitutionnel*, June 11, 1866; Émile Abraham, "Chronique théâtrale", August 17, 1863.

101   Théophile Gautier, "Revue dramatique", *Le Moniteur Universel*, September 11, 1860.

102   B. Jouvin, "Théâtres", *Le Figaro*, September 13, 1860.

103   Saint-Victor, "Théâtres", March 11, 1862.

104   Jouvin, "Théâtres", September 13, 1860.

105   Paul de Saint-Victor, "Théâtres", *La Presse*, September 30, 1860; Théophile Gautier, "Revue dramatique", *Le Moniteur Universel*, January 18, 1858. The kaleidoscope was a recurring comparison for Saint-Victor; see also his review of *Rothomago* ("Théâtres", March 11, 1862). For Gautier, the effect of watching such spectacles could be exhausting and overwhelming. His review of *Rothomago* begins: "The play hardly finished, and we are here leaning on a desk, beginning our review, our eyes still completely dazzled by this kaleidoscope of sets, of costumes and of tricks that we call the féerie" (Théophile Gautier, "Revue dramatique", *Le Moniteur Universel*, March 3, 1862). While being dazzled by such a "kaleidoscope" might lead to a criticism of the play's lack of narrative or meaning, Gautier adds: "What does it matter? It is enough that the tableaux replace themselves rapidly and unravel ceaselessly in new decompositions."

106   Théophile Gautier, "Revue dramatique", *Le Moniteur Universel*, June 4, 1866.

107   Louis Ulbach, "Revue théâtrale", *Le Temps*, March 11, 1862.

108   G. Vapereau, *L'année littéraire et dramatique* (Paris: L. Hachette, 1863), 7:195.

109   Louis Ulbach, "Revue théâtrale", *Le Temps*, October 12, 1863. Ulbach would elaborate on this a year later in "Revue théâtrale", *Le Temps*, September 26, 1864.

110   "Fête de nuit", *L'Exposition de Paris 1889*, July 13, 1889, 154.

111   Henri de Parville, "Exposition universelle", *Journal des Débats*, May 31, 1889; Louis Figuier, *L'Année Scientifique et Industrielle*, 1889, 381.

112   Ibid., 388.

113   Ibid., 389.

114   Eugène-Melchior de Vogüé, "À travers l'exposition", *Revue des Deux Mondes*, July 15, 1889, 449.

115   Ibid., 450.

116   "Fête de nuit", 154.

117   Parville, "Exposition universelle".

118   Vogüé, "À travers l'exposition", 451.

119   Ibid., 449.

120 "Loitering Through the Paris Exposition", *Atlantic Monthly*, March 1890, 371.
121 Ibid., 372–73.
122 Ibid., 373.
123 Ibid.
124 Ibid., 374.
125 Un monsieur de l'orchestre, "La soirée théâtrale", *Le Figaro*, July 12, 1889.
126 Francisque Sarcey, "Chronique théâtrale", *Le Temps*, July 22, 1889.
127 Hector Pessard, "Les premières", *Le Gaulois*, July 12, 1889.
128 Marcel Fouquier, "Chronique du théâtre", *La Nouvelle Revue*, July 1889, 583.
129 Ibid.
130 Ibid., 582.

Chapter 2

1   Roxane Martin discusses the version of *Le pied de mouton* which premiered in 1860, noting how certain scenes were changed to allow for more emphasis on spectacular effects, and particularly transformations (Martin, *La féerie romantique*, 401–7). For instance, like this film version, rather than having the main character arrive on a horse, he enters a scene on an enormous snail which undergoes a series of transformations.

2   Richard Abel, *The Ciné Goes to Town: French Cinema, 1896–1914* (Berkeley: University of California Press, 1994), 61; Richard Abel, *The Red Rooster Scare: Making Cinema American, 1900–1910* (Berkeley: University of California Press, 1999), 7.

3   Quoted in Henri Bousquet, ed., *Catalogue Pathé des années 1907–1909* (Paris: Henri Bousquet, 1996), 866.

4   See Abel, *Ciné Goes to Town*, 278–97.

5   Bousquet, ed., *Catalogue Pathé*. These féeries were: *Cendrillon ou la pantoufle merveilleuse*, *Ali Baba*, *Barbe bleue*, *Le pied de mouton*, *La légende de Polichinelle*, *Geneviève de Brabant*, *La bonne aventure*, *Le pêcheur de perles* and *Le secret de l'horloger*.

6   For example, Charles Musser notes the connections between *Jack and the Beanstalk* (Porter, 1902) and pantomime and magic-lantern shows (Charles Musser, *Before the Nickelodeon: Edwin S. Porter and the Edison Manufacturing Company* (Berkeley: University of California Press, 1991), 200–1); Andrew Higson examines the relation of *Alice in Wonderland* (Hepworth, 1903) with its earlier incarnation as an illustrated book (Andrew Higson, "Cecil Hepworth, *Alice in Wonderland* and the Development of the Narrative Film", in *Young and Innocent?: The Cinema in Britain, 1896–1930*, ed. Andrew Higson (Exeter: University of Exeter Press, 2002), 42–64); Ian Christie traces connections between *The Magic Sword* (Booth, 1901) and a variety of nineteenth-century entertainments, including magic theatre, fairy extravaganzas, magic-lantern shows and pantomime (Ian Christie,

"The Magic Sword: Genealogy of an English Trick Film", *Film History* 16, no. 2 (2004): 163–71).

7   For example, Georges Sadoul's writing on Méliès draws attention to the relationship between theatrical and cinematic fantasies (Georges Sadoul, *Georges Méliès* (Paris: Seghers, 1961). Katherine Kovács has traced the connections between theatrical and cinematic *féeries* in some detail in "Georges Méliès and the Féerie", in *Film Before Griffith*, ed. John L. Fell (Berkeley: University of California Press, 1983), 244–57. A. Nicholas Vardac also explores the relation between the staging of fantasy and the films of Méliès in *Stage to Screen: Theatrical Method from Garrick to Griffith* (Cambridge, MA: Harvard University Press, 1949).

8   On the relation of the cinema of attractions to the films of Méliès, see especially André Gaudreault, "Theatricality, Narrativity, and Trickality: Reevaluating the Cinema of Georges Méliès", *Journal of Popular Film and Television* 15, no. 3 (Fall 1987): 110–19; Tom Gunning, "'Now You See It, Now You Don't': The Temporality of the Cinema of Attractions", in *The Silent Cinema Reader*, ed. Lee Grieveson and Peter Krämer (London: Routledge, 2004), 41–50.

9   Abel, *Ciné Goes to Town*, 70. Abel discusses the term "transformation view" on pp. 61–62.

10   Bousquet, ed., *Catalogue Pathé*, 13.

11   Remy de Gourmont, "Epilogues: Cinématographe", trans. Richard Abel, in *French Film Theory and Criticism: A History/Anthology, 1907–1939*, vol. 1, ed. Richard Abel (Princeton: Princeton University Press, 1988), 49–50.

12   Ibid., 49.

13   Ibid., 48.

14   Remy de Gourmont, "'The Funeral of Style (1902)' and 'The Dissociation of Ideas (1900)'", in *Symbolist Art Theories: A Critical Anthology*, ed. and trans. Henri Dorra (Berkeley: University of California Press, 1994), 302.

15   Ibid., 300.

16   Ibid., 303.

17   Ibid., 304.

18   Paul Hammond notes "the metaphorical possibilities of the substitution trick" in *Marvellous Méliès* (London: Gordon Fraser, 1974), 34–35. Elizabeth Ezra discusses how transformations can be usefully situated in the context of metaphor. She writes that with substitutions, like parallel editing, "an impression of structural equivalence, or parallelism between the two subjects shown in succession, is conveyed… This structural equivalence has a poetic value, like any trope… Méliès's use of filmic substitution is metaphor in motion" (*Georges Méliès* (Manchester: Manchester University Press, 2000), 43).

19   Georges Méliès, "Cinematographic Views", trans. Stuart Liebman, in *French Film Theory and Criticism: 1907–1939*, vol.1, ed. Richard Abel (Princeton: Princeton University Press, 1988), 44. I have replaced the translation of "trolley" with "omnibus", as it is in the original French.

20   Elizabeth Ezra, for example, notes that the anecdote is "in all likelihood, apocryphal" (Ezra, *Georges Méliès*, 28).

21   André Gaudreault situates such substitution splices (or trick shots) as instances of "discontinuity", writing that "one image (*or rather part of the content*) drives out another" (André Gaudreault, "Méliès the Magician: The Magical Magic of the Magic Image", *Early Popular Visual Culture* 5, no. 2 (July 2007): 172). Such a substitution splice, Gaudreault continues, "is the complete opposite, then, of the editing found in the paradigm of narration, which – and this is a factor of continuity – is founded upon the *sequence* of shots, on their *suture.*"

22   See Ben Singer, "Modernity, Hyperstimulus and the Rise of Popular Sensationalism", in *Cinema and the Invention of Modern Life*, ed. Leo Charney and Vanessa Schwartz (Berkeley: University of California Press, 1995), 72–99.

23   Masha Belenky, "From Transit to *Transitoire*", *Nineteenth-Century French Studies* 35, no. 2 (Winter 2007): 416.

24   This has been examined particularly in terms of the *flâneuse*. See, for example, Janet Wolff, "The Invisible Flâneuse: Women and the Literature of Modernity", *Theory, Culture & Society* 2, no. 3 (1985): 37–46.

25   Paul Ricoeur, *The Rule of Metaphor*, trans. Robert Czerny with Kathleen McLaughlin and John Costello (London: Routledge, 2003), 29, 37, 38.

26   The tableaux, accompanied by their descriptive text, are reprinted in Maurice Bessy and Lo Duca, *Georges Méliès, mage: Édition du centenaire* (Paris: Pauvert, 1961), 105–15.

27   Ibid., 109.

28   Ibid.

29   Méliès, "Cinematographic Views", 36.

30   Ibid., 37.

31   Ibid., 38.

32   For a related discussion of metaphor and cinema, see Dudley Andrew, *Concepts in Film Theory* (Oxford: Oxford University Press, 1984), 94–95.

33   Ricoeur, *Rule of Metaphor*, 48.

34   Méliès, "Cinematographic Views", 39.

35   Odilon Redon, "Confessions of an Artist", in *Symbolist Art Theories: A Critical Anthology*, ed. and trans. Henri Dorra (Berkeley: University of California Press, 1994), 56.

36   Quoted in *Symbolist Art Theories*, ed. and trans. Henri Dorra, 300.

37   Redon, "Confessions of an Artist", 55.

38   Barbara Larson, *The Dark Side of Nature: Science, Society, and the Fantastic in the Work of Odilon Redon* (University Park, PA: Pennsylvania State University Press, 2005), xv.

39   Ibid., 107–8.

40   Wilhelm Grimm, "Preface to Volume 1 of the First Edition (1812)", in Maria Tatar, *The Hard Facts of the Grimms' Fairy Tales*, 2nd ed., ed. and trans. Maria Tatar (Princeton: Princeton University Press, 2003), 254–55.

41   Simon During, *Modern Enchantments: The Cultural Power of Secular Magic*

(Cambridge, MA: Harvard University Press, 2002); Marina Warner, *Phantasmagoria: Spirit Visions, Metaphors, and Media into the Twenty-first Century* (Oxford: Oxford University Press, 2006).

42   Edmond Stoullig, *Les annales du théâtre et de la musique*, 1906, 347.

43   Méliès, "Cinematographic Views", 35.

44   Martin, *La féerie romantique*, 351.

45   John Frazer examines links between the work of Doré and the films of Méliès in *Artificially Arranged Scenes* (Boston: G. K. Hall & Co., 1979), 15–16.

46   See Aimée Boutin, "'Ring Out the Old, Ring In the New': The Symbolism of Bells in Nineteenth-Century French Poetry", *Nineteenth-Century French Studies* 30, nos. 3 & 4 (Spring–Summer 2002): 277.

47   See "Complete Catalogue of Genuine and Original 'Star' Films (Moving Pictures) (1903)", in *Motion Picture Catalogs by American Producers and Distributors, 1894–1908*, ed. Charles Musser et al. (Frederick, MD: University Publications of America, 1985); "Urban Films Catalogue (June 1905)", in *A History of Early Film*, ed. Stephen Herbert (London: Routledge, 2000); Henri Bousquet, ed., *Catalogue Pathé*.

48   Ezra, *Georges Méliès*, 162.

49   Reprinted in Bessy and Duca, *Georges Méliès*, 92.

50   "No. 135, Edison Films (September 1902)", in *Motion Picture Catalogs*, ed. Charles Musser et al., 57.

51   For a discussion of the lecturer and the tableau, see Jacques Malthête, "Méliès et le conférencier", *Iris*, no. 22 (Autumn 1996): 117–29.

52   "Complete Catalogue", in *Motion Picture Catalogs*, ed. Charles Musser et al., 57.

53   "Urban Films Catalogue", in *A History of Early Film*, ed. Stephen Herbert, 283.

54   Ben Brewster and Lea Jacobs write that in addition to referring to a new setting, the term "tableau" can also refer to "the French *scène*, for a division of an act marked by the entrance or exit of a speaking character without a change of setting…" (Ben Brewster and Lea Jacobs, *Theatre to Cinema: Stage Pictorialism and Early Feature Film* (Oxford: Oxford University Press, 1997), 37). Georges Sadoul describes how the term was used to suggest the establishment of a definite composition rather than a change of scene (*Georges Méliès*, 37). Tom Gunning, in a discussion of *A Trip to the Moon*, suggests a more malleable approach, writing that "tableaux indicate key actions in the film and do not correspond to cinematic shots…" (Tom Gunning, "A Trip to the Moon", in *Film Analysis: A Norton Reader*, ed. Jeffrey Geiger and R. L. Rutsky (New York: W. W. Norton & Company, 2005), 74–75).

55   Martin, *La féerie romantique*, 256–57.

56   "Clever Moving Pictures", *Los Angeles Times* (October 11, 1903), in Abel, *Red Rooster*, 13.

57   "Urban Films Catalogue", in *A History of Early Film*, ed. Stephen Herbert, 283.

58 I am referring to the English and French catalogue descriptions; the American catalogue included an intermediary tableau titled "The Queen of Air in Her Domain", presumably to increase the sense of spectacle and add to the number of tableaux that could be advertised ("Supplement No. 5, Fairyland, (1903)", in *Motion Picture Catalogs*, ed. Charles Musser et al., 6).

59 Ibid.

60 Antonia Lant, "Haptical Cinema", *October* 74 (Fall 1995): 46.

61 Paul Ricoeur, *Time and Narrative*, trans. Kathleen McLaughlin and David Pellauer (Chicago: University of Chicago Press, 1984), 1:x.

62 Ricoeur, *Rule of Metaphor*, 114.

Chapter 3

1 Grace Kingsley, "Week's News and Views", *Los Angeles Times*, October 14, 1917.

2 "Written on the Screen", *New York Times*, June 24, 1917.

3 "Jack and the Beanstalk", *Motion Picture Magazine*, September 1917, 51.

4 "At One Theatre 60,000 See 'Jack and the Beanstalk'", *Motion Picture News*, September 8, 1917, 1482.

5 "Seventh Motion Picture News Chart of National Film Trade Conditions", *Motion Picture News*, December 30, 1916, 4192–4193.

6 Jolo, "Aladdin", *Variety*, September 28, 1917, 38.

7 "Children's Shows a Failure", *Photoplay*, February 1918, 60.

8 Jolo, "Aladdin".

9 "Jack and the Beanstalk", *Motion Picture Magazine*, 51.

10 "États-Unis", *La Cinématographie Française*, December 14, 1918, 38.

11 Lindsay, *Art of the Moving Picture*, 8.

12 Hugo Münsterberg, *The Photoplay: A Psychological Study*, in *Hugo Münsterberg on Film*, ed. Allan Langdale (1916; repr., London: Routledge, 2002), 54.

13 Émile Vuillermoz, "Devant l'écran", *Le Temps*, January 10, 1917.

14 Münsterberg quotes from Lindsay's book in *Photoplay*, 69.

15 Münsterberg, *Photoplay*, 172.

16 Allan Langdale, "S(t)imulation of Mind: The Film Theory of Hugo Münsterberg", in *Hugo Münsterberg on Film*, ed. Allan Langdale (London: Routledge, 2002), 2.

17 "Kellerman in Mermaid Role", *Los Angeles Times*, June 7, 1914; Walter H. Bernard, "Annette Kellerman as Neptune's Daughter", *Motion Picture Magazine*, July 1914, 57.

18 Langdale suggests that there were personal associations that piqued Münsterberg's interest in the film ("S(t)imulation of Mind", 7).

19 Münsterberg, *Photoplay*, 54. *Neptune's Daughter* is also described as a major example of the new feature-length film in Walter Rosenberg, "The Exhibitor's View", *Variety*, December 25, 1914, 35.

20 Münsterberg, *Photoplay*, 59.

21 Ibid., 61.
22 Ibid., 62.
23 Ibid.
24 Ibid., 63.
25 Ibid., 149.
26 In the *New York Times*, this turn away from narrative was alluded to in a review of Münsterberg's *Photoplay*, which discussed it alongside Lindsay's work. The review noted that there had been books on movies before, but these had tended to be guides for scenario writers or accounts of the struggles of filming; here, however, were "two books on the photoplay which constitute tentative criticism, which seek gropingly a basis for aesthetic appreciation of the cinema" ("Notable Books in Brief Reviews: Professor Münsterberg and Vachel Lindsay in Appreciations of the Cinema – Some Recent Publications", *New York Times*, June 4, 1916).
27 Münsterberg, *Photoplay*, 90, 63, 114, 114, 119, 127, 129. All italics in the original.
28 See Pascal Manuel Heu, *Le temps du cinéma: Émile Vuillermoz, père de la critique cinématographique, 1910–1930* (Paris: L'Harmattan, 2003).
29 Émile Vuillermoz, "Devant l'écran", *Le Temps*, December 27, 1916.
30 Émile Vuillermoz, "Devant l'écran", *Le Temps*, June 20, 1917.
31 Émile Vuillermoz, "Devant l'écran", *Le Temps*, March 28, 1917.
32 Émile Vuillermoz, "Devant l'écran", *Le Temps*, May 23, 1917.
33 Vuillermoz, "Devant l'écran", June 4, 1919.
34 Richard Abel, *French Film Theory and Criticism: A History/Anthology*, (Princeton: Princeton University Press, 1988), 1:108.
35 Ibid., 106.
36 Vuillermoz, "Devant l'écran", June 4, 1919; Émile Vuillermoz, "Devant l'écran", *Le Temps*, April 25, 1917; Émile Vuillermoz, "Devant l'écran", *Le Temps*, July 4, 1917.
37 Vuillermoz, "Devant l'écran", January 10, 1917.
38 Émile Vuillermoz, "L'écran", *Le Temps*, November 23, 1916.
39 Unlike Münsterberg, Lindsay was dismissive of *Neptune's Daughter*. He did draw attention to certain fairy-tale features, writing of its "story akin to the mermaid tale of Hans Christian Andersen", but wonders why filmmakers return to artificiality or conventions drawn from other genres in such films, "flatten[ing] out at the moment the fancy of the tiniest reader of fairy-tales begins to be alive" (Lindsay, *Art of the Moving Picture*, 66). Instead of a fairy-tale film, he sees *Neptune's Daughter* as a type of action film emphasizing the human figure in motion (ibid., 67).
40 Lindsay, *Art of the Moving Picture*, 38.
41 Ibid., 39.
42 Ibid., 110.
43 Charlie Keil, for example, writes of how, during the so-called transitional period of cinema between 1907 and 1913, "the object becomes the site of character (and hence viewer) knowledge and serves as a powerful tool of narration as well as narrative structure" (Charlie Keil, *Early American*

Cinema in Transition: Story, Style, and Filmmaking, 1907–1913 (Madison: University of Wisconsin Press, 2001), 58).

44 Lindsay, *Art of the Moving Picture*, 41.

45 On the subject of the Pathé trick film, see ibid., 40; on the subject of fairy-tale footwear, see ibid., 85.

46 Ibid., 95, 87, 39.

47 Ibid., 41, 85, 87.

48 Rachel O. Moore has discussed how this fascination with animate objects aligns Lindsay with a kind of primitivism and commodity fetishism (Rachel O. Moore, *Savage Theory: Cinema as Modern Magic* (Durham: Duke University Press, 2000), 57–58).

49 Lindsay, *Art of the Moving Picture*, 66.

50 Ibid., 162.

51 Ibid., 163.

52 Ibid., 42.

53 The Editor, "Close-Ups", *Photoplay*, September 1915, 92.

54 Minna Irving, "The True Wonderland", *Motion Picture Story Magazine*, June 1911, 13.

55 Sam J. Schlappich, "The Fairies of the Screen", *Motion Picture Magazine*, March 1915, 32.

56 Minna Irving, "The Magic Film", *Motion Picture Story Magazine*, July 1911, 50.

57 Maurice Maeterlinck, *The Blue Bird*, trans. Alexander Teixeira de Mattos (New York: Dodd, Mead & Company, 1909), 10.

58 "Maeterlinck's 'Blue Bird' Tests Ingenuity of New Theatre", *New York Times*, September 18, 1910.

59 "A Fairy Play: Maeterlinck's Pantomime Morality", *New York Daily Tribune*, December 19, 1909.

60 Edward Morton, "'The Blue Bird' at the Haymarket", *The Playgoer and Society Illustrated*, January–February 1910, 146.

61 "'The Blue Bird' A Fairy Drama", *New York Times*, April 10, 1909.

62 Henri de Régnier, "La Semaine dramatique", *Journal des Débats*, March 13, 1911. Drawing attention to some of the more successful plays in this regard, Régnier points to Shakespeare's *Tempest* and *A Midsummer Night's Dream*, Flaubert's *Le château des cœurs*, Théodore de Banville's *Riquet à la houppe*, Jean Richepin's *La belle au bois dormant* and, with some qualifications, Maeterlinck's *The Blue Bird*.

63 Adolphe Brisson, "Chronique théâtrale", *Le Temps*, March 6, 1911.

64 M. V., "Paris qui cause", *La Presse*, June 1, 1909.

65 Mae Tinée, "The Blue Bird", *Chicago Daily Tribune*, May 6, 1918.

66 Ibid. The review of the play in the *New York Daily Tribune* noted, "If in some scenes the 'atmosphere' was missing, the illusion far to seek, the cause may have been due to a poverty of invention on somebody's part, not on Maeterlinck's part, by any means" (Jeanette Dix, "The Drama: Maeterlinck's 'Blue Bird', Produced at The New Theatre", *New York Daily Tribune*, October 2, 1910). Similarly, the *New York Times* noted, "It must

have been obvious to anyone who has read the fantasy that not all of its significance and not all of its attractiveness would stand the disillusioning glare of the footlights…" ("Lovely Fantasy on New Theatre Stage", *New York Times*, October 2, 1910). Perhaps responding to such criticisms, the play's staging was altered months later "so that the unreal part of it is left unreal. To speak in plain technicalities, they have arranged the scenes now so that the entrances are masked in gray gauze, and there are no sharp, realistic lines to disturb the eyes" ("New Scene in 'Blue Bird'", *New York Times*, February 7, 1911).

67   Anthony Anderson, "Films: 'The Blue Bird', Charming Picturization of Maeterlinck's Play", *Los Angeles Times*, April 2, 1918.

68   "'The Blue Bird' a Hit on Screen, Many Opportunities in Maeterlinck's Work to Exploit Stage Magic", *New York Times*, April 1, 1918.

69   Mae Tinée, "The Blue Bird".

70   D. O. Coate, "D. O. Coate Gives Description of 'The Blue Bird' Drama", *La Crosse Tribune and Leader-Press*, March 31, 1918.

71   Victor O. Freeburg, *The Art of Photoplay Making* (1918; repr., New York: Arno, 1970). Lindsay discusses Freeburg's use of *The Art of the Moving Picture* as a textbook while teaching at Harvard (*Art of the Moving Picture*, 21–22).

72   Freeburg, *Art of Photoplay Making*, 132–33, 133.

73   "Awarded to Maeterlinck", *New York Times*, November 10, 1911.

74   Vuillermoz, "Devant l'écran", April 25, 1917.

75   Lindsay, *Art of the Moving Picture*, 172, 173, 179.

76   Dorothy Nutting, "Monsieur Tourneur", *Photoplay*, July 1918, 55.

77   Ibid., 56.

78   Jennifer L. Shaw, *Dream States: Puvis de Chavannes, Modernism and the Fantasy of France* (New Haven: Yale University Press, 2002), 175–76.

79   Mae Tinée, "The Blue Bird".

80   Shaw, *Dream States*, 11.

81   Ibid., 9.

82   Ben Carré, "Décorer l'Oiseau Bleu", *Positif*, no. 344 (October 1989): 47.

83   Maurice Maeterlinck, "The Tragical in Daily Life", in *The Treasure of the Humble*, trans. Alfred Sutro (London: Ballantyne Press, 1905), 105–6.

84   Émile Vuillermoz, "Devant l'écran", *Le Temps*, June 6, 1917.

85   Gilles Deleuze, *Cinema 2*, trans. Hugh Tomlinson and Robert Galeta (London: Continuum, 2005), 42, 43, 44.

86   Ibid., 44, 53.

87   Maeterlinck, "Tragical in Daily Life", 110.

88   Remy de Gourmont, "'Funeral of Style' and 'Dissociation of Ideas'", 305.

89   Kristin Thompson, "The International Exploration of Cinematic Expressivity", in *The Silent Cinema Reader*, ed. Lee Grieveson and Peter Krämer (London: Routledge, 2004), 254.

90   Laura Marcus, *The Tenth Muse* (Oxford: Oxford University Press, 2007), 211.

91   Émile Vuillermoz, "Devant l'écran", *Le Temps*, August 15, 1917.

92   Constantin Stanislavski, "The Mysterious World of *The Blue Bird*", in
      Stanislavski's Legacy, rev. ed., ed. and trans. Elizabeth Reynolds Hapgood
      (New York: Routledge, 1999), 160.

Chapter 4

1   Eleanor Brewster, "The Enchanted Threshold", *Motion Picture Magazine*,
      December 1917, 108.
2   Ibid., 108, 112.
3   Charles Warnerby, "Child Screen Star's Career a 20th Century Fairy Tale",
      Movie Weekly, February 10, 1923, 10.
4   Ben Singer and Charlie Keil, "Introduction: Movies in the 1910s", in
      American Cinema of the 1910s, ed. Charlie Keil and Ben Singer (Piscataway,
      NJ: Rutgers University Press, 2009), 21.
5   Gaylyn Studlar, "Oh, 'Doll Divine': Mary Pickford, Masquerade, and the
      Pedophilic Gaze", *Camera Obscura* 16, no. 3 (2001): 208. John C. Tibbetts
      situates Pickford's roles in the context of a more specific tradition, describing
      how her "growing girl" roles drew upon a popular image of childhood and
      femininity ("Mary Pickford and the American 'Growing Girl'", *Journal of
      Popular Film and Television* 29, no. 2 (2001): 50–62).
6   Studlar, "Oh, 'Doll Divine'", 216.
7   Peter Stoneley, *Consumerism and American Girls' Literature, 1860–1940*
      (Cambridge: Cambridge University Press, 2003), 2.
8   Cal York, "Studio News and Gossip East and West", *Photoplay*, November
      1924, 55. The next year, Cinderella came first in a fan poll of which film
      roles Pickford should take on next ("Pickford Role Poll", *Photoplay*, October
      1925, 45).
9   Gordon Gassaway, "What Makes a Good Screen Story?", *Picture-Play
      Magazine*, May 1923, 19.
10   Sumiko Higashi, *Cecil B. DeMille and American Culture: The Silent Era*
      (Berkeley: University of California Press, 1994), 92.
11   Vuillermoz, *Le Temps*, June 4, 1919.
12   "On the Films – and Behind: Illustrations from the 'Cinderella' Film,
      Produced by the Famous Players Company", *Photoplay*, January 1915.
13   Ibid., 141.
14   Pearl Gaddis, "The Cinderella of the Cooper-Hewitts", *Motion Picture
      Magazine*, June 1917, 27.
15   Jerome Shorey, "Do You Believe in Fairies?", *Photoplay*, September 1918,
      47.
16   H. H. Van Loan, "The Doll Lady: Disclosing the Peter Pan-ishness of
      Mary Fuller", *Motion Picture Magazine*, April 1917, 112–13.
17   For a discussion of the different versions of the story, see Janice Kirkland,
      "Frances Hodgson Burnett's Sara Crewe Through 110 Years", *Children's
      Literature in Education* 28, no. 4 (1997): 191–203.
18   Randolph Bartlett, "The Shadow Stage", *Photoplay*, January 1918, 110.

19   "Once upon a Time", *Picturegoer*, December 1921.

20   Ibid., 23.

21   "Miss Burkes's 'Peggy' Seen on the Screen", *New York Times*, January 17, 1916. The subtitle to the article highlights the fairy-tale interlude: "Actress' First Picture Is Interpolated with Scenes from Fairy Stories".

22   Higashi, *Cecil B. DeMille*, 100.

23   "Cinderella's Ball", *Picturegoer*, December 1921, 32–33.

24   Claude Fayard, "Le cinéma: La féerie", *La Semaine à Paris*, June 17, 1922, 10.

25   Pickford describes the film as pivotal in her career, helping her regain independence and artistic control, in Mary Pickford, *Sunshine and Shadow* (London: William Heinemann Ltd, 1956), 184.

26   Quoted in Deanna M. Toten Beard, "American Experimentalism, American Expressionism and Early O'Neill", in *A Companion to Twentieth-Century American Drama*, ed. David Krasner (Malden, MA: Blackwell, 2005), 55.

27   Ibid., 54.

28   Pickford, *Sunshine and Shadow*, 179.

29   On the image of the "social butterfly", see Janet Staiger, *Bad Women: Regulating Sexuality in Early American Cinema* (Minneapolis: University of Minnesota Press, 1995).

30   Tibbetts notes that this scene "prefigur[es] the counterfeiting scene in Fritz Lang's *Dr Mabuse, the Gambler*, made five years later" ("Mary Pickford", 57).

31   Richard deCordova, *Picture Personalities: The Emergence of the Star System in America* (Champaign, IL: University of Illinois Press, 2001), 12.

32   "Miss Clark in Film Farce", *New York Times*, November 20, 1916; "Here Are All the Winners of the Great Popular Player Contest", *Motion Picture Magazine*, February 1917. Pickford received 462,190 votes, Bushman 411,800 and Clark 410,820 (ibid., 128).

33   William Curtis Nunn, *Marguerite Clark, America's Darling of Broadway and the Silent Screen* (Fort Worth: Texas Christian University Press, 1981).

34   C. I. D., "Knotty Problems for the Stage Manager in 'The Blue Bird'", *New York Daily Tribune*, September 4, 1910.

35   Marguerite Clark, "Filming Fairy Plays", *Motion Picture Magazine*, February 1918, 99–100. Some of the passages about another Paramount film from the time suggest a larger studio aim than simply marketing Clark's film, perhaps indicating outside input.

36   George Vaux Bacon, "Little Miss Practicality", *Photoplay*, March 1916, 37, 40.

37   Edward S. O'Reilly, "She Says to Me, Says She—", *Photoplay*, January 1918, 49, 50.

38   Ibid., 51, 51, 52.

39   Clark, "Filming Fairy Plays", 102, 104.

40   "Fairyland Busy Making Little Words of Big Ones", *New York Times*, November 10, 1912.

41   Clark, "Filming Fairy Plays", 101.

42   Ibid., 99.
43   Ibid., 162.
44   Ibid., 103, 102, 102.

Chapter 5

1   Vachel Lindsay, *The Progress and Poetry of the Movies*, ed. Myron Lounsbury (1925; repr., Lanham: Scarecrow Press, 1995), 166, 155.

2   Émile Vuillermoz, "Courrier cinématographique: Le Voleur de Bagdad", *Le Temps*, September 20, 1924.

3   Laurence Reid, "The Picture of the Month", *Motion Picture Classic*, June 1924, 47.

4   Ibid.

5   *The Thief of Bagdad* also drew upon an artistic context outside of film; for example, Gaylyn Studlar has explored its relation to the Ballets Russes (Gaylyn Studlar, "Douglas Fairbanks: Thief of the Ballets Russes", in *Bodies of the Text: Dance as Theory, Literature as Dance*, ed. Ellen W. Goellner and Jacqueline Shea Murphy (New Brunswick, NJ: Rutgers University Press, 1994), 107–24).

6   René Clair, *Cinéma d'hier, cinéma d'aujourd'hui* (Paris: Gallimard, 1970), 96.

7   For a discussion of "Orientalism" in film, see especially Ella Shohat, "Gender and Culture of Empire: Towards a Feminist Ethnography of the Cinema", in *Visions of the East: Orientalism in Film*, ed. Matthew Bernstein and Gaylyn Studlar (London: I.B.Tauris, 1997), 19–66; Robert Irwin, "A Thousand and One Nights at the Movies", *Middle Eastern Literatures* 7, no. 2 (July 2004): 223–33. *The Thief of Bagdad* was indebted to *Destiny* and *Waxworks* for more than just its Arabian spectacle; it used a magic carpet in a similar manner to both films. A similar use of exotic locales and subjects was evident in French cinema of the 1920s, with productions drawing upon what Richard Abel characterizes as "the *conte arabe* tradition of *A Thousand and One Nights*" (Richard Abel, *French Cinema: The First Wave, 1915–1929* (Princeton: Princeton University Press, 1984), 151).

8   Other examples of fairy-tale films from the period include *Peter Pan* (Brenon, 1924), *The Wizard of Oz* (Semon, 1925) and *A Kiss for Cinderella* (Brenon, 1925). Early films directed by René Clair (*The Imaginary Voyage* (1925)), Lotte Reiniger (*The Adventures of Prince Achmed* (1926)), Jean Renoir (*La petite marchande d'allumettes* (1928)) and Luis Buñuel (*Un chien andalou* (1929)) also invoked fairy tales in their explorations of film fantasy.

9   "The Screen: Arabian Nights Satire", *New York Times*, March 19, 1924.

10   William A. Johnston, "The Thief of Bagdad", *Motion Picture News*, April 5, 1924.

11   "Our Honours List: A Guide to the Best Films of the Month", *Pictures and the Picturegoer*, November 1924, 12.

12   Ibid.

13   *The Arabian Nights: Tales From a Thousand and One Nights*, trans. Richard
      Burton (New York: Modern Library, 2001), p. 3. My emphasis.

14   Ibid., xxiv.

15   Ibid., xxiii.

16   Danny, "Praise", *The Film Daily*, March 20, 1924, 1.

17   "Film Banquet is Dazzling", *Los Angeles Times*, July 11, 1924.

18   "The New Pictures", *Time*, March 31, 1924.

19   Adele Whitely Fletcher, "Across the Silversheet", *Motion Picture Magazine*,
      June 1924, 53.

20   "Film Banquet is Dazzling", *Los Angeles Times*.

21   Fletcher, "Across the Silversheet", 53; Danny, "Bagdad", *The Film Daily*,
      March 19, 1924, 1.

22   Reid, "Picture of the Month", 47.

23   Ibee, "Thief of Bagdad", *Variety*, March 26, 1924, 26.

24   For an account of the illustrated gift book, see Michael Felmingham, *The
      Illustrated Gift Book, 1880–1930* (Aldershot: Scolar Press, 1988).

25   Laurence Housman, preface to *Arabian Nights: A Selection of Tales from the
      Book of a Thousand and One Nights* (1907; repr., Ware: Omega, 1985), ix.

26   Ibid.

27   Kate Douglas Wiggin, preface to *Arabian Nights, Their Best-Known Tales*,
      ed. Kate Douglas Wiggin and Nora A. Smith (1909; repr., New York:
      Atheneum, 1993), ix.

28   "Police Clear Jam at Movie Premier", *New York Times*, March 19, 1924.

29   "The Screen: Arabian Nights Satire", *New York Times*.

30   "Gest Will Get Young Fortune Handling Fairbanks' Picture", *Variety*,
      March 5, 1924, 16.

31   Kenneth Macgowan, "The Play of the Month", *Motion Picture Classic*,
      April 1924, 47.

32   Laurence Reid, "The Thief of Bagdad – A Fantasy", *Motion Picture News*,
      March 29, 1924, 1415.

33   See Richard Koszarski, *An Evening's Entertainment: The Age of the Silent
      Feature Picture, 1915–1928* (Berkeley: University of California Press,
      1990), 9–25.

34   E. C. A. Bullock, "Theater Entrances and Lobbies (1925)", in *Moviegoing
      in America: A Sourcebook in the History of Film Exhibition*, ed. Gregory A.
      Waller (Malden, MA: Blackwell, 2002), 104.

35   John F. Barry and Epes W. Sargent, "Building Theatre Patronage (1927)",
      in *Moviegoing in America: A Sourcebook in the History of Film Exhibition*,
      ed. Gregory A. Waller (Malden, MA: Blackwell, 2002), 110.

36   Giuliana Bruno, *Atlas of Emotion: Journeys in Art, Architecture, and Film*
      (New York: Verso, 2002), 48–49.

37   Stephen Fox, *The Mirror Makers: A History of American Advertising and
      its Creators* (New York: Illini Books, 1997), 70.

38   T. J. Jackson Lears, *Fables of Abundance: A Cultural History of Advertising
      in America* (New York: Basic Books, 1994), 212–13.

39   Léon Moussinac, "Notre point de vue: L'atmosphère", *L'Humanité*, December 23, 1932, 4.

40   William Leach, *Land of Desire: Merchants, Power, and the Rise of a New American Culture* (New York: Vintage Books, 1994), 9.

41   Ibid.

42   See, for example, Holly Edwards, "A Million and One Nights", in *Noble Dreams, Wicked Pleasures: Orientalism in America, 1870–1930*, ed. Holly Edwards (Princeton: Princeton University Press, 2000), 11–57.

43   Elaine S. Abelson, *When Ladies Go A-Thieving: Middle-Class Shoplifters in the Victorian Department Store* (Oxford: Oxford University Press, 1989), 5.

44   For a discussion of the importance of the circulation of customers, see Leach, *Land of Desire*, 73–74.

45   Lindsay, *Progress and Poetry*, 201.

46   Raoul Walsh, *Each Man in His Time: The Life Story of a Director* (New York: Farrar, Straus and Giroux, 1974), 166.

47   Lindsay, *Progress and Poetry*, 190–91.

48   A Scenario Writer, "The Evolution of a Picture", *New York Times*, March 16, 1924.

49   Leach, *Land of Desire*, 72.

50   "Doug Fairbanks Brings Romance of Arabian Nights", *Oakland Tribune*, November 3, 1924.

51   For a discussion of the importance of the "central decorative idea", see Leach, *Land of Desire*, 298–348.

52   Gaylyn Studlar, *This Mad Masquerade: Stardom and Masculinity in the Jazz Age* (New York: Columbia University Press, 1996), 85.

53   Leora Auslander, *Taste and Power: Furnishing Modern France* (Berkeley: University of California Press, 1996), 298.

54   Ibid., 302. Auslander quotes Honoré de Balzac in her epigraph to the discussion: "[Collecting] is the hunt for masterpieces!… one finds onseself face to face with adversaries who defend the quarry! it's trick against trick!… it's like in fairy tales, a princess guarded by sorcerors!" (Ibid., 296).

55   T. J. Jackson Lears, "From Salvation to Self-Realization: Advertising and the Therapeutic Roots of the Consumer Culture, 1880–1930", in *The Culture of Consumption: Critical Essays in American History, 1880–1980*, ed. Richard Wightman Fox and T. J. Jackson Lears (New York: Pantheon Books, 1983), 4.

56   "General Advance Stories about the Picture", in *The Thief of Bagdad* press book, British Film Institute, London.

57   "How Douglas Fairbanks Produces His Pictures", *New York Times*, June 7, 1925.

58   Edwin Schallert, "Doug Rubs the Magic Lamp", *Picture-Play Magazine*, August 1923, 44.

59   Marjorie Mayne, "A Dream Princess", *Pictures and the Picturegoer*, December 1924, 58.

60   Ibid., 59.

61   Ibid., 58.

62   Charles Henry Steele, "Spotlight for Julanne", *Picture-Play Magazine*, December 1923, 82.

63   Kathleen G. Donohue, *Freedom from Want: American Liberalism and the Idea of the Consumer* (Baltimore: Johns Hopkins University Press, 2003), 115.

64   For an account of the speech, see "Coolidge Praises Advertising as Aid to Our Prosperity", *New York Times*, October 28, 1926. Lears notes that the speech was written by the advertising executive Bruce Barton (Lears, *Fables of Abundance*, 224).

65   "Coolidge", *New York Times*.

66   Ibid.

67   Lindsay, *Progress and Poetry*, 157.

68   Ibid., 166, 176, 178, 176.

69   Ibid., 180, 180, 183, 183, 184.

70   Lears, *Fables of Abundance*, 198.

71   Ibid., 41–42.

72   Reid, "Picture of the Month", 92.

73   "Two Feature Stories and Paragraphs During Run of Picture", in *The Thief of Bagdad* press book, British Film Institute, London. This was a "feature story, to be signed by a fictitious person, who will represent the Filmland correspondent of the paper accepting it".

74   "Film Efforts Rewarded", *Los Angeles Times*, February 18, 1929.

75   Jeanine Basinger, *Silent Stars* (New York: Alfred A. Knopf, 1999), 441.

76   Cynthia Felando, "Clara Bow is *It*", in *Film Stars: Hollywood and Beyond*, ed. Andy Willis (Manchester: Manchester University Press, 2004), 19.

77   Marsha Orgeron, "Making *It* in Hollywood: Clara Bow, Fandom, and Consumer Culture", *Cinema Journal* 42, no. 4 (Summer 2003): 78.

78   See Amelie Hastie, *Cupboards of Curiosity: Women, Recollection, and Film History* (Durham: Duke University Press, 2007), 19–71.

79   Lori Landay, "The Flapper Film: Comedy, Dance, and Jazz Age Kinaesthetics", in *A Feminist Reader in Early Cinema*, ed. Jennifer M. Bean and Diane Negra (Durham: Duke University Press, 2002), 224.

80   Ibid., 241.

81   Leslie Midkiff DeBauche, *Reel Patriotism: The Movies and World War I* (Madison: University of Wisconsin Press, 1997), 182.

82   Mordaunt Hall, "An Intelligent Pictorial Comedy", *New York Times*, October 30, 1927.

83   "Glamour or Realism", *Picturegoer*, May 1928, 14.

84   Marshall Berman, "Women and the Metamorphoses of Times Square", *Dissent* 48, no. 4 (September 2001), http://www.dissentmagazine.org/article/?article=906.

85   For a discussion of the motif of viewing in *Sunrise*, see Lucy Fischer, *Sunrise* (London: British Film Institute, 1998), 62–65.

Chapter 6

1   See Robin Allan, *Walt Disney and Europe* (Bloomington: Indiana University Press, 1999).
2   Paul Wells, *Understanding Animation* (London: Routledge, 1998), 76.
3   Norman M. Klein, "Animation and Animorphs", in *Meta-Morphing: Visual Transformation and the Culture of Quick-Change*, ed. Vivian Sobchack (Minneapolis: University of Minnesota Press, 2000), 28.
4   Wells, *Understanding Animation*, 75.
5   Émile Vuillermoz, "Chronique cinématographique", *Le Temps*, February 23, 1935.
6   Vuillermoz would use a similar rhetoric in other descriptions of Disney films and animated films, characterizing *King Neptune* (Gillett, 1932), for example, as an "underwater féerie" (Émile Vuillermoz, "Le Cinéma. Chronique. Indications", *Le Temps*, January 14, 1933).
7   J. Michael Barrier, *Hollywood Cartoons: American Animation in its Golden Age* (Oxford: Oxford University Press, 1999), 124.
8   Sergei Eisenstein, "On Disney", trans. Alan Y. Upchurch, in *The Eisenstein Collection*, ed. Richard Taylor (London: Seagull Books, 2006), 88.
9   Erwin Panofsky, "Style and Medium in the Motion Pictures", in *The Visual Turn: Classical Film Theory and Art History*, ed. Angela Dalle Vacche (New Brunswick, NJ: Rutgers University Press, 2002), 83.
10 Tino Balio, *Grand Design: Hollywood as a Modern Business Enterprise, 1930–1939* (New York: Charles Scribner's Sons, 1993), 179.
11 "Mouse & Man", *Time*, December 27, 1937.
12 Karen Merritt, "Marguerite Clark as America's Snow White: The Resourceful Orphan Who Inspired Walt Disney", *Griffithiana* 64 (October 1998): 17.
13 Ibid., 17–18.
14 Lindsay, *Art of the Moving Picture*, 34–35.
15 "Fairyland Busy Making Little Words of Big Ones", *New York Times*.
16 Robin Allan, drawing on Jonathan Rosenbaum's observation, links the presentation of the book to a German film released a few years earlier, *The Blue Light* (Riefenstahl, 1932), which begins and ends its main story with an iconographically similar image (Allan, *Walt Disney and Europe*, 45).
17 Tatar, *The Hard Facts of the Grimms' Fairy Tales*, 108–9.
18 Ibid., 109–10.
19 Ruth Bottigheimer, "The Ultimate Fairy Tale: Oral Transmission in a Literary World", in *A Companion to the Fairy Tale*, ed. Hilda Ellis Davidson and Anna Chaudhri (Cambridge: D. S. Brewer, 2003), 69.
20 Roger Chartier, *The Cultural Uses of Print in Early Modern France*, trans. Lydia G. Cochrane (Princeton: Princeton University Press, 1987).
21 Ibid., 5.
22 Wanda Gág, *Tales from Grimm*, trans. and illus. Wanda Gág (1936; repr., London: Faber, 1973), 17.

23   Lears, *Fables of Abundance*, 383.

24   Megan Benton, *Beauty and the Book: Fine Editions and Cultural Distinction in America* (New Haven: Yale University Press, 2000), 3.

25   Ibid., 192.

26   Ibid., 37.

27   Watts, *Magic Kingdom*, 167.

28   Lewis Jacobs, *The Rise of the American Film* (1939; repr., New York: Teachers College Press, 1968), 504–5.

29   Benton, *Beauty and the Book*, 167–68.

30   Douglas E. Schoenherr, "A Note on Burne-Jones's 'Pocket Cathedral' and Ruskin", *Journal of William Morris Studies* 15, no. 4 (Summer 2004): 91.

31   Quoted in Schoenherr, "A Note on Burne-Jones's 'Pocket Cathedral'", 92.

32   Walter Crane, *Of the Decorative Illustration of Books Old and New* (London: Bell, 1921), 184.

33   In a discussion of Eisenstein's writing on this subject, Giuliana Bruno describes how "the relation between film and architectural ensemble involves an embodiment, for it is based on the inscription of an observer in the field. Such an observer is not a static contemplator, a fixed gaze, a disembodied eye/I. She is a physical entity, a moving spectator, a body making journeys in space" (Bruno, *Atlas of Emotion*, 56).

34   Eleanor Byrne and Martin McQuillan describe the film as a "paean to all things domestic" (Eleanor Byrne and Martin McQuillan, *Deconstructing Disney* (London: Pluto, 1999), 59).

35   Anne Carroll Moore, "The Three Owls' Notebook", *The Horn Book* 14, no. 1 (January–February 1938): 32.

36   Anne Carroll Moore, "The Three Owls' Notebook", *The Horn Book* 14, no. 2 (March–April 1938): 91.

37   Ibid., 92.

38   Bertha Mahony Miller, "Twenty Years of Children's Books", in *A Horn Book Sampler: On Children's Books and Reading*, ed. Norma R. Fryatt (Boston: The Horn Book, 1959), 105.

39   Ibid., 106.

40   Arjun Appadurai, "Introduction: Commodities and the Politics of Value", in *The Social Life of Things: Commodities in Cultural Perspective*, ed. Arjun Appadurai (Cambridge: Cambridge University Press, 1986), 48.

41   Ibid., 44–45.

42   Allan, *Walt Disney and Europe*, 46.

43   Lears, *Fables of Abundance*, 65.

44   Ibid., 102, 95.

45   Roland Marchand, *Advertising the American Dream: Making Way for Modernity, 1920–1940* (Berkeley: University of California Press, 1985), 276.

46   Leach, *Land of Desire*, 63.

47   Quoted in Louise Krasniewicz, *Walt Disney: A Biography* (Santa Barbara: Greenwood, 2010), 69.

48   Charles Eckert, "ShirleyTemple and the House of Rockefeller", in *Stardom: Industry of Desire*, ed. Christine Gledhill (London: Routledge, 1991), 60.

49   Ibid., 68.

50   Gaylyn Studlar, *In the Realm of Pleasure: Von Sternberg, Dietrich, and the Masochistic Aesthetic* (Urbana: University of Illinois Press, 1988), 95.

51   Marcia Landy, *Cinematic Uses of the Past* (Minneapolis: University of Minnesota Press, 1996), 177.

52   Studlar, *In the Realm of Pleasure*, 94.

53   Landy, *Cinematic Uses of the Past*, 151–90.

54   Quoted in Landy, *Cinematic Uses of the Past*, 155–56.

55   I am referring to: Diane Waldman, "'At Last I Can Tell It to Someone!': Feminine Point of View and Subjectivity in the Gothic Romance Film of the 1940s", *Cinema Journal* 23, no. 2 (Winter 1983): 29–40; Mary Ann Doane, *The Desire to Desire: The Woman's Film of the 1940s* (Bloomington: Indiana University Press, 1987); Maria Tatar, *Secrets Beyond the Door: The Story of Bluebeard and His Wives* (Princeton: Princeton University Press, 2004).

56   Tatar, *Secrets Beyond the Door*, 92.

57   See Helen Hanson, *Hollywood Heroines: Women in Film Noir and the Female Gothic Film* (London: I.B.Tauris, 2007), 69–77; Tatar, *Secrets Beyond the Door*, 82–83.

58   Tania Modleski, *The Women Who Knew Too Much: Hitchcock and Feminist Theory* (New York: Routledge, 1988), 45.

59   Tatar, *Secrets Beyond the Door*, 94.

60   Anthony Giddens, *The Consequences of Modernity* (Stanford: Stanford University Press, 1990), 38.

61   Ibid., 37.

62   Miriam Hansen, "Mass Production of the Senses", 343.

63   Raymond Knapp, *The American Musical and the Performance of Personal Identity* (Princeton: Princeton University Press, 2006), 126.

Afterword

1   See, for example, Margaret Atwood, *Bluebeard's Egg* (Toronto: McClelland and Stewart, 1983) and Angela Carter, *Burning Your Boats: The Collected Short Stories* (New York: Penguin, 1997).

2   Cristina Bacchilega, *Postmodern Fairy Tales: Gender and Narrative Strategies* (Philadelphia: University of Pennsylvania Press, 1997), 3.

3   Tom Shippey, "Rewriting the Core: Transformations of the Fairy Tale in Contemporary Writing", in *A Companion to the Fairy Tale*, ed. Hilda Ellis Davidson and Anna Chaudhri (Cambridge: D. S. Brewer, 2003), 253. Shippey argues that critics and authors in the 1980s (although reaching back a decade earlier) worked to make the ideological mechanisms of fairy tales transparent, their social force suggestive and their tales pliable (256–58).

4   Lindsay, *Art of the Moving Picture*, 40.
5   Alison McMahan, *The Films of Tim Burton: Animating Live Action in Contemporary Hollywood* (New York: Continuum, 2005), 71.
6   Washington Irving, *The Legend of Sleepy Hollow & Other Stories* (London: Minster Classics, 1968), 22.
7   Eisenstein, "On Disney", 108.
8   Ibid., 106.
9   Jonathan Crary, *Techniques of the Observer: On Vision and Modernity in the Nineteenth Century* (Cambridge, MA: MIT Press, 1990), 106.
10   Erwin Panofsky, *Perspective as Symbolic Form*, trans. Christopher S. Wood (New York: Zone Books, 1991), 27.
11   Ibid., 72.
12   J. K. Rowling, *Harry Potter and the Prisoner of Azkaban* (Bloomsbury: London, 2004), 394–95.
13   Garrett Stewart, *Framed Time: Toward a Postfilmic Cinema* (Chicago: University of Chicago Press, 2007), 7.
14   Ibid.
15   Ben Hibon, "Lights, Camera…", *Los Angeles Times*, January 31, 2011.
16   Lotte Reiniger, *Shadow Theatres and Shadow Films* (London: Batsford, 1970), 30.
17   Hibon, "Lights, Camera…"
18   Lev Manovich, *The Language of New Media* (Cambridge, MA: MIT Press, 2001), 314–22.

Bibliography

Abel, Richard. *French Cinema: The First Wave, 1915–1929*. Princeton: Princeton University Press, 1984.

Abel, Richard. *French Film Theory and Criticism: A History/Anthology*. Vol. 1. Princeton: Princeton University Press, 1988.

Abel, Richard. *The Ciné Goes to Town: French Cinema, 1896–1914*. Berkeley: University of California Press, 1994.

Abel, Richard. *The Red Rooster Scare: Making Cinema American, 1900–1910*. Berkeley: University of California Press, 1999.

Abelson, Elaine S. *When Ladies Go A-Thieving: Middle-Class Shoplifters in the Victorian Department Store*. Oxford: Oxford University Press, 1989.

Abraham, Émile. "Chronique théâtrale". *Le Petit Journal*, August 17, 1863.

Abraham, Émile. "Théâtres". *Le Petit Journal*, August 16, 1869.

Allan, Robin. *Walt Disney and Europe*. Bloomington: Indiana University Press, 1999.

Anderson, Anthony. "Films: 'The Blue Bird', Charming Picturization of Maeterlinck's Play". *Los Angeles Times*, April 2, 1918.

Andrew, Dudley. *Concepts in Film Theory*. Oxford: Oxford University Press, 1984.

Appadurai, Arjun. "Introduction: Commodities and the Politics of Value". In *The Social Life of Things: Commodities in Cultural Perspective*, edited by Arjun Appadurai, 3–63. Cambridge: Cambridge University Press, 1986.

The Arabian Nights: Tales From a Thousand and One Nights. Translated by Richard Burton. New York: Modern Library, 2001.

Atlantic Monthly. "Loitering Through the Paris Exposition". March 1890.

Atwood, Margaret. *Bluebeard's Egg*. Toronto: McClelland and Stewart, 1983.

Auslander, Leora. *Taste and Power: Furnishing Modern France*. Berkeley: University of California Press, 1996.

Bacchilega, Cristina. *Postmodern Fairy Tales: Gender and Narrative Strategies*. Philadelphia: University of Pennsylvania Press, 1997.

Bacon, George Vaux. "Little Miss Practicality". *Photoplay*, March 1916.

Balio, Tino. *Grand Design: Hollywood as a Modern Business Enterprise, 1930–1939*. New York: Charles Scribner's Sons, 1993.

Bapst, Germain. *Essai sur l'histoire du théâtre: la mise en scène, le décor, le costume, l'architecture, l'éclairage, l'hygiène*. Paris: Hachette, 1893.

Barrier, J. Michael. *Hollywood Cartoons: American Animation in its Golden Age*. Oxford: Oxford University Press, 1999.

Barry, John F. and Epes W. Sargent. "Building Theatre Patronage (1927)". In *Moviegoing in America: A Sourcebook in the History of Film Exhibition*, edited by Gregory A. Waller, 110–15. Malden, MA: Blackwell, 2002.

Bartlett, Randolph. "The Shadow Stage". *Photoplay*, January 1918.

Basinger, Jeanine. *Silent Stars*. New York: Alfred A. Knopf, 1999.

Baudelaire, Charles. *The Flowers of Evil*. Edited by Marthiel Mathews and Jackson Mathews. New York: New Directions, 1989.

Baudelaire, Charles. "The Painter of Modern Life". In *Selected Writings on Art and Literature*, translated by P. E. Charvet, 390–435. London: Penguin, 2006.

Baudelaire, Charles. "Théophile Gautier". In *Selected Writings on Art and Literature*, translated by P. E. Charvet, 256–284. London: Penguin, 2006.

Beard, Deanna M. Toten. "American Experimentalism, American Expressionism and Early O'Neill". In *A Companion to Twentieth-Century American Drama*, edited by David Krasner, 53–68. Malden, MA: Blackwell, 2005.

Belenky, Masha. "From Transit to *Transitoire*". *Nineteenth-Century French Studies* 35, no. 2 (Winter 2007): 408–23.

Bénichou, Paul. *Romantismes français*. Vol. 2. Paris: Gallimard, 2004.

Benton, Megan. *Beauty and the Book: Fine Editions and Cultural Distinction in America*. New Haven: Yale University Press, 2000.

Berman, Marshall. *All That Is Solid Melts into Air: The Experience of Modernity*. New York: Penguin, 1988.

Berman, Marshall. "Women and the Metamorphoses of Times Square". *Dissent* 48, no. 4. September 2001. http://www.dissentmagazine.org/article/?article=906.

Bernard, Walter H. "Annette Kellerman as Neptune's Daughter". *Motion Picture Magazine*, July 1914.

Bessy, Maurice and Lo Duca. *Georges Méliès, mage: Édition du centenaire*. Paris: Pauvert, 1961.

Bettelheim, Bruno. *The Uses of Enchantment: The Meaning and Importance of Fairy Tales*. London: Penguin, 1976.

Booth, Michael R., ed. *English Plays of the Nineteenth Century. V. Pantomimes, Extravaganzas and Burlesques*. Oxford: Oxford University Press, 1976.

Bottigheimer, Ruth. "The Ultimate Fairy Tale: Oral Transmission in a Literary World". In *A Companion to the Fairy Tale*, edited by Hilda Ellis Davidson and Anna Chaudhri, 57–70. Cambridge: D. S. Brewer, 2003.

Bousquet, Henri, ed. *Catalogue Pathé des années 1907–1909*. Paris: Henri Bousquet, 1996.

Boutin, Aimée. "'Ring Out the Old, Ring In the New': The Symbolism of Bells in Nineteenth-Century French Poetry". *Nineteenth-Century French Studies* 30, nos. 3 & 4 (Spring–Summer 2002): 267–81.

Brewster, Ben and Lea Jacobs. *Theatre to Cinema: Stage Pictorialism and Early Feature Film*. Oxford: Oxford University Press, 1997.

Brewster, Eleanor. "The Enchanted Threshold". *Motion Picture Magazine*, December 1917.

Brisson, Adolphe. "Chronique théâtrale". *Le Temps*, March 6, 1911.

Brooke, Maude. "Her Health is Her Fortune". *Motion Picture Magazine*, November 1917.

Brooks, Peter. *The Melodramatic Imagination: Balzac, Henry James, Melodrama, and the Mode of Excess*. New Haven: Yale University Press, 1976.

Bruno, Giuliana. *Atlas of Emotion: Journeys in Art, Architecture, and Film*. New York: Verso, 2002.

Buczkowski, Paul. "J. R. Planché, Frederick Robson, and the Fairy Extravaganza". *Marvels & Tales: Journal of Fairy-Tale Studies* 15, no. 1 (2001): 42–65.

Bullock, E. C. A. "Theater Entrances and Lobbies (1925)". In *Moviegoing in America: A Sourcebook in the History of Film Exhibition*, edited by Gregory A. Waller, 104–105. Malden, MA: Blackwell, 2002.

Byrne, Eleanor and Martin McQuillan. *Deconstructing Disney*. London: Pluto, 1999.

C. I. D. "Knotty Problems for the Stage Manager in 'The Blue Bird'". *New York Daily Tribune*, September 4, 1910.

Cardwell, Douglas. "The Well-Made Play of Eugène Scribe". *The French Review* 56, no. 6 (May 1983): 876–84.

Carré, Ben. "Décorer l'Oiseau Bleu". *Positif*, no. 344 (October 1989): 46–48.

Carter, Angela. *Burning Your Boats: The Collected Short Stories*. New York: Penguin, 1997.

Chartier, Roger. *The Cultural Uses of Print in Early Modern France*. Translated by Lydia G. Cochrane. Princeton: Princeton University Press, 1987.

Christie, Ian. "The Magic Sword: Genealogy of an English Trick Film". *Film History* 16, no. 2 (2004): 163–71.

Clair, René. *Cinéma d'hier, cinéma d'aujourd'hui*. Paris: Gallimard, 1970.

Clark, Marguerite. "Filming Fairy Plays". *Motion Picture Magazine*, February 1918.

Coate, D. O. "D. O. Coate Gives Description of 'The Blue Bird' Drama". *La Crosse Tribune and Leader-Press*, March 31, 1918.

Crane, Walter. *Of the Decorative Illustration of Books Old and New*. London: Bell, 1921.

Crary, Jonathan. *Techniques of the Observer: On Vision and Modernity in the Nineteenth Century*. Cambridge, MA: MIT Press, 1990.

Danny. "Bagdad". *The Film Daily*, March 19, 1924.

Danny. "Praise". *The Film Daily*, March 20, 1924.

DeBauche, Leslie Midkiff. *Reel Patriotism: The Movies and World War I*. Madison: University of Wisconsin Press, 1997.

deCordova, Richard. *Picture Personalities: The Emergence of the Star System in America*. Champaign, IL: University of Illinois Press, 2001.

Deleuze, Gilles. *Cinema 2*. Translated by Hugh Tomlinson and Robert Galeta. London: Continuum, 2005.

Dix, Jeanette. "The Drama: Maeterlinck's 'Blue Bird,' Produced at The New Theatre". *New York Daily Tribune*, October 2, 1910.

Doane, Mary Ann. *The Desire to Desire: The Woman's Film of the 1940s*. Bloomington: Indiana University Press, 1987.

Dochez, Louis. *Nouveau dictionnaire de la langue française*. Paris: C. Fouraut, 1859.

Donohue, Kathleen G. *Freedom from Want: American Liberalism and the Idea of the Consumer*. Baltimore: Johns Hopkins University Press, 2003.

Dorra, Henri, ed. and trans. *Symbolist Art Theories: A Critical Anthology*. Berkeley: University of California Press, 1994.

During, Simon. *Modern Enchantments: The Cultural Power of Secular Magic*. Cambridge, MA: Harvard University Press, 2002.

Eckert, Charles. "Shirley Temple and the House of Rockefeller". In *Stardom: Industry of Desire*, edited by Christine Gledhill, 60–73. London: Routledge, 1991.

The Editor. "Close-Ups". *Photoplay*, September 1915.

Edwards, Holly. "A Million and One Nights". In *Noble Dreams, Wicked Pleasures: Orientalism in America, 1870–1930*, edited by Holly Edwards, 11–57. Princeton: Princeton University Press, 2000.

Eisenstein, Sergei. "On Disney". Translated by Alan Y. Upchurch. In *The Eisenstein Collection*, edited by Richard Taylor, 79–175. London: Seagull Books, 2006.

The Era. "The Drama in Paris". August 29, 1891.

Ezra, Elizabeth. *Georges Méliès*. Manchester: Manchester University Press, 2000.

Fay, C. R. *Palace of Industry, 1851*. London: Cambridge University Press, 1951.

Fayard, Claude. "Le cinéma: La féerie". *La Semaine à Paris*, June 17, 1922.

Felando, Cynthia. "Clara Bow is *It*". In *Film Stars: Hollywood and Beyond*, edited by Andy Willis, 8–24. Manchester: Manchester University Press, 2004.

Felmingham, Michael. *The Illustrated Gift Book, 1880–1930*. Aldershot: Scolar Press, 1988.

Figuier, Louis. *L'Année Scientifique et Industrielle*, 1889.

Fischer, Lucy. *Sunrise*. London: British Film Institute, 1998.

Fletcher, Adele Whitely. "Across the Silversheet". *Motion Picture Magazine*, June 1924.

Fouquier, Marcel. "Chronique du théâtre". *La Nouvelle Revue*, July 1889.

Fox, Stephen. *The Mirror Makers: A History of American Advertising and its Creators*. New York: Illini Books, 1997.

Frank Leslie's Illustrated Newspaper. "Paris in New York". October 6, 1866.

Frank Leslie's Illustrated Newspaper. "Musical and Dramatic". February 26, 1870.

Frazer, John. *Artificially Arranged Scenes*. Boston: G. K. Hall & Co., 1979.

Freeburg, Victor O. *The Art of Photoplay Making*. 1918. Reprint edition. New York: Arno, 1970.

Gaddis, Pearl. "The Cinderella of the Cooper-Hewitts". *Motion Picture Magazine*, June 1917.

Gág, Wanda. *Tales from Grimm*. Translated and illustrated by Wanda Gág. 1936. Reprint, London: Faber, 1973.

Gassaway, Gordon. "What Makes a Good Screen Story?" *Picture-Play Magazine*, May 1923.

Gaudreault, André. "Theatricality, Narrativity, and Trickality: Reevaluating the Cinema of Georges Méliès". *Journal of Popular Film and Television* 15, no. 3 (Fall 1987): 110–19.

Gaudreault, André. "Méliès the Magician: The Magical Magic of the Magic Image". *Early Popular Visual Culture* 5, no. 2 (July 2007): 167–74.

Gautier, Théophile. "Théâtres". *La Presse*, March 31, 1845.

Gautier, Théophile. "Théâtres". *La Presse*, June 16, 1851.

Gautier, Théophile. "L'Inde". In *Caprices et Zigzags*, 232–271. Paris: V. Lecou, 1852.

Gautier, Théophile. "Revue dramatique". *Le Moniteur Universel*, January 18, 1858.

Gautier, Théophile. *Histoire de l'art dramatique en France depuis vingt-cinq ans*. 4 vols. Brussels: Hetzel, 1858–1859.

Gautier, Théophile. "Revue dramatique". *Le Moniteur Universel*, August 17, 1858.

Gautier, Théophile. "Revue dramatique". *Le Moniteur Universel*, November 21, 1859.

Gautier, Théophile. "Revue dramatique". *Le Moniteur Universel*, September 11, 1860.

Gautier, Théophile. "Revue dramatique". *Le Moniteur Universel*, March 3, 1862.

Gautier, Théophile. "Revue dramatique". *Le Moniteur Universel*, June 1, 1863.

Gautier, Théophile. "Revue dramatique". *Le Moniteur Universel*, June 4, 1866.

Gautier, Théophile. *Mademoiselle de Maupin*. Translated by Helen Constantine. London: Penguin, 2005.

Giddens, Anthony. *The Consequences of Modernity*. Stanford: Stanford University Press, 1990.

Ginisty, Paul. *La Féerie*. Paris: L. Michaud, [1910].

Gledhill, Christine. "Rethinking Genre". In *Reinventing Film Studies*, edited by Christine Gledhill and Linda Williams, 221–43. London: Arnold, 2000.

Gourmont, Remy de. "'The Funeral of Style (1902)' and 'The Dissociation of Ideas (1900)'". In *Symbolist Art Theories: A Critical Anthology*, edited by Henri Dorra, 299–305. Berkeley: University of California Press, 1994.

Gourmont, Remy de. "Epilogues: Cinématographe". Translated by Richard Abel. In *French Film Theory and Criticism: A History/Anthology, 1907–1939*, vol. 1, edited by Richard Abel, 47–50. Princeton: Princeton University Press, 1988.

Grimm, Wilhelm. "Preface to Volume 1 of the First Edition (1812)". In Maria Tatar, *The Hard Facts of the Grimms' Fairy Tales*, 2nd ed., edited and translated by Maria Tatar, 252–59. Princeton: Princeton University Press, 2003.

Gunning, Tom. "'Now You See It, Now You Don't': The Temporality of the Cinema of Attractions". In *The Silent Cinema Reader*, edited by Lee Grieveson and Peter Krämer, 41–50. London: Routledge, 2004.

Gunning, Tom. "A Trip to the Moon". In *Film Analysis: A Norton Reader*, edited by Jeffrey Geiger and R. L. Rutsky, 64–81. New York: W. W. Norton & Company, 2005.

Gunning, Tom. "The Birth of Film Out of the Spirit of Modernity". In *Masterpieces of Modernist Cinema*, edited by Ted Perry, 13–40. Bloomington: Indiana University Press, 2006.

Hall, Mordaunt. "An Intelligent Pictorial Comedy". *New York Times*, October 30, 1927.

Hammond, Paul. *Marvellous Méliès*. London: Gordon Fraser, 1974.

Hamrick, Lois Cassandra. "Gautier as 'Seer' of the Origins of Modernity in Baudelaire". In *Baudelaire and the Poetics of Modernity*, edited by Patricia A. Ward, 29–41. Nashville: Vanderbilt University Press, 2001.

Hansen, Miriam. "The Mass Production of the Senses: Classical Cinema as Vernacular Modernism". In *Reinventing Film Studies*, edited by Christine Gledhill and Linda Williams, 332–50. London: Arnold, 2000.

Hanson, Helen. *Hollywood Heroines: Women in Film Noir and the Female Gothic Film*. London: I.B.Tauris, 2007.

Harris, Augustus. "'The National Theatre', 1885". In *Victorian Theatre: The Theatre in its Time*, edited by Russell Jackson, 276–281. New York: New Amsterdam Books, 1989.

Hastie, Amelie. *Cupboards of Curiosity: Women, Recollection, and Film History*. Durham: Duke University Press, 2007.

Hemmings, F. W. J. *The Theatre Industry in Nineteenth-Century France*. Cambridge: Cambridge University Press, 1993.

Herbert, Stephen, ed. *A History of Early Film*. Vol. 1. London: Routledge, 2000.

Heu, Pascal Manuel. *Le temps du cinéma: Émile Vuillermoz, père de la critique cinématographique, 1910–1930*. Paris: L'Harmattan, 2003.

Hibon, Ben. "Lights, Camera..." *Los Angeles Times*, January 31, 2011.

Higashi, Sumiko. *Cecil B. DeMille and American Culture: The Silent Era*. Berkeley: University of California Press, 1994.

Higson, Andrew. "Cecil Hepworth, *Alice in Wonderland* and the Development of the Narrative Film". In *Young and Innocent?: The Cinema in Britain, 1896–1930*, edited by Andrew Higson, 42–64. Exeter: University of Exeter Press, 2002.

Housman, Laurence. Preface to *Arabian Nights: A Selection of Tales from the Book of a Thousand and One Nights*, v–x. 1907. Reprint, Ware: Omega, 1985.

Ibee. "Thief of Bagdad". *Variety*, March 26, 1924.

Irving, Minna. "The Magic Film". *Motion Picture Story Magazine*, July 1911.

Irving, Minna. "The True Wonderland". *Motion Picture Story Magazine*, June 1911.

Irving, Washington. *The Legend of Sleepy Hollow & Other Stories*. London: Minster Classics, 1968.

Irwin, Robert. "A Thousand and One Nights at the Movies". *Middle Eastern Literatures* 7, no. 2 (July 2004): 223–33.

Jacobs, Lewis. *The Rise of the American Film*. 1939. Reprint, New York: Teachers College Press, 1968.

Johnson, Ray. "Tricks, Traps and Transformations: Illusion in Victorian Spectacular Theatre", *Early Popular Visual Culture* 5, no. 2 (July 2007): 151–65.

Johnston, William A. "The Thief of Bagdad". *Motion Picture News*, April 5, 1924.

Jolo. "Aladdin". *Variety*, September 28, 1917.

Jouvin, B. "Théâtres". *Le Figaro*, September 13, 1860.

Jouvin, B. "Théâtres". *Le Figaro*, August 20, 1863.

Kearns, James. *Théophile Gautier, Orator to the Artists: Art Journalism in the Second Republic*. London: Legenda, 2007.

Keil, Charlie. *Early American Cinema in Transition: Story, Style, and Filmmaking, 1907–1913*. Madison: University of Wisconsin Press, 2001.

Kingsley, Grace. "Week's News and Views". *Los Angeles Times*. October 14, 1917.

Kirkland, Janice. "Frances Hodgson Burnett's Sara Crewe Through 110 Years". *Children's Literature in Education* 28, no. 4 (1997): 191–203.

Klein, Norman M. "Animation and Animorphs". In *Meta-Morphing: Visual Transformation and the Culture of Quick-Change*, edited by Vivian Sobchack, 21–39. Minneapolis: University of Minnesota Press, 2000.

Knapp, Raymond. *The American Musical and the Formation of National Identity*. Princeton: Princeton University Press, 2005.

Knapp, Raymond. *The American Musical and the Performance of Personal Identity*. Princeton: Princeton University Press, 2006.

Koszarski, Richard. *An Evening's Entertainment: The Age of the Silent Feature Picture, 1915–1928*. Berkeley: University of California Press, 1990.

Kovács, Katherine. "A History of the Féerie in France". *Theatre Quarterly* 8, no. 29 (Spring 1978): 29–38.

Kovács, Katherine. "Georges Méliès and the Féerie". In *Film Before Griffith*, edited by John L. Fell, 244–57. Berkeley: University of California Press, 1983.

Krasniewicz, Louise. *Walt Disney: A Biography*. Santa Barbara: Greenwood, 2010.

Kriegel, Lara. "Narrating the Subcontinent in 1851: India at the Crystal Palace". In *The Great Exhibition of 1851: New Interdisciplinary Essays*, edited by Louise Purbrick, 146–78. Manchester: Manchester University Press, 2001.

L'Exposition de Paris 1889. "Fête de nuit". July 13, 1889.

La Cinématographie Française. "États-Unis". December 14, 1918.

Laloue, Ferdinand, Anicet Bourgeois, and Laurent. "Les pilules du diable". *Magasin théâtral: choix de pièces nouvelles jouées sur tous les théâtres de Paris* 33 (1842).

Landay, Lori. "The Flapper Film: Comedy, Dance, and Jazz Age Kinaesthetics". In *A Feminist Reader in Early Cinema*, edited by Jennifer M. Bean and Diane Negra, 221–248. Durham: Duke University Press, 2002.

Landy, Marcia. *Cinematic Uses of the Past*. Minneapolis: University of Minnesota Press, 1996.

Langdale, Allan. "S(t)imulation of Mind: The Film Theory of Hugo Münsterberg". In *Hugo Münsterberg on Film*, edited by Allan Langdale, 1–41. London: Routledge, 2002.

Lant, Antonia. "Haptical Cinema". *October* 74 (Fall 1995): 45–73.

Larousse, Pierre. *Grand dictionnaire universel du XIXe siècle*. Vol. 8. Paris: Administration du grand dictionnaire universel, 1866–1877.

Larson, Barbara. *The Dark Side of Nature: Science, Society, and the Fantastic in the Work of Odilon Redon*. University Park, PA: Pennsylvania State University Press, 2005.

Leach, William. *Land of Desire: Merchants, Power, and the Rise of a New American Culture*. New York: Vintage Books, 1994.

Lears, T. J. Jackson. "From Salvation to Self-Realization: Advertising and the Therapeutic Roots of the Consumer Culture, 1880–1930". In *The Culture of Consumption: Critical Essays in American History, 1880–1980*, edited by Richard Wightman Fox and T. J. Jackson Lears, 1–38. New York: Pantheon Books, 1983.

Lears, T. J. Jackson. *Fables of Abundance: A Cultural History of Advertising in America*. New York: Basic Books, 1994.

Lindsay, Vachel. *The Art of the Moving Picture*. 1915, revised edition 1922.

Reprinted with an introduction by Stanley Kauffmann and appendix by Kent Jones. New York: The Modern Library, 2000.

Lindsay, Vachel. *The Progress and Poetry of the Movies*. 1925. Edited by Myron Lounsbury. Lanham: Scarecrow Press, 1995.

Lloyd, Rosemary. *Baudelaire's Literary Criticism*. Cambridge: Cambridge University Press, 1981.

Los Angeles Times. "Kellerman in Mermaid Role". June 7, 1914.

Los Angeles Times. "Film Banquet is Dazzling". July 11, 1924.

Los Angeles Times. "Film Efforts Rewarded". February 18, 1929.

Lucas, Hippolyte. "Théâtres". *L'Artiste* 2, no. 2 (1839): 223.

M. V. "Paris qui cause". *La Presse*, June 1, 1909.

Macgowan, Kenneth. "The Play of the Month". *Motion Picture Classic*, April 1924, 47.

Maeterlinck, Maurice. "The Tragical in Daily Life". In *The Treasure of the Humble*, translated by Alfred Sutro, 95–119. London: Ballantyne Press, 1905.

Maeterlinck, Maurice. *The Blue Bird*. Translated by Alexander Teixeira de Mattos. New York: Dodd, Mead & Company, 1909.

Malthête, Jacques. "Méliès et le conférencier". *Iris*, no. 22 (Autumn, 1996): 117–29.

Manovich, Lev. *The Language of New Media*. Cambridge, MA: MIT Press, 2001.

Marchand, Roland. *Advertising the American Dream: Making Way for Modernity, 1920–1940*. Berkeley: University of California Press, 1985.

Marcus, Laura. *The Tenth Muse*. Oxford: Oxford University Press, 2007.

Martin, Roxane. *La féerie romantique sur les scènes parisiennes, 1791–1864*. Paris: Honoré Champion Éditeur, 2007.

Martineau, Jane, ed. *Victorian Fairy Painting*. London: Royal Academy of Arts, 1997.

Mayne, Marjorie. "A Dream Princess". *Pictures and the Picturegoer*, December 1924.

McMahan, Alison. *The Films of Tim Burton: Animating Live Action in Contemporary Hollywood*. New York: Continuum, 2005.

Méliès, Georges. "Cinematographic Views". Translated by Stuart Liebman. In *French Film Theory and Criticism: 1907–1939*, vol. 1, ed. Richard Abel, 35–47. Princeton: Princeton University Press, 1988.

Merritt, Karen. "Marguerite Clark as America's Snow White: The Resourceful Orphan Who Inspired Walt Disney". *Griffithiana* 64 (October 1998): 4–25.

Miller, Bertha Mahony. "Twenty Years of Children's Books". In *A Horn Book Sampler: On Children's Books and Reading*, edited by Norma R. Fryatt, 104–110. Boston: The Horn Book, 1959.

Modleski, Tania. *The Women Who Knew Too Much: Hitchcock and Feminist Theory*. New York: Routledge, 1988.

Moi, Toril. *Henrik Ibsen and the Birth of Modernism*. Oxford: Oxford University Press, 2006.

Moore, Anne Carroll. "The Three Owls' Notebook". *The Horn Book* 14, no. 1 (January–February 1938): 31–33.

Moore, Anne Carroll. "The Three Owls' Notebook". *The Horn Book* 14, no. 2 (March–April 1938): 91–92.

Moore, Rachel O. *Savage Theory: Cinema as Modern Magic*. Durham: Duke University Press, 2000.

Morning Chronicle. "Christmas Holiday Amusements". December 28, 1857.

Morton, Edward. "'The Blue Bird' at the Haymarket". *The Playgoer and Society Illustrated,* January–February 1910.

Motion Picture Magazine. "Here Are All the Winners of the Great Popular Player Contest". February 1917.

Motion Picture Magazine. "Jack and the Beanstalk". September 1917.

Motion Picture News. "Seventh Motion Picture News Chart of National Film Trade Conditions". December 30, 1916.

Motion Picture News. "At One Theatre 60,000 See 'Jack and the Beanstalk'". September 8, 1917.

Moussinac, Léon. "Notre point de vue: L'atmosphère". *L'Humanité,* December 23, 1932.

Münsterberg, Hugo. *The Photoplay: A Psychological Study.* 1916. Reprinted in *Hugo Münsterberg on Film.* Edited by Allan Langdale. London: Routledge, 2002.

Musser, Charles et al., eds. *Motion Picture Catalogs by American Producers and Distributors, 1894–1908.* Frederick, MD: University Publications of America, 1985.

Musser, Charles. *Before the Nickelodeon: Edwin S. Porter and the Edison Manufacturing Company.* Berkeley: University of California Press, 1991.

New York Daily Tribune. "A Fairy Play: Maeterlinck's Pantomime Morality". December 19, 1909.

New York Times. "'The Blue Bird' A Fairy Drama". April 10, 1909.

New York Times. "Maeterlinck's 'Blue Bird' Tests Ingenuity of New Theatre". September 18, 1910.

New York Times. "Lovely Fantasy on New Theatre Stage". October 2, 1910.

New York Times. "New Scene in 'Blue Bird'". February 7, 1911.

New York Times. "Awarded to Maeterlinck". November 10, 1911.

New York Times. "Fairyland Busy Making Little Words of Big Ones". November 10, 1912.

New York Times. "'The Blue Bird' a Hit on Screen, Many Opportunities in Maeterlinck's Work to Exploit Stage Magic". April 1, 1918.

New York Times. "Coolidge Praises Advertising as Aid to Our Prosperity". October 28, 1926.

New York Times. "Miss Burkes's 'Peggy' Seen on the Screen". January 17, 1916.

New York Times. "Notable Books in Brief Reviews: Professor Münsterberg and Vachel Lindsay in Appreciations of the Cinema – Some Recent Publications". June 4, 1916.

New York Times. "Miss Clark in Film Farce". November 20, 1916.

New York Times. "Written on the Screen". June 24, 1917.

New York Times. "Police Clear Jam at Movie Premier". March 19, 1924.

New York Times. "The Screen: Arabian Nights Satire". March 19, 1924.

New York Times. "How Douglas Fairbanks Produces His Pictures". June 7, 1925.

Nunn, William Curtis. *Marguerite Clark, America's Darling of Broadway and the Silent Screen.* Fort Worth: Texas Christian University Press, 1981.

Nutting, Dorothy. "Monsieur Tourneur". *Photoplay,* July 1918.

O'Reilly, Edward S. "She Says to Me, Says She—". *Photoplay,* January 1918.

Oakland Tribune. "Doug Fairbanks Brings Romance of Arabian Nights". November 3, 1924.

Olds, Marshall C. *Au pays des perroquets: Féerie théâtrale et narration chez Flaubert.* Amsterdam: Rodopi, 2001.

Orgeron, Marsha. "Making *It* in Hollywood: Clara Bow, Fandom, and Consumer Culture". *Cinema Journal* 42, no. 4 (Summer 2003): 76–97.

Panofsky, Erwin. *Perspective as Symbolic Form.* Translated by Christopher S. Wood. New York: Zone Books, 1991.

Panofsky, Erwin. "Style and Medium in the Motion Pictures". In *The Visual Turn: Classical Film Theory and Art History,* edited by Angela Dalle Vacche, 69–84. New Brunswick, NJ: Rutgers University Press, 2002.

Parville, Henri de. "Exposition universelle". *Journal des Débats,* May 31, 1889.

Pessard, Hector. "Les premières". *Le Gaulois,* July 12, 1889.

Philip, Neil. "Creativity and Tradition in the Fairy Tale". In *A Companion to the Fairy Tale,* edited by Hilda Ellis Davidson and Anna Chaudhri, 39–55. Cambridge: D. S. Brewer, 2003.

Photoplay. "Children's Shows a Failure". February 1918.

Photoplay. "On the Films – and Behind: Illustrations from the 'Cinderella' Film, Produced by the Famous Players Company". January 1915.

Photoplay. "Pickford Role Poll". October 1925.

Pickford, Mary. *Sunshine and Shadow.* London: William Heinemann Ltd, 1956.

Picturegoer. "Cinderella's Ball". December 1921.

Picturegoer. "Once upon a Time". December 1921.

Picturegoer. "Glamour or Realism". May 1928.

Pictures and the Picturegoer. "Our Honours List: A Guide to the Best Films of the Month". November 1924.

Planché, J. R. *The Recollections and Reflections of J. R. Planché.* Vol. 2. London: Tinsley Brothers, 1872.

Rearick, Charles. *Pleasures of the Belle Époque: Entertainment and Festivity in Turn-of-the-Century France.* New Haven: Yale University Press, 1985.

Redon, Odilon. "Confessions of an Artist". In *Symbolist Art Theories: A Critical Anthology,* edited and translated by Henri Dorra, 54–56. Berkeley: University of California Press, 1994.

Régnier, Henri de. "La semaine dramatique". *Journal des Débats,* March 13, 1911.

Reid, Laurence. "The Thief of Bagdad – A Fantasy". *Motion Picture News,* March 29, 1924.

Reid, Laurence. "The Picture of the Month". *Motion Picture Classic,* June 1924.

Reiniger, Lotte. *Shadow Theatres and Shadow Films.* London: Batsford, 1970.

Ricoeur, Paul. *Time and Narrative.* Vol. 1. Translated by Kathleen McLaughlin and David Pellauer. Chicago: University of Chicago Press, 1984.

Ricoeur, Paul. *The Rule of Metaphor.* Translated by Robert Czerny with Kathleen McLaughlin and John Costello. London: Routledge, 2003.

Roqueplan, Nestor. "Théâtres". *Le Constitutionnel,* March 27, 1865.

Roqueplan, Nestor. "Théâtres". *Le Constitutionnel,* June 11, 1866.

Roqueplan, Nestor. "Théâtres". *Le Constitutionnel,* August 21, 1869.

Rosenberg, Walter. "The Exhibitor's View". *Variety,* December 25, 1914.

Rowling, J. K. *Harry Potter and the Prisoner of Azkaban*. Bloomsbury: London, 2004.

Sadoul, Georges. *Georges Méliès*. Paris: Seghers, 1961.

Saint-Victor, Paul de. "Théâtres". *La Presse*, September 30, 1860.

Saint-Victor, Paul de. "Théâtres". *La Presse*, March 11, 1862.

Sarcey, Francisque. "Chronique Théâtrale". *Le Temps*, August 23, 1869.

Sarcey, Francisque. "Chronique Théâtrale". *Le Temps*, July 22, 1889.

Sarcey, Francisque. "Théophile Gautier". In *Quarante ans de théâtre: feuilletons dramatiques*. Vol. 1. Paris: Bibliothèque des "Annales politiques et littéraires", 1900–1902.

A Scenario Writer. "The Evolution of a Picture". *New York Times*, March 16, 1924.

Schallert, Edwin. "Doug Rubs the Magic Lamp". *Picture-Play Magazine*, August 1923.

Schlappich, Sam J. "The Fairies of the Screen". *Motion Picture Magazine*, March 1915.

Schoenherr, Douglas E. "A Note on Burne-Jones's 'Pocket Cathedral' and Ruskin". *Journal of William Morris Studies* 15, no. 4 (Summer 2004): 91–93.

Shaw, Jennifer L. *Dream States: Puvis de Chavannes, Modernism and the Fantasy of France*. New Haven: Yale University Press, 2002.

Sherson, Erroll. *London's Lost Theatres of the Nineteenth Century*. London: John Lane the Bodley Head Ltd, 1925.

Shippey, Tom. "Rewriting the Core: Transformations of the Fairy Tale in Contemporary Writing". In *A Companion to the Fairy Tale*, edited by Hilda Ellis Davidson and Anna Chaudhri, 253–74. Cambridge: D. S. Brewer, 2003.

Shohat, Ella. "Gender and Culture of Empire: Towards a Feminist Ethnography of the Cinema". In *Visions of the East: Orientalism in Film*, edited by Matthew Bernstein and Gaylyn Studlar, 19–66. London: I.B.Tauris, 1997.

Shorey, Jerome. "Do You Believe in Fairies?". *Photoplay*, September 1918.

Singer, Ben. "Modernity, Hyperstimulus and the Rise of Popular Sensationalism". In *Cinema and the Invention of Modern Life*, edited by Leo Charney and Vanessa Schwartz, 72–99. Berkeley: University of California Press, 1995.

Singer, Ben and Charlie Keil. "Introduction: Movies in the 1910s". In *American Cinema of the 1910s*, edited by Charlie Keil and Ben Singer, 1–25. Piscataway, NJ: Rutgers University Press, 2009.

Sobchack, Vivian. Introduction to *Meta-Morphing: Visual Transformation and the Culture of Quick-Change*, edited by Vivian Sobchack, xi–xxiii. Minneapolis: University of Minnesota Press, 2000.

Staiger, Janet. *Bad Women: Regulating Sexuality in Early American Cinema*. Minneapolis: University of Minnesota Press, 1995.

Stanislavski, Constantin. "The Mysterious World of *The Blue Bird*". In *Stanislavski's Legacy*, rev. ed., edited and translated by Elizabeth Reynolds Hapgood, 159–61. New York: Routledge, 1999.

Steele, Charles Henry. "Spotlight for Julanne". *Picture-Play Magazine*, December 1923.

Stewart, Garrett. *Framed Time: Toward a Postfilmic Cinema*. Chicago: University of Chicago Press, 2007.

Stoneley, Peter. *Consumerism and American Girls' Literature, 1860–1940*. Cambridge: Cambridge University Press, 2003.

Stoullig, Edmond. *Les annales du théâtre et de la musique*, 1906.

Studlar, Gaylyn. *In the Realm of Pleasure: Von Sternberg, Dietrich, and the Masochistic Aesthetic*. Urbana: University of Illinois Press, 1988.

Studlar, Gaylyn. "Douglas Fairbanks: Thief of the Ballets Russes". In *Bodies of the Text: Dance as Theory, Literature as Dance*, edited by Ellen W. Goellner and Jacqueline Shea Murphy, 107–24. New Brunswick, NJ: Rutgers University Press, 1994.

Studlar, Gaylyn. "Oh, 'Doll Divine': Mary Pickford, Masquerade, and the Pedophilic Gaze". *Camera Obscura* 16, no. 3 (2001): 197–227.

Studlar, Gaylyn. *This Mad Masquerade: Stardom and Masculinity in the Jazz Age*. New York: Columbia University Press, 1996.

Tatar, Maria. *The Hard Facts of the Grimms' Fairy Tales*. 2nd ed. Princeton: Princeton University Press, 2003.

Tatar, Maria. *Secrets Beyond the Door: The Story of Bluebeard and His Wives*. Princeton: Princeton University Press, 2004.

The Thief of Bagdad press book. British Film Institute, London.

Times. "The Christmas Pantomimes and Entertainments". December 28, 1857.

Times. "The Christmas Pantomimes, Burlesques, &c". December 28, 1858.

Times. "Holiday Amusements". December 27, 1859.

Times. "The Christmas Pantomimes and Burlesques". December 27, 1859.

Thompson, Kristin. "The International Exploration of Cinematic Expressivity". In *The Silent Cinema Reader*, edited by Lee Grieveson and Peter Krämer, 254–69. London: Routledge, 2004.

Tibbetts, John C. "Mary Pickford and the American 'Growing Girl'". *Journal of Popular Film and Television* 29, no. 2 (2001): 50–62.

Time. "The New Pictures". March 31, 1924.

Time. "Mouse & Man". December 27, 1937.

Tinée, Mae. "The Blue Bird". *Chicago Daily Tribune*, May 6, 1918.

Ulbach, Louis. "Revue théâtrale". *Le Temps*, March 11, 1862.

Ulbach, Louis. "Revue théâtrale". *Le Temps*, October 12, 1863.

Ulbach, Louis. "Revue théâtrale". *Le Temps*, September 26, 1864.

Ulbach, Louis. "Revue théâtrale". *Le Temps*, March 27, 1865.

Un monsieur de l'orchestre. "La soirée théâtrale". *Le Figaro*, July 12, 1889.

Van Loan, H. H. "The Doll Lady: Disclosing the Peter Pan-ishness of Mary Fuller". *Motion Picture Magazine*, April 1917.

Vapereau, G. *L'année littéraire et dramatique*. Vol. 5. Paris: L. Hachette, 1863.

Vapereau, G. *L'année littéraire et dramatique*. Vol. 7. Paris: L. Hachette, 1866.

Vardac, A. Nicholas. *Stage to Screen: Theatrical Method from Garrick to Griffith*. Cambridge, MA: Harvard University Press, 1949.

Variety. "Gest Will Get Young Fortune Handling Fairbanks' Picture". March 5, 1924.

Vitu, Auguste. *Les mille et une nuits du théâtre*. Vol. 5. Paris: P. Ollendorff, 1888.

Vogüé, Eugène-Melchior de. "À Travers L'Exposition". *Revue des Deux Mondes*, July 15, 1889.

von Franz, Marie-Louise. *Shadow and Evil in Fairy Tales*. Dallas: Spring Publications Inc., 1974.

Vuillermoz, Émile. "L'écran". *Le Temps*, November 23, 1916.

Vuillermoz, Émile. "Devant l'écran". *Le Temps*, December 27, 1916.

Vuillermoz, Émile. "Devant l'écran". *Le Temps*, January 10, 1917.

Vuillermoz, Émile. "Devant l'écran". *Le Temps*, March 28, 1917.

Vuillermoz, Émile. "Devant l'écran". *Le Temps*, April 25, 1917.

Vuillermoz, Émile. "Devant l'écran". *Le Temps*, May 23, 1917.

Vuillermoz, Émile. "Devant l'écran". *Le Temps*, June 6, 1917.

Vuillermoz, Émile. "Devant l'écran". *Le Temps*, June 20, 1917.

Vuillermoz, Émile. "Devant l'écran". *Le Temps*, July 4, 1917.

Vuillermoz, Émile. "Devant l'écran". *Le Temps*, August 15, 1917.

Vuillermoz, Émile. "Devant l'écran: Lueurs". *Le Temps*, June 4, 1919.

Vuillermoz, Émile. "Courrier Cinématographique: Le Voleur de Bagdad". *Le Temps*, September 20, 1924.

Vuillermoz, Émile. "Le Cinéma. Chronique. Indications". *Le Temps*, January 14, 1933.

Vuillermoz, Émile. "Chronique cinématographique". *Le Temps*, February 23, 1935.

Waldman, Diane. "'At Last I Can Tell It to Someone!': Feminine Point of View and Subjectivity in the Gothic Romance Film of the 1940s". *Cinema Journal* 23, no. 2 (Winter 1983): 29–40.

Walsh, Raoul. *Each Man in His Time: The Life Story of a Director*. New York: Farrar, Straus and Giroux, 1974.

Warner, Marina. *From the Beast to the Blonde: On Fairy Tales and Their Tellers*. London: Vintage, 1995.

Warner, Marina. *Fantastic Metamorphoses, Other Worlds: Ways of Telling the Self*. Oxford: Oxford University Press, 2002.

Warner, Marina. *Phantasmagoria: Spirit Visions, Metaphors, and Media into the Twenty-first Century*. Oxford: Oxford University Press, 2006.

Warnerby, Charles. "Child Screen Star's Career a 20th Century Fairy Tale". *Movie Weekly*, February 10, 1923.

Watts, Steven. *The Magic Kingdom: Walt Disney and the American Way of Life*. Columbia: University of Missouri Press, 1997.

Wells, Paul. *Understanding Animation*. London: Routledge, 1998.

Wiggin, Kate Douglas. Preface to *Arabian Nights, Their Best-Known Tales*, edited by Kate Douglas Wiggin and Nora A. Smith, vii–x. 1909. Reprint Edition. New York: Atheneum, 1993.

Wolff, Janet. "The Invisible Flâneuse: Women and the Literature of Modernity". *Theory, Culture & Society* 2, no. 3 (1985): 37–46.

York, Cal. "Studio News and Gossip East and West". *Photoplay*, November 1924.

Zipes, Jack. *When Dreams Came True*. London: Routledge, 1999.

Zipes, Jack. Introduction to *The Oxford Companion to Fairy Tales*, edited by Jack Zipes, xv–xxxii. New York: Oxford University Press, 2000.

Zipes, Jack. *The Enchanted Screen*. London: Routledge, 2011.

Zola, Émile. *Le naturalisme au théâtre*. Paris: G. Charpentier, 1881.

Index

Les 400 coups du diable, 57

Abel, Richard, 39, 86, 246n7
Abraham, Émile, 1
Academy Awards, 143, 163, 169, 171, 173, 196, 197
Adventures of Prince Achmed, The (1926), 224
advertising: atmosphere, 150; *The Blue Bird* (1918) and, 95, 111; children's literature and, 190; consumer culture and, 151, 157–160, 162–163; fairy tales and, xv; féerie (film) and, xx, 65–67; *L'Inhumaine*, 142; *Snow White and the Seven Dwarfs* and, 178, 186, 195; *The Thief of Bagdad* and, 148; traditionalism, 184; *Ye Belle Alliance* (play) and, 14
Affairs of Anatol, The (play), 135
"Aladdin", 25, 40, 92, 159
Aladdin and the Wonderful Lamp (1917), 75, 77, 142
Aladin (play), xix, 32
"Ali Baba and the Forty Thieves", 125–126
Ali Baba and the Forty Thieves (1918), 75
Alias Jimmy Valentine (1915), 97
"Alice in Wonderland", 75, 199
Alice in Wonderland (1903), 236n6
Alice in Wonderland (2010), 213
Allan, Robin, 192, 250n16
Ames, Winthrop, 181
Andersen, Hans Christian, 94, 138, 230n7, 241n39

animated film, xvii, 176–179, 181, 183, 211, 212, 216, 219, 224–226, 250n6; *Snow White and the Seven Dwarfs* and, 175–176, 178–179, 180, 181, 192, 196
apotheosis, 8, 14, 16, 22, 30, 31, 67, 69
Appadurai, Arjun, 190–191
Arabian Nights. See Thousand and One Nights, The
Aristotle, 46, 52
Around the World in 80 Days (play), 36
Arts and Crafts, 185, 187
atmosphere, 145, 148–151, 187
Atwood, Margaret, 212
Auslander, Leora, 156, 248n54

Babes in the Woods (1932), 177, 216
Babes in the Woods, The (1917), 75
Bacchilega, Cristina, 212
Bacon, Francis, 226
Ball of Fire (1941), xxiii, 179, 206–209
Balzac, Honoré de, 156, 248n54
Barrier, J. Michael, 177
Barry, John F., 150
Barton, Bruce, 249n64
Basinger, Jeanine, 165
Baudelaire, Charles, xx, 22–23, 27–29, 54, 86, 233n76, 234n96; "Parisian Dream", 27–29
Baum, L. Frank, 75
Baxter, Peter, 200
Beard, Deanna M. Toten, 130
Beauty and the Beast (1991), 216
Belenky, Masha, 46
La Belle et la Bête (1946), 216

Bénichou, Paul, 22
Benton, Megan L., 185–186
Bergson, Henri, 84, 109
Berman, Marshall, xiv, 172
Betty Boop, 176, 183
Beverley, William, 13, 232n40
La biche au bois (play), 11, 15, 16, 30, 40, 66
Bijou (play), 10
Black Crook, The (play), 15
Blue Bird, The (play), 93, 106, 112, 181, 242n66; as a féerie, 94, 95; as cinematic, 96, 97; *The Poor Little Rich Girl* (play) and, 130; Marguerite Clark and, 136
Blue Bird, The (1918), xv, xxi, 79, 92, 93–112, 129, 198, 216; Pierre Puvis de Chavannes and, 98, 99–101; public art and, 102, 129; "The Tragedy of Everyday Life" and, 98, 106–107, 110; the crystal image and, 109–110; *The Poor Little Rich Girl* and, 130
Blue Bird, The (1940), 197–198
Blue Light, The (1932), 250n16
"Bluebeard", 40, 62, 200–202, 205–206
Bluebeard (1901), 49, 61–62, 64, 183
Bluebeard cycle, 200–202
Bluebeard's Eighth Wife (1938), xxiii, 204, 205–206
book: *Alice in Wonderland* (1903), 236n6; in *Bluebeard*, 61; *The Blue Bird* (1940) and, 198; children's, 188–190; fairy tale, xv, 182–183, 230n7; fine, 185–187; *Harry Potter and the Prisoner of Azkaban* and, 222; *The Scarlet Empress* and, 199; *Shrek* and, 211; *Snow White and the Seven Dwarfs* and, xxii–xxiii, 180–192, 196, 250n16; féerie (theatre) and, 30, 40; *The Thief of Bagdad* and, xxii, 146–147. *See also* illustrations
Borzage, Frank, 169
Bottigheimer, Ruth, 182
Bow, Clara, xv, 165–167
Brackett, Charles, 204, 206

Brewster, Ben, 239n54
Brisson, Adolphe, 94
Brothers Grimm, 56–57, 136, 138, 175, 178, 182, 183, 187, 217, 224, 230n7
Bruno, Giuliana, 150, 251n33
Bullock, E. C. A., 149–150
Burke, Billie, 127
Burne-Jones, Edward, 187
Burnett, Frances Hodgson, 123
Burton, Richard, 144–145
Burton, Tim, 213
Bushman, Francis X., 135

Calloway, Cab, 176
Cape Fear (1991), 212
Caprice, June, 122–123
Carré, Ben, 104, 130
Carter, Angela, 212
cartoon. *See* animated film
Cendrillon (play), 30, 31
changement à vue, 7, 8–10, 19; *The Blue Bird* and, 95. *See also* transformation scene
Chaplin, Charles, 135
Chartier, Roger, 182–183
La chatte blanche (play), 1–2
Chéret, Jules, 167
Children in the House (1916), 127
children: as audience for fairy-tale films, 75–77, 105–106, 119; as audience for féerie (theatre), 2–3; *The Blue Bird* and, 94, 105–106; fairy tales and, xiii, 80, 88, 112, 137, 163; fantasy and, 90, 92, 123, 124, 136, 139, 170, 180, 203; literature and, xxii, 114, 180–181, 183, 188–190, 199, 212; Mary Pickford performing as, 114–115, 131, 244n5; *Snow White and the Seven Dwarfs* and, 178; *The Thief of Bagdad* and, 144–145, 146, 157, 162, 163
Christie, Ian, 236n6
Christmas Dream, The (1900), 64
Christmas in July (1940), 202
chromatrope, 31

Chronicles of Narnia, The: The Lion, The Witch and the Wardrobe (2005), 213

"Cinderella", 2, 62, 75, 88, 128; and stardom, 113–114, 115–116, 122, 244n8; the Bluebeard Cycle and, 201–202; *Bluebeard's Eighth Wife* and, 206; *Ella Cinders* and, 166; *The Golden Chance* and, 117, 118; *Midnight* and, 204–205; *Rebecca* and, 20; *Seventh Heaven* and, 170–171; *Shrek 2* and, 214, 215; *Snow White and the Seven Dwarfs* and, 175, 180; *Wings* and, 165

Cinderella (play), 30

Cinderella (1899), xx, 40, 49, 58–60, 61, 62, 63, 64, 65, 117

Cinderella (1914), 114, 115–123, 126, 135, 155

cinema of attractions, 40, 237n8

"Cinematographic Views", xx, 45, 47, 50–53, 57–58

Clair, René, 142

Clark, Marguerite, 115, 135–139, 141, 179–180

Colbert, Claudette, xxiii, 204

commercial aesthetic, xxii, 151, 163. *See also* advertising; consumer culture

Company of Wolves, The (1984), 212

consumer culture, xiv, xviii, xxii, 151, 156–160, 162–163, 194; cinema and, 152, 154–155, 163; fairy tales and, 151, 191; masculinity and, 156–157; *Midnight* and, 205; *Shrek 2* and, 214–216; *Snow White and the Seven Dwarfs* and, 187, 190–191, 194–196; *The Thief of Bagdad* and, 143, 151–160, 163. *See also* commercial aesthetic

Coolidge, Calvin, 158–159, 249n64

Crane, Walter, 187, 230n7

Crary, Jonathan, 220–221

Cruikshank, George, 230n7

Cruise of the Make-Believes, The (1918), 123

Crystal Palace. *See* Great Exhibition of 1851

d'Aulnoy, Catherine, 1, 2, 138

Daughter of the Gods, A (1916), 80, 126

David Copperfield (1935), 181

Dawley, J. Searle, 138

DeBauche, Leslie Midkiff, 168

Deburau, Jean-Gaspard, 8

Debussy, Claude, 84, 98

deCordova, Richard, 135

"Deer in the Woods, The", 2. *See also La biche au bois*

Deleuze, Gilles, 109–110

DeMille, Cecil B., 127–128, 154–155

department stores, xxii, 151, 153–154, 156, 161, 162, 165, 166

Déserteuse (1917), 85

Destiny (1921), 142, 246n7

Dietrich, Marlene, 198, 200

Disney, Walt, xvi-xvii, 176–178, 183, 186, 196, 211, 214, 216, 250n6

Dizzy Red Riding Hood (1931), 176

"Donkeyskin", 2. *See also Peau d'âne*

Donohue, Kathleen G., 158

Doré, Gustave, 30, 62, 230n7

Dorra, Henri, 44

dreams: *The Blue Bird* and, 94, 96, 97, 102, 109; *Cinderella* and, 116–119, 123; cinema and, xiii, 42–43, 82, 85, 86–87, 112, 119; Marguerite Clark and, 136, 139; féerie (film) and, 53, 59, 62, 64, 70–71; féerie (theatre), 1, 2, 11–12, 16, 21–22, 29, 232n33; *The Golden Chance* and, 119; interludes and, 126; *The Little Princess* (1917) and, 123, 124; *The Little Princess* (1939) and, 197; "Parisian Dream", 27–28; Mary Pickford and, 135; *The Poor Little Rich Girl* (1917) and, 129, 130, 133–134; *Sleepy Hollow* and, 217, 219–220; *Snow White and the Seven Dwarfs* and, 181; stardom and, 157–158; "The Theatre of Which We Dream", 17–18, 23, 27; *The Thief of Bagdad* and, 152–153, 157

Dulac, Edmund, 146–147

During, Simon, 57

Eberson, John, 150, 151
Eckert, Charles, 197, 198
Eisenstein, Sergei, 178, 219, 251n33
Ella Cinders (1926), 166
exhibitions, 29–30. *See also* Great
    Exhibition of 1851; Universal
    Exposition of 1889
Ezra, Elizabeth, 45, 237n18, 237n20

Fairbanks, Douglas: fairy tales and,
    163; stardom, 135, 141, 143, 158,
    161; *The Thief of Bagdad* and, 141–
    144, 146, 148, 149, 153, 154, 155,
    157–158, 163
fairies, xiii, 26, 42, 82, 85, 87, 91;
    The Blue Bird (1918) and, 93, 99,
    103–105; *The Blue Bird* (1940) and,
    198; *Bluebeard* and, 62; *Cinderella*
    (1899) and, 59; *Cinderella* (1914)
    and, 116–117, 118, 119; Marguerite
    Clark and, 136; féerie (theatre)
    and, 6, 8, 9, 26; *The Good Fairy*
    and, 203–204; pantomime and,
    13, 16; *The Poor Little Rich Girl*
    (1917) and, 133–134; *Shrek 2* and,
    214–215; stardom and, 122–123;
    Wings and, 165. *See also Kingdom
    of the Fairies, The*
"Fairies, The", 26
fairy extravaganzas, 16, 236n6
fairy play. *See* féerie (theatre)
fairy tales, xiii-xxiii, 17, 57, 78, 95,
    229n7, 230n7, 252n3; Academy
    Awards and, 169; aesthetics of film
    and, 79, 91–92, 96, 112, 116, 133,
    135, 161, 198, 227; animation and,
    176–177, 179; *Ball of Fire* and, 206–
    207; *The Blue Bird* and, 93, 94–95,
    96, 98, 111; the Bluebeard cycle
    and, 200–202; *Bluebeard's Eighth
    Wife* and, 204, 205–206; books and,
    180–183, 187, 189–190; children
    and, xiii, 2, 75, 77, 80, 88, 144,
    189–190, 212; *Cinderella* (1914)
    and, 116–117; Marguerite Clark,
    135–138; consumer culture and,

151–152, 248n54; contemporary,
    212–213, 217; cultural value and,
    179, 186–187, 191, 196; féerie
    (film) and, 40, 62–63, 234n88;
    féerie (theatre) and, 1, 2, 4–5, 30,
    78, 128; *The Golden Chance* and,
    118; *The Good Fairy* and, 203–204;
    in relation to the Great Exhibition
    of 1851, 23–27; *Harry Potter and
    the Deathly Hallows Part 1* and, 224;
    illustrated books and, 146–147; as
    interludes, 125–128, 166; *The Little
    Princess* and, 124–126; *Midnight*
    and, 204–205; modernity and, 112,
    113, 173, 206, 209, 213; moralism
    and, xiii, 5, 144; *Neptune's Daughter*
    and, 80, 241n39; pantomime and,
    12–13; Mary Pickford and, 114,
    135; *The Scarlet Empress* and, 198–
    200; *Seventh Heaven* and, 169–171;
    Shrek and, 211–212; *Shrek 2* and,
    214–216; *Sleepy Hollow* and, 217–
    218, 219, 222; *Snow White and
    the Seven Dwarfs* and, 175–176,
    178–182, 186, 189, 191, 193, 202,
    216; as source material for films,
    xvii, 75–76, 126, 163, 179, 212–213;
    spectacle and, 1, 77, 128, 147, 179;
    stardom and, 113–114, 115, 123,
    136, 158, 165–166; *Sunrise* and,
    172; theorists of film and, 78–82,
    84, 86, 87–90, 92, 141, 216; *The
    Thief of Bagdad* and, 141–147,
    151–152, 157, 161, 163; *Wings*
    and, 163–165, 166, 168, 173. *See
    also* illustrations; storytelling
fantastic view, 51–53
fantasy. *See* dreams; fairy tales; fantastic
    view
féerie (film), xx, xxi, 39–43, 56, 58,
    60, 64, 80, 171, 236n5; *The Blue
    Bird* (1918) and, 95; catalogue
    descriptions and, 65–69;
    "Cinematographic Views" and,
    50–51; féerie (theatre) and, 39,
    40–41, 62, 66, 68; modernity and,

41; transformation and, 39–43, 45, 47, 51, 60, 64, 65, 73, 226; visual continuities and, 69. *See also* *Bluebeard*; *Christmas Dream, The*; *Cinderella* (1899); *Impossible Voyage, The*; *Kingdom of the Fairies, The*; *Little Red Riding Hood*; Méliès, Georges; *Merry Frolics of Satan, The*; *Palace of the Arabian Nights*; *Le pied de mouton* (1907); *Trip to the Moon, A*

féerie (theatre), xix-xx, xxii, 1–12, 15–37, 57, 78, 202, 230n9, 235n105, 242n62; authored by industry and technology, 31–32; Baudelaire and, 28; *The Blue Bird* and, 94–95; as cinematic, 42, 79–80, 84–86, 92, 141, 142; exhibitions and, 29–30; Great Exhibition of 1851 and, 24–27, 28; fairy-tale interludes and, 128; féerie (film) and, 39, 40–41, 60, 62, 66, 68; Fox Kiddes and, 78; *The Goddess of Spring* and, 177; *A Good Little Devil* and, 115; illustrations and, 30–31; *L'Inhumaine* and, 142; *King Neptune* and, 250n6; luminous fountains and, 33–35, 36; modernism and, 21–22; modernity and, 23, 28; narrative structure, 6–7; optical devices and, 31; pantomime and, 15–17; scientific, 36, 37; *The Thief of Bagdad* and, 141; in the United States, 15, 78

Felando, Cynthia, 165

Figuier, Louis, 33, 34

fire: Bengal, 8; *The Blue Bird* (1918) and, 95, 104–106; *Sleepy Hollow* and, 218–219, 222; storytelling and, 124, 193, 218–219

Fischer, Lucy, 172

flapper, 164, 166, 167

Flaubert, Gustave, 22, 44, 54

Fleischer, Dave, 176

Folies-Bergère, 4, 164, 166, 167

Forbidden Fruit (1921), 128

Fouquier, Marcel, 36

Fox, Stephen R., 150

Fox, William, 76, 78

Fox Kiddies, 75–78

Freeburg, Victor O., 95–96, 243n71

Freud, Sigmund, 90

Fuller, Loïe, 4–5, 104

Fuller, Mary, 123

Gág, Wanda, 183

Gates, Eleanor, 129

Gaudreault, André, xx, 40, 238n21

Gautier, Théophile: *The Blue Bird* and, 94, 110; cinema and, 42; fairy tales and, 24–27; fantasy and, 19–20, 29; féerie (theatre) and, xx, 1, 5, 7–12, 17–23, 26, 27, 28–29, 30, 31, 232n25, 232n33, 233n76, 234n88, 234n89, 235n105; the Great Exhibition of 1851 and, 23–27; modernism and, 20–22; modernity and, 22–23, 28; "The Theatre of Which We Dream", 17–18, 20, 27, 94, 110

Gaynor, Janet, 169

Geddes, Norman Bel, 149

Gest, Morris, xxii, 148–149

Giddens, Anthony, 206

Ginisty, Paul, 6

Gledhill, Christine, xviii

Goddess of Spring, The (1934), 177

Golden Chance, The (1915), 117–119, 128, 202

Good Fairy, The (1935), xxiii, 179, 202–204

Good Little Devil, A (play), 115

Good Little Devil, A (1914), 115

Gourmont, Remy de, 42–45, 46, 47, 53–54, 110

Great Exhibition of 1851, 23–28, 29, 234n89. *See also* exhibitions

Grimms. *See* Brothers Grimm

Gunning, Tom, xx, 4, 40, 239n54

Guys, Constantin, 234n96

Hammond, Paul, 45, 237n18

Hamrick, Lois Cassandra, 22–23

Hansen, Miriam, xiii, xvi, 206
Harris, Augustus, 232n40
Harry Potter and the Deathly Hallows Part 1 (2010), 224–226
Harry Potter and the Prisoner of Azkaban, xxiii, 213, 222–223, 226–227
Hastie, Amelie, 166
Hepworth, Cecil, 40
Hibon, Ben, 224, 225
Higashi, Sumiko, 118, 128, 154
Higson, Andrew, 236n6
Hitchcock, Alfred, 201
Housman, Laurence, 147
Hugo (2012), 227

idealism, 21, 92
illustrated book. *See* book
illustrations: fairy tales and, xv, 230n7; féerie (film) and, 62–63; féerie (theatre) and, 30–31; *Jack and the Beanstalk* (1917) and, 77; *The Thief of Bagdad* and, 146–147
Imagism, 42
Impossible Voyage, The (1904), 49, 63–64, 71
Indian Court. *See* Great Exhibition of 1851
L'Inhumaine (1925), 142
interludes, 125–128, 142, 155, 166, 168–169, 171, 173, 197
intermediality, xv, xxii, 5, 98, 146
Intolerance (1916), 86
Irving, Minna, 91–92
Irving, Washington, 218
Island of Jewels (play), 13
It (1927), 165

Jack and the Beanstalk (1902), 236n6
Jack and the Beanstalk (1917), 75–77
Jack and the Beanstalk (1931), 176
Jacobs, Lea, 239n54
Jacobs, Lewis, 186
Jannings, Emil, 173
Johnston, Julanne, 157–158
Johnston, William A., 142

Jouvin, B., 30, 31

kaleidoscope, 4, 31, 235n105
Kearns, James, 20
Keil, Charlie, 241n43
Kellerman, Annette, 80–81
Kid, The (1921), 128
King Neptune (1932), 250n6
Kingdom of the Fairies, The (1903), xx, 49, 66–72
Klein, Norman M., 176
Knapp, Raymond, 15, 207
Kovács, Katherine, 40, 237n7
Kriegel, Lara, 23
Krupa, Gene, 208

Landay, Lori, 167
Landy, Marcia, 199, 200
Langdale, Allan, 240n18
Lant, Antonia, 72
Larson, Barbara, 54–55
Last Command, The (1928), 173
Leach, William, xxii, 151, 154, 195
Lears, T. J. Jackson, xxii, 150, 157, 162–163, 184, 194, 249n64
Lee, Lila, 122–123
Lindsay, Vachel, xv, xxi, 78, 79, 87–90, 91, 92, 96, 97, 106, 180, 216, 241n26, 241n39, 242n48, 243n71; *The Thief of Bagdad* and, 141, 153–154, 160–162
Little Princess, A (1995), 213
Little Princess, The (1917), 114, 123–129, 135, 142, 182
Little Princess, The (1939), 197
"Little Red Riding Hood", 40, 63, 205, 212
Little Red Riding Hood (1901), 65
Lloyd, Rosemary, 22, 233n76, 234n93
Lucas, George, 213
Lucas, Hippolyte, 9, 232n25
luminous fountains, 4, 33–35, 36, 177

Macgowan, Kenneth, 149
Mademoiselle de Maupin, 17, 20
Maeterlinck, Maurice: *The Blue Bird*

(play) and, xxi, 93–95, 98, 106, 130, 242n66; cinema and, 96–97, 98; "The Tragedy of Everyday Life" and, 98, 106–107, 110

magic, xiv, 57, 236n6; animation and, 177; *The Blue Bird* (1918) and, 95, 103, 104, 110, 216; *The Blue Bird* (1940) and, 198; carpet, 144, 148, 150; *Cinderella* and, 117; cinema and, xvi, 82, 89, 91, 92, 113, 127, 150, 173; consumer culture and, 159–160, 163; féerie (film) and, 41, 42, 47, 48, 61, 62, 68; féerie (theatre) and, 6, 9, 29, 60; *Harry Potter and the Deathly Hallows Part 1* and, 224; *Harry Potter and the Prisoner of Azkaban* and, 222, 223; *The Little Princess* (1917) and, 123; *Shrek 2* and, 215, 223; *Sleepy Hollow* and, 217, 218, 220–222, 223; *Snow White and the Seven Dwarfs* and, 175, 176, 178, 192, 194, 207; stardom and, 113, 122–123, 158; *The Thief of Bagdad* and, 144, 145, 147, 151, 153, 155–156, 157, 158, 161, 162, 163

magic lantern, 31, 40, 223, 236n6

Magic Sword (1901), 236n6

Male and Female (1919), 128

Manovich, Lev, 226

Marchand, Roland, 195

Marcus, Laura, 112

Marion, Frances, 130

Mark of Zorro, The (1920), 142

Martin, Roxane, 6, 68, 236n1

Matrix, The (1999), 213

McMahan, Alison, 217

Méliès, Georges, xv, xviii, xx, 39–40, 45–53, 56–58, 62–69, 72–73, 202; animate objects and, 58–64; catalogue descriptions and, 65–69; *Cinderella* (1914) and, 117; "Cinematographic Views" and, 50–53, 57–58; Gustave Doré and, 62–63; féerie (film) and, 39–40, 171; gender roles and, 46–47, 49;

metaphor and, 45, 110; modernity and, 46; substitution splice and, 45–47; urban life and, 46–47; visual continuities and, 69–72. *See also Bluebeard*; *Christmas Dream, The*; *Cinderella* (1899); *Impossible Voyage, The*; *Kingdom of the Fairies, The*; *Little Red Riding Hood*; *Merry Frolics of Satan, The*; *Palace of the Arabian Nights*; *Trip to the Moon, A*

melodrama, xix, 6, 8, 114, 168, 169

Merely Mrs. Stubbs (1917), 126

Merritt, Karen, 179–180

Merry Frolics of Satan, The (1906), xx, 47–49, 57, 70

metamorphosis. *See* transformation

metaphor, 44–47, 52–54, 57, 58, 70, 73, 89, 110, 133–134, 237n18

Metempsychosis (1907), 41–42

Mickey Mouse, 177

Midnight (1939), xxiii, 204–205

Miller, Bertha Mahony, 190

Miracle, The (play), 149

Modern Cinderella, A (1917), 123

modernism, xiv, xvi-xvii, xx, 5, 142; *The Blue Bird* (1918) and, xxi, 98; féerie (theatre) and, 5, 21–22; Théophile Gautier and, 20–22; *Wings* and, 167. *See also* modernity

modernity, xiv, xvi-xviii, xix, xx, xxiii, 4–5, 22–23, 112, 113, 115, 139, 143, 206, 213; *The Blue Bird* and, 112; fantasy and, 22–23, 27–28; féerie (film) and, 41, 49; féerie (theatre) and, 5, 23; Théophile Gautier and, 22–23, 28; Georges Méliès and, 46; *The Poor Little Rich Girl* (1917) and, 132; *Seventh Heaven* and, 171; stardom and, 113, 139; *Sunrise* and, 172–173; *Wings* and, 167, 169. *See also* modernism

Modleski, Tania, 201

Les Mohicans, 17

Moi, Toril, 21

Molnár, Ferenc, 202

Moore, Anne Carroll, 188–190
Moore, Colleen, 166
Moore, Rachel O., 242n48
moralism, xiii, xiv, xvii, 20, 23, 229n7; *The Blue Bird* and, 93, 95, 96, 101; féerie (theatre) and, 5, 6–8, 9, 12; *The Good Fairy* and, 203; *Snow White and the Seven Dwarfs* and, 185, 191; *The Thief of Bagdad* and, 144, 146, 155–157
Morris, William, 185–186, 187
Mother Goose, 87, 183
Mother Goose Land (1933), 176, 183
Mother Goose Melodies (1931), 183
Moussinac, Léon, 151
Münsterberg, Hugo, xv, xxi, 78, 79, 80–84, 86, 87, 89, 92, 106, 112, 240n18, 241n26, 241n39
murals, 98, 99–102
Musser, Charles, 236n6
mutability. *See* transformation

Nathan, George Jean, 130
Neptune's Daughter (1914), 80–81, 82, 85, 240n19, 241n39

Ocean (1916), 85
Olds, Marshall C., 22
Orgeron, Marsha, 165–166
Oz series, 75

Palace of the Arabian Nights (1905), 72
Pan's Labyrinth (2006), 212
Panofsky, Erwin, 178, 221
pantomime, xix, 12–17, 232n40, 236n6; *Forbidden Fruit* and, 128; *The Goddess of Spring* and, 177; *Seventh Heaven* and, 170
paranoid woman's film. *See* Bluebeard cycle
Parrish, Maxfield, 146–147
Parville, Henri de, 33
Pathé, 40, 42, 88
Peau d'âne (play), 30, 234n88
peddler, 192–195
Peggy (1916), 126–127

La Péri, 17
Perrault, Charles, 2, 26, 62, 182
Pessard, Hector, 36
Peter Pan (play), 94, 136
Piano, The (1993), 212
Pickford, Mary, xv, xxi, 114–116, 135, 141, 197, 244n5, 244n8; *Cinderella* and, 115, 122, 123; *The Little Princess* and, 125, 128–129; *The Poor Little Rich Girl* and, 129–130, 133, 134, 135, 244n25
Le pied de mouton (play) 4, 6, 9, 30, 31, 37, 39, 236n1
Le pied de mouton (1907), 39, 40
Pied Piper, The (1933), 177
Les pilules du diable, 4, 9–10, 11, 18, 29, 232n33
Pinocchio (1940), 181
Planché, J. R., 13, 16
Poor Little Rich Girl, The (play), 129–130
Poor Little Rich Girl, The (1917), 97, 114, 129–135
Porter, Edwin S., 40
Le prince Soleil, 35–37
Prunella (play), 136
Prunella (1918), 126, 136
Puvis de Chavannes, Pierre, 98, 99–102

Queen of the Sea (1918), 80

Rackham, Arthur, 146
Rancière, Jacques, 109
"Rapunzel", 214
Rearick, Charles, 4
Rebecca (1940), xxiii, 200, 201
Redon, Odilon, 53–56
Régnier, Henri de, 242n62
Reinhardt, Max, 82, 149
Reiniger, Lotte, 224–226
Ricoeur, Paul, 46, 52–53, 73
Riquet à la houppe (play), 16
Robin Hood (1922), 142, 161
Rodin, Auguste, 97–98
Romanticism, 2, 22, 112, 134
Roqueplan, Nestor, 2, 16, 30

Rosenbaum, Jonathan, 250n16
Rothomago, 4, 30, 31–32, 235n105
Ruskin, John, 187

Sadoul, Georges, 40, 237n7, 239n54
Saint-Victor, Paul de, 31
Sarcey, Francisque, 1, 7, 18, 20, 36
Sargent, Epes W., 150
Scarlet Empress, The (1934), xxiii, 179,
    198–200
Schlappich, Sam J., 91
Schoenherr, Douglas E., 187
Scribe, Eugène, 18
Secret Beyond the Door, The (1948), 200
Les sept châteaux du diable, 8–9, 40
Seven Swans, The (1917), 136
Seventh Heaven (1928), 143, 169–171,
    173
shadow plays, 224–225
Shaw, Jennifer L., 100, 102
Sheik, The (1921), 142
Shippey, Tom, 212, 252n3
Shrek (2001), 211–212, 214
Shrek 2 (2004), 213, 214–216, 217, 223
Siegfried (1924), 142
Silly Symphonies, 176–177
Sirens of the Sea (1917), 80–81, 126
"Sleeping Beauty", 40, 63, 175, 202
Sleepy Hollow (1999), xxiii, 213, 217–
    222, 223, 226
"Snow White", 176, 179, 215, 217–218
Snow White (play), 136, 138, 179–181
Snow White (1916), 126, 136, 179–180
Snow White (1933), 176
Snow White and the Seven Dwarfs
    (1937), xviii, xxii, 175–176, 178–
    182, 184–196, 202, 219; *Ball of
    Fire* and, 207–209, 219; *The Blue
    Bird* (1940) and, 198; *Shrek* and,
    211; *Shrek 2* and, 215, 216; *Sleepy
    Hollow* and, 218
Sobchack, Vivian, 231n13
Le Soleil noir, 55
Spielberg, Steven, 213
Stanislavski, Constantin, 112
stardom, xiv, xv, xvi, xviii, 135, 143,

197; *Cinderella* (1914) and, 122;
    Fairbanks and, 141, 158; fairy
    tales and, xxi-xxii, 113–114, 123,
    136–139, 165–166; the fairy-tale
    interlude and, 127; *The Scarlet
    Empress* and, 200; *Shrek 2* and,
    214; transformation and, 113, 115,
    122, 158, 165–166. *See also* Mary
    Pickford
Stewart, Garrett, 223
Stoneley, Peter, 114
storytelling: children's literature, 190;
    fairy tales and, 57, 181–183, 206,
    212; fairy-tale interlude and,
    126–127; *The Good Fairy* and, 203,
    205; images and, 30; *The Little
    Princess* (1917) and, 124–125, 129;
    The Little Princess (1939) and, 197;
    The Scarlet Empress and, 198–199;
    Shrek and, 211; *Sleepy Hollow*
    and, 218–220; *Snow White and
    the Seven Dwarfs* and, 181–183,
    187, 192–193; *The Thief of Bagdad*
    and, 144–145
Strindberg, August, 138
Studlar, Gaylyn, 114, 155, 199
Sturges, Preston, 202
substitution splice, 41, 43, 45–47, 49,
    50, 51, 52, 58, 237n18, 238n21. *See
    also* trick effects
Sullivan's Travels (1941), 202
Sumurun (1920), 142
Sunrise (1927), 143, 171–173
Le sylphe d'or, 7
Symbolism, xvi, xx, 42, 86, 98

Tale of the Fox, The (1930), 183
Talmadge, Norma, 127
Tatar, Maria, 182, 200, 202
Temple, Shirley, 196–198
thaumatrope, 219–222, 223
theatres, motion picture, 148, 149–151
Thief of Bagdad, The (1924), xv, xxii,
    141–149, 151–163, 164, 173, 182,
    246n5, 246n7; exhibition of, 147–
    149, 151

Thompson, Kristin, 111

Thousand and One Nights, The, 2, 4, 25, 34, 126, 144–145, 146–147, 157, 162, 169

Three Little Pigs, The (1933), 177

Tibbetts, John C., 244n5, 245n30

Tourneur, Maurice, 95, 97–98, 101, 111, 130

transformation, xvii, xxii–xxiii, 17, 19, 37, 54, 78, 113, 143, 169, 231n13; animation and, 176–178, 216, 219; *The Blue Bird* (play) and, 96, 106; *The Blue Bird* (1918) and, 95, 103–104, 106, 108, 110, 129; the Bluebeard cycle and, 201–202; *Bluebeard's Eighth Wife* and, 205–206; Clara Bow and, 165–167; *Cinderella* (1914) and, 116–117, 118, 122–123; consumer culture and, 151–152, 163; *Ella Cinders* and, 166; fairy tales and, xiv-xv, xxiii, 5, 229n7; fairy-tale interlude and, 127; féerie (film) and, xx, 39, 40–43, 45, 47–49, 58–61, 63–64, 66–73; féerie (theatre) and, xix, 1, 4, 5–12, 15–17, 22, 23, 30, 32, 34, 37, 41, 236n1; film aesthetics and, xv, xxi, 42, 50–52, 53, 73, 82–84, 89–92, 96, 106, 112, 132, 135, 213; film stars and, xvi, 113–115, 122–123, 129, 135, 158; Loïe Fuller and, 5, 104; *The Golden Chance* and, 118; *The Good Fairy* and, 204; *Harry Potter and the Deathly Hallows Part 1* and, 224–225; *Harry Potter and the Prisoner of Azkaban* and, 222–223, 226–227; *The Little Princess* (1917) and, 124, 127–128; *The Little Princess* (1939) and, 197; luminous fountains and, 33–35; metaphor and, 45–47, 52–54, 73, 89, 110; *Midnight* and, 205; modernity and, xiv, xvi, xx, xxiii, 23, 46, 112, 169, 172; *Neptune's Daughter* and, 81; nineteenth-century spectacle and, xix, 4; pantomime and, 12–17; *The*

Poor Little Rich Girl (play) and, 130, 132; *The Poor Little Rich Girl* (1917) and, 132–134; *The Scarlet Empress* and, 198, 200; *Seventh Heaven* and, 171; *Shrek* and, 212; *Shrek 2* and, 214–216; *Sleepy Hollow* and, 222; *Snow White* (1916) and, 180; *Snow White and the Seven Dwarfs* and, 178–179, 181, 187, 192–194, 196, 216; substitution splice and, 45–46; *Sunrise* and, 172; *The Thief of Bagdad* and, xxii, 152, 155, 163; *Wings* and, 164–165, 167–169

transformation scene, 12–16, 232n40; *Forbidden Fruit* and, 128; the luminous fountains and, 35; *Seventh Heaven* and, 170

transformation view, xx, 41, 50, 51, 71. See also fantastic view

trick cuts. See substitution splice; trick effects

trick effects: féerie (film) and, 39, 41, 62; féerie (theatre) and, xix, 7, 10, 30, 32, 94, 235n105; film aesthetics and, 43, 82, 84, 89, 106; pantomime and, 12, 16; *Seventh Heaven* and, 170; *The Thief of Bagdad* and, 141. See also substitution splice

trick films, 51, 88–89, 216, 226. See also transformation view

Trip to the Moon, A (1902), 40, 56, 63–64, 65, 66, 71, 239n54

Turlututu (play), 31

Twelve Temptations, The (play), 15

Twister (1996), 212

Two Arabian Knights (1927), 169

Ugly Duckling, The (1931), 177

Ulbach, Louis, 16, 29–30, 32

Undine (1916), 80

Universal Exposition of 1889, 33–36

Vardac, A. Nicholas, 40, 237n7

Verlaine, Paul, 84, 98

Verne, Jules, 2

Viehmann, Dorothea, 182

Vitu, Auguste, 7
Vogüé, Eugène-Melchior de, 34
Vuillermoz, Émile, xiii, xv, xxi, 78, 79–80, 84–87, 88, 92, 106, 108, 112, 119, 250n6; *The Goddess of Spring* and, 177; Maeterlinck and, 96–97; *The Thief of Bagdad* and, 141

Walsh, Raoul, 154
Warner, Marina, xiv, 57, 231n13
Water Babies (1935), 177
Watts, Stephen, xvi-xvii
Waxworks (1924), 142, 246n7
well-made play, the, 18
Wells, Paul, 176
Whip, The (1917), 97
Whispering Chorus, The (1918), 128
"White Cat, The", 2. *See also La chatte blanche*

Wiggin, Kate Douglas, 147
Wild at Heart (1990), 212
Wilder, Billy, 204, 206
Wings (1927), 143, 163–169, 171, 173, 202
Wishing Ring, The (1914), 97
"Wizard of Oz, The", 212. *See also Oz* series
Wizard of Oz, The (1939), xxii, 197–198, 214
world's fairs, xix, 23, 90. *See also* exhibitions; Great Exhibition of 1851; Universal Exposition of 1889

Ye Belle Alliance (play), 14

Zecca, Ferdinand, 40
Zipes, Jack, xiv, xvii, 229n7
Zola, Émile, xx, 18, 21–22